Love's Sacred Song

A Novel

Mesu Andrews

Revell
a division of Baker Publishing Group
Grand Rapids, Michigan

© 2012 by Mesu Andrews

Published by Revell
a division of Baker Publishing Group
P.O. Box 6287, Grand Rapids, MI 49516-6287
www.revellbooks.com

Printed in the United States of America

Library of Congress Cataloging-in-Publication Data
Andrews, Mesu, 1963-
    Love's sacred song : a novel / Mesu Andrews
        p.   cm.
    Includes bibliographical references.
    ISBN 978-0-8007-3408-4 (pbk.)
    1. Title
PS3601.N55274L74 2012
813′.6—dc23   2011041152

Scripture quotations are from the Holy Bible, New International Version®. NIV®. Copyright © 1973, 1978, 1984 by Biblica, Inc.™ Used by permission of Zondervan. All rights reserved worldwide. www.zondervan.com

This is a work of historical reconstruction; the appearance of certain historical figures is therefore inevitable. All other characters, however, are products of the author's imagination, and any resemblance to actual persons, living or dead, is coincidental.

The internet addresses, email addresses, and phone numbers in this book are accurate at the time of publication. They are provided as a resource. Baker Publishing Group does not endorse them or vouch for their content or permanence.

12   13   14   15   16   17   18   7   6   5   4   3   2   1

To those who wouldn't let me quit.
My husband, my mom, Meg . . .

CHARACTER LIST

Abiathar	David's high priest
Abishag	Shulammite maiden chosen as David's bed warmer
Absalom	David's third son; ima—Maacah; attempted rebellion when Solomon was a boy
Adonijah	David's fourth son; ima—Haggith; attempted coup while David was on his deathbed
Adoniram	Solomon's administrator of foreign labor
Ahishar	palace high steward; Son of Judah
Ammizabad	Benaiah's son; killed in battle
Amnon	David's firstborn son; ima—Ahinoam; raped his sister and was then killed by brother Absalom
Arielah	daughter of Jehoshaphat and Jehosheba; Shunem's treaty bride
Bakari	Egyptian ambassador
Barzillai	remained loyal to David during Absalom's rebellion
Bathsheba	Solomon's ima; David's wife (taken in adultery)
Benaiah	David's captain of the guard; Solomon's army commander
Bethuel	abba of Daughters of Jerusalem; royal tailor
Dalit	Bathsheba's handmaid
David	second king of Israel
Dodo	weaver in Shunem
Edna	matchmaker in Shunem

Elihoreph	Solomon's chief secretary; Son of Judah
Eleazar	one of Benaiah's Mighty Men
Elisheba	Reu's ima; palace cook
Hannah	Abishag's sister; Arielah's handmaid
Hezro	one of Benaiah's Mighty Men
Hiram	king of Tyre (Phoenician)
Igal	Arielah's middle brother
Jehosheba	Arielah's ima
Jehoshaphat	Arielah's abba; Shunem's judge
Joab	David's army commander
Kemmuel	Arielah's oldest brother
Mahlon	Reu's surrogate abba; scribe
Marah	prostitute of Shunem; moves business to Jerusalem
Miriam	ima of Daughters of Jerusalem
Naamah	Solomon's Ammonite wife; ima of crown prince
Nahum	one-eyed palace guard
Nathan (prince)	Solomon's brother; son of David and Bathsheba
Nathan (prophet)	prophet; loyal to Solomon during Adonijah's coup
Oliab	watchman in Jerusalem
Phaltiel	chief elder in Shunem after Jehoshaphat
Psusennes	successor pharaoh to Sekhet's father
Rehoboam	Solomon's firstborn; son of Naamah
Reu	palace courier; Jehoshaphat's aide
Ruth	kind old woman in Shunem
Sarah	widow in Shunem
Sekhet	Pharaoh's daughter; Solomon's wife
Sherah	younger twin Daughter of Jerusalem
Shimei (Baal Hamon)	vinedresser at Baal Hamon
Shimei (Benjamite)	cursed David during Absalom's rebellion
Shiphrah	older twin Daughter of Jerusalem
Siamun	Pharaoh; Sekhet's father
Solomon	son of David and Bathsheba
Yoshim	Jehoshaphat's steward while in Jerusalem
Zadok	Solomon's high priest

PART 1

1

These are the numbers of the men armed for battle . . .
men of Issachar, who understood the times and knew
what Israel should do.

A rielah tiptoed around the sleeping forms of her surly
brothers. Empty wineskins served as silent witnesses
to their drunken slumber. Kemmuel and Igal would be snoring till dawn. They'd been a disgrace to Abba Jehoshaphat
and to the tribe of Issachar since they were old enough to
tend sheep.

Kemmuel rolled on his side and smacked his lips, and Arielah stood like a stone. A moment later, she reached for the
iron handle and tugged open the rough-hewn cedar door.
The bottom corner scraped the dirt and creaked on leather
hinges. She held her breath. Glancing slowly over her shoulder, she sighed her relief at the steady rise and fall of her
brothers' chests.

A shadow of melancholy swept over her. They looked so
peaceful lying there, but their rage was a living thing boiling just beneath the surface. If only they would let her love
them. But her big brothers rebuffed even the love Abba and

11

Ima tried to offer. Arielah had learned at an early age to keep her distance or reap her brothers' wrath, and now she spent most of her time avoiding them. Tears blurred her vision.

Focusing beyond them, she saw Ima Jehosheba seated by the cooking stones, waving her out the door. Ima's wink and loving smile nudged Arielah into the shadowy courtyard. Abba Jehoshaphat had already gone to Shunem's well for the elders' meeting. Both parents had known Arielah planned to observe the meeting from a distance, since a woman was never welcome there. And though Abba was a righteous man of faith and prayer, tonight he condoned Arielah's deception.

Keeping to the shadows, Arielah left their courtyard and slipped behind a few stacked water jars, feeling more like a bandit than the daughter of Shunem's most revered judge. Silently she moved among the merchants' stalls toward the well at the center of Shunem. There every town meeting was held and every bit of gossip found its voice. Crouching behind crates and tables, she remained under the shadow of goatskin canopies covering the empty booths. No merchants lingered this late to hawk their wares. Only dogs and vermin loitered to clean up the scraps.

She smiled, remembering a time when her childish spying had taken her into the busy streets of Jerusalem. She was only seven when King David had summoned Abba as a northern advisor to consult on a civil matter. The whole family accompanied Jehoshaphat to the capital city. *That was the first time I saw Solomon.* Arielah's heart skipped a beat at the thought of the young king. Tonight's meeting would be very different from the one in Jerusalem so many years ago.

Inching closer to Shunem's well, she could hear the buzz of the crowd. Tension showed on men's perspiring brows, though the early spring winds whipped their robes. Over two hundred men, leaders from all ten of Israel's northern tribes, now gathered at the city's center. The fury that brought these men to Shunem had been building for years, but the disgrace of one Shulammite maiden provided the straw that broke the proverbial dromedary's back.

Arielah remembered the day Ahishar arrived in Shunem nine new moons ago as the palace high steward. His grand escort was pompous and proud, but his close-set eyes and thinning, straight hair reminded her of a weasel. Abba Jehoshaphat had taught Arielah that outward appearance wasn't the defining measure of a man; however, after only a day in Ahishar's presence, Arielah was quite sure the steward's weaselly appearance matched his character. He had stood at the very well where the angry northern leaders now gathered and announced the search for the most beautiful Israelite maiden to care for the aging King David. Abishag, a girl just one year older than Arielah, won the distinction and was immediately taken to Jerusalem. Word of the girl's true fate had come through a Shulammite merchant whose sister served in the king's kitchens. Abishag had become nothing more than David's belly warmer—taken to his bed but never becoming wife or concubine.

Now the question that burned in every heart had become an inferno. What would become of Abishag when King David cast her aside? No man would want her after she'd been defiled in another man's bed—even if the palace vowed the relationship was never consummated. Would King Solomon toss her away like refuse, or would he include her in the ongoing care of David's wives and concubines?

While Arielah's heart broke for the girl she'd seen drawing water at Shunem's well, the men of their town and tribe felt a different emotion. Disgrace blighted the whole tribe of Issachar. Fury over Abishag's rejection spread like wildfire. Their most beautiful daughter was sacrificed to the whims of Judah's royalty. Men from Shunem traveled from one tribe to another, stirring the emotions of other hardworking, honest men of the north.

These were the common folk of Israel, faithful in their

annual treks to Gibeon for Passover. These were shepherds, farmers, fishermen, men of the soil and stream. They cried when they were sad and laughed when they were happy. They made no apologies for their lifestyle, or for their emotions. Much to the contrary, they drank deeply from all the well-springs of life. And tonight, these hardworking, deep-feeling northern officials would spew their fury.

Arielah searched the crowd for her abba's silver-streaked head and finally spotted him at the front by the well curb. Her heart swelled, love and pride competing for first place. Her wise abba stood a head taller than the rest of the men, full in form, yet not an ounce of unmuscled flesh. His reputation as a shepherd, vinedresser, and elder had earned him not only the respect of every man in northern Israel but also the approval of King David. Frequently, he sat on the king's council, each time representing the tribe of Issachar—the tribe famous for understanding their times and knowing what Israel should do.

Arielah stubbed her toe on an awning post and pressed her lips together to keep from crying out. She must hurry to find an appropriate hiding place. Finally, spotting a donkey attached to a small cart, she knelt between the beast and a merchant's booth not far from the last row of men in the crowd. She felt as though she needed the reassuring sight of her abba's strong features, and this vantage point would provide the perfect cover for her to see his changing expressions.

For weeks, they had tended his flocks together, speaking of the plan Jehoshaphat would present tonight. They had contemplated Israel's fate and Arielah's future—and tonight the two would merge.

"To be used in the king's bed but rejected as a true bride . . ." one of the tribal leaders bellowed. "Abishag's humiliation will not be ignored! It's an insult to our tribe!"

Another man beat the air with his fist. "The house of David will abuse us no more!"

"Let David answer to *all* of Israel for this abomination!" a third cried.

Arielah settled into her quiet hiding place for the long night of blustering, and her mind wandered again to that moment when she saw Solomon for the first time. *How could I, at seven years old, know I would marry Solomon someday?* The question had never occurred to her before. She'd always just *known* the young prince would be hers—like one knows her own name.

More than ten Passovers ago, King David had summoned her abba to Jerusalem as an advisor when a northern landowner cheated a Judean merchant. Arielah's brothers had begged to go, and Jehoshaphat agreed, telling Ima he hoped to use the journey as a bonding time with his sons.

Kemmuel, the older of the boys, seemed especially contrary toward Abba. When Jehoshaphat disciplined, Kemmuel's sullen countenance screamed of injustice. When Jehoshaphat was merciful, Kemmuel's smirk challenged his abba's perceived weakness. Igal, the younger of the boys, simply worshiped the ground his brother walked on and followed his lead in every matter.

When Arielah heard her brothers were accompanying Abba to Jerusalem, she asked Ima, "Why can't women travel to Jerusalem too?"

After a few strategic whispers from his wife, Jehoshaphat agreed to take Jehosheba and Arielah as well.

"We must travel as quickly as possible," he said, feigning a stern gaze at his wife and daughter. "No dawdling over intriguing desert animals or flowers."

The two earnestly nodded their agreement.

"It is only one day's journey for a man on a camel, but we'll take the donkey and make it in three days."

On the fifth day of the journey, Jehoshaphat's family arrived in Jerusalem with necklaces of woven desert flowers draped around every family member's neck—including the donkey's.

Arielah remembered traveling the long road up to Jeru-salem, thinking the city resembled a long-necked queen with a crown on her head. Three sides of the city's walls were bordered by deep valleys, and the towering fortress of Zion stood guard on the northern edge of the City of David. As their family entered the eastern gate, Jehosheba tightened her grip on Arielah's hand. Merchants shouted. Goats and chickens ran through the streets as children chased them. Beggars reached out, and musicians strummed their six-string lyres. Looking to see her ima's reaction, Arielah caught sight of the magnificent fortress that Abba had described from previous visits. Its imposing walls had been created as empty rooms and then filled with dirt and stones. He had called the fortress *impenetrable*. She hadn't known what he meant until she saw the grand structure. Now she understood.

As she gawked, her gaze wandered to an army officer on the wall near one of the fortress parapets. He was leading five finely dressed soldiers in military drills with swords and shields. That's when she saw him. Solomon. All five young sol-diers wore royal purple tunics under their leather breastplates, and each bore David's insignia on his shoulder. But Solomon was easy to distinguish. Just as Abba had once described the fortress as *impenetrable*, he had described Bathsheba's favored son as *extraordinary*. There was indeed nothing or-dinary about Prince Solomon.

With luminous dark eyes and raven hair more silky than curly, Prince Solomon wore an air of royalty. He was the tall-est of his brothers, his shoulders square. Arielah guessed him the same age as Kemmuel—twelve Passovers old. As she was pondering, Solomon rested a moment from his training and glanced through the crowd, catching sight of little Arielah's bold inspection. When she didn't turn away, he studied her and finally offered an amused nod. She returned it—a sort of truce. She knew in that moment Solomon would be hers someday.

Ima Jehosheba tugged on her hand, and their family arrived at one of Jerusalem's small inns. Abba kissed Jehosheba good-bye, and she resumed unpacking the supplies. Abba gave each of his sons a piece of carved leather to barter in the bustling marketplace and hurried off to the palace. Arielah slipped out the door behind him, finding dozens of hiding places in the narrow streets of the City of David. Abba looked back once as though he felt her presence, but he soon turned and continued on his way.

Pretending she was the daughter of a woman with a basket, she walked past the guards at the fortress gate and entered a different world on the unwalled northern side of the city. David's luxurious Phoenician-style palace hummed with ac-tivity. It didn't squawk or shout or screech. The palace built as a gift by King Hiram's carpenters and stonemasons purred with elegance. Arielah watched Abba Jehoshaphat ascend the stone stairway and disappear into the grand cedar doors. Quickly giving up the hope of sneaking past palace guards, she skipped back to the inn. Ima Jehosheba had finished unpacking and asked, "Where are your brothers?"

Arielah shrugged her shoulders and quickly joined in Ima's meal preparation, hoping to let the matter drop. Kemmuel and Igal returned at sunset, as did Abba, and Arielah's spying expedition was almost a secret success—almost.

"I think I know why King David built his palace on the other side of the fortress of Zion," she said, munching ab-sently on her last crust of bread. The room fell utterly silent, and she realized she'd revealed her afternoon mischief.

Jehosheba balled her fists on her hips. "And just when did you see the king's palace?"

Arielah swallowed the last bite of bread past the lump in her throat. "I'm sorry, Ima. I wanted to see where Abba was going."

Jehoshaphat raised an eyebrow. The gesture seemed to Arielah like both a reprimand and a request to hear more.

Glancing from one parent to the other, she decided to address Abba's curiosity rather than Ima's wrath. "North Jerusalem is much quieter than the southern City of David. A shepherd king needs peace to sleep soundly at night."

Abba combed his fingers through his beard as he often did when deep in thought. His frown gave way to a slight grin. "You are perceptive, my lamb. The king said to me this afternoon, 'I'm quite safe on the north side of the fortress since any enemy would have to conquer our ten northern tribes before arriving on my doorstep. I'd have plenty of time to move my household into the fortress before they reached Jerusalem.'"

The memory jolted Arielah like a splash of cold water, and she became suddenly aware of the cries of revolt resounding from beside Shunem's well.

"What if it's my daughter next time?" one of the elders at Shunem's well shouted.

"We should be sharpening our plowshares."

"Judah must pay for their arrogance, and David's family repent of their pride."

The sun had taken its leave behind the foothills of Mount Gilboa, and torchlight cast eerie shadows across the distorted faces of angry men. How could King David have guessed that his most dangerous enemy might be Israel's northern ten tribes?

A shiver crept up Arielah's spine, raising the hairs on her arms to attention. *Why do I feel as though I'm being watched?* She glanced behind and around her, then set aside the thought, straining to hear what another elder was saying. It seemed the crowd was beginning to quiet, a sure sign that Abba would soon speak. Jehoshaphat always listened well and spoke last.

2

Then David rested with his fathers. . . . He had reigned forty years over Israel.

Israel's great warrior king lay shivering on a straw mattress, reduced to a mass of withered flesh by the inescapable weapon of time. Levites circled David's bed, waving censers full of incense and beseeching the God of their abbas for mercy on behalf of their beloved king. But the aromatic censers couldn't disguise the smell of death in the opulent royal chamber.

"Can't we do something else to warm him?" Solomon asked the palace physician as Abba David convulsed with yet another chill.

The old man bowed his head. "I'm sorry, my king. We've done all we can."

Servants scurried about, jostling the glowing embers in the bronze braziers, trying to look busy. Solomon recognized the hopelessness on their faces. He knew no more could be done. The trade routes he was working to establish with Egypt and Tyre would soon avail them of the mysterious herbs from the Far East, but they would arrive too late to help Abba David.

Medicinal scents of balsam and myrrh mingled with stale sweat to create an aura Solomon would not soon forget. He'd stayed in Abba's chamber through the night, bound by cords of love after the physician's prediction of David's imminent passing. In dawn's early glow, Solomon stared glassy-eyed into the round braziers filled with burning grapevines. The fragrant warming pots surrounding Abba's bed fought the relentless chill that plagued the old king. But what of the chill in the *young* king? The icy dread that skittered up his spine and the sweat dripping down his back? Solomon's linen robes hung in a mass of sweaty rags, testifying to his enduring vigil at David's bedside. Tears joined the beads of perspiration on his cheeks. *I don't want to lose my abba, Lord, but I can't bear to see him linger like this.*

The mound of blankets atop the king moved. The great King David groaned. His suffering continued. So it had continued day after day. Solomon looked away, unable to bear the scene. *The strongest man I know, now lying at death's door, unable to cross the threshold.*

Tilting his head up like a child, Solomon was comforted by Benaiah's presence. As captain of the king's guard, Benaiah now protected Solomon as he had shielded David all these years. Solomon smiled at the big man, their eyes communicating more than words.

The captain stood nearly five cubits tall, almost eye to eye with a camel. His wide neck and broad shoulders made his military exploits even more fantastic. But his victories couldn't express his full character. Brave? Yes. Loyal? To a fault. Yet the tears brimming on his long lashes comforted Solomon more than a thousand fallen enemies. Benaiah was more than a soldier. He was a friend, and his heart was breaking too. Even the great Benaiah couldn't protect King David from age's cruel grip.

Seated on the other side of David's bed was Bathsheba, Solomon's ima and the most powerful—and persecuted—of the king's wives. Long ago, David had taken her to his bed and arranged her first husband's death. Nathan the prophet faithfully delivered God's message of judgment. David had listened, as he often did, and God forgave, as He always did.

Now the faithful prophet Nathan stood watching in a distant corner, his face a mask of unreadable papyrus. He lived in perpetual listening with a spirit only the voice of God could reach. Solomon smiled as he studied the old prophet. The man of God moved his lips but made no sound. What did one pray when he already knew the will of Jehovah?

Zadok the priest stood directly to Nathan's left, quietly chanting, entreating the Lord for His mercy. Prophet and priest interceding for king. *I must remember to speak with Zadok about the burial procession and the order of the princes. The princes* . . . Solomon winced. Only a few days ago, his brother Adonijah had tried unsuccessfully to usurp Solomon's reign. Thanks to Ima Bathsheba and the brave efforts of the three loyal men in this room—Zadok, Nathan, and Benaiah—Solomon had secured his abba's blessing and reestablished his right to the throne. Since then, these allies had not left Solomon's side.

Abba David had been Israel's great warrior king for forty years, but most of his final battles were fought in his own palace. How Solomon wished he could have shielded his abba from the pain of their family's sordid upheaval. Brother raping sister. Brother killing brother. Brother stealing abba's throne—well, almost stealing it. Subduing the Philistines, Ammonites, and other nations must have seemed mundane compared to the conflicts among David's own children.

Solomon stroked his abba's forehead. Israel's beloved shepherd king made all his sons advisors after they celebrated their twelfth Passover, and in the ten Passovers since Solomon had observed the way of kings, he'd learned one thing. Israel's fiercest enemies didn't fight with javelin, spear, or sword. They fought with sharp minds and poisoned tongues. If he hoped to build Israel from nation to kingdom, he must reason first and fight last.

Solomon's gaze fell again on his abba's sunken eyes and gaunt cheeks. The shell of a man before him was a stranger. All his life Solomon had heard of King David's rise from the shepherd's field to the battlefield with a rock and a sling and faith big enough to slay a giant. Abba united twelve unruly tribes and governed them as one nation.

Solomon rested his elbows on the straw mattress and let his head drop into his hands. Digging his fingers into his raven hair as though he would pull out fistfuls, he whispered, "Oh, Abba, how can I rule this unruly nation without you to guide me?"

"Your abba believes you have great wisdom, my lord." A muffled female voice rose from beneath the blankets.

Solomon snapped to attention. He hadn't intended his words to be heard.

Abba David smiled weakly. "She s-speaks t-t-truth, my s-son." His teeth chattered as he spoke.

The young king reached out to pull the blankets nearer his abba's face, but a delicate hand met his, and warmth like fire raced from his fingertips to his cheeks.

"Here, let me do it, my lord." The girl, Abishag, spoke again, her melodic voice dancing amid the priest's whispered prayers. She tucked the blankets tightly around herself and the royal charge lying beneath her. Silky black hair lay in sweaty clumps against her face.

Solomon studied the outline of her soft curves—the long, slender woman that draped Abba like a blanket. He marveled at the depth of intimacy shared between a dying king and a poor northern maiden. They lived a pure and transparent love. Love without the consummation of body, it was a deeper consummation of the heart that spoke without words.

Solomon glanced at his ima. Even Bathsheba's undying love couldn't match the inner connectedness between Abba and the Shulammite. Abishag's relationship with the king had been cultivated over endless hours—undisturbed, heartwarming, meaningful hours—in which words were useless and physical intimacy unnecessary.

Leaning closer, Solomon kissed David's cheek and whispered, "Rest now, Abba. I'm sorry I disturbed you. Save your strength."

Solomon watched as Abishag stroked Abba's hair, and he wondered again, *Would it be so wrong to take Abishag as my concubine after Abba dies? She's not a concubine or wife in the physical sense, after all.*

With a voice full of death's rattle, David croaked through trembling lips, "Be strong! Show yourself a man."

Solomon glanced sheepishly at Abishag, feeling his neck and cheeks flame at his abba's rebuking tone. "Yes, Abba. You've instilled in me the courage of a strong man." Though God had told Abba personally that Solomon would rule Israel with peace on every side, the warrior king seemed hardpressed to believe a strong ruler could manage without a sword in his hand.

"No!" the old king rasped through chattering teeth. "Listen. You must remember the Lord's commands, my son—use your strength to walk in His ways and keep His laws and requirements, as written in the law of Moses."

Again, Solomon's eyes found Abishag's. A single tear made its way across the bridge of her nose as she lay on Abba David's chest.

Solomon's heart softened. Let Abba speak a hundred instructions—each word was a treasure in these final moments. "Yes, Abba. I will be strong. I will follow God's laws."

"You know that General Joab killed two innocent men in times of peace. Deal with him according to your wisdom, my son, but don't let his gray head go down to the grave in peace." He shivered violently, and Abishag curled herself tightly around him. Abba David closed his eyes, determination lining his brow as he choked out more words. "Show kindness to the s-sons of Barzillai, who stood by m-me when I fled from your b-brother Absalom's treachery."

Solomon nodded but remained quiet.

David paused too and then laid a shaky hand atop the blanket on Abishag's back. "Do you remember when your brother Absalom tried to steal my kingdom?"

Solomon frowned. "I remember our whole family left Jerusalem and fled to Mahanaim for safety."

David gently patted Abishag, waiting until Solomon's attention rested on her. "And do you remember the sins your brother Absalom committed against the ten concubines I left to care for my palace when the rest of our family fled?"

Solomon felt the blood drain from his cheeks. He stared mutely at Abishag, then David. "Abba, I would never defile your wives or concubines as Absalom did. I have made provision for *all* your women to be cared for in a new wing on the north side of the palace."

No response. Only silence. Solomon saw fear flicker in Abishag's eyes. The girl had been misled by royal promises before—promised a king's bed, refused a bride's rights.

Determination welled up inside Solomon. "Though I will inherit all your wives and concubines, Abba, I assure you that it will be in name only. I am simply following the advice of our advisors to adopt the custom of neighboring countries."

David nodded, seemingly appeased, and Abishag drew the blanket over his arm once more, surrounding him in their warm cocoon. Solomon sighed heavily and prepared to leave, his mind wandering to the calendar changes necessary according to the astronomical charts he'd been studying.

A cold, weak hand reached out and grabbed his wrist. "Solomon!"

His heart nearly leapt from his chest. "Abba, what?"

David's cloudy eyes glistened. "Remember that you have with you Shimei son of Gera, who called down bitter curses on me the day we fled Absalom's rebellion and went to Mahanaim. I swore before the Lord that I would not put him to death by the sword, but you are a man of wisdom, Solomon. You will know what to do."

Solomon let his full weight fall onto the wooden stool beside David's bed. "Abba, you say I have wisdom to know what to do with General Joab, and that I'll know how to deal with Shimei. But what makes you think I have this wisdom? Until a few days ago, you were still officially king of Israel, and I was one of the advisor princes. City elders were deciding disputes among the people, and you still passed down national rulings through your royal officials. What makes you think I will suddenly have the wisdom to secure this kingdom under my reign?" The final words came out in more of a whine than Solomon intended, but truth be told, he'd wanted to ask Abba that question for weeks.

King David smiled through chattering teeth. Abishag's large, doe eyes blinked from one king to the other, seemingly waiting for someone to rule on something.

"Well?" Solomon said, chuckling. "Are you going to let me in on whatever you find so amusing?"

"Have I ever told you your real name, Solomon?"

A slight gasp escaped Bathsheba's lips, and Solomon's world tilted a little. "My real name?" He couldn't stem his tears when he saw Ima Bathsheba reach for David's quaking hand. Abba and Ima had always known a deeper love than had David with his other wives.

"Your ima and I named you Solomon, which means peace, and that name was confirmed when Yahweh spoke to me and said you would build His temple and reign in peace over Israel. But on the night you were born, Nathan the prophet delivered a message from the Lord, giving you a special name."

"Ima? What is he saying?" Solomon asked, but Ima Bathsheba's gaze was fixed on her husband.

Adoration, memories, perhaps some regret—all were

etched into the fine lines of Ima's beautiful face. "After our first son died, your abba comforted me," she said, "and you were born a year later. We named you Solomon in hopes that your life would be characterized by peace rather than the turmoil that surrounded our union—"

"My lord," the prophet Nathan interrupted, "Jehovah sent word to your parents through me that you were to be called Jedidiah, loved of the Lord."

"What? Jedidiah?" The word sounded strange in his ears. "I don't understand. Why am I hearing this name for the first time?"

Nathan looked first at David and then at Bathsheba. "Because though your parents have known since your birth that you are beloved of the Lord, such knowledge among the princes would have placed your life in grave danger."

A sob escaped Solomon's lips before he could muffle it.

"Last year," David said, "when we held the temple preparation assembly, I announced four things in the hearing of all Israel. You are God's choice as Israel's king and will be the builder of His temple. Your reign will be characterized by peace, and most astounding of all—Yahweh will be your Abba." A single tear slid down King David's cheek. "You are Jedidiah, my son, and with His love will come the wisdom to rule His people."

A fierce cough shook the old king's body, and Solomon reached for a steaming cloth. David pushed it away, fighting for words. "Remember those in Israel who must be dealt with before our nation can live in peace—before *you* can live in peace." Tears blurred Solomon's vision as Abba David continued his charge. "Shalom-on. Establish your throne . . . and then . . . seek peace, for yourself and for Israel." The old king shivered uncontrollably, and Abishag's slender form curled tightly around him. "Live your name, my son, Shalom-on." He struggled to say more, but his words were choked off by a weak cough and a gasp for life's breath.

Nathan and Zadok emerged from the corner, their prayers silenced by Jehovah's whisper to the prophet's spirit. Bathsheba's quiet sobs turned to wails as she saw their approach. She too must have sensed the inevitable coming quickly.

Solomon leaned in to kiss his abba's cheek, his face now almost touching Abishag's forehead. He could feel her breath on his beard. She rolled aside, snuggling into the curve of David's arm, leaving her lingering scent of cinnamon and saffron.

The three remained motionless, suspended in time. Each was afraid to move lest they lose the moment to eternity, each knowing death would be the victor in the warrior king's final battle.

Gathering his last breath, David whispered, "Peace, Solomon. Seek peace, Jedidiah."

"Yes, Abba. I will." The young king laid his head on his abba's chest and heard mighty King David's last heartbeat.

3

The war between the house of Saul and the house of David lasted a long time. David grew stronger and stronger, while the house of Saul grew weaker and weaker.

Arielah searched for Jehoshaphat's face in the crowd. Smiling to herself, she realized he had followed his usual custom—remaining silent until every other argument was heard. A hush fell over the crowd, and every face turned expectantly toward her abba. It seemed the heavens themselves drew near to hear the words of Shunem's highest city official.

"Men of Israel," Jehoshaphat began in low tones, "our twelve tribes have brawled and battled since the desert wanderings in Moses's day. But Israel's recent past is most painful. After King Saul died, do you recall the bloody civil war that consumed our country?" He scanned the crowd, and his gaze fell on a few younger officials. "Some of you are too young to remember it, but you've learned about it at your abbas' knees." Then looking at one of the older officials, he prodded, "But you, Zophar, you remember the days of blood in Israel, don't you?"

The older man nodded and then lowered his gaze. No one wanted to speak of Israel's dreadful days before David's rule.

Jehoshaphat scanned the crowd, the majority of gray-bearded faces now noticeably subdued. "The tribes of Israel have always acted like a family with too many children in one tent. We bicker and fight, jealousy and suspicion fueling the fires of resentment and rage. Brothers, open your eyes and see the hand of God. The tribe of Judah has prospered and grown while the rest of Israel's tribes have waned. God has given David success, and to the king's credit, instead of using God's blessing for his own gain, King David has proven faithful, seeking Jehovah's heart and maintaining a united Israel."

The night air fell silent. Jehoshaphat removed a torch from the hand of a man beside him and then shouted and slammed the torch against the well post, snapping it in two. "We are a holy people chosen by the Lord as the apple of His eye! We must act like it!"

Every eye was upon him, and the silence that followed echoed louder than any of the evening's shouts. It seemed even the locusts stopped their song until Jehoshaphat spoke again.

Arielah watched Abba in stunned awe but noticed a mischievous grin working its way across his lips.

"Elder Reuben," he said, "are you awake now?"

Laughter erupted as a drowsy elder patted out the torch's sparks kindling in his beard. Abba's antics had relieved the crowd's tension like a hole in a wineskin. Yet he conveyed his point—King David deserved respect because he had received God's favor. Arielah stifled a giggle and marveled anew at Abba's wisdom.

Consumed by her thoughts, she didn't feel the man's breath on her neck until it was too late. A huge, calloused hand clamped over her mouth. Instinctively, she grabbed at the hand and turned, trying to free herself and identify her attacker. Before she could break away, another shadowy figure cast a musty woolen blanket over her head, blinding her to the direction she was now being dragged.

Her mind reeled, panic warring with reason. She dared not cry out, for if her presence at the meeting was discovered, Abba would be disgraced. So she fought silently, tenaciously; her legs and arms jerked and squirmed. The first attacker kept his hand over her mouth and carried her under his arm like a sack of grain, trapping her arms at her sides. The second man clamped her legs in the same side-armed grip and held the blanket in place to hide their identity. The elders' voices were growing faint, and Arielah knew the men were hauling her away from the crowd.

The first man stumbled over a rock in the street, and the blanket swayed just enough for her to glimpse their surroundings. Old Ruth's small home was directly beside them, just past the baker's market stall. Fear rose to terror when she realized these men were carrying her toward the city gate. She couldn't let them violate her—or worse.

Lord Jehovah, she prayed silently, *if they carry me outside the gate, I have no hope of rescue*. Certain Abba would rather forgive her for disgracing him than attend her funeral or mourn her lost honor, Arielah fought like an animal against the men whose plans were unclear but unthinkable. She bit the hand covering her mouth and released the screams he'd held captive.

"Ouch!" came a muffled voice, just before she felt a blow to her cheek. "Shut up, you little fool," he whispered, replacing his hand over her mouth.

The familiar voice robbed her of breath.

"See how she fights, this little lion of God." The other man chuckled, low and foreboding. "Abba named her well."

Arielah's body went limp. Kemmuel. Igal. She could never overpower her brothers.

"What's the matter, little sister? Why not fight like a man if you want to attend a man's meeting?"

30

Like a limp rag, Arielah lay motionless in their arms, afraid to move or speak. Her submission seemed to fuel their fury, for Kemmuel suddenly yanked her legs, pulling her from Igal's grip. Her shoulders and head hit the ground with a thud.

Kemmuel released her legs and tore away the blanket, staring down at her with hate in his eyes. Arielah tried to scurry to her feet, but he lunged forward. "Oh no you don't." His hand clamped onto her wrist like a vise.

"No! Please!" she said, sobbing. Searing pain shot up her arm.

"Grab her other wrist," he ordered Igal. "We'll drag her outside the gate, where no one can hear her scream." When Arielah tried to twist away, they tightened their grasps, painfully crushing the delicate tendons and bones in her wrists. They yanked her backward, her arms extended overhead. She left a single, meandering trail in the dark, dusty street of Shunem.

Why? Why do you hate me? She wanted to plead, but she knew they would only laugh and prolong the ridicule. Her brothers had always been cruel, but their cruelty had lately intensified to violence. They were careful to leave wounds and bruises Abba couldn't see.

"Oh!" she cried out as a discarded piece of pottery tore into her robe and flesh.

"Ah, little sister found her tongue, Igal. We'll have to make sure she doesn't tell Abba."

Jehoshaphat knew of his sons' failings but didn't realize the extent of their brutality. Abba had disciplined and taught all three children as a wise abba should, but rather than accept his love, Kemmuel and Igal shunned familial ties and blamed Arielah for every hardship in their lives.

"Please, brothers," she whimpered, "I won't tell Abba. Please let me go. Stop before you do something you'll regret." Arielah wriggled in their grasp, trying to position her torn robe between raw flesh and the littered street.

Kemmuel spit in her face. "My only regret is that you were born. Before you came along, Igal and I held at least a portion of Abba's heart." Arielah saw a moment of vulnerability on the moonlit features towering above her—just before an iron gate slammed shut on Kemmuel's emotions.

Her heart broke at the pain beneath his hatred. At least now she understood the source of her brothers' cruelty. But they believed a lie. Abba loved his sons deeply. Could anyone convince them they'd cheated themselves all these years?

When they were finally beyond Shunem's walls, the men released her. She rolled on her back, appreciating the softness of her woolen robe.

The brothers positioned themselves at her hands and feet. "You take her wrists, Igal, and I'll grab her ankles."

Arielah's reaction was quick and instinctive. Like a crab beside the Great Sea, she pulled her hands and feet under her and tried to scoot away. But before she could escape, Igal's meaty hands found her wrists again, and Kemmuel grabbed her ankles.

"Let's see how high our sister can fly, Igal!" The two swung Arielah from side to side, lifting her higher with each rhythmic sway. Finally, Kemmuel began the count. "One, and two, and threeeeee!"

Arielah sailed into the air and hit the cold, unyielding ground with a sickening thud. She saw torchlight flash at the corners of her vision and then welcomed the sweet darkness that would spare her further torment.

Arielah's eyes opened slowly as from a dream, but her throbbing head reminded her of the nightmare she'd endured. Nervously glancing right and left to be sure her brothers were gone, she stood on wobbly legs. The blood rushing to her head pounded like a wooden spoon on Ima's cooking pots. The fresh wounds on her right side and leg stung like a thousand bees. Her robe, shredded by the dragging, offered no protection from the cool night air.

Arielah slowly regained her bearings. Outside the city gate, she saw torches amid the distant crowd gathered at the well. Moonlight surrounded her, casting an eerie glow on her torn robe and bloodstained mantle. Beneath her mantle, the headpiece binding her hair was soaked with blood, and she could feel a warm trickle seeping down the back of her neck. Touching a lump on the back of her head, she winced when her fingers found a small cut in its center.

Not so bad this time, she thought, making her way toward the gate. She would slip quietly back to their home and wash her wounds using the water jar in the far corner of the courtyard. Hopefully Ima would be busy inside and wouldn't notice her return. The cuts and scrapes from her dragging would be easy enough to clean up, but the head wound would require more care. She must hurry. When Abba presented his plan, she must be ready. Israel's treaty bride could hardly appear to the northern officials looking like a tattered beggar.

Arielah limped back toward the city, thankful their house was one of those nestled within the high protective walls surrounding Shunem. Entering the southern gate, she walked a few paces toward their courtyard, where a fenced garden lay just outside their home. Here Arielah could tend her wounds and still faintly hear some of the elders' meeting. Pausing just a moment before entering the courtyard, she heard Abba's raised voice wafting on the crisp night air.

"My northern brothers, we have fought our Judean brothers and eyed them with suspicion for too long. We are too quick to condemn, too slow to listen."

Arielah hurried into the courtyard to retrieve the water jar and stool. Picking up an old rag, she began washing the wounds on her right leg and ribs, wondering all the while how she might slip into the house unnoticed for a fresh robe and headpiece.

The sound of hoofbeats intruded. They were approaching the city, heavy and pounding. The lumbering gallop of a camel, not the clipped pace of a mule or horse. She stood and limped toward the city gate as quickly as her bruised leg would carry her. Just as she reached the gate, a camel and rider bearing King David's banner passed in a flurry of dust.

What is a royal messenger doing alone in Shunem—at night, on a camel? With the known tension between the king's household and Shunem, sending a royal representative alone was unusual. "But to come at night . . . and on a camel rather than a horse." She whispered her confusion to no one.

The messenger and his rumbling mount raced toward the well and awkwardly halted—but not before knocking over four or five slow-moving officials. The men seemed about to raise a fuss, but the messenger atop his perch cried out, "My lords!" The panic in the young man's voice gave everyone pause.

"Speak, sir," Jehoshaphat said from the front of the crowd.

"King David is dead!" the young man sobbed more than shouted. He tapped the camel on the shoulder, and it knelt. The messenger rolled off the beast and made his way to the front of the gathering, where Jehoshaphat awaited him.

Confusion reigned, giving Arielah a chance once again to slink to the same donkey cart where she'd found cover before her attack.

The torchlight revealed the royal messenger as a chubby young man who must have been twenty years old to be in the king's service, but he looked more like twelve. Tears streamed down his round cheeks. "Our king is dead!" he cried. "King David rests with his abbas and will be buried in the City of David tomorrow morning."

Silence hung like a shroud as each man weighed the effects of those words. David had reigned in Israel for forty years, and his would be the first royal burial in Israel. Saul, the nation's first king, had been killed in battle by the Philistines and his bones buried in Jabesh-Gilead. *How does one bury a legend?* Arielah wondered.

What do we do? was echoed in the chill wind of silence.

What do we do? was written on the furrowed brows of the elders.

What do we do? was even etched on the faces of Jehoshaphat's rebellious sons. They too had found their way into the noble crowd.

What would become of God's chosen people now that God's chosen leader was dead?

What do I do? Arielah's question was more imminent. Would Abba reveal his plan tonight? Would her future still be decided at this meeting of Israel's northern officials?

4

*From birth I was cast upon you; from my mother's
womb you have been my God.*

Jehoshaphat scanned the sea of frightened faces surrounding Shunem's well. "Take heart, my brothers. King David
has died; God has not."

His own heart was breaking at the thought of the great
man's death, but he dare not show it. Not yet. "Remember that God has placed young Solomon on the throne, and
competent men—Benaiah the captain, Zadok the priest, and
Nathan, God's prophet—stand at his side."

He stepped up on the well curb to regain control before the
mournful beating of breasts and rending of garments began.
"Listen, brothers. Those of you who wish to honor the years
of King David's faithfulness, meet me at the southern city gate
as soon as you can pack your camels. Only dromedaries for
this swift trip, and only one man per beast. If we leave soon,
we should arrive in Jerusalem by midmorning tomorrow to
join the burial procession of our king."

Stunned faces in the crowd remained silent, and Jehoshaphat knew he must address the raw emotion that still

bubbled beneath the surface. "Our king's death does not make right the wrongs done by his household, but he was God's anointed." A few muted tongues began to whisper, and heads nodded their assent. "All of Israel will grieve the customary thirty days, and then I will return to Jerusalem a second time to offer condolences to King Solomon personally. At that time, I will present the concerns of our northern tribes." Relief eased the tension on the elders' weathered faces as Jehoshaphat offered his final remark. "If our young king is a righteous man like his abba, he will hear our grievances and my plan for peace."

At the mention of a plan for peace, the crowd seemed to lean forward as if waiting for more details. When no explanation came, one official voiced the group's collective concern. "Good Jehoshaphat, we know you are wise, and your past faithfulness persuades us to trust you, but we would sleep easier tonight if—" The man stammered, but nods and jabs from his peers spurred him to complete his thought. "We want to know what plan you will propose to the king."

Jehoshaphat paused, meeting the frightened stares of many longtime friends. "I have never failed you before. You must trust me now—without knowing all the details."

A nervous buzz filled the air as Shunem's judge reached his arm around the shoulders of the king's messenger. "Please come to my home tonight, son. We'll get you a fresh camel for the return trip to Jerusalem."

"Thank you, my lord. King Solomon sent out messengers to all northern tribes this morning, and my dromedary has maintained a quick pace to reach Shunem by nightfall. I'm grateful for your hospitality." The camel squawked and spit as if realizing it had been mentioned.

Jehoshaphat grinned at the surly beast and patted the messenger's shoulder. "We'll be sure both you and your camel get plenty of food and water."

Relief was written in the rotund youngster's tear-streaked

face. "My camel wondered if she would find food and shelter this evening."

Jehoshaphat laughed at the boy's clever reply. Straightforward. Tenderhearted. Quick-witted. Yes, the palace had sent the right man for the job.

While the two moved through the crowd toward home, some men called out their support and promises to accompany Jehoshaphat to Jerusalem this evening, but Shunem's judge still heard murmurs rippling on the breeze.

"I'd feel better if I knew what he planned to present to the king," one said.

"Perhaps he'll tell us more during the mourning period before he returns to Jerusalem," another said.

Jehoshaphat was determined to focus on his guest and the imminent journey to Jerusalem. Leading the palace messenger toward home, Jehoshaphat asked, "What is your name, young man?"

"Reu, my lord."

They passed the last stragglers from the crowd, and Jehoshaphat noticed Kemmuel and Igal loitering near one of the market stalls. Waving them over, he said, "Reu, these are my sons, and they will help you tend your camel." Kemmuel scowled his disapproval, but Jehoshaphat ignored his foul mood. "And then they will escort you to our home for a fine meal."

Igal mirrored his brother's sour expression, neither son masking his impatience. Kemmuel kicked a rock across the path while Igal kept his gaze averted. Jehoshaphat was tempted to apologize for their rudeness, but when he turned to Reu, the young man bowed and addressed his grumbling caretakers.

"My camel's name is Delilah," he said to Kemmuel, who tried to ignore the jovial young man. "I named her thus because she is a willful female that leads me into sin wherever we go."

Kemmuel's eyes bulged and searched Igal's face as if making sure his slow-witted brother had heard. Suddenly both of Jehoshaphat's sons collapsed in a fit of laughter and finally gathered their wits enough to move toward the waiting Delilah. The young messenger looked over his shoulder and winked at Shunem's judge. Jehoshaphat wished he could win his sons' fondness so readily.

With a sad shrug, he turned toward home, dreading the news he must give Arielah. She would be disappointed that the treaty bride announcement must wait, but she would understand. Leaving the crowd behind, he saw only a delicate silhouette in the moonlight, waiting by his courtyard gate. He could hear gentle sniffing and knew his daughter was crying. *Of course*, he thought. *She must have heard everything from her hiding place in the market.*

Approaching in the darkness, Jehoshaphat spoke only when close enough to whisper. "Your ima chose your name rightly." Tilting her chin up, he said, "Truly, from the womb you have been our lion of God, and tonight is yet another circumstance in which you must stand strong."

A new wave of tears overtook her, and she melted into his arms, releasing giant, heaving sobs.

"I'm so sorry, little one," he said, holding her tightly. "I could not pronounce you as Israel's treaty bride tonight—as the one who will salve the wounds of Abishag's disgrace. In light of King David's death, I felt in my spirit that Solomon should hear the proposal first, before the northern tribes approve it." Arielah's tears quieted, and he whispered to his daughter's broken heart, "I ask you the same question I asked the elders of Israel's northern tribes. Can you trust me to do what is best for you without knowing all the details?" Jehoshaphat held her at arm's length, awaiting her response, searching her eyes for the truth.

"I trust you wholeheartedly," she said. "I know you will do what is right for me—and what is best for Israel."

Jehoshaphat felt the dampness of her sleeve. *She must have wet it with her tears*, he thought. Then a cool breeze blew, and her robe fluttered. The clouds cleared, and the moonlight revealed the complete trust on Arielah's face—and something more.

Blood.

Jehoshaphat was stricken. He studied her torn robe and for the first time noticed the bloodstains on her head covering and mantle. The control he'd displayed as Shunem's judge vanished, the restraint of his emotions evaporating like morning mist.

"Arielah, are you all right?" He gathered her in his arms again, grief nearly choking him, and his heart was torn in two. "What happened?" he whispered in her ear. But in his spirit, he knew. Arielah's silence confirmed her brothers' involvement. From the time they were children, she had yearned for their acceptance, hoped for their repentance, but only reaped their wrath.

Jehoshaphat squeezed his eyes shut. *Jehovah, wisdom fails me when it comes to these rebellious sons of mine. What am I to do?* He had been praying for his sons' transformation for years and loved all three of his children deeply; yet how does one separate hatred for deeds from the persons themselves?

Arielah pulled away to meet his gaze. "I thought tonight would be the beginning of my escape from my brothers' cruelty. I thought I could hold on as long as I knew the treaty bride plan was in place, as long as I knew God had a plan for me . . ." Her voice trailed away into quiet sobs, muffled in her abba's shoulder.

Jehoshaphat felt a tear slide down his cheek. Surely his heart would break in two. "Oh, my precious lamb," he said, "Jehovah *does* have a purpose for all this." As he held her tightly, their shoulders shook, unified in sorrow.

When their tears had ebbed, she nestled her head against him. "I believe it is as you said, Abba. From the womb, Jehovah has called me to be a lion of God, but when my brothers' hatred flares, I feel like a frightened lamb."

"My precious girl," he said, "I have tried to protect you—"

"Abba, this is *not* your fault!" she said, stepping away, passion in her tone. "You can't change their hearts. And you can't protect me every moment."

Gathering her into his arms again, he continued. "I know I can't watch over you all the time, but if you were married . . . sometimes I wish you were called to an ordinary life, to marry a shepherd and give me a multitude of grandchildren." His words were choked by the tightness in his throat. When he could speak again, he did so in a whisper. "But when one is called to great heights, Arielah, the pathway up the mountain is often riddled with deep ruts."

Just then, Jehoshaphat felt a hand on his shoulder. Releasing Arielah, he slipped his arm around his wife's petite waist. Jehosheba must have heard the elders' meeting adjourn and saw the two standing by the courtyard gate. She melted into her husband's side and looked tenderly at Arielah.

"Come, daughter. I've heard enough and seen enough to know that our sons have again dealt with you harshly." Jehosheba turned and stroked Jehoshaphat's cheek. "And I can see from the look in your eyes that the meeting with the officials must not have gone well." She reached for Arielah's hand without waiting for her husband's confirmation. "The news of the meeting can wait, my love, but our daughter's wounds cannot. Come, precious one." Arielah cast a backward glance at him while Jehosheba guided her to the back corner of their courtyard for privacy.

Jehoshaphat gathered the water jar and stool, followed the women, and positioned the stool so that Arielah could sit between them. Jehosheba reached for the rag to tend the head wound, but Jehoshaphat stopped his wife's hand and gently reached for the cloth. He met his wife's gaze, united in their grief as only parents of suffering children can be.

Caring little about the propriety of his actions, he removed his daughter's mantle and tenderly unwound her blood-caked headpiece while Jehosheba tended Arielah's side and leg. When he lit a clay lamp to see the cut on her head, a soft groan escaped his lips.

"It's not so bad, Abba," she said, squeezing his hand. "It will heal quickly." Love and tears formed an unbroken circle as two weeping parents ministered to their beloved girl. Finally, Arielah stood, ready to go inside for fresh clothes.

"Arielah," Jehoshaphat called. She stopped, waiting for him to speak, but his throat was clenched tight. Washing her wounds had magnified the very real dangers that awaited Arielah as Israel's treaty bride. Did she fully understand, or was she blinded by her dreams of Solomon? "My lamb, as Israel's treaty bride, you will experience great joy, and our nation will reach unparalleled unity." He paused, emotion constricting his throat. "But joy and unity come at a price. You'll face great danger in Jerusalem. This commitment could require enormous sacrifice."

Eyes glistening, she nodded. "As I said, Abba, I believe the hardships I've borne have prepared me—"

Jehoshaphat stepped toward her, taking her hands in his. "But here I've been able to provide some protection for you. In Jerusalem you'll be alone in the king's household."

"Abba, I am never alone." She reached up to brush a tear from his cheek. "When I was a child, you protected me from Kemmuel and Igal. I am not a child anymore, and now only Jehovah can protect me—whether in Shunem from my brothers or in Jerusalem as Israel's treaty bride."

Jehoshaphat's resolve shattered into a thousand teardrops. "Are you sure you want to do this? Do you want to give your life to Solomon—knowing the turmoil of our country and the fate of life in a king's harem?"

Arielah fell silent, her eyes searching. "I admit that I'm afraid of what awaits in Jerusalem. But I have loved Solomon all my life, and because of what I suffer at my brothers' hands, I am learning to call on Jehovah as my only helper. It is a good lesson, Abba." Arielah turned toward the house but was stopped abruptly by a figure from the shadows.

Even Jehoshaphat's breath caught as Kemmuel's dark presence dimmed the light of hope in their midst.

Fear strangled Arielah and threatened to rob her of air. She exhaled slowly, and her heart stilled as she recalled the words she'd spoken moments ago. *Only Jehovah can protect me.* She recalled that unveiled glimpse of vulnerability in Kemmuel's eyes, a hatred rooted in his belief that she'd stolen their abba's love. Kemmuel wasn't a leviathan; he was her brother. And for the first time in many years, she met his dark, foreboding gaze. She saw hate and the pain beneath it.

Igal rounded the corner with the king's messenger and stopped short in awkward silence. His eyes darted from the bloody rags in his parents' hands to Arielah, and then to Kemmuel. His gaze fell to his sandals and lingered there. Arielah wondered, as she so often had, if her impressionable second brother would do the right thing if Kemmuel weren't there.

"Arielah seems to have met with some ill fate this evening," Kemmuel said with a sneer. "How fortunate that she has an ima and abba to fawn over her like servants." Then, as though disgusted by their presence, he began marching toward the house while Igal and Reu shifted nervously at the courtyard gate.

"Kemmuel!" Jehoshaphat's shout split the silence, but rather than turn to face Abba, Kemmuel merely stopped, forcing Jehoshaphat to address his back. "Your disrespect will not go unpunished forever, my son. The sins you've committed against your sister will return to you one day."

Kemmuel whirled around. "And who will punish me, Abba? You? Do you have the strength to fight me? What can you do to me, you weak and foolish old man?"

A collective gasp rose from the courtyard. Kemmuel's brazen disrespect—especially shown in the presence of a guest—was unthinkable. Arielah glanced at the royal messenger; his cheeks and neck were crimson. Even Igal looked horrified.

Arielah saw Abba's inner battle through the windows of his soul. Something shifted in his eyes, and she knew Abba's response would be different this time. He had given his first-born countless opportunities to repent. Kemmuel, the boy, had squandered them all. Now Kemmuel, the man, would answer to Abba's firm—but merciful—hand.

"Kemmuel, you are no longer welcome in my home," Jehoshaphat said. "You may sleep in my barns or my sheepfolds, but from this day forward, you will be to me as a hired hand until you repent of your rebellion. I love you, my son, but I cannot allow you to destroy yourself and this family."

Kemmuel looked dumbstruck.

Jehoshaphat turned to his younger son and said softly, "Igal, you have always followed your brother's evil ways. Choose now the way you will go."

Arielah could feel her heart pounding. *Lord, please give Igal the strength to break free from Kemmuel's influence.*

Igal's face was ashen. Turning toward Jehosheba, Arielah witnessed the silent exchange between a loving ima and her lost son. Jehosheba stood beside Arielah but held out her hand to Igal. The second son smiled faintly, but when his eyes met his sister's, his deadly glare was accusing. *This is all your fault*, he seemed to say.

Igal looked to Kemmuel then, his older brother's expression as hard as the bricks in Egypt.

"Yes, Igal, choose which way you will go," Kemmuel taunted.

Igal squeezed his eyes shut. A decision of this magnitude seemed to cause the slow-witted brother physical pain.

"Now! Choose now!" Kemmuel screamed, bullying his brother as usual. Like a confused lamb, Igal looked from Ima to Abba and then to his older brother who had always held an invisible strap around his neck. It was only a moment—just a brief hesitation. Then he walked into the house with Kemmuel to gather his things and move to the barns.

Ima buried her face on Arielah's shoulder. "How could our sons treat their abba like this? Don't they realize they could be stoned for such rebellion?" Arielah moved Ima to the farthest corner of the courtyard. She didn't want to be near the house when her brothers returned.

Jehoshaphat extended his hand to his guest, guiding him to join the women. "Reu, I'm sorry you had to witness the shame that stains my family."

Reu's sincerity was evident as he placed his hand on the judge's shoulder. "My lord, I will not pretend to know the difficult relationships between abbas and sons since my own abba died when I was a young boy. But I have never seen a man love as you love your sons."

Arielah's heart warmed at the kindness of this stranger. His words seemed like a balm to her abba's wounded spirit.

"The law says you could have Kemmuel and Igal stoned for the way they cursed you tonight. In fact, I don't know any other Israelite who would allow repentance after being treated this way." Then, nodding at Jehosheba and Arielah, he said, "I believe the house of Jehoshaphat is not a house stained with shame but one made of mercy."

A loud *crack!* sounded as Kemmuel tried to slam the cedar door closed, but its corner caught on the dirt floor and splintered. Arielah's brothers rushed by, their belongings in sacks slung over their shoulders. Neither offered a word of farewell, nor did they look back.

The little band in the courtyard watched in silence until the two silhouettes faded in the moonlight. Arielah felt the cool spring breeze and suddenly remembered her torn robe. Thankful that Ima Jehosheba stood beside her and blocked Reu's view of her injuries, Arielah would allow Abba and his guest to enter the house first, while Ima brought a new robe and headpiece outside.

Jehoshaphat offered a sad smile to their royal guest. "Reu, you have been more than patient. Now let me show you the hospitality of Shunem. My honorable wife is a fine cook, and my daughter plays beautifully on her shepherd's flute." Abba wrapped his arm around the messenger's shoulders and guided him to the house, casting a backward glance at his wife and daughter. "Jehosheba and Arielah will be along in a little while."

Reu patted his ample middle. "I thought I remembered you promising food before we began our journey back to Jerusalem."

As the two men made their way into the house, Arielah whispered through tears, "Ima, why must Kemmuel and Igal continue to hurt themselves and others, when all we want to do is love them? How can we make them understand?"

Jehosheba cupped Arielah's cheek and wiped away her tears. "We are all given stones with which we build our lives, Arielah. Love is the cornerstone upon which your abba has chosen to build this family. When Kemmuel refused to make it *his* cornerstone, his life became unsteady, unstable—and his character unsound with it." She gently kissed Arielah's forehead. "Kemmuel must choose his cornerstone, my little lion of God. We cannot build his life for him."

Ima brushed her arm and then disappeared into the house, leaving Arielah to meditate on her words. Indeed, her parents' love had been the bedrock of her life, that unshakable, sacred cornerstone upon which Arielah had grown in safety and confidence. Her brothers had been offered the same love but had rejected it. Why? How could anyone resist it?

She suddenly remembered Solomon. He had just lost his abba. Was King David *his* unshakable cornerstone?

Jehosheba reappeared with a fresh robe and head covering. Arielah exchanged her tattered garments and donned her clean woolen robe, wondering, *On what cornerstone will Solomon build his life? His nation?*

5

*[As Jacob lay dying, he] called for his sons and said:
... "Judah, your brothers will praise you; ... your father's sons will bow down to you."*

Professional mourners began wailing the moment King David's eyes closed in death. But in the depths of the palace dungeon, screams melted into the incoherent mumblings of the tortured. It was here in this dark kingdom that Ahishar, the palace high steward, reigned supreme. After Prince Adonijah's failed attempt to steal the throne, Ahishar was the highest-ranking palace official still undetected in the covert Sons of Judah. Fear was Ahishar's greatest weapon, and he wielded it expertly in his underground kingdom.

Holding a clean white cloth over his nose and mouth, he examined his most recent betrayer. "How long, Mahlon, have you been a scribe in my service?"

The man reeked of blood and excrement, but the sweet smell of his fear seeped through Ahishar's cloth. "Twenty ... years, my ... lord." The scribe slumped between two guards, his face and lips swollen after long hours of torture.

"And in those twenty years, how many times have you

spoken to Elisheba the cook about matters of politics in Israel?"

"Lord Ahishar," Mahlon said, "truly, I . . . I spoke to Elisheba . . . of palace matters . . . very few times . . . hardly ever."

At Ahishar's nod, one of the guards seized Mahlon's hair and jerked his head back. "Tell me, my friend. Recount the exact words you found necessary to gush to the palace cook."

"Please, my lord, I offered no details. I just said you wished Judah to rule the northern tribes of Israel." He paused as though considering whether to tell all.

Ahishar smiled. *Smart fellow. Consider carefully.* "I can bring Elisheba down and ask her if you'd prefer."

Mahlon's eyes were wild. "No! I told her the Sons of Judah planned to . . . conquer the Israelites in the north . . . to make Judah a nation . . . royal and powerful." His begging and hysteria deteriorated until Ahishar's once refined scribe became a babbling idiot.

But the high steward felt no compassion. How ridiculous that a highly respected scribe would risk his position, his reputation—even his life—to impress the palace cook. Compassion? No. He felt disgust. This flawlessly dutiful scribe threw away a lucrative career for a few moments of boasting.

Stroking his patchy beard, Ahishar considered his own carelessness. He should never have conducted the business of the Sons of Judah in the presence of someone like Mahlon. A scribe who mingled with servants was unworthy to enter the secret society's membership of select palace officials and influential Judean leaders. It was a tight circle of trust, and too much talk could forfeit generations of planning. King Solomon must never discover their existence. He, like King David, was under the impression that Israel should remain a nation of equality among the tribes. If only Adonijah's coup had succeeded. As leader of the Sons of Judah, he would have immediately declared war on the northern tribes.

A slow smile crept across Ahishar's face. *Now that Adonijah is gone and I command the Sons of Judah, who would dare challenge me for Judah's new throne?* Perhaps it was to his benefit that Adonijah had failed.

Mahlon's piteous moan drew the high steward's attention, and the scribe resumed his pleading. "As you know, my lord, I too am of the tribe of Judah. I applauded your loyal support of the tribe of Judah to Elisheba. So please, master, have mercy on me, your brother Judean."

"Enough!" Ahishar screeched, taking three quick steps to close the gap. With their noses almost touching, Ahishar whispered, "Say one more word and I will cut out your tongue."

Mahlon hesitated only a moment. "Yes, my lord."

A slow, satisfied chuckle began at the base of Ahishar's throat. "I did warn you, my friend." He watched with delight as the realization dawned on his prisoner's face.

"No! Please, master, I didn't mean to say another word!" Mahlon fought the guards valiantly but, of course, to no avail.

"Hold his jaws apart!" Ahishar shouted over the scuffle. "A mute scribe can still write beautiful letters on a clay tablet."

Exhausted, Solomon concentrated on putting one foot in front of the other, walking deliberately from the astronomers' tower near the Valley Gate toward the palace. Benaiah walked with him, and the pounding of the big man's sandals shook the ground, a familiar cadence that had accompanied him since Abba's death this morning.

After leaving David's bedside, Solomon had thrown himself into pressing matters of state. Time was precious since all work would cease when he announced the thirty-day grieving period tomorrow. Solomon's final task of the day took him to the celestial experts in the watchtower to discuss his proposed calendar changes. Hoping to reach a decision tonight, since the changes would affect the beginning of Passover, he lifted his eyes to the cloudy sky. "How can I track the path of the moon and stars, Benaiah, when the night is as dark as the tents of Kedar?"

The captain followed the king's gaze upward. "It seems even the moon and stars are shrouded to mourn King David's death."

Trudging uphill through the fortress gate, they entered the unwalled portion of the new city. Clouds cleared, and the moon shone on Mount Moriah, the plot of land north of the palace that would become God's temple site.

"How will Israel remember my abba, Benaiah?" Solomon asked, studying the vacant hill. "Will they remember this as Araunah's threshing floor, where Abba went after his disobedient census caused seventy thousand Israelite deaths before he offered sacrifices to God? Or will they remember that this was Mount Moriah, where Abraham was willing to sacrifice Isaac but God provided a miracle instead?" Benaiah remained silent, eyes forward. Solomon wasn't looking for an answer, and the big man seemed to realize it. "Will Israel remember David the warrior, his provision of wealth and foreign laborers to build God's temple? Will they recall my abba's friendship with Hiram, king of Tyre, that provided the necessary cedar logs and shipping lanes to transport them?"

More silence passed. Finally, Benaiah ventured a gentle answer. "Perhaps you will ask Israel these things tomorrow at the royal tombs. They are your people now, my lord. They will remember the things of which you remind them."

My people now. Solomon's mind continued to spin. As they ascended the palace steps, sounds of professional mourners wafted on the night breeze. The soft moans would last through the night, reminding the city of a legend lost.

With a slight chuckle, Solomon asked, "And what will Israel remember of me, my friend? Calendar changes?"

The big man smiled in return. "With your inquisitive mind, young Solomon, I believe Israel will never forget you. Only Jehovah knows the extent of your reign."

Glancing above them, Solomon noted extra guards near the palace parapets and the eastern wall bordering the Kidron Valley. For the first time, he realized Benaiah had seemed especially on edge today, more than grief silencing him. He'd been on alert. "Judging by the extra guards," Solomon said, shifting their topic once more, "I sense you're expecting some sort of increased threat."

His captain raked his large hand over his weary face and then turned with a respectful grin. "You are indeed inquisitive, my lord."

Solomon nodded, bidding his friend to continue.

"We have received word that some of the foreign ambassadors have inquired about the storehouses of wealth your abba gathered to build the temple. King David wisely distributed the riches into three separate citadels at Megiddo, Hazor, and of course here, in the fortress of Zion. When we dispatched word of your abba's death to the surrounding tribes and nations, we added guards in and around the palace. Additional men have been assigned to King David's—I'm sorry. I mean, they've been assigned to *your* private chambers since your chamber wall shares the northern wall of the fortress."

It all sounded so matter-of-fact, so routine when Benaiah said it. But when Abba's heart stopped beating, Solomon's whole world had shifted. Nothing felt routine. Now he alone ruled Israel. He must keep his nation and his family safe.

Suddenly overwhelmed with the need to see his only son, he choked out the command. "Benaiah, send one of the guards to summon my wife Naamah. Have her bring Prince Rehoboam." Struggling to keep his composure, he said, "I need to hold my future so I can let go of my past."

With a nod and a directive glance, Benaiah obeyed, issuing the command to a guard as they entered the palace. Winding through the grand halls, Solomon continued his silent contemplations amid the eerie echoes of mourners' wails. "I can't believe he's gone," he whispered. Benaiah's meaty hand rested around his shoulder, the gentle giant his constant support.

Solomon's sackcloth slippers made no sound on the mosaic tiles leading to his chambers. Two Mighty Men stood guard at the double cedar doors between twin lion statues. The lion had long been the symbol of Judah's tribe, and the Mighty Men had long been David's mercenary bodyguards, many of whom were Cherethite and Pelethite warriors. The doors of Abba David's chamber—now Solomon's—opened at the clang of the guards' crossed spears. The king walked beneath the canopied weapons of his fiercest defenders.

Naamah stood before him, breathless, hurried. Though Solomon had walked leisurely between the palace entrance and his chamber, his summons had obviously been issued with urgency.

His wife's exquisite dark eyes flashed like a flame against polished obsidian. "Why have I been called, and why would you command your son to be awakened to see you at this hour?"

Rehoboam lay on his nursemaid's shoulder, sound asleep, and Solomon felt torn between anger and regret. Naamah never offered him a kind word anymore, but she was right this time. He should have considered the late hour. Taking a step toward his Ammonite wife, he noted a shadow of fear in her eyes and then her quick recovery. She was every measure a king's daughter, but he occasionally caught glimpses of the atrocities she must have witnessed of her abba's defeat at General Joab's hand. The Ammonites had been a vassal nation since Solomon was born; in fact, it was while Joab was winning that battle that Abba David seduced Ima Bathsheba. Naamah had been saved with other Ammonite noblemen's daughters, and though she was several years Solomon's senior, her sad eyes had captured his heart. But tonight those eyes cast daggers.

Reaching out his hand, he said, "Please, Naamah. It's been

a long day. I didn't want to be alone tonight." He waited for her response. Nothing.

Rehoboam nuzzled into his nursemaid's shoulder, releasing the contented sigh of one too young to know true sorrow. Solomon reached for the boy, but Naamah grabbed him out of the maid's arms. "Stop, he's sleeping," she whispered, her anger smoldering. "Why must you wake a peaceful boy from his dreams?"

Rehoboam stirred and began to whimper. "Mi-ma?"

"See what you've done?" she spat while smoothing the toddler's curly dark hair. Naamah took a wool-stuffed doll from the maid's hand, the likeness of a man with the head of an ox. Rehoboam cuddled the toy god Molech and contentedly sucked his thumb, nestling to sleep in his ima's arms.

All blood drained from Solomon's face. "Give the child to his nurse. Now!"

Naamah jumped, startling Rehoboam awake, and the boy began to wail.

"Benaiah, escort Naamah's maid back to the nursery, and return to us when you have news that our son is sleeping peacefully."

Tears welled in his wife's eyes as she transferred her son to the maid's arms and watched Benaiah lead them from the room. With the precision learned from a lifetime among nobility, Naamah turned gracefully to meet Solomon's gaze. "I did not expect to be called to the king's chamber this evening." She removed her head covering and began untying her belt with shaking hands. "I have not been properly oiled and lotioned."

Solomon covered the distance between them in two steps, stilling her hands in his grasp. "Naamah, we must talk about that pagan god you have given Rehoboam. You cannot teach my son to embrace any god but El Shaddai." He spoke quietly, tenderly, trying to control his already frayed emotions.

She tilted her head up slowly, and Solomon saw her eyes

drowning in pain. "Your father's soldiers killed my father and brothers. Israel has made slaves of my people and taken possession of all Ammonite cities." Blinking, she released the river of tears down her cheeks. "If I don't teach my son of his mother's people, how can he know that the blood of two great nations flows through his veins?" She laid her head on Solomon's chest, and instinctively he enfolded her in a protective embrace. He could feel her trembling from head to toe with her final plea. "Please don't take away the last remnant of my Ammonite heritage. I am only one of five foreign wives in your harem, and the Israelite wives and concubines spurn us. All we have are the traditions of our homelands to keep us sane, Solomon. Please . . . please." The floodgate of tears burst, and her shoulders shook uncontrollably. Gone was the dignity of her nobility. Gone was her arrogance. He held a broken treasure, and his heart broke with her.

How could he help her? The harem was like a kingdom—of women. While other nations allowed eunuchs to provide male levelheadedness, Israel refused them, calling their disfigurement an abomination. Solomon remembered Ima Bathsheba's torturous days in Abba's harem until Abba built her a home on the western ridge. Ima, at least, worshiped Jehovah. The foreign wives were spurned for blasphemy as well as for beauty. Solomon ruled Israel, but his wives ruled the harem—a complex world of bitterness and betrayal.

"Shhh." He held her as she cried. "I didn't realize how difficult the last two years have been." The lovely faces of his Moabite and Edomite wives flashed before him. At least Naamah had conceived right away, which had positioned her as first wife. Stroking Naamah's hair, he let her tears subside before tilting up her chin. "I cannot allow you to teach my son to worship a pagan god, Naamah." She started to protest, but Solomon pressed a silencing finger to her lips. "However, you may teach him of the Ammonite people." He paused to read her expression and consider his next words. "And you may continue to worship Molech in the privacy of your chamber—as long as you don't announce it to the Israelite women." The smile that lit her face soothed his soul, and the kiss placed on his lips sent fire through his blood.

"Thank you, my lord," she said with a hurried retreat. "May I go check on Rehoboam, to see if he's at rest?"

Solomon's heart plummeted. "Of course. Go." He watched her disappear behind the double cedar doors, a new concern now foremost on his mind. He and Abba had reached a trade agreement with Egypt, and Pharaoh's daughter was scheduled to arrive within the moon's cycle as Solomon's new treaty bride. What if this Egyptian princess became as unsettled as Naamah? Women's tears were troubling, but if Pharaoh's daughter sent embittered reports back to her homeland, Solomon would deal with more than a disquieted harem. He could be faced with an Egyptian invasion.

"Guard!" he shouted, walking toward the doors. The great cedar panel swung open on iron hinges.

"Yes, my lord?" The man nodded.

"Summon Ahishar to my chamber. I must speak with the high steward immediately." As the soldier backed out of the room, Solomon added, "You might as well assemble the full council in the throne hall. Despite the late hour, Ahishar will need to meet with them after he hears what's on my mind."

6

❧ 1 Kings 1:7–8 ❧

*[Before David died,] Adonijah conferred with Joab . . .
and with Abiathar the priest, and they gave him their
support. But Zadok the priest, Benaiah son of Jehoiada,
[and] Nathan the prophet . . . did not join Adonijah.*

A hishar scanned the faces of the most powerful men
in Israel. Eight royal officials slumped and yawned on
cushioned couches, lining both sides of the long aisle leading
to Solomon's throne.

"Why were we yanked from our dreams in the middle of
the night?" groused old Abiathar, the high priest.

"We haven't even gone home yet," one of the younger
priests said. "We just finished anointing King David's body
after the servants prepared and washed him." A moment of
sadness paused the group before more complaining began.

Ahishar listened as protests filled the two-story throne hall.
Of the king's ten royal officials, four of those seated were devout
Sons of Judah and four were loyal to a united Israel. Benaiah, the
ninth advisor, was loyal to the king alone and attended council
meetings only when Solomon was present. Ahishar, the tenth
advisor and leader of the Sons of Judah, held the majority vote,

thereby wielding the greatest power of all. He stood before the king's council and allowed himself a cryptic smile. *When I lead Judah to victory over Israel's northern tribes, I will be your king, and you will not complain like nagging wives.*

"Thank you for gathering so quickly at such a late hour," Ahishar said, bowing in feigned humility. Fixing his eyes on the royal secretary, he scratched his long, slender nose—an established signal that the next topic was significant to the Sons of Judah. "Elihoreph, King Solomon has considered this a matter of extreme urgency. We must vote on it tonight and fill the necessary positions before the burial procession in the morning."

As chief secretary and fellow Son of Judah, Elihoreph was Ahishar's most trusted ally—if a snake could trust a fox. The secretary sat a little straighter, poised his hand over the wax tablet, and gripped the stylus with white knuckles.

"King Solomon has asked that I choose two young virgins to facilitate his foreign wives' transition into Judean life."

When Ahishar took a breath, old Abiathar inserted a sarcastic snort. "You called me out of my warm bed to talk about women in King Solomon's harem?" The old priest's bristly gray eyebrows knit together.

Ahishar pinned him with a stare. "Is it only conspiracies that wrest you from slumber, my lord?" He could see the verbal jab hit its mark. Color drained from Abiathar's cheeks. The old high priest had recently changed allegiance like the Great Sea changes tide. Though Abiathar was a Levite priest and had no proof the Sons of Judah existed, he had been helpful in Adonijah's attempt to steal Solomon's throne. When the coup failed, both the prince and the priest received mercy from King Solomon in return for their promised loyalty. Now Abiathar's word held as much honor as a cracked clay cup.

"A conspiracy would indeed stir my ire," the old priest answered, stoic now. "I do not wish to see King Solomon hurt again."

Uneasy eyes searched the marble tiles. All the king's advisors felt the sting of Prince Adonijah's rebellion—for very different reasons. Those loyal to King David realized they should have publicly supported Solomon earlier. The Sons of Judah mourned the loss of their leader when Solomon banished Prince Adonijah to his home in En Rogel.

The day after the uprising, Ahishar had sent word to the secret society: *We meet tomorrow to choose a new leader.* At the meeting, when others voiced fear that the investigation of Adonijah's coup would uncover their centuries-old existence, Ahishar disagreed. "It provides the perfect distraction for the ultimate civil war. Judah will finally conquer the northern ten tribes," he'd said. His rousing speech had secured his leadership, which had reached new heights with tonight's commission from the king.

"As I was saying . . ." Ahishar cleared his throat and continued. "Solomon's foreign wives bring handmaids from their native lands, and the two virgins I choose—we'll call them 'friends'—will teach the foreign wives about harem life. These 'friends' must be thoroughly familiar with palace propriety, the City of David, and the unique . . . shall we say, *challenges* of royal living."

"Why now, Ahishar?" Zadok asked.

The throne hall fell silent, and Ahishar's heart skipped a beat.

Zadok was an old priest like Abiathar, but he was vastly different in wisdom and integrity. Zadok spoke little and said much. He heard the message behind words and read the intentions of a glance. He was one of the three men responsible for Adonijah's defeat, and Ahishar knew Zadok was measuring him now.

Swallowing hard, Ahishar said, "The Egyptian princess is scheduled to arrive after the thirty-day grieving period, and King Solomon asks that the maidens be ready to assist his new wife immediately upon her arrival. Since our king will announce the beginning of grieving tomorrow, and no work may be done during the time, I must choose the two maidens tonight." Ahishar's words tumbled out like a naughty child offering excuses.

Zadok nodded. Silence. His cloudy eyes seemed to search the corners of Ahishar's soul. Did he know the two women Ahishar had chosen were at the core of his plan to become king?

The high steward's mouth was too dry to swallow, too dry to speak. He must say something! "Good question, Zadok!" he blurted out, much louder than intended. "Anyone else?"

Elihoreph lifted his eyes from his stylus and clay tablet, offering a calming stare. "And who do you have in mind for this distinguished position of 'Wives' Ambassadors'?"

The palace steward dragged in a deep breath, squared his shoulders, and nodded gratefully to Elihoreph. "Though the chief secretary's title, 'Wives' Ambassadors,' is quite suitable, I've chosen a more descriptive label—'Daughters of Jerusalem.'" Elihoreph offered a disappointed sniff and recorded the title on his tablet while Ahishar continued. "'Daughters of Jerusalem' rings like a well-played timbrel and emphasizes their indisputable heritage. I've chosen the twin daughters of Bethuel, the royal tailor." Ahishar paused for the length of a heartbeat and added, "I believe many of you know their ima, Miriam." He watched with wicked delight as every face registered recognition, and silence wrapped the room like burial rags.

Miriam was well acquainted with most of the men in the room. Her husband, Bethuel, had become the city's most fashionable tailor and the court's most gullible buffoon. While Bethuel sewed ornate couches and pillows for the king's highest-ranking officials, his wife enjoyed intimate relations with his customers, opening political doors a tailor's needle and thread could never unlock. Their twin daughters spent most of their lives waiting for their parents at the palace and had consequently grown up alongside royal heirs and noblemen's children.

But the maidens had learned more than manners of royalty. They were experts in deceit and seduction, second only to their ima Miriam.

"Our Daughters of Jerusalem will teach Solomon's current foreign wives to worship Jehovah and respect our heritage," Ahishar explained lightly, keeping his true intent carefully hidden. "And I will work with Shiphrah and Sherah to ensure that any future foreign wives report a joyous marriage to their homeland. In this way, we will aid the Lord's prophecy for Solomon's reign and enjoy peace with nations on every side." A wry smile raised one corner of his lips. "After all, a happy harem means a peaceful palace."

The advisors nodded and murmured congratulations to each other, though none had participated in the decision. Ahishar masked a wave of disgust. How could these men be satisfied with their crumbs of power when a banquet of ambition lay before them? Had they no imagination? Even his fellow Sons of Judah seemed fooled by the duties he'd concocted for the Daughters of Jerusalem. Couldn't they see that when Shiphrah and Sherah served the exact *opposite* purpose in Solomon's harem, Judah and Israel would finally be forced into civil war?

The twins would encourage the king's five foreign wives to worship their pagan gods, thereby enraging Judeans and Israelites alike. The Daughters of Jerusalem would then ostracize the few northern Israelite wives of both David's and Solomon's harems, showing blatant favoritism to the royal Judean women. When the Israelite wives complained—and they would most certainly complain—Shiphrah and Sherah would facilitate their grievances to their families back in northern Israel, hoping to stir more hostility. With reported paganism and favoritism rampant in the harem, northern Israel would undoubtedly strike, and King Solomon would be forced to declare war.

Ahishar's smile widened. *But will Judah fight for a king who allows his women to worship pagan gods and rule his household?* Judah would demand a stronger leader, and Ahishar would muster allegiance from the well-trained Judean military. Their five hundred thousand professional soldiers could overpower the ill-prepared eight hundred thousand northern tribesmen armed with winnowing forks and scythes. *Solomon's youth will be his downfall*, Ahishar delighted silently, *and Judah will be mine—the nation she was meant to be.*

Realizing the room was silent and all eyes were on him, Ahishar felt his cheeks burn. "Forgive me, my friends," he said, shaking his head as if rattling stray thoughts aside. "I was just contemplating how much more smoothly King Solomon's daily life can progress if he can live in peace with his women." Unfurling a parchment, Ahishar laid it on the edge of the platform and lifted a candle from its base. "This decree affirms your support of the Daughters of Jerusalem. You may affix your personal seals to this document as your vote of approval." Tipping the candle, he dripped a dollop of beeswax at the bottom and tugged at his leather necklace, lifting his seal from beneath his robe. He rolled his small cylinder across the warm wax as the first vote. "Next?"

Seven of the men rose from their couches, but Abiathar, the old high priest, shouted, "Wait!" The advisors paused and glanced in his direction. "I have more questions. I believe we should discuss this further," he said, searching the faces of his compatriots for support.

Instead, the other council members exchanged awkward glances and looked to Ahishar for rescue. The palace high steward issued a subtle nod to four rough-looking soldiers at the rear of the throne hall. The guards advanced and stood directly behind Abiathar's couch.

"Palace matters fall under my purview, my friend," Ahishar said. "And as you said before, it's hardly a matter to pull you away from your warm bed. Why discuss it further?"

Elihoreph was the first council member to step forward and press his seal into a fresh dollop of wax. The other Sons of Judah followed, their confident strides assuring Ahishar of their support, even in matters of which they had no knowledge. The high steward nodded graciously, more certain than ever that the less they knew, the more power he wielded.

Next came the Israelite loyalists, and finally Abiathar. Hesitating beside the parchment, seal poised in his hand, he whispered, "I know you are up to something, Ahishar, but without proof or Benaiah's strong presence, I cannot determine what." His bristly eyebrows drew together, creating a single tuft like lamb's wool above his eyes. "But I suppose two silly maidens in a harem can't cause much harm." Abiathar sighed and affixed his final seal to the parchment.

Nodding silent direction to the burly Judean watchmen, Ahishar left no doubt that the meeting was over. "Thank you, gentlemen, for your faithful service to our king." The watchmen opened the rear doors, and the soft sounds of mourners' wails filled the courtroom. "Please return to your chambers and get some sleep. We convene court early for a few last items of business before we bury our beloved King David in the morning."

Sober nods and glistening eyes were the only answer. As retreating sandals exited the throne hall, Ahishar's expression remained somber, but he silently reveled in this victory. One step closer to Judah's rise to power, he ascended the marble stairs and gazed at King David's throne. Glancing right and then left to ensure privacy, he melted into the finely embroidered purple cushions, placing his hands on the lion's-head armrests. *This throne will be mine someday*, he thought, inhaling the overpowering aroma of cedar.

A heavy wall tapestry fluttered. "Who's there?" he said, leaping from the throne.

"So, my palace weasel, it appears the Sons of Judah continue undaunted though my rebellion failed." Prince Adonijah appeared out of the shadows and approached the dais. "Shall I bow, Ahishar?"

The steward's heart pounded. "No, my lord! No! I had no idea anyone was watching!"

"Obviously. A man can be executed as a traitor for sitting on the king's throne."

Adonijah's smirk sent Ahishar's mind reeling. *I am leader of the Sons of Judah now. You had your chance to be king and squandered it with shortsighted planning.* But his success rested on the ability to deceive. "My lord Adonijah, I fear for your safety. It was my understanding that King Solomon banished you to your home in En Rogel."

Adonijah's face shaded, red as a pomegranate. "Solomon did not banish me! I chose to return home for a time, but I am the rightful leader of the Sons of Judah, and I will be king!"

Ahishar bowed once more. "I meant no disrespect, my lord, and of course, you as King David's son are the rightful leader of the Sons of Judah." Ahishar had to think quickly. Adonijah's return could draw unwanted attention to the Sons' activities. The Mighty Men would undoubtedly be scrutinizing Adonijah's every move. *I must divert his attention from the Sons of Judah.*

"What is this plan about the Daughters of Jerusalem, Ahishar? If you're taking care of the details, I assume it somehow benefits the Sons of Judah—and you." Adonijah tugged at his collar, covering the fingernail scars on his neck.

Ahishar smiled at the rogue prince. "Ah, yes. I believe you might remember Shiphrah and Sherah, my lord. The twin virgins of Bethuel, the royal tailor. They once resisted your advances"—the steward paused and then bowed—"foolishly, of course."

The prince's neck turned crimson, making the lingering claw marks more noticeable. "Yes, I remember them." He scowled. "Why were they bathing with my sisters in the palace if they were daughters of a common merchant?"

"Bethuel is no common tailor, and their ima's skill in seduction won Shiphrah and Sherah lives of leisure among children of nobility. Neither twin has ever cooked a meal or carded wool, but in the arts of lotions and paints, they are flawless."

Adonijah waved away the explanation. "Other than

winning for yourself the pleasurable gratitude of their ima, I don't understand how two spoiled, manipulative virgins in Solomon's harem benefit the Sons of Judah."

With every kernel of restraint he possessed, Ahishar refused to unleash his anger on this small-minded prince. But neither would he waste his time on long-winded explanations. "Their ima's gratitude is indeed enticing, my lord; however, it is King Solomon's appreciation for the Daughters' diligent service that will aid our cause. When they recount the impossible role of keeping peace in his harem, your brother's sympathy will no doubt lead him to underestimate their treachery."

He offered a perfunctory bow, hoping the simple explanation would suffice. Then, as suddenly as Adonijah had appeared, the idea for Ahishar's diversion materialized. *Solomon's sympathy!* The thought was so simple yet so profound.

"My lord!" he nearly shouted, and Adonijah jumped like a startled shepherd. "I have a plan that only you can accomplish. It will require all your wit and charm."

Adonijah looked suspicious. "Don't waste your cheap manipulations on me, steward. Tell me the plan, and I will decide its merit."

Ahishar nodded demurely. "The queen mother is resting in the palace tonight. Go to her and ask that she beg Solomon to give you Abishag, David's Shulammite nursemaid, as your wife."

Adonijah paused, searching Ahishar's face. "Solomon would never give me Abishag. He knows giving me one of Abba's women would be like handing me part of his kingdom."

"True, my lord, but one of the servants told me that King Solomon had grown quite attached to the girl, and—"

"All the more reason not to ask for her!" Adonijah's eyes sparked dangerously.

"Please, my lord, hear me out." Smoldering, the prince fell silent, and Ahishar continued. "A loyal servant reported that Solomon had spoken of his sympathy for Abishag's plight.

She will live in the harem of David's women, never to marry or bear children because King David made Solomon vow that he would never bed Abishag or any of his women."

Adonijah lifted a single eyebrow. "So why would Solomon give one of Abba's women to me?"

"The same servant has observed Bathsheba's jealousy of the girl Abishag. David's queen knows her son shares his abba's lust for beauty. She will be your ally, my lord, to remove this lovely temptation from Solomon's presence." Ahishar paused to allow the prince a moment's consideration, hoping beyond hope Adonijah would show the same shortsighted ambition that foiled his first coup. "You could win Bathsheba's goodwill and steal one of Solomon's treasures."

The two men shared a conspiratorial smile. "Abishag is quite beautiful," Adonijah said. "But what makes you think Solomon would agree to give her to me?"

"King Solomon cannot have her because of his promise to your abba, and the king's tender heart will be moved by Bathsheba's argument for the girl's happiness." Pausing only a moment, he added, "We both know your brother can't deny a pleading woman."

Adonijah crossed his arms and then cupped his chin, deep in thought. "All right. I'll do it!" he said with boyish delight.

"I believe you should go at once, my lord, to speak with Bathsheba. I'm sure she's still awake. Who can sleep with this constant droning of mourners?"

Ahishar bowed to the prince and remained in the penitent position until he heard Adonijah's footsteps retreating across the marble floor. Lifting his head, he reveled in almost certain victory. *Yes, foolish prince, Bathsheba will hear your request. She may even present it to her son. Then you'll face Solomon's fury, and I'll once again be the undisputed leader of the Sons of Judah.*

7

Now Adonijah, the son of Haggith, went to Bathsheba,
Solomon's mother. Bathsheba asked him, "Do you come
peacefully?"

Bathsheba yawned and snuggled into her double-stuffed
woolen mattress. She hadn't slept since . . . well, she
couldn't remember when she last laid on a sleeping couch.
After David's death this morning, she had joined the servants in preparing his body for burial. It was one of the last
times she'd ever see her beloved husband's earthly shell. The
thought pierced her.

After she had helped the servants wash, wrap, and anoint
David's body for burial, Solomon had seen her exhaustion
and begged her to remain at the palace rather than return to
her private home on the western ridge. She recognized the
same weariness on his face and agreed. Glancing around the
large, ornately decorated private chamber, she wished she'd
returned home. This newly constructed chamber in David's
harem was lovely, filled with fine linen, pottery, and trinkets
from distant lands. But she'd escaped the confines of harem
life years ago when David built her private home. It was the

grandest house in Israel, but David had called it their shepherd's hut because it was secluded and peaceful, and during
the hours he visited there, he could forget palace life.

Tonight, staring out this ivory-latticed window, she wished
she could forget palace life and sleep. She tried counting
stars. Before that, she'd counted sheep, goats, even herding
dogs. But sleep was a miser unwilling to share its peace. Her
mind whirred with memories of this morning's bittersweet
moments. She remembered Solomon's tormented features,
watching his abba slip away, but she also recalled David's
confidence in their wise son's ability to rule.

Then came the dagger to her heart. The beautiful Shulammite lying atop David. Warming him. Caressing him. Loving
him.

Tears wet her pillow. *I could have warmed him like that—
before five children rounded my figure.* She knew the thought
was ridiculous. David loved her. She'd always known she was
his favorite, but sharing her husband with other women still
tormented her. *Why must a king rule first and love last?*

When David took Bathsheba from her first husband, Uriah,
she knew that a relationship with the king of Israel would
never be normal. But when David's love for her blossomed,
she consoled herself thinking, *Other women share his body,
but I possess his heart.* And when their son Solomon was
named his successor, she knew that she had won not only
David's heart but also Jehovah's favor.

Then the Shulammite arrived.

Abishag's presence had not only shaken the foundation
of David's love for her, it had unsettled an already boiling
pot of unrest in the northern tribes. Had Jehovah removed
his blessing too?

She snuggled further under a lion-skin cover that David
had given her years ago and breathed in the musky scent of
her husband. Thankful now that she hadn't taken all of her
personal items to her private home, she listened to the hum of

midnight mourning and squeezed her eyes shut. She dreaded tomorrow. Solomon would lead the burial procession to their family's tomb, and she would follow him on a white donkey. Her eldest son would be the king of Israel—alone, without his abba to guide him.

Can Solomon stem the tide of unrest in the north? Her heart pounded, and she tried to calm herself, recalling David's affirmation of his wisdom. *But who will our son turn to for guidance now that you're gone, my love?* she asked the memory of her beloved. Fresh tears rolled onto her pillow as fear battled with despair.

Their quiet, intellectual son was indeed wise, as David pointed out, but he was young and easily distracted by beauty. Bathsheba remembered how impressed David had been when Solomon suggested the conquered Ammonites serve as temple construction laborers, their work to be considered a portion of their vassal payment. She also remembered David's frustration when Solomon's desires squelched his judgment, and their son took the Ammonite princess, Naamah, to be his wife.

Bathsheba squeezed her eyes shut at the memory. "You are too much like your abba," she whispered in the darkness. "You can't take a woman simply because she pleases you."

Solomon had watched Abishag with the same growing fascination. David had recognized it too and challenged their son to rise above the temptation that had almost destroyed his kingdom—and nearly withered his soul. Solomon had promised he wouldn't bed any of his abba's women.

"You promised, my son. You promised," she whispered.

Just then she heard a faint tapping on her door. Puzzled, she wondered who would disturb her this late. "Who is it?"

The iron hinges creaked, and Bathsheba's handmaid peeked through the narrow opening. "My lady," she whispered, "please forgive me for intruding, but—"

"Come in, Dalit. I wasn't sleeping."

The old woman's round face glowed with kindness regardless of the hour. "I have some troubling news, my lady, but I've already called for an escort of Benaiah's Cherethite guards to attend us."

Bathsheba's heart pounded. Dear Dalit had been her childhood nurse and was no stranger to peril. It had been Dalit who delivered the news that Bathsheba's first husband had been killed in battle—at David's sly command. "What is it, Dalit? What's happening?"

"Prince Adonijah has returned from En Rogel, and he's asked to see you immediately."

"At this hour?" Fear sliced through her, cutting off her ability to think clearly. "No! I won't see him! Have the escort prepare my donkey to return home." Bathsheba leapt from her bed and reached for her sackcloth robe and slippers.

Dalit reached out to steady her. "Bathsheba." The use of her familiar name startled her but cleared her mind to hear Dalit's words. "I don't know what the prince wants, but he says it's urgent. I've asked him to wait in the wives' garden." Guiding her mistress to a low stool, Dalit began fitting her head covering in place. "Your quick mind and clever forethought secured the throne for your son once before, my lady. Perhaps this rogue prince is up to no good again." She placed a silver-handled mirror in Bathsheba's hand and spoke to her reflection. "Find out what the prince wants, and then—as you did before—determine the best course of action."

Allowing her maid's words to calm her, Bathsheba took a deep breath and donned her robe and slippers. "All right, Dalit. When the guards arrive, have them escort Prince Adonijah to my chamber."

The woman bowed quickly and left just as Bathsheba considered summoning Nathan the prophet. It had been his plan that thwarted Adonijah's coup before. But because of the late hour, she decided to wait and see what the prince wanted before bothering the man of God.

Moments later, Adonijah arrived, and Bathsheba marveled that her beloved David's features rested on such a hateful young man. Adonijah was only a dozen years younger than Bathsheba herself, and he was truly one of the most handsome men she'd ever seen. But he was spoiled and selfish, and David had never corrected his wayward behavior. So he pranced about the palace as if the world owed him its praise.

"Do you come peacefully?" she said in her most regal voice.

Adonijah's face softened and he looked . . . well, almost kind. "Yes, Queen Mother. Of course I come peacefully."

Bathsheba almost wept with relief. But could he be trusted? As she studied him further, she noticed his eyes bore dark circles and he appeared thinner than he had days ago, when he'd attempted to steal Solomon's throne. Tonight he looked almost like the adolescent boy she'd known when she first came to the palace. Her heart softened.

Realizing she hadn't invited him to sit down, she said, "Would you like some refreshment—honeyed spring water, perhaps?" She moved toward her couch and directed Adonijah to an ivory stool opposite her.

"No thank you, my lady. I come with one humble request. I'm embarrassed, really, but my heart won't let me sleep, and I haven't eaten since I left the palace several days ago."

"All right, Adonijah. You may ask it."

"As you know, the kingdom was mine and all Israel looked to me as their king, but things changed, and the kingdom is now in Solomon's capable hands." He paused and then added, "As was the Lord's wish." He began wringing his hands. "I only have one request to make. Please, Queen Mother, please don't refuse me. I've already lost so much."

Bathsheba shifted uncomfortably on her couch at his uncharacteristic emotional outburst. "Adonijah, I cannot refuse or allow it if I don't know what you want. Now, what is your request?"

"Please ask your son to give me Abishag the Shulammite as

my wife. I have loved her since I first laid eyes on her." Tears welled on his lower lashes. "I know King Solomon respects you and will listen to your counsel."

Bathsheba stared at Adonijah, her mind whirring like a spindle. If Abishag married Adonijah, Solomon would no longer need to resist her as a temptation. He would be better able to concentrate on kingdom duties and perhaps even find a lovely bride with whom he could build a true relationship.

Focusing again on Adonijah, she noted his tears. They seemed sincere, and he certainly appeared to be tormented. She had last seen him on the day of the failed coup, after being dragged into Solomon's courtroom. On that day, he still exuded an air of pompous superiority, though he was obviously defeated. Solomon spared his life on the condition of future allegiance.

Eyes narrowing to slits, Bathsheba asked, "Do you want Abishag because you hope to use her as leverage for another coup since she was David's concubine?"

He seemed genuinely stricken. "No, my lady. As I said, the kingdom is now in Solomon's hands. I love the girl." He bowed. "As Abba loved you."

The words pierced her. "You know nothing of your abba's love for me," she said coolly, remembering the battles in the harem with Adonijah's ima, Haggith. No doubt he'd grown up with an earful of complaints about the favored wife before him. "I will speak to Solomon on your behalf before tomorrow's burial procession, Adonijah." He looked up with a hopeful grin, but she continued before he dared thank her. "Don't make me regret helping you. I will ask this of my son, but you must remember whom God has chosen as the rightful ruler of Israel."

Adonijah's smile never dimmed. "I promise, my lady. I will never forget who the rightful ruler of Israel is."

Arielah tossed and turned on her straw mattress, unable to sleep in the eerie absence of her brothers' snoring. She and Ima were alone in their home. Perhaps for the first time ever. Arielah replayed the awful scene in the courtyard when Kemmuel dishonored their abba and Abba banished both sons to the sheepfolds. Her face twisted at the memory. *Why do you insist on hurting him, Kemmuel?* The question haunted her.

Using both hands to rub away the tension in her forehead, she turned her thoughts toward Jerusalem. Abba Jehoshaphat and Reu, the royal messenger, left Shunem shortly after the moon's zenith. Both men had been exhausted, but they were determined to honor King David and arrive in Jerusalem for the burial procession. Reu thought they could get to the city by sunrise, but Abba knew the northern elders couldn't travel as quickly as a single courier. He reminded them all that if they arrived too late to join the procession, they could still offer condolences by leaving remembrance stones at the royal tomb.

Glancing again out the small window above her sleeping mat, Arielah saw the first glow of sunrise. *Finally!* she thought. *If I go to the well early, I'll miss the old gossips, and perhaps I can return to the house before Kemmuel and Igal find me.* She rose quietly and slipped on her woolen robe and leather sandals. When she emerged from behind the cooking stones, she nearly bumped noses with Ima Jehosheba.

"Oh!" Ima stepped back, eyes wide. "Arielah, I was trying to be so quiet. Did I wake you?"

Giggling, she fell into her ima's arms. "No, I don't think I've slept all night. It's too quiet." Pulling away, she saw tears welling in Ima's eyes. A nod said she missed her sons' thunderous snoring too. "I'll go fetch some water from the well and return shortly."

Ima swiped at her eyes. "Yes," she said, "but go quickly. Your brothers will have seen your abba leave last night. They'll know he isn't here to protect you."

Arielah reached for the large water jar to balance on her

head and carried the smaller pitcher in her hand. Ima opened
the door and followed her to the courtyard gate. Glancing
toward the well, Ima said, "I see old Ruth is already at the
well. Stay in sight of other women and your brothers will leave
you alone." She opened the gate and let her daughter pass.

Arielah pecked her cheek with a kiss and winked. As the
sky grew brighter, women descended on Shunem's well like
flies on date cakes. For most, it was the sweetest part of their
day, an oasis of gossip, grins, and girl talk. For Arielah, it
was pure torture.

"What news?" Edna the matchmaker shrieked when she
saw Arielah approaching. "Surely your abba said something
of King David's last hours. And that *messenger*!" she continued without giving Arielah a chance to reply. "He was barely
sprouting a beard. I'll bet he's not married yet. I wonder if
we could make a match for him here in Shunem. Although
I realize we normally try to match within our own tribes. I
wonder if he's Judean—"

"Edna!" old Ruth shouted. The women encircling the well
fell silent, and Edna looked like a camel chewing its cud.

Arielah stifled a giggle, and Ruth offered a kind smile.
"Good morning, dear."

"Good morning," Arielah said, stepping forward to kiss
Ruth's feathery, wrinkled cheek. "How are you feeling today,
my friend?"

The old woman waved her hand as if shooing flies. "Never
ask an old woman that question, my dear. She might answer
you." She winked one hooded eye and returned her attention
to her matchmaking friend. "Edna, let's not ask Arielah to
discuss politics this early in the morning. Let's talk about
something far more interesting."

Women around the well lifted questioning brows.

"Men," Ruth said. "Let's talk about men."

Raucous laughter echoed in the well, resounding as if an
entire town had gathered for entertainment.

Once again Edna turned her attention to Arielah. "All right, let's talk about men," she said, a twinkle in her eye. "When is your abba going to pay me a visit, Arielah? You're not getting any younger, you know. The time for your match is well past due."

Arielah's cheeks flamed as the women began offering suggestions for Arielah's potential husband. *This is why I hate gathering water at the well.* She smiled and nodded, trying to act interested, while the whole time her heart ached for a young prince who was now Israel's king.

8

Then King Solomon swore by the LORD: "May God deal with me, be it ever so severely, if Adonijah does not pay with his life for this request!"

Solomon had been awake since the first shaft of dawn's light shone through his abba's garden doorway. Would it ever feel like *his* garden, *his* personal chamber? The servants had cleaned, perfumed, and fanned every nook and cranny to clear away the scent of Abba David's long illness, but they couldn't wash away the memories.

The king's private garden, its archway just a few cubits from Solomon's sleeping couch, once held the wild beasts of King David's hunts. When his abba fell ill, Solomon ordered that the caged lions and panthers be taken away, jokingly threatening to lead the hunt if they escaped. The advisors laughed with him at the absurdity of Solomon wielding a weapon, but Benaiah's stern gaze chided the young regent's self-scorn. Though Solomon had endured the same military drills as David's other sons, the prince whose name embodied peace never excelled at war.

"Good morning, my lord." Benaiah's deep voice resonated

from the captain's private entrance. His brow furrowed in concern. "You look awful, Solomon."

"Good morning, my lord," came Ahishar's nasally greeting from the double cedar doors. "My, my, you look well rested. Ready to tackle this morning's difficult tasks, your majesty?"

A wry smile creased Solomon's lips. The two greetings summarized the difference in his closest advisors. Benaiah's comfortable honesty, brutal yet trustworthy. Ahishar's fawning flattery, ever dutiful and efficient.

"Come, let's break our fast together," he said, inviting them both to the small ivory table in his meeting chamber. "I'd like to share what Jehovah has whispered to my soul."

Again Solomon observed with interest the difference in each man's response. Benaiah moved to his familiar place at the table, his expression filled with anticipation, while Ahishar fumbled nervously with the clay tablet and stylus in his hand.

"My lord," Ahishar began hesitantly, "I have so much to accomplish before you initiate the official grieving period. Though I would love to break my fast with you, I—"

"Sit down, Ahishar."

"Yes, my lord." The steward folded his wiry legs beneath him and plopped down on a goatskin rug.

Chamber servants hurried from Solomon's private suite and out the garden door. They would wind through the back stairway to the kitchen, retrieving Solomon's usual breakfast of goat's milk, bread, and cheese—and figs, of course. He loved figs. Studying the Mighty Men whom Benaiah had stationed in his chamber last night, he asked his captain, "What in creation do they eat? Their biceps are as big as my thighs."

Benaiah's eyes sparkled with mischief. "They eat high stewards who argue with kings."

The comment drew a sneer from Ahishar and a chuckle from Solomon. "All right, you two," the king said, again playing peacemaker between his clever officials. "I've been up most of the night contemplating King David's final words to me." His words sobered Benaiah and Ahishar, who now offered their full attention. "I keep recounting Abba's words, 'Establish your throne and then seek peace, for yourself and for Israel.' I feel as though I must deal swiftly with Joab and Shimei, pronounce judgment before I institute the thirty-day grieving period."

Ahishar and Benaiah exchanged concerned glances. Benaiah spoke first, compassion shadowing his features. "Did you sleep at all last night?"

Solomon swallowed hard and watched Benaiah do the same. "I fell asleep just before dawn, but the nightmares returned." Solomon averted his gaze, studying the shabby sackcloth covering his feet.

"You've been working night and day since your abba made you his successor." Benaiah's giant hand clamped down on Solomon's shoulder. "The mourning period will give us all some much-needed time for reflection and rest. Are you sure these matters of state can't wait until your mind is clearer?"

"Perhaps," Solomon said, then searched both advisors' faces. "I spent most of the night staring at my chamber doors, imagining an invasion of hostile nations taking over my kingdom before I've even had a chance to rule. And it's not just foreign invasion I dread. The messengers we dispatched to the northern tribes to announce Abba David's death returned with reports of a clandestine elders' meeting in Shunem."

Ahishar gasped, but Benaiah remained steady, having been the one to share the report with Solomon.

"So tell me," the king continued, "why did the northern leaders gather, Benaiah? Are they preparing for civil war?" His voice had risen to a shrill whine, like a frightened boy.

Benaiah remained silent, but Ahishar looked panicked. Solomon couldn't tell if he feared war or the delay in his morning schedule, and the thought gave the king a moment to regain control. "How can we hope for peace with neighboring nations—or even peace with our own northern tribes—if I don't establish the peace of my abba's dying wish?"

Tears brimmed on Benaiah's lashes. "You must do what Jehovah whispers to your spirit, King Solomon. Pronounce judgment on the traitors, and I will be faithful to mete out their punishment."

"But, my lord!" Ahishar's voice erupted. "I don't understand how we can postpone the burial procession to the royal tomb. Surely you have considered the effect of the warm spring sun on King David's wrapped body." The steward looked stricken, alternating pleading glances from captain to king.

Solomon swallowed hard. He was trying *not* to think of his abba's body wrapped in the myrrh and spices of a burial shroud. Pinning his steward with a sharp stare, he said, "Send orders that the servants add more spices to dispel the odor. I will obey my abba's final wishes before I say my last good-bye."

Ahishar straightened his shoulders and righted his posture. Looking as if he might bite off his tongue, he offered no further argument. "Yes, my lord."

The servants arrived with the customary meal, and all three ate in relative silence, the droning of mourners now the routine setting of every thought, word, and deed.

Solomon exited his private chamber through the veiled corner door leading into the great throne hall. When he emerged from behind two heavy tapestries, trumpets blared and servants bowed. Solomon ascended the stairs to his throne as usual, ready to quiet the customary applause. But the sound of trumpets dwindled; the routine ovation faded.

Every sound was shrouded by the eerie echoes of mourning.

Scanning the sea of grief before him, Solomon was touched and humbled. He extended grateful hands to his people, his throat too tight to speak. As one, the gathered Israelites bowed to their new king, and Solomon could hold back his tears no longer.

Suddenly distracted by a commotion on his right, he glanced

toward the archway between the throne hall and courtyard. There stood Ima Bathsheba, waiting to be recognized. "Come, Ima. Join me," he said, wiping his cheeks and beckoning her to the dais.

She glided across the floor as if carried on a cloud. She was stunning. Even after the torturous days of Abba's illness, even in a grieving robe and slippers, she was breathtaking, and for the first time, Solomon saw Ima as a woman.

He recognized the distinctive beauty that had won his abba's love. She had never dressed like the other wives with seductive makeup, ornate robes, and heavy jewelry. Ima Bathsheba was a farmer's daughter, showcasing her supple olive skin and natural glow. The shepherd king of Israel had cherished his earthy queen. Abba David had shared a special bond with Ima, and Solomon hoped to one day enjoy a love with a woman just as rare.

Gliding up the three-stepped dais, the queen mother met him on the platform and touched her forehead to his hand—a sign of obeisance to her new king. "Solomon, my son," she whispered, "I have seen the burden of Israel weigh heavy on your shoulders—just as I saw it press down on your abba."

He wiped a tear from her cheek. "It's all right, Ima. Benaiah is a good friend. He'll help me." The revelation of her humanity was startling. He'd been consumed with his loss and fears about ruling this nation. What about her feelings? He rubbed his thumb over the soft skin on her hand. "Don't shed tears for me, Ima. I'm not a child anymore. I am the king of Israel. You can't rush in and kiss my skinned knees."

Before he realized what she was doing, she pulled her hand from his grasp and knelt before him.

"No, Ima! What are—Ima, stand up!" He had never seen her bow to Abba, and she would certainly never bow to him!

But as he reached for her elbow, she gently refused his efforts. A tender smile framed her words. "I know better than anyone that you are the king of Israel. But first and foremost"—her chin quivered—"you are my son. And I will always help you if I see a way to be useful."

Solomon didn't know whether to chuckle, cry, or hug her. The determined set of her jaw, the sparkle in her eye—yes, this was the headstrong ima he knew. She'd spent her life making decisions for him and then ensuring those in power followed through. Truly, if Ima and Nathan hadn't responded so quickly to Adonijah's coup, Solomon would have lost the throne while Abba lay dying. She had gained his respect long ago. Today she deserved his honor.

Bending to help her stand, Solomon lifted his voice. "Ahishar, bring Abba David's throne from my chamber for the queen mother." An excited flutter rolled over the crowd, and the high steward issued orders to four hulking servants.

"Solomon, what are you doing?" Bathsheba's cheeks pinked. "I don't want to sit beside—"

He silenced her with a smile and a single finger to her lips. "Please, Ima. You will sit beside me today as I fulfill Abba's last wishes." Understanding dawned on her face, and she reached up to brush his cheek. The affectionate act heightened the crowd's hum. Such a public display would provide market gossip for weeks.

They waited in amiable silence until the servants arrived with the throne and Bathsheba took her place of honor at Solomon's right hand. Glancing up at Benaiah, Solomon saw his reassuring nod and knew the time had come to deal with Joab and Shimei. *Lord, give me wisdom*, he prayed.

Drawing a breath for his first judgment, Solomon nearly choked when Bathsheba leaned over and whispered, "My son, I have one small request before you begin your proceedings. Do not refuse me."

Heart pounding, Solomon offered a sideways glance. She was full of surprises today. "Make it, Ima. I will not refuse you."

Offering no preamble or conditions, she spoke clearly for

the audience to hear. "Let Abishag the Shulammite be given in marriage to your brother Adonijah."

Solomon felt as if he'd taken a blow. His face stung as if he'd walked through a swarm of bees. "What?" he roared. "Why would you request Abishag for Adonijah, Ima?"

The warm rumble of the crowd died to cold silence.

"You might as well give my older brother the throne! Have you joined Abiathar the priest and Joab the general in their efforts to give him the kingdom?" He stood, towering over her, panting with rage as if he'd run a long race.

Bathsheba stared at him in silence, her face white with fear. He'd never spoken to Ima with such fury. He'd never spoken to *anyone* with such fury.

Turning to the stunned crowd, he trembled with unspent anger. "May God deal with me severely if Adonijah doesn't pay with his life for making this request. Benaiah!" he shouted over the crowd, and his captain descended the platform and bowed before him. "Adonijah must die today for his treachery. He has deceived the queen mother and threatened my throne."

"Yes, my lord. It will be as you say."

His captain turned, but Solomon halted him. "We are not finished here, Benaiah." Exchanging a knowing glance with Solomon, the captain signaled his elite guards to join him at the king's feet. The captain knew of Joab and Shimei, but there was another Solomon must deal with now.

"You, Abiathar!" The king turned his ire on the traitorous priest seated among his advisors just a few cubits from the throne. "It was you and Joab who conspired with Adonijah to steal my throne when Abba lay dying. I suspect you have a hand in this new treachery—"

"No, my lord! No!" The old priest stood, his eyes as round as horses' hooves. "I'm not. I mean we did, but no more—"

"Silence!" Solomon shouted. "You are no longer an advisor to the king or a priest before the sovereign Lord. Go back to your fields in Anathoth. You deserve to die, but because you shared in my abba's hardships, I will spare your life." The old man's shoulders slumped, but he knew better than to speak. One of Benaiah's guards stepped forward, seized his brittle arm, and escorted him from the throne hall.

Every eye followed the old priest's progress, but Solomon remembered Benaiah's charge from the night before. *They are your people now, my lord. They will remember the things of which you remind them.*

"Elihoreph!" Solomon shouted. His chief secretary nearly jumped from his cushioned couch. "Record in the annals of the king, 'Concerning Joab, son of Zeruiah and commander of Israel's hosts, he will die today for his sins against Abner son of Ner and Amasa son of Jether, whom he killed in peacetime." He paused slightly, giving the secretary time to scribble.

"Concerning Shimei, son of Gera, the Benjamite from Bahurim who called down curses on King David when our family fled to Mahanaim from my brother Absalom—though my abba showed him mercy, Shimei's guilt remains. He must build a house in Jerusalem and live there, never leaving the city. On the day he crosses the Kidron Valley, Shimei will surely die. His blood will be on his own head." An approving rumble rolled over the audience, and Solomon waited for silence while Elihoreph wrote furiously, recording the detailed decree. "And finally, it is my desire to show kindness to the sons of Barzillai of Gilead and welcome them to eat at my table because they provided for our family when Absalom sought to steal Abba's throne."

Solomon watched as Elihoreph feverishly worked the stylus over his clay tablet, waiting for the customary nod to signal he had finished the record. When the secretary finally met his gaze, the king announced, "We will reconvene after the midday meal, at which time I will officially inaugurate our nation's grieving period for our beloved King David."

He watched Benaiah lead his Pelethite and Cherethite guards up the center aisle, their size and weaponry a sobering punctuation to Solomon's judgment. Two men were about to die at his command, and he would undoubtedly determine the fate of nations from this platform in years to come. The thought was staggering, humbling. *Lord Jehovah, give me wisdom.* In his contemplation, he heard one woman's weeping, not because she was loudest but because her heart was crushed.

Ima Bathsheba.

Solomon returned to his throne and reminded himself of his most recent revelation. His ima was a woman. Hurting. Vulnerable. "Why?" he whispered. "Why would you ask that I give Abishag to Adonijah?"

She sniffed, keeping her voice low. "It's hard to believe this was a conspiracy. He seemed so sincere when he came to me last night and said he loved the girl." She looked into Solomon's eyes, pleading. "You must know that if I thought he presented any real danger, I would never have asked."

"I know, Ima," he said and started to wipe her tears. But the renewed buzz of the crowd stilled his hand. Conscious of their private moment in this public place, he said to Ahishar, "I will escort the queen mother to her chamber. You may return King David's throne to my private meeting room."

Bathsheba stood, and Solomon joined her. She whispered while they descended the steps, "I trust your judgment of Adonijah's motives, my son, but I hope your anger at his request for Abishag had nothing to do with the place she holds in your heart." Halting on the bottom step, she pierced him with her gaze. "You have enough on your mind without stirring up trouble in your abba's harem."

Before Solomon could respond, she released his arm and bowed again, effectively ending their discussion and halting his accompaniment. The queen mother disappeared through the courtyard archway and beyond its central fountain, leaving Solomon at the foot of his throne, pondering. *Being the king in Israel would be much simpler were it not for all the women.* A wry smile pulled at the corner of his lips. *But the color they bring to my world is worth every stripe in the pattern of life.*

9

Pharaoh king of Egypt had attacked and captured Gezer. He had set it on fire. He killed its Canaanite inhabitants and then gave it as a wedding gift to his daughter, Solomon's wife.

Solomon thanked his council members and listened to the last of the professional mourners echo down the halls of the palace. His cedar doors clicked shut, and he turned to find Benaiah ending the biggest yawn he'd ever seen. A long, pink scar stretched from the left corner of his mouth to the center of his brow.

The gesture proved contagious, and Solomon stretched, releasing a simultaneous groan.

"Well, we avoided war on my first day as king," he said with a coy grin. "Abba David would be proud."

Benaiah's stoic expression caught the king's attention. "Yes, young Solomon. King David would have been proud of his son today."

Immediately tears welled in Solomon's eyes. "Thank you, my friend. And I am proud of our nation." Both men shared a nod and scanned the room, hearing quiet sniffs and kind affirmations from his chamber stewards and guards. Abba had been the first king of Israel honored by a national burial, and the outpouring of support had been nothing short of miraculous. Israelites from Dan to Beersheba had traveled through the night to arrive in Jerusalem to pay tribute. Even some of the leaders reported to have attended the clandestine Shulammite meeting had arrived in time, thanks to the burial delay because of Adonijah's and Joab's executions. The threat of the northern tribes was real, but in spite of the unrest, Israelites loved their king. No war cries had erupted, only the wailing of mourners.

"You should get some rest, my friend," Solomon said, taking his place on the low grieving stool in his bedchamber. "I'll return this morning's compliment: you look awful." Benaiah finally grinned, and Solomon added one more goad. "But at least you get to wear your battle armor and sandals. I'm stuck in this torn sackcloth robe and slippers for thirty days." He looked longingly at his empty washbasin, hardly able to imagine the passing of a full moon's cycle without washing, working, or enjoying the pleasure of a woman.

Benaiah tugged at the tunic beneath his leather breastplate. "I'll have you know your guards wear sackcloth beneath their armor, my lord." The mountainous man itched and wriggled like a fidgety child. "We will feel the discomfort of grief while remaining faithful to our king." Bowing, he said, "Now, if you'll excuse me, I'm going to remove this armor and try to get some much-anticipated rest."

Solomon watched him walk away, but stopped him with one last thought. "Benaiah?"

His friend turned with a furrowed brow and cocked his head.

"Thank you for helping me carry out Abba's last wishes. You even searched out that weasel Shimei and brought him to the throne hall for sentencing. I feel like you've given me a fresh start, a new beginning."

Benaiah shrugged, offering an impish grin. "Would you like to wager a wineskin on how long it will be before Shimei leaves Jerusalem and brings down judgment on himself?"

"I'll wager you will be waiting for him when he does!" Solomon chuckled but sobered as he carefully fashioned his next words. "*Thank you* hardly seems appropriate when speaking of executing my traitorous brother and cousin, but I'm deeply grateful for your faithfulness to execute Adonijah and Joab. It couldn't have been easy to enter the Lord's tent and strike down that coward Joab while he held on to the horns of the altar."

Benaiah nodded, seeming to accept the appreciation given. An uneasy silence settled between them. Hoping to assuage whatever doubts his friend might be feeling, Solomon added, "Joab was calculating and cold, my friend. He was a manipulator, and he knew your abba was a priest. He never dreamed you'd obey my command to kill him at the altar."

Benaiah lifted his left eyebrow, stretching the imposing battle scar extending up from his jawbone. "Joab seriously miscalculated my loyalty to my king." His words were unadorned, matter-of-fact, and they put to rest any concern Solomon had that his new commander second-guessed today's events.

Solomon watched his friend's scar throb and realized he hardly noticed it—except at times like these. He often forgot Benaiah was first and foremost a warrior. "Do you ever doubt, Benaiah? Isn't there *something* I might ask of you that you wouldn't do?"

His commander returned, covering the distance between them in two steps. Towering above Solomon, he said, "I will disobey you only if it will save your life, my king."

They stood in silence, Solomon contemplating the weight of such a statement, until a knock on the king's door interrupted the moment. Benaiah stepped away, and Solomon shouted, "Come!"

A disheveled Egyptian courier stood before them, escorted by one of Benaiah's Pelethite guards. The courier was panting, dust-covered, but worse—he looked haunted, as if he himself couldn't believe what he was about to say. "My lord, Pharaoh's ambassador and caravan will arrive in Jerusalem before dawn . . ." He spoke perfect Hebrew, but he hesitated, seemingly uncertain as to whom he should direct his news. He glanced first at the king and then at the servants and soldiers.

"Why is the Egyptian ambassador coming now?" Solomon asked, exasperated. It had been an extraordinarily long day—a long week and year. Trying to calm himself, he continued more patiently. "Our plan was to finalize our agreement with Egypt's ambassador after the next new moon."

"The Egyptian caravan carries your new bride, Pharaoh's daughter, and—"

"What?" Solomon's heart skipped a beat. His harem wasn't ready for the Egyptian princess. His nation, his palace was grieving. She wouldn't understand their customs, and Ahishar surely hadn't had time to implement the Daughters of Jerusalem.

"And they bring loads of plunder from their victory over the Canaanite city of Gezer."

"What?" Benaiah and Solomon shouted at once.

"Pharaoh Siamun planned to offer Gezer as a wedding gift to his daughter, but Pharaoh was killed in the battle." Solomon stumbled back, reaching for his stool as he grasped the enormity of the courier's report. "The Egyptian ambassador now speaks for Egypt's new king, Pharaoh Psusennes, to ensure the success of Egypt's trade agreement with Israel."

Ahishar burst through the chamber doors that had been left partially open when the courier entered. "I just heard the news. How long before the ambassador and princess arrive?"

Solomon spoke as if in a dream. "Pharaoh Siamun is dead, Ahishar. The man with whom we made this treaty attacked an innocent Canaanite city in order to give its wealth to his daughter as a wedding gift and provide its strategic thoroughfare for our trade routes." The words tasted bitter on his tongue. Shifting his attention back to the Egyptian courier, he asked, "And what did your pharaoh imagine I would do with all the Canaanites living in Gezer after he took the city?" Solomon knew it was silly to ask a mere courier such a question, but the whole situation was so outrageous he asked anyway.

"My lord, he . . . well, he . . ." The young man glanced nervously at each waiting expression, seemingly hesitant to answer. Finally, he said, "Pharaoh destroyed the city with fire and then killed all the Canaanites living there. He offers a perfect shell with which the king of Israel may build a mighty fortress of your liking."

All breath left Solomon's chest. The courier's answer had been practiced, perfected, to flaunt Egypt's power and foster Solomon's greed. It accomplished neither. "My steward will see that you are housed in the servants' quarters," he said, watching Ahishar enlist a chamber servant's aide. "You will be reunited with your caravan when they arrive at dawn." The young man bowed and stepped backward out of the king's meeting area, and soldiers closed the double doors behind them.

Ahishar immediately drew a breath, no doubt to recount a list of tasks to complete before the caravan's arrival, but Solomon silenced him with an upraised hand. "I realize some very important guests are on their way."

Ahishar nodded, seemingly relieved that the king hadn't missed that detail.

"However, I also realize something far more important than our guests."

The steward's nodding stopped, his eyes shifting nervously to Benaiah, the mountain of calm standing at Solomon's right hand.

"I had no idea Pharaoh would have such wild disregard for

human life. Killing an entire city for a wedding gift." Shaking his head, Solomon continued. "I feel like a child with much to learn about ruling a nation, and I'm afraid I'll be eaten alive by predators like Pharaoh Siamun and his successor, Pharaoh Psusennes, if I don't learn to hear from Jehovah as Abba David did."

For the first time ever, perhaps, Ahishar appeared totally befuddled. "But, my lord, you don't even play the harp."

The steward's absurd comment prompted a thought. *How did Abba David receive such favor with Jehovah, and why—when he sinned like any other man—did God condescend to speak to David so clearly?*

"A man need not play a harp to hear from Jehovah, my lord." Benaiah's deep voice soothed the recesses of Solomon's soul. "What do you propose?"

"I think a visit to Gibeon is in order," he said to Benaiah, more a question than an answer.

"But we've just started mourning," Ahishar quickly pointed out.

A full-fledged smile creased Benaiah's face. "I'm the son of a priest, and I've never heard a law forbidding *worship* during the grieving period."

A flutter of fear worked through Solomon's belly. "Benaiah, tell me why Abba David seldom visited Gibeon. It seemed to me he was almost frightened of the Tent of Meeting housed at that most holy high place. Why did he worship only at the ark here in Jerusalem?"

"Your abba *did* fear the Lord." Benaiah allowed a comfortable silence. "But he didn't fear God at Gibeon alone. He was afraid many times during his reign as Israel's king. When the Lord struck down Uzzah for steadying the ark on the oxcart—David feared Him. When the Lord punished King David and your ima by taking their firstborn son—David feared Him. And when your abba saw the angel of the Lord sheathe his sword and end the plague at the threshing floor in Jerusalem—King David feared ever inquiring of the Lord in His presence at the tabernacle of Gibeon." Benaiah's eyes were kind but piercing. "But the fear of the Lord is the beginning of wisdom, young Solomon. Go to Gibeon. Seek God's presence. Be afraid. For it is in your fear that you will establish your own relationship with Jehovah. You don't need to rule like King David to be a great king."

Solomon's heart raced. Benaiah's words felt like spring water splashed on hot coals. Sizzling. Refreshing. Exhilarating. "Yes, my friend. *Israel* and I will go to Gibeon."

"Israel?" Ahishar chirped. "So should I organize a processional, your majesty?"

Solomon chuckled. "No, Ahishar, but I will make an announcement to all the leaders still gathered in Jerusalem for Abba's burial—the commanders, judges, and family leaders. All are welcome to join me in Gibeon, to seek Jehovah at the bronze altar before the Lord in the Tent of Meeting."

"Yes, right. As you wish, my lord." Ahishar took out his clay tablet and stylus, poised to record a list of the king's next words. "I assume you'll plan to leave after the first week of grieving restrictions have been lifted. The second stage of mourning is far more lenient. Perhaps by then, the Egyptian ambassador and your new bride will be more accustomed to their new surroundings and might even be inclined to join you, my lord. What exactly would you like me to plan for the Egyptians when they arrive?"

As Ahishar pressed the iron pen into damp clay, Solomon said, "I leave tomorrow morning, Ahishar. I will greet the ambassador and princess when their caravan enters the city after dawn, and I'll ask them to break the fast with me."

The steward's hand began to shake.

"I will extend my deepest sympathies to Princess Sekhet at the loss of her abba and invite her to join me in the consolation of El Shaddai at Gibeon's altar. If they refuse to accompany us, thereby refusing to honor King David's death and his son's grieving, they may remain in Jerusalem until I return in thirty days." Solomon met Benaiah's approving grin. "When I enter Jerusalem's gates again, I will discuss our trade agreement with Egypt's ambassador, and if the terms benefit both our nations, I will at that time establish the treaty and wed Princess Sekhet."

Ahishar looked as if he had swallowed a bad fig. He let the clay block and stylus hang limp at his sides. "May I at least introduce to you the Daughters of Jerusalem, who are waiting to welcome your Egyptian princess and help with her transition to Jerusalem?"

Solomon smiled. He should have known his able steward would already be preparing for the wedding. "Yes! By all means," he said, patting Ahishar's shoulder. "Are they here now? Bring them in!"

Ahishar's nod prompted the guards to pull open the heavy cedar doors. At the threshold stood two apparitions, identical in form and beauty. Solomon heard himself gasp and noted even Benaiah's posture straighten. The glow of lamplight shone through the women's sackcloth robes, illuminating perfect curves beneath unusually well-fitted clothes.

"The twin daughters of Bethuel, the royal tailor," Ahishar said, and Solomon reconciled the oddity of the customized grieving garb.

The women stepped forward at the steward's introduction. They were obviously familiar with court protocol. Wavy black hair cascaded over their shoulders beneath head coverings of rough-woven cloth, but their honey-brown eyes softened everything about them.

"I welcome you to the palace," Solomon said, watching them kneel before him, yearning to stroke their alabaster cheeks. "The high steward has chosen you for an important task."

Both faces tilted upward, and again he marveled at their likeness. Identical but for a small beauty mark above one sister's lip and a crooked front tooth when the other sister smiled.

"I am Shiphrah, my king," said the crooked-toothed sister, inclining her head.

"And I am Sherah," the other girl said, as if not to be forgotten.

"I am the older and wiser twin," Shiphrah said, a look silencing her sister before she turned back to the king. "And we are honored to have been chosen to serve in your harem."

Sherah's pout accentuated the beauty mark above her lip, and he tried to imagine their exquisite beauty when they weren't veiled by grieving attire. "Well, it seems we'll have need of your service sooner than anticipated," he said, casting a glance at his two advisors. "I'd like you to begin your hospitality to the Egyptian princess, Sekhet, as soon as she arrives—tomorrow morning at dawn."

The maidens bowed their heads in silent submission.

"I'm not sure if she speaks Hebrew." Solomon looked to Ahishar, and the steward's shrug conveyed uncertainty. "I'll need you to do the best you can—"

"My lord," Shiphrah interrupted, "my sister and I would be happy to learn some Egyptian phrases from the courier we saw leave your chamber. Your princess may feel less alone if her new homeland shows interest in her heritage." She glanced up—only a moment, a seductive, enticing moment. "Perhaps we might even learn some phrases to teach the king so that he might woo his new bride."

Solomon could feel his heart race and crimson rise on his neck. Ahishar had indeed chosen these so-called Daughters of Jerusalem wisely. How smoothly might his other foreign marriages have started if he'd had Shiphrah and Sherah to soothe the Ammonite princess, Naamah, or the Moabitess or Edomitess? "I would like that very much," he said, succumbing to the urge to touch their cheeks. He lifted both hands to barely brush each girl's face but drew back quickly—though both smiled rather than recoil. "Rise, my friends. Together we will create harmony in my harem."

He extended both hands to urge the maidens to their feet. Each grasped the hand offered, turned it, and kissed his palm—the act in perfect unison. The hairs on Solomon's arms stood at strict attention, and a shudder worked through him.

This time Sherah spoke. "We are indeed your friends, my king, and will do everything in our power to create a harem that honors Judah."

10

Solomon went up to the bronze altar before the Lord in the Tent of Meeting and offered a thousand burnt offerings on it.

That night God appeared to Solomon and said to him, "Ask for whatever you want me to give you."

Solomon answered God, ". . . Give me wisdom and knowledge, that I may lead this people." . . .

God said to Solomon, "Since this is your heart's desire and you have not asked for wealth, riches or honor, nor for the death of your enemies, and since you have not asked for a long life . . . therefore wisdom and knowledge will be given you. And I will also give you wealth, riches and honor, such as no king who was before you ever had and none after you will have."

Benaiah, take me home." Solomon skipped a rock across the clear waters of Gibeon's great pool, the leisurely gesture now a habit of his thirty days at rest. "Jehovah has spoken, and I have heard Him, my friend." His throat tightened.

"I'm no longer ruling Israel based on the promise made to Abba David. Now I'm reigning over Jehovah's people with the wisdom and blessing He promised to me." Skipping another rock, he allowed time for his emotions to settle before speaking again. "I'm glad the Egyptians remained in Jerusalem. I've needed every moment of this time to gain a clear vision of the Lord's plan for our nation."

He heard Benaiah chuckle. "You'd better hope your new bride doesn't see you before your bath, or all trade agreements may be forfeit."

Solomon laughed and tugged on his overgrown beard. "Yes, my friend. It will feel good to bathe and trim this ragged beard. And we have a week to settle the treaty and initiate reforms before the Passover celebration begins."

"And have a wedding?" Benaiah lifted his left eyebrow, stretching his long battle scar, reminding Solomon of the lives already lost in Gezer for the marriage.

"Egypt is a powerful nation, my friend, and the singular fact that Pharaoh Siamun offered his daughter as my bride is a testimony to Abba David's leadership and rising power." He dropped the remaining rocks he was holding, letting them fall gently to Gibeon's soil. "But Egypt is a nation in turmoil, and I will not fall prey to her inner strife. If the successor Psusennes will abide by Pharaoh Siamun's terms, I will honor our agreement and marry Princess Sekhet. But we will be distant relatives with a guarded relationship."

"I believe Jehovah's wisdom already bears fruit, my king." Benaiah bowed, heaping respect on top of friendship.

Solomon acknowledged his captain's approval with misty eyes. "How can it be, Benaiah? Why did God choose Abba? Why did he appear to me in that dream, asking me to name whatever I desired and He would give it? And furthermore, what possessed me to say *wisdom*?" Both men laughed aloud. "Why didn't I ask for peace in my harem or a hundred noble sons?"

Their laughter dwindled into the silence of friends who need no words to speak. Finally Solomon said, "When the Lord granted me wisdom and knowledge beyond the measure of any man before me or any man yet to come, I remember thinking, *I must be dreaming*. And when He added to the blessing wealth, riches, and honor, I was so overwhelmed. In my dream, I was on my knees before Him, buried my face in my hands, and cried." Turning to his captain, he said, "That's how I woke up—on the floor by my couch, facedown. Crying."

"It was more than a dream," the mountainous man said.

"It was more than a dream."

They stood watching the breeze comb the flowering wheat. "My lord," Benaiah whispered, "we must be on our way if we hope to reach Jerusalem before midday."

Solomon didn't budge. "I've decided to redefine the boundary lines of Israel's tribes." He noted his captain's shocked expression but continued. "I believe that creating twelve new districts will blur the established borders and create more unity in our nation."

Benaiah bent over, plucked a sprig of grass, and began chewing on it. "And how will you implement this new plan?"

"I will choose twelve governors—designated 'princes'—to rule under me as administrators. They'll be responsible to oversee a foreign workforce that we'll use as builders and common laborers within each district." He turned now to face his captain, excitement bubbling up inside him. "We'll fortify Hazor, Megiddo—and even Gezer. The district princes will send their foreign workers in shifts to build the temple and other public buildings." Seeing his commander wasn't yet convinced, he hesitated before adding, "And the princes will be responsible to collect Israelite taxes."

"Taxes?" Benaiah's scar danced as he chewed the grass with gusto. "What sort of taxes do you propose?"

"Each of the twelve districts will be responsible to supply the needed provisions of my household for one moon cycle each year. I also plan to send an immediate request to Hiram, king of Tyre, asking that Israelite craftsmen be trained to work with his Sidonian lumbermen. I plan to send thirty thousand Israelites—ten thousand each new moon on a three-moon rotation—to Lebanon to fell the giant cedars we'll use to construct the temple. Then more laborers will be necessary to harvest the wheat and olive oil I'm sure Hiram will ask for in return for his trees."

His captain's fist clenched. "And will Judah be included in this taxing and labor? How many in the City of David bend their backs to a plow and cut cedars in Lebanon?"

Benaiah's words slapped Solomon as if he'd used his clenched fist. The king stared at his friend, too shocked to be offended. "The tribe of Judah will be exempt from redistricting—and taxation—because most of them are members of my household either by birth or by service." The shock began to lessen, and the offense increased. "What are you saying, Benaiah? Are you accusing me of—of the very betrayal our northern tribes claim as grounds for revolt?"

Benaiah removed the now decimated blade of grass from his mouth, bowed his head, and massaged his temples. "No, of course not, but I want you to hear my warnings before you face the objections of your council and the northern tribes. Consider carefully how you will gain the confidence and trust of experienced men who don't have the privilege of witnessing your good intentions and godly integrity." Placing a steady hand on Solomon's shoulder, he added, "Nor did they see your face—as I did—when you awoke from the vision of God's promise."

Solomon knew his friend was right. *But there is so much to do!* "How do I gain their confidence and trust, Benaiah?"

"I believe that in this too, Jehovah will grant you wisdom, my king." A mischievous smile creased his lips. "But you will win no one's favor until you take a bath." With a wink and a nudge, he said, "Now, may we go back to Jerusalem?"

Having had a good meal and a refreshing bath, Solomon expected to feel energized for the day ahead. Instead, the palace felt oppressive after so many days encamped on the lush terraces outside Gibeon's city wall. He studied the heavy embroidered curtains separating his bedchamber from the adjacent meeting area, the grand tapestries on his walls, and the mosaic tiles that graced his floors. Tawdry attempts to match the grandeur of God's creation. A knock on the door piqued his longing for a mourning dove's song.

But the mourning was over.

"Come!" he shouted, allowing his chamber servants to wind the golden waistband around his purple linen robe.

Ahishar rushed in, stylus poised, happier than Solomon had seen him since many new moons had passed.

"Well, my buzzing high steward, you must be delighted at the impossible demands of my schedule today."

Barely containing his delight, the man grinned, shaking his iron pen at the king. "Oh, my lord, after hearing of your Gibeon encounter and the reforms you have planned, I have no doubt today's court proceedings will be the most memorable in Israel's history."

Solomon wondered if Ahishar had carefully chosen his words as a snide threat or if his steward was truly supportive of the proposed reforms. "Well then, why don't you read me the order of business so I can prepare my heart and mind."

The steward withdrew a rolled papyrus from beneath his robe and began reciting. "First will be a private meeting with your council members. We will then throw open the doors of the throne hall and welcome the representatives from visiting nations who have come to congratulate you as Israel's new king."

"But what of the countless Israelites," Solomon interrupted, "who have waited for judgment since before Abba's death? When will their disputes be heard?"

Ahishar shifted uncomfortably but maintained his pleasant smile. "They will of course be heard, my lord, just as soon as we uphold the laws of hospitality that govern the nations." He bowed submissively, but Solomon was not appeased. As keeper of the court proceedings, Ahishar wielded great power—power to determine who spoke to the king and when.

"Go on," Solomon said, receiving the gold-leafed crown on his head. "Hurry, I'm almost ready." Ahishar blathered on as Solomon studied his reflection in the polished bronze shield. *One week. I have one week before the idle days of the Passover Feast to prove that God's promise at Gibeon wasn't just a dream.*

Ahishar's voice fell silent, and Solomon looked into the expectant face of his high steward.

"Ready, my lord?"

As if hearing the question through the chamber walls, Benaiah entered in full dress armor, followed by a contingent of his elite guard. Solomon's surprise must have been evident.

"The Egyptians have made it clear to the other national contingents that they plan to address the king before anyone else." Benaiah's scar pulsed as he addressed Ahishar. "After King Solomon meets with his council, announce the Egyptians immediately and then excuse them as quickly as possible." The three nodded their agreement and moved in unison toward the chamber's veiled corner door.

Stepping over the threshold, Solomon emerged into his hall of justice from behind the heavy tapestries covering the hidden portal. No trumpets announced his presence, only the welcoming bows of his council members beside their cushioned couches.

"Please, sit down," Solomon said, motioning to their comfortable stools. "I trust that each of you received and read the scroll I sent to you this morning. In it, I thoroughly outlined proposed reforms for our nation." Anxious glances passed among the advisors, but Solomon continued, pointing now to the empty couch of the traitorous priest Abiathar and a new couch arranged in the left row. "I have appointed a new position to the council and a new man to fill it. Adoniram will coordinate the efforts of a national corvee, our foreign labor force. And Zadok will replace Abiathar as high priest."

Both men appeared from the king's hidden chamber door and assumed their places among the council amid congratulatory nods. Solomon spoke over their distraction to continue with the business at hand.

"I'm sure you have questions and concerns; however, the scroll of court proceedings is lengthy today, so I'd like to postpone our discussion on reforms to another time."

After waiting a moment, Ahishar, who stood at the king's right side, said, "Hearing no objection from my fellow counselors, I suggest we let our new king begin to rule!"

Wide smiles and gracious nods soothed Solomon's anxious soul. Undoubtedly these men would argue with his reforms, but they were at least willing to respect his request for patience.

"Guards!" Ahishar's voice echoed in the sparsely filled room. "You may open the doors of King Solomon's hall of justice!"

The grand doors opened, and the sight left Solomon breathless. Lithe, dark women covered in oil—and hardly anything else—danced and bounded up the center aisle, leading a contingent of six Nubian soldiers matching Benaiah's size. The Nubians' bare chests glistened, their arms banded with gold, their faces and forearms scarred by brutally artistic carvings. A portly, sandy-skinned man dressed in a long white robe preceded a gilded conveyance borne on the shoulders of four more Nubians. Within the sheer-curtained transport reclined a most intriguing figure. A woman. Or was it a lion?

Solomon smiled. *Do I flee, or do I hunt her?* Leaning over to Ahishar, he whispered, "Princess Sekhet seems to have changed her attire since we met the morning I left for Gibeon."

Clearing his throat and shielding their conversation with

a hand to his mouth, Ahishar said, "Princess Sekhet honors her patron goddess, Sekhmet, for whom she was named. The image representing the deity bears a woman's body and the head of a lion." Solomon heard satisfaction in his steward's voice. "Quite appropriate for a treaty with the son of David, whose crest is widely recognized as the Lion of Judah. Don't you think, my lord?"

"Hmmm." Solomon fell silent, and Ahishar resumed his posture. He had inferred by the princess's name that she worshiped the patron goddess of physicians and healers, but to flaunt her pagan god in Solomon's court was brazen indeed.

The Egyptian procession divided at the council couches, and only the ambassador approached the king's throne. The Nubians lowered the veiled chamber, revealing six golden-clad priestesses who were previously hidden. Their voluminous leonine wigs matched that of their princess, making all seven women appear more feral than tame.

The ambassador bowed, resting his forehead on the marble floor. "I am Bakari, humble servant and bearer of gifts from the high priest of Amun-Re, the god on earth, Pharaoh Psusennes."

Solomon shuddered, waiting for a lightning bolt to split the roof of his palace. Would Jehovah allow a mortal to claim His divinity? Spectators had filed in but remained utterly still.

Extending his scepter, Solomon finally said, "You may rise, Bakari."

The king was vaguely aware of others entering the throne hall amid the ambassador's broken Hebrew. "Magnificent king, ruler of Israel, son of the mighty King David, our pharaoh Siamun gave his life in battle to secure the dowry city of Gezer for his daughter, Princess Sekhet." He paused as if waiting for tribute. Solomon would give none. Instead the king glanced at the princess to measure her reaction. Her face was chiseled stone. Elegant but cold.

When Solomon's gaze rested again on Bakari, the

ambassador continued, "Pharaoh Psusennes's last words before we parted at the gates of Gezer were these: 'I will uphold the treaty agreement of Pharaoh Siamun with Israel as long as the son of David honors the mighty princess with the privileges of an Egyptian wife.'"

Solomon lifted an eyebrow, exchanging a glance with Benaiah, who had positioned his Pelethite and Cherethite guards between the Nubians and the throne. "And to what *privileges* specifically is your new pharaoh referring, Bakari?" He wanted to remind the pompous windbag that she would be an Israelite wife when she married him, but he resisted.

Bakari spread his hands and tilted his head as if explaining to a child. "Our divine pharaoh Psusennes simply asks that Princess Sekhet maintain her personal priestesses and altars for worship while living in Jerusalem. Her servants and priestesses will accommodate all her wishes. She will be no burden to the king." He ended with an awkward smile that looked utterly foreign on his face.

Solomon's heart raced as he wavered between indignation and triumph. Abba David had worked for years to cultivate friendly relations with Pharaoh Siamun. Now Psusennes dared to propose new terms? Yet a treaty with Egypt would expand Israel's influence in world trade, providing access to horses, chariots, spices, ivory, gold. The possibilities were endless.

He glanced again at the fascinating princess in her golden cage and was suddenly distracted by two other womanly shapes. The Daughters of Jerusalem had entered amid the crowd and advanced to stand at the back corner of the princess's conveyance. Gone were their well-fitted grieving robes and rough-woven veils. They were adorned in scarlet and purple robes tailored to reveal the perfect V at their throats. Solomon could hardly catch his breath.

"Shiphrah, Sherah. Come to me." His command caused an excited flutter through the now crowded courtroom. The twin beauties bowed low until Solomon extended his scepter and then addressed the Egyptian ambassador. "Princess Sekhet will receive greater honor than any of my previous wives," he said, motioning to the Daughters of Jerusalem, "for she will be attended by these lovely maidens, who will teach her the ways of Israelite women." The ambassador's smile disappeared, but Solomon continued, emphasizing his next words. "I will honor my new *wife* by allowing her priestesses to remain in her service, but she will also learn the ways of El Shaddai while she worships the gods of Egypt." The crowd stirred, and Solomon noted the concerned glance Benaiah cast over his shoulder.

"The son of King David is wise," the ambassador said, inclining his head but not conceding a full bow. "Pharaoh Psusennes has given me authority to bind our nations for the greater good of expanded trade and lasting dynasties. The divine pharaoh offers Princess Sekhet, her name meaning 'she who is powerful,' to unite our nations in a firm and unyielding friendship."

Solomon returned the nod, and a deafening cheer rattled the cedar rafters of his courtroom. He sought Benaiah's face and found his friend smiling, and the two shared a faint shrug. Egypt a friend? Only time would tell.

Quieting the crowd with an upraised scepter, Solomon said, "I accept Princess Sekhet as my wife. She is now Queen Sekhet, and I will treat her with the honor and privilege that Jehovah's law requires. Furthermore, I invite our new Egyptian friends to join me at this time tomorrow, when I will stand before the ark of the Lord and sacrifice burnt offerings and fellowship offerings in numbers never before equaled."

The ambassador's sandy-brown complexion suddenly turned as white as goat's milk.

"As you have asked—and I have agreed—to honor my new wife's personal worship," Solomon explained, barely containing his mischief, "so tomorrow begins my new queen's lessons of praise to El Shaddai!"

Bakari's face regained its color, now a vivid shade of crimson. His lips pressed into a thin line, the ambassador bowed and then issued heated commands. His Egyptian words were muddled, but their intent was clear. The Nubian guards hoisted the litter to their shoulders, the lioness within baring her teeth as if ready to strike. The Egyptians' hurried departure was quite unlike their opening display.

Solomon raised his voice over the commotion and announced to the lingering Israelites outside the courtroom doors, "Spread the word throughout the city. I invite my whole household—those belonging to it by service or by birth—to celebrate a feast of God's faithfulness after we sacrifice at the ark of God. Every family in Jerusalem will receive a loaf of bread from their king at tomorrow's feast!"

Renewed cheers resounded from visiting nations and Israelites alike. Solomon thought Benaiah appeared to be chuckling, and Ahishar leaned down, again hiding their conversation behind his hand.

"Your first celebration as Israel's king will certainly be popular with the crowd, but I daresay Elisheba, our palace cook, will be wringing her hands when she discovers she must bake bread for the whole tribe of Judah."

Solomon's stomach tightened at the mention of Judah as his household. Ahishar agreed with his decision, it was plain. *But can I really justify the tribe of Judah as my household— exempting them from the redistricting and the taxation of other tribes?* He would need to seek Jehovah's wisdom on the matter. But for now, there were more treaties and more brides to consider.

"Call the next ambassador, Ahishar."

11

The Lord said to Moses and Aaron in Egypt, ". . . The first month of your year . . . on the tenth day of this month each man is to take a lamb for his family . . . year-old males without defect. . . . Take care of them until the fourteenth day of the month . . . [and] slaughter them at twilight."

Thirty days after King David's death, the outward signs of mourning ceased in northern Israel. Torn and dusty sackcloth robes were washed and used as rags. The men's unkempt beards were combed and trimmed, and the village women no longer covered their faces. Shunem hummed with activity, and Jehoshaphat prepared for his second journey to Jerusalem since the death of his friend and king. David had not summoned Shunem's judge often, but over the years their hearts had been knit together in friendship, sharing their devotion to El Shaddai and the heartbreak of wayward sons.

"Kemmuel!" Jehoshaphat caught sight of his elder son and rushed to meet him just outside the city gate. "Would you like to join me in Gibeon to celebrate Passover this year?" He planned to incorporate the sacred feast with his journey to Jerusalem for his business with the king. "Perhaps you or your brother would like to choose the lamb for our family's sacrifice." His voice sounded too eager, forced, but he couldn't hold back. His heart yearned for a fresh start with his sons on this most sacred of celebrations.

But his hopes met a dead stare and familiar scorn. "No, my lord. I have no family," Kemmuel said. "I am merely a hired hand in my master's fields." He turned, and Jehoshaphat watched him disappear into the light mist that loomed over Mount Moreh.

Reu had arrived just in time to hear the exchange. "Perhaps his heart will soften during your extended time away."

Jehoshaphat's fading smile found new life in Reu's optimism. "Perhaps," he said, clapping his hand on the boy's shoulder. The two turned and began walking toward home. The young messenger had returned to Shunem after King David's burial, invited by Jehoshaphat for an unofficial visit during the lull of palace business during the grieving period. "I'm glad you're here, Reu," Jehoshaphat said. "Your presence has given new joy to my household."

Reu's short legs shuffled twice as fast to keep pace with Jehoshaphat. "I have appreciated your hospitality, my lord. I never expected to ride into Shunem bearing news of King David's death and then be invited to return as a guest in your home. Thank you, my lord, for your friendship. I'm honored."

"We've learned how to laugh again." Jehoshaphat kept his eyes forward, not daring to glance at the young man who had been like balm to an abba's broken heart.

A gentle rain began to fall, and Reu held out his hands, catching raindrops. The simple childlike gesture inspired Jehoshaphat. "Reu, will you join me in Gibeon for the Passover Feast?"

Jehoshaphat sensed uneasiness in the silence. Though David had united the people of Israel to worship only Jehovah, their Passover Feast remained divided. Judeans celebrated in Jerusalem, before the ark of God, and northern tribesmen celebrated at Gibeon, where the Tent of Meeting stood. Discrimination against northerners at Jerusalem's Passover was as common as women's well gossip. It was the tribes' way. It was tradition. It wasn't the law of Moses, but it was engraved on the hearts of Israel.

"Thank you, my lord," Reu finally said, "but I must get back to the palace. Now that the official grieving has ended, palace business will resume."

Jehoshaphat pursed his lips, determined not to press. *Lord Jehovah*, he prayed, *give me wisdom to bridge the gap that divides our nation.*

Rain fell in large droplets now, dripping from Jehoshaphat's beard. "Well, Reu, if you can't join me in the celebration, will you honor me by choosing the Passover lamb for our family, a year-old male without defect?"

Reu stopped, his expression awed. "I would be honored, Lord Jehoshaphat." He glanced down at his sandals and created a small canal in the dirt for the raindrops to flow. He seemed to be gathering his thoughts, so Jehoshaphat waited. When the young man finally looked up, his eyes were raining as steadily as the clouds. "I never knew my abba, and I was fortunate to love and respect the man who helped raise me. But I've never met anyone like you." Before Jehoshaphat could respond, Reu wiped his face and hurried toward the sheepfolds.

Arielah heard her abba stirring inside the house. She'd been waiting in the courtyard with the Passover lamb since before dawn. When Reu had chosen the lamb last night, he had brought it into the courtyard so the family could care for it as the law required.

Holding its little black nose in her hand, she whispered, "Abba will take good care of you on the journey to Gibeon."

She remembered their family journeys of years past, when

Kemmuel or Igal had been chosen to shepherd the lamb. They chose the unblemished male on the tenth day of the first new moon, feeding it, tending it, protecting it. And then on the fourteenth day, when they arrived in Gibeon, their family watched the priests slaughter their precious lamb at twilight. For almost five hundred years, Israelites had been remembering their flight from Egyptian slavery this way, commemorating the joy of their freedom and the passing over of the death angel that ultimately swayed Pharaoh's heart to release the Israelites from servitude.

"Good morning, my lamb," Jehoshaphat said, interrupting her thoughts. "The cock hasn't even said good morning, and you're already coddling the newest member of our family."

"Yes, and he's hungry. He's been nibbling on my robe." Arielah sat perched on an old olive tree stump with new sprouts shooting out its sides. The lamb was cuddled up next to her feet as she stroked its muzzle. "It's a good thing Reu chose one of the tame lambs. I'd hate to think of you chasing a wild little beast all over the mountains by yourself."

Her abba stood silent for a few moments. She couldn't look at him or her tears would surely fall.

"You understand why you cannot journey with me this time, don't you?"

He had guessed her disappointment, though she hadn't spoken of it. Arielah stood, and the lamb bleated his protest at losing his soft pillow. "Yes, Abba, I understand," she said, leading the way out the courtyard gate. "I'm not the same seven-year-old girl who begged to go to Jerusalem the first time. I know Jehovah must work without my interference, and I must wait on His timing." She tried to sound brave. Could he hear her voice quiver?

Jehoshaphat smiled. "How is it you have learned that lesson at such a young age?"

"I'm learning, Abba." She laced her arm through his. "I'm *learning* that lesson."

He opened the courtyard gate and allowed her to precede him. She bowed like a princess and waited until Abba latched it closed. "Let's go to the barn and gather some grain for our new friend," she said, holding his arm again.

Jehoshaphat's laughter split the morning air. "Oh, you are spoiling this little one, aren't you?"

Arielah tried to stem the tears, but they were stubborn this morning and splashed onto her cheeks. "Considering how short the lamb's life is going to be, I think a little grain is the least we can do." Offering a weak smile, she let out a disgusted sigh and swiped at the tears that refused to end.

Jehoshaphat squeezed her arm to his side. "I'll take some grain with me to feed our little lamb on the way to Gibeon." The two walked in silence for a time, enjoying the sweet fellowship they'd always shared.

"Abba," Arielah said, pausing their leisurely pace and turning to meet his gaze, "I wanted to tell you . . ." She stammered, uncharacteristically devoid of words. "Before you go, I just . . . I mean . . ." She looked away. How could she express all that was bursting from her heart? Her inexplicable love for Solomon. Her fear of Kemmuel and Igal when Abba left. Her desire to see Israel united.

He turned her chin with a single finger, his smile inviting her words.

"I love you, Abba."

Jehoshaphat gathered her into his arms. "Yes, my lamb. King Solomon will know what a prize he gains in my beautiful treaty bride. And though your brothers have not yet repented of their rebellion, I still hold out hope."

How was it possible that he read her heart as if she were a scroll and he a scribe? She snuggled into his embrace and voiced her only remaining concern. "When will you return, Abba?"

Resting his chin on top of her head, he recounted the days of his journey. "Three days to Gibeon, then a week's celebration of Passover and the Feast of Unleavened Bread. After that, to Jerusalem. I don't know what awaits me there. I have no idea how long I must wait to see the king, but Jehovah will make a way."

A rooster crowed in the distance, breaking the intimate moment. She pulled away, sniffed, and dried her eyes with the corner of her mantle. Shunem was coming alive, and though the Shulammites acknowledged the special bond between abba and daughter, such public affection wouldn't be appropriate. Resuming their step, they passed old Ruth, who was making her way to the well, and Dodo as he hobbled out to feed his pigeons.

Arielah whispered as they passed, "When I marry the king, this is what I'll miss most."

Jehoshaphat squeezed his eyes shut, and Arielah watched the pain leak from the corners of his eyes. She offered the corner of her veil to wipe his tear. "Why must things change, Abba? Why does Jehovah allow us to care so deeply and then later require us to sacrifice?"

"Oh, my precious lamb. Jehovah only asks that we sacrifice in order to prepare our hearts for the greater gifts He has to give."

The Passover Feast was especially poignant for Jehoshaphat this year. He had made the journey south with a caravan of northern villagers, as usual, enjoying the camaraderie of the yearly trek. But this year was different. Israelites feared change, and as a leader among the northern tribes, he felt compelled to offer reassurance.

"Passover has always signified a new beginning," Jehoshaphat said on the second night around the fire. "And this Passover promises not only a new year but also a new era in Israel's history!"

"Poor Jehoshaphat," one Shulammite said with a twinkle in his eye. "One of the lambs must have kicked him in the head."

Those around the fire laughed, and Jehoshaphat willingly joined them. "All right, my friends," he said, feigning a wounded ego. "Surely you think me too optimistic, but Passover gives us a chance to be born again."

Solemn nods and a genial hush fell over the camp. Men from various northern tribes discussed their fears, and Jehoshaphat listened long and well. After he heard their concerns and offered counsel, his enthusiasm proved contagious, and soon everyone, no matter how pessimistic, held high hopes for their Passover celebration in Gibeon.

When they arrived at the sacred high place, a familiar old Levite greeted Jehoshaphat with news. "King Solomon's grief birthed sacrifices, my friend." The Levite's face still glowed with wonder. "Burnt offerings and fellowship offerings to Jehovah—a quest beyond anything even the oldest of Jehovah's servants could recall." He described a strong king, an empowered son of David, now anointed with true devotion and God's promised wisdom.

When Jehoshaphat stood at the altar at twilight on the fourteenth night of the first new moon, he offered his Passover lamb to the priest. *Lord Jehovah*, he prayed, *let the death angel pass over your people Israel once more. Let the blood of the lamb save us from ourselves.*

The sobering night gave way to the seven-day Feast of Unleavened Bread, drawing families together from Dan to Beersheba. At the end of the celebration, faithful pilgrims loaded their beasts of burden and prepared for their journeys home.

But not Jehoshaphat. Waving good-bye to friends new and old, he loaded his small donkey and mounted a second mule he'd borrowed from one of the Shulammites. Though his heart longed for Shunem, his future waited in Jerusalem—a future for his nation and his daughter.

12

Now two prostitutes came to the king and stood before him. . . . When all Israel heard the verdict the king had given, they held the king in awe, because they saw that he had wisdom from God to administer justice.

The short but harsh wilderness between Gibeon and Jerusalem was a sea of rocks and hills. "I don't know which is worse," he said to his mule. "The fact that you're the only one I have to talk to, or the torture of riding your bony back." The forlorn creature replied by swishing a fly with its tail.

Rounding a large boulder and cresting the final rise, Jehoshaphat saw Jerusalem perched high on Mount Zion. "Ah, David's crown," he breathed. He'd first glimpsed the city as a boy of twelve just after David's army conquered the impregnable fortress of the Jebusites. Then a shabby town with dirt streets and one-room dwellings, Jerusalem had become God's crown of blessing on David's reign.

Jehoshaphat dug his heels into the mule's sides and began the slow ascent up the narrow road to the unwalled new Jerusalem. He noted King Solomon was indeed continuing many changes that King David had begun. Construction on the northern wall was under way and would expand Jerusalem to more than twice the size of the current City of David, which lay south of the palace. Stakes driven into the ground proved progressing plans for God's temple in the open space north of the palace. No doubt the City of David on the south side of the fortress remained a haven for the ferociously devoted tribe of Judah.

"My lord, fine silk from the East," a merchant said, sidling up to Jehoshaphat's heavily loaded donkey. Jehoshaphat tightened his grip on the reins, tugging the pack animal closer so he didn't lose anything to shifty fingers.

Vendors from all over the world lined both sides of the road, offering spices, pottery, and more. When Jehoshaphat finally entered the city through the new northern gate, he dismounted his mule and pulled the second beast alongside, scanning the open expanse. God's temple would rest on this very spot.

Leaving both animals with a stable boy, Jehoshaphat approached the north side of the palace. He discovered more street vendors, the finer artisans of Israel, whose place of honor was secured by their talent, the quality of their goods, and their political finesse. Their bangles and baubles held no interest for Shunem's judge, but the casual conversation of two merchants snagged his interest.

"I've never been so happy to be Judean," one man said, sampling a raisin cake from his own supplies.

A merchant in the neighboring stall raked his fingers through his overgrown beard and reached for a clay lamp from his shelves. "I too am thankful that my back won't be broken to fill the stomachs of the king's household. When the northern tribes discover King Solomon's redistricting plan *and* the monthly tax for his household, we may finally see war in Israel." The merchant examined his lamps as though inspecting rare Cushite gems and looked at the baker with a sly grin. "My clay lamps will be much more valuable than your raisin cakes."

"Shalom, and forgive my intrusion, brothers," Jehoshaphat said, "but I thought I heard you say the king is going to re-district the tribes of Israel."

"We are not your *brothers*, Galilean," the baker growled, throwing his suddenly devalued raisin cakes in a basket. "Your northern accent tells me you should go back home and tell your friends that the winds are changing in Israel, and they won't like the way the winds blow." The man spit on the ground, barely missing the fresh basket of raisin cakes.

Jehoshaphat was stunned by the man's rudeness and chose to believe his short temper rose from the imminent decrease in raisin cake profit. He nodded a pacifying farewell and continued to the palace.

From the city gates to the palace guard tower, beggars and merchants alike whispered rumors of Solomon's reforms. Reports varied from proposed calendar changes, building projects, centralized government, and yes—the redistricting of Israel's tribes. Jehoshaphat pondered the news, sorting through every detail like an old woman pulling straw from her wool. Though dread had been his initial response, he pondered a subtle outcome. Perhaps tearing down those ancient tribal boundaries could unite their nation.

As Shunem's judge rounded the northwest corner of the palace, he quickened his pace. Maybe the rebirth of Israel that he'd lauded at Passover was truer than he had imagined. But with these changes in the works, the treaty bride proposal was more important than ever.

"What business have you with the king?" An imposing palace guard startled Jehoshaphat from his thoughts. The leather armor the man wore distinguished him as a leader in the king's army. However, the grotesque scar where one eye used to dwell revealed a soldier whose military career had abruptly ended.

"I come as a representative of the northern tribes to seek a hearing before King Solomon."

A timid scribe appeared from behind the large guard and made sounds but formed no intelligible words. His tongue was as absent as the guard's left eye. However, he motioned to the soldier, and the two men seemed to understand each other completely.

"What is your name?" the guard asked impatiently. "The high steward's scribe needs your name for the court proceedings."

"Jehoshaphat, son of Paruah, from Shunem." He glanced to the right and left, noting additional watchmen stationed around the square palace perimeter. "It would seem you've added extra security since the last time I visited Jerusalem."

The one-eyed guard glared. "We have closed every other entrance to the palace and are on high alert." He didn't explain further. He didn't need to.

Jehoshaphat understood that more to lose meant more to protect. The testimony of Israel's rising power and wealth marched around the palace perimeter wearing javelins and bows strapped to their backs. The palace's grand pillars, intricately engraved with pomegranates, grapes, and palms, were a lovely façade for the prison of prosperity Jerusalem was becoming.

"You may enter." The guard nodded, and Jehoshaphat crossed the threshold into the entrance hall, its stone walls cold and unyielding. He lingered there with other afternoon petitioners while the king undoubtedly enjoyed his midday meal and respite.

Listening intently, Jehoshaphat heard the one-eyed soldier repeat, "What business have you with the king?" And each time, another supplicant was admitted to the entrance hall, waiting for the cedar doors to release the tide of petitioners into the throne hall. The crowd grew until it became a living thing, buzzing and shoving, squeezed into the shrinking space of the entrance hall.

None too soon, a shofar sounded, and a voice resounded from inside the hall of justice. "Come all who have matters of judgment for the king of Israel, King Solomon!"

The massive cedar doors opened, and Jehoshaphat gaped like a child. On his previous trips to Jerusalem, he'd never visited the famed courtroom. He'd met with King David in the fortress of Zion or walked around the wall of the southern City of David. Now his eyes devoured every detail of the majestic spectacle. Nearly a hundred people jostled for position near the railing on a second-story boardwalk from which extraordinary tapestries hung. Another two hundred stood on both sides of a long center aisle that split the lower level. The air swelled with the pungent odor of Phoenician cedar.

A second aisle in the main hall angled right, leading to Solomon's magnificent throne. This aisle was lined on either side with ornate couches. The crowd hushed. No trumpet sounded. None was necessary. The parting of bodies announced the entry of Solomon's wise council members. Dressed in blue and scarlet robes, they filed in and settled onto their cushioned stools like colorful peacocks perched on roosts.

The crowd noise swelled, and Jehoshaphat tuned his ear to those around him. Petitioners from bordering nations spoke in foreign phrases, but the waiting Israelites chatted about Solomon's insightful rulings during the seven-day interval after his return from Gibeon and before Jerusalem's Passover Feast.

Interestingly, their conversations had nothing to do with the matters of state Jehoshaphat had heard rumored in the marketplace. Instead they talked of his treaties, his brides, and his profound judgments. In fact, the king's most famous ruling involved a babe and two prostitutes.

"The two harlots both claimed parentage of a baby boy," the old man shouted over the din. "King Solomon resolved it by asking for a sword to cut the baby in half." Those around the old man gasped, and his cloudy eyes twinkled. "Ah, yes, exactly the reaction of the crowd that day, but when the rightful ima gave up her petition so as to save the babe's life, the wise young king's ploy proved her parentage." The toothless old man grinned wide at the oohs and aahs he'd expected and received, and Jehoshaphat pondered the young king whose name meant "peace." Solomon had donned the robe of authority through a mantle of wisdom.

Studying the sea of expectant faces around him, Jehoshaphat wondered how long he would have to wait to gain an audience. *Lord Jehovah, each person in this room desires a moment of the king's time.* He had barely formed the thought when trumpets announced the royal arrival.

A reverent hush fell over the crowd, and Jehoshaphat recognized Ahishar, the palace high steward, pushing aside the heavy tapestries behind the king's throne. His heart plummeted. When they'd met in Shunem almost a year ago, Jehoshaphat suspected Ahishar's deception and tried to stop him from taking Abishag to Jerusalem. He and the steward had parted on less than cordial terms, and now Ahishar, as gatekeeper to the king, would determine when—or if—Jehoshaphat spoke to Israel's new regent. *Please, Jehovah. Work in Ahishar's heart to give me an audience with the king—soon.*

As Jehoshaphat prayed, King Solomon ascended the dais to his throne. He was dressed in royal robes with a gold-leafed crown settled atop shoulder-length, raven hair. His well-trimmed beard bespoke a lifetime of palace privilege, and he bore the striking masculine features that made his abba David the desire of every Israelite maiden. His dark eyes and complexion, however, reflected Queen Bathsheba's beauty, and the regal grace with which she moved translated into a powerful stride in this confident young king.

Jehoshaphat watched the high steward and two formidable soldiers take up their positions as the king assumed his place

on his gilded throne. Solomon laid his hands atop the lions'
heads carved into the sides of his perch. Jehoshaphat had
heard the armrests were inlaid with jewels from David's military conquests: onyx, carnelian, topaz, amethyst, and more.

Ahishar leaned over to whisper something to the king, and
Jehoshaphat wondered if Solomon's reported gift of wisdom
was accompanied by discernment. Of course, David's son
hadn't the years of experience necessary to develop an intuitive judge of character, but perhaps Jehovah had warned
him that his steward couldn't be trusted. He wondered if—

"Let all who have come to King Solomon's court draw
near to hear the wisdom of the Lord," Ahishar boomed,
interrupting Jehoshaphat's surveillance.

Shunem's judge glanced at those around him, measuring
the response to the steward's claim. Dare Solomon equate
his rulings to God's own wisdom? But the expectant faces
shone with anticipation. Not one seemed to question the
declaration of divine understanding.

"Come now to be heard, Jehoshaphat, the righteous judge
of Shunem!" Ahishar's voice echoed off the walls, and Jehoshaphat's feet became molten lead on the marble floor.

The buzz of the crowd rose to fever pitch as everyone waited
on the supplicant to present himself before the king. Ahishar's black eyes found Jehoshaphat and challenged him to
step forward.

Jehoshaphat's mind reeled. *What is this sly fox up to?*
Though he had prayed for a chance to speak with the king,
he hadn't expected it quite so soon. But the confidence of his
righteous cause unbound his feet, and he shouldered his way
through the crowd to bow before Israel's king.

"I bring you greetings, my king, from the people of the
north." Lifting his head ever so slightly, he met the king's
gaze. "Indeed, I represent the northern districts that will
benefit by our nation's new design." In a crucial moment
of decision, Jehoshaphat purposely avoided any mention

of the condolences that led him to Jerusalem. Instead, he would focus solely on the king's new plan and how it could complement the treaty bride proposal.

Solomon's previously ho-hum demeanor burst into attentive interest. "Greetings, faithful Jehoshaphat. Please rise. My abba spoke highly of you many times."

Seeing the king's interest piqued, Jehoshaphat was inspired with a new approach to present his plan. "I come with a proposal that must be weighed privately. May I request a personal audience with the king tomorrow morning?"

Solomon smiled wryly, an intriguing sparkle in his eyes. "Yes, Jehoshaphat, I would be delighted to hear your proposal and to break our fast tomorrow morning—privately—in my chamber." The king seemed about to say more but hesitated and whispered something to Ahishar.

Jehoshaphat waited, heart pounding, watching the interchange. He relaxed a bit when the steward scowled.

"I invite you to remain in the palace tonight," the king offered. "My high steward will have one of the servants assigned to meet your needs."

Jehoshaphat deepened his bow. "I am honored beyond words, my king," he said. "Until tomorrow then, King Solomon." He backed away, noting the challenge in Ahishar's eyes. A night in the palace . . . Perhaps he would sleep with his chamber door locked.

The sun was sinking over the western hills, and Arielah took a final count of the flock before leading them home. "Twenty-six, twenty-seven, twenty-eight, twenty-nine—" *Where is Edna's lamb?* The troublesome ewe she'd named after the crotchety matchmaker had birthed a lamb yesterday. "The lamb was here at last count. One, two, three, four . . ." She began again, hoping she'd simply overlooked the babe. But Edna's bleating had changed from occasional to constant and confirmed the count before Arielah finished. "Twenty-nine. One missing." She scanned the rocky mountain path above her, considering every step they'd traveled. "Where did we lose you, precious lamb?"

Her mind began to race. Abba had warned her before last Sabbath to be extra alert for bears awakening from their long winter's hibernation. The western sky was changing to a deeper orange glow. The lions would begin prowling for prey. If she herded the rest of the flock back to Shunem's sheepfolds, it would be too dark to return and search for the lost lamb. But she couldn't go search for the lamb and leave the whole flock unprotected—could she?

Jehovah, what should I do? Glancing from the horizon to the rocky path above and behind her, Arielah listened for that silent inward voice. She felt the familiar tingle up her spine, and her palms began to sweat. Jehovah often warned her of danger like this. Some might have said it was her own fear talking; regardless, she must find the lamb.

"Protect your women, Samson," she said to the ram among the ewes. "I'll be back as quickly as I can." He blinked his liquid black eyes and munched on a new shoot of green grass, calm amid unknown danger.

Retracing her steps up the path of Mount Moreh, she veered right and left, checking behind rocks and searching for any sign of struggle. Blood. Tufts of black wool. A predator would have taken the lamb off the path to feast in a cave or behind a rock. Thankfully, she found no sign of violence but regrettably no signs of the lamb either.

The sun had now turned red and kissed the earth. *Jehovah, help me find the babe!* Frantic, Arielah tugged on her shepherd's flute, releasing it from the strap on her belt, and trilled the song she often played for the flock at midday. Playing with all her heart, she allowed the evening breeze to carry the sound.

And then she waited.

Even the distant bleating of her flock stilled. A faint little *bahaha* came from a cluster of rocks below her. She rushed to the ledge and peered over, and there was her precious lamb. His right front leg was misshapen, obviously from a fall. Carefully Arielah climbed down and gathered him into her arms. "Oh, little one," she said, tears streaming down her cheeks, "I thought I'd lost you." His black nose nuzzled into that warm place on her neck. She kissed his muzzle and then lifted him over her head to place him around her shoulders. He bleated when she moved his broken leg. "I know it hurts, but I bet you'll never get too close to a ledge again."

With one hand securing her little friend and the other hand helping her climb, she returned to the rocky path and was on her way back to the flock. The sun was now half hidden and the sky darkening fast. "You'll be spending a lot of time in my arms, little one," she said to the furry black face bleating in her ear. "Sometimes pain means more comfort from the shepherd." The words pierced her heart, their truth resonating through her conflicts with her brothers and the comfort she gained from Abba and Jehovah. "I will call you *Arieh* because, like me, you will be loved through your pain."

13

*Solomon also had twelve district governors over all
Israel, who supplied provisions for the king and the
royal household. Each one had to provide supplies for
one month in the year.*

The king requests your company at his table to break the
fast." The messenger's high-pitched voice propelled
Jehoshaphat from a dead sleep, and the incessant knocking
nearly rattled the door from its hinges.

"What? Where am I? Who's there?" Blurry-eyed, Jehoshaphat searched his strange surroundings.

A lighthearted voice repeated the invitation. "The king
requests . . ."

"Reu, my friend, is that you?" Jehoshaphat stumbled out
of bed. "I wondered if I might see you during my stay at the
palace." The king's messenger, who had become so dear to
Jehoshaphat's family, had found him. Fumbling with the iron
lock above the handle, Shunem's judge tugged at the cedar
door. "Oh, I don't know why I locked this cursed thing."
He heard Reu's light chuckle on the other side. "I can't get
it unlatched!"

"My lord, if you'll just pull up on the——"

Jehoshaphat flung open the door and bowed as if he were the most hospitable of servants. "Please, my friend, come in."

Reu chuckled again, but Jehoshaphat thought he noted a tinge of sadness on his friend's face. "I cannot stay long, my lord. I've brought a refreshing cup of honeyed water before you break your fast with the king." Stepping over the threshold, Reu tried to steady the goblet on the silver tray in his shaking hands. He turned and locked the door behind him.

Seeing the young man's apprehension, Jehoshaphat fought the dread he'd felt since yesterday's silent exchange with Ahishar in the throne hall. "How did you find me so quickly, my friend? Who told you I was here?"

Reu kept his voice barely above a whisper. "My ima Elisheba is the head cook, and her kitchen has always been the center of palace gossip. No detail—great or small—escapes her notice, my lord." He paused, looking left and right as if a conspirator might peek out from beneath the goatskin rug. "And believe me, you are a big detail." Reu lifted the silver goblet to his lips and drank deeply of Jehoshaphat's morning refreshment.

Jehoshaphat grinned at his friend's absentminded gesture. "And why am I a big detail?"

Reu's eyes grew large as he gulped and then wiped the sweet nectar from his lips. "Because you arrived in Jerusalem a day early!" he said, setting down the goblet.

Thoroughly confused, Jehoshaphat asked, "How could I be a day early when the king didn't know I was coming?"

"Please, my lord, sit down." Reu rushed the few steps from the door to a cushioned couch. "I will tell you everything, but I must hurry before your steward arrives to escort you to the king's chamber." Sitting down heavily beside the judge, Reu took a deep breath and began. "I am one of twelve couriers who were commissioned last night to disperse the king's edicts of reform to twelve new districts in Israel. The royal command erases the tribal lines established by Moses, imposes a labor tax on each district to supply food for the king's household one moon cycle per year, and mandates an Israelite workforce to assist Sidonian lumbermen with the felling of cedars in Lebanon."

"I heard of some of these reforms in the market yesterday," Jehoshaphat said while Reu gulped another mouthful of honeyed water. "But I don't understand what they have to do with me." He paused, a sudden realization squeezing his heart. "Reu, you shouldn't be telling me this." He glanced at his locked chamber door and prayed no one was listening on the other side. "What if someone hears you?"

His friend's expression was undecipherable. "I'm faithfully discharging my duty," he said. "I'm delivering my decree to the governor of King Solomon's tenth district."

Silence. Gut-wrenching silence as the two locked eyes and measured the weight of his statement.

"There's more," Reu said in barely a whisper. Jehoshaphat nodded, and his friend continued. "An ancient sect of Judean zealots called the Sons of Judah has set a plan into motion that will rend Israel in two, making Judah the crown and the northern tribes her slaves. They have infiltrated the king's council and the Judean military . . ." He paused, his eyes misting. "They have even placed two virgins in the king's harem, the Daughters of Jerusalem, to control the political influence of Solomon's foreign wives."

At the mention of the king's harem, Jehoshaphat felt his heart race. "Arielah." The whisper of her name brought tears. "She'll be walking into a boiling pot of intrigue far greater than I'd imagined."

Reu nodded sadly. "And she'll be fighting the second most powerful man in the kingdom." The normally rosy-cheeked, jovial courier turned a vengeful, hard stare on Jehoshaphat. "Ahishar is the leader of the rebellion and found a way to dispose of Prince Adonijah. He'll stop at nothing to steal Solomon's throne."

Shunem's judge felt as if every drop of blood had rushed from his face. "Are you sure, Reu? How can your ima be certain of all this?"

"Do you remember when I told you that my abba was killed in David's army and another good man helped Ima Elisheba raise me?"

Jehoshaphat nodded.

"It was Ahishar's scribe, Mahlon, who was like an abba to me, and Ahishar cut out his tongue because he told my ima about the Sons of Judah."

Jehoshaphat's stomach rolled. "Jehovah, help us all," he whispered, wiping his face as if he could wipe away the sordidness of the details. "How has your ima escaped Ahishar's wrath if he knows she's aware of the Sons of Judah?"

The young man's eyes welled with tears. "Ahishar has told both my ima and Mahlon that if information goes any further, he will have me arrested and tortured."

"Oh, Reu!" Jehoshaphat's heart pounded. "What a nightmare." He pulled the young courier into a ferocious embrace. Holding the boy tightly, he suddenly connected Reu's relationships. "I believe I met your friend at the palace entrance. Is he the scribe who works with the one-eyed guard to assemble the list of court petitioners?"

Reu sat back and wiped his face on his sleeve. "He still serves Ahishar, recording names on a clay tablet and then transferring them to the papyrus scroll used in court. Ahishar keeps him close since Mahlon knows so many of the high steward's secrets."

Jehoshaphat ran his fingers through his hair, releasing a long, slow sigh. "Well, my friend, we—"

A knock on the door startled them both. "Just a moment," Jehoshaphat shouted. Turning to Reu, he whispered, "Pray, my friend. Pray that Jehovah grants me wisdom and favor as

I meet with our king." His heart ached for Arielah. Should he still offer his precious lamb when the sacrifice had become so dangerous? "How can I get word to you if I must see you before I leave Jerusalem?"

Another knock. "My lord Jehoshaphat," came a young male voice on the other side of the door. "Please, we must hurry. The king awaits your meeting in his private chamber."

"Send word through a messenger to my ima's kitchen if you need me, my lord," Reu said. With a sad smile, he added, "The governor to which I was delivering my news already knows his position as one of the king's new princes. I suspect I'll have the day at leisure." Opening the door, Reu greeted the chamber steward. "Be kind to him, Yoshim. This man is a good friend."

Jehoshaphat walked beside the quiet servant boy, Yoshim, and realized he was gaping again at the palace grandeur. "Don't lose me!" he teased. "I could wander for weeks and never find my chamber." The servant cast a coy smile over his shoulder and then ducked his head, continuing down a long marble hallway.

Approaching the mosaic entryway of double doors, Jehoshaphat admired the thumb-sized pieces of stone arranged in lovely patterns. Intricate designs of palm trees, pomegranates, and cherubs were etched on the doors and door frames, and stone lions resting on their haunches stood like sentries on both sides. Next to each lion, the king's elite soldiers guarded the door—each man twice the size of other Israelites. Yoshim stepped confidently between them as though they were statues themselves. Rising up on tiptoes, he lifted the large round circlet of iron and let it fall once—*clang!* Then again—*clang!*

After a rush of hurried footsteps, the doors opened wide. King Solomon stood framed in the doorway. "Come, Jehoshaphat, you are welcome at my table."

Shunem's judge was again awed at the luxury of a king's

world. Directly before him was a large olive-wood table that could have accommodated twenty people, raised two handbreadths off the floor by four beautifully carved legs. Jehoshaphat was accustomed to the table in his own home—a piece of leather placed on the floor and then folded after each meal to provide space to walk in the common room.

Solomon guided his guest past the splendid table and settled beside a small ivory table in the corner. Ahishar stood waiting, his expression forcibly pleasant. Four goatskin rugs circled the table, revealing the imminent arrival of one more guest.

"I thought we'd eat here," the king said, inviting Jehoshaphat to be seated.

Just as they folded their legs to take their places, Benaiah burst through the door. "Please forgive me, my lords. I'm sorry to delay our meal."

King Solomon glared a silent reprimand at his captain and then turned a forced smile on his guest. "Jehoshaphat, soon to be my prince of Shunem, I'd like to introduce the commander of Israel's army."

Jehoshaphat was still pondering the "prince of Shunem" comment as Solomon continued. "Benaiah has been my most trusted advisor since Abba's death."

Ahishar tried to hide a wince, no doubt envious of the captain's favored status.

Discerning tension between the king's two advisors, Jehoshaphat offered his hand to the captain. "It is an honor to finally meet you. When I saw you in court yesterday, I had hoped a man of your size was friendly!"

Locking his hand against Jehoshaphat's wrist, Benaiah nodded briefly, released his grip, and cast a suspicious glance at Ahishar. "And when I saw *you* in court yesterday, Jehoshaphat, I hoped our palace steward had not breached confidentiality and leaked the king's decision to a member of our northern tribes."

"I'll not have him speak to me this way in front of—" Ahishar shouted.

"Enough!" Solomon said, lifting his hands to silence his advisors. After sufficiently chastising them with a stare, the king returned his attention to Jehoshaphat. "I apologize for my friends' outbursts, but we were all a little surprised to see one of my district princes arrive in the throne hall hours before I confided your new position to my council and a full day before I sent a courier to Shunem with the news."

Jehoshaphat finally grasped the title "prince of Shunem." King Solomon had used *prince* and *governor* interchangeably, a label for his new district administrators. Shunem's judge had been confused and concerned, even though he'd heard the news this morning from a friend. He could only guess how the northern tribesmen would feel when they received royal decrees from impersonal couriers.

"I must confess, my king," Jehoshaphat began, adjusting his position on the curly white rug, "I had no idea that I was to become a governor or prince, and my visit to your courtroom was planned on the night King David died." The three men at the table exchanged puzzled glances, obviously gauging their trust of this northern visitor. "I assure you, my knowledge of the redistricting was based on a rumor I heard in the market yesterday from a particularly unpleasant Judean."

"A rumor?" the king and commander asked at the same time, both raising an eyebrow.

Benaiah's skepticism was much more intimidating, stretching the long scar on the left side of his face. "You asked for an audience with the king based on nothing more than a rumor?"

The room had fallen utterly silent.

"Well, I . . . I heard of other reforms the king was considering, and I thought, well . . ."

The commander stood, and Jehoshaphat's heart leapt to his throat. Would he be arrested? Tortured?

And then erupted one of the deepest belly laughs

Jehoshaphat had ever heard. "Stand up, my lord," Benaiah said to him. "Let me shake the hand of the cleverest official I've ever met!"

Tension drained from the room like water from an overturned jar. Grins and good-natured shoves opened the men's hearts to speak on level terms.

"So you had no idea I planned to name you as prince of my tenth district?" Solomon asked.

"No, my lord," Jehoshaphat said. "Not until the courier you assigned pounded on my door this morning." Again, laughter soothed the souls of the cautious leaders.

Solomon clapped Jehoshaphat's shoulder soundly. "Let's get started on our meal. I'm starving. Your steward awaits your request, *Prince* Jehoshaphat."

"Well, Yoshim," Jehoshaphat said, "I'll have whatever the king is having. That is, unless you have a better suggestion, my friend."

Solomon's warm smile faded, and Ahishar's expression glowed. Jehoshaphat realized he'd erred but wasn't sure how.

"Why is a northern tribesman on such friendly terms with a palace servant?" Ahishar asked. "I train the chamber stewards to be invisible, *Prince* Jehoshaphat, neither seen nor heard by those they serve. So how would you know the young man's name is Yoshim?" When Jehoshaphat drew a breath to explain that Reu had addressed the boy by name, Ahishar demanded more answers. "And how did a royal courier know to deliver his message to you at the palace this morning? Do you have spies among us, Jehoshaphat? Are there vengeful Shulammites who conspire to harm the king in retribution for Abishag's treatment?" He leaned forward, challenging. "Ask Benaiah what we do with traitors in Jerusalem."

Before Jehoshaphat could dispel Ahishar's accusations, Benaiah released a burst of air from between pursed lips, and his imposing scar began to dance. Yoshim's eyes grew as round as the lemons on the table. But Solomon's face was a blank clay tablet, as he awaited Jehoshaphat's reply to etch his opinion.

Ahishar's aim was clear. Reu's warnings were proving true. The high steward was seeking to drive a wedge between Solomon and his northern brothers in hopes of civil war. Jehoshaphat didn't yet understand how Ahishar planned to use the king's harem, but he knew without a doubt that offering Arielah as a treaty bride would risk her life.

Calmly Jehoshaphat directed his reply to the king. "Yoshim and I met just this morning, and if it weren't for Yoshim and the royal courier, Reu, I might never have successfully unbolted my door, nor would I ever find my way back to my chamber." His easy manner and attempt at humor softened the king's features. Jehoshaphat would gain nothing by growing defensive or accusing Ahishar without proof. The king must judge his new prince for himself. "So what does a king eat for breakfast?"

"I'm rather predictable," Solomon said with a lingering gaze. "I have a propensity for goat's milk, bread, and cheese." Reaching for a dried fig, he began rolling it under his hand on the table. "And figs, fresh, dried, or candied—doesn't matter. I love figs, and I eat the same thing every morning."

"Well, then," Jehoshaphat said, "I'll have goat's milk, bread, and cheese." He reached for a fig and popped it in his mouth. "And figs."

Solomon offered a slight nod, tossed a fig in the air, and caught it in his mouth. Jehoshaphat applauded. Even Benaiah's jaw relaxed, and a slight grin cracked his hard exterior. Yoshim and the other servants hurried toward a door at the far corner of the king's chamber, and Jehoshaphat tried to guess what they would report to Reu's ima, the palace cook.

"So, tell me," Solomon said when the four men had settled into silence, "if you didn't know of my reforms when you came to Jerusalem, what prompted your journey?" His brow furrowed. "Did I hear you say you planned the journey the night of my abba's death?"

"Yes, my lord." Jehoshaphat's heart pounded as he prayed, *Jehovah, give me wisdom. How much do I reveal? Do I offer my lamb for our nation's peace?* Raising his eyes, he searched the faces of the men seated with him. "May I ask each of you a question before I answer?"

Solomon smiled, offered a forbearing nod.

"I understand that you have a son. Rehoboam, is it?" he asked Solomon.

"Yes, he is my firstborn."

The king was noticeably aloof, but Jehoshaphat moved on. "And what about you, Ahishar? Do you have children?"

"No. I never married," he said as if thoroughly bored. "I have dedicated my life to serving my kings."

"What about you, Benaiah?"

The commander appeared quite uncomfortable, glancing first at the king and then back at Jehoshaphat. "Yes," he said barely above a whisper. "I once had a son."

"What?" Solomon's remoteness disappeared. "Benaiah, I didn't know you were ever married."

Bathed in silent prayer, Jehoshaphat pressed on. "Would you mind sharing what happened to your son, Captain?"

"How do you know about my son?" Benaiah leaned dangerously close, his scar dancing.

Jehoshaphat drew a calming breath. "I had no idea you once had a son, but I've been praying that Jehovah would guide my conversation, Captain." The two locked gazes. Measuring. Waiting. "Perhaps what you have to say will impact the proposal I will present to the king."

With one last twitch of his left eyebrow, the big man spoke. "I was a young commander in King David's army when my wife died giving birth to our son. His name was Ammizabad. When he became of age, David placed me over the Mighty Men, and I put my son in charge of my army division. He

was killed the next day when the Edomites rioted." Turning
to Solomon, he said, "I'm sorry I didn't tell you, my king, but
you were too young to remember those days. I didn't think
the past mattered to my current post."

"Well, this is all very moving." Ahishar's nasally whine split
the air. "But what does it have to do with the night of King
David's death and Jehoshaphat's more-than-coincidental
arrival in Jerusalem?"

"Because I am offering my child to fight for the king,"
Jehoshaphat said almost before Ahishar finished. "And the
battle might just cost my child's life."

Solomon exchanged puzzled glances with his two advisors.
"Prince Jehoshaphat, Israel is not at war," he said amiably.
"If your son is twenty or older, he has already been counted
in the eight hundred thousand fighting men in Israel. And he
would not be needed in Judah's ranks. Our soldiers already
number five hundred thousand." Offering a kindly tilt of
his head, he said, "You didn't need an audience with me to
request that your son enlist in the army."

When Jehoshaphat smiled brightly, he expected all three
men to call for the physicians, for his next words would surely
tip the scales toward insanity. "It is not a son I offer to fight
for Israel, King Solomon. It is my beloved daughter."

14

Solomon also had twelve district governors over all Israel. . . . These are their names: Ben-Hur . . . Ben-Deker . . . Ben-Hesed . . . Ben-Abinadab . . . Baana . . . Ben-Geber . . . Ahinadab . . . Ahimaaz . . . Baana . . . Jehoshaphat son of Paruah—in Issachar; Shimei . . . Geber.

Solomon studied the prince of his tenth district. What was he up to? This man, whom Abba David had lauded for his keen wisdom and integrity, knew better than to offer a woman for military service.

"My lord," Ahishar sputtered, "surely you must reconsider your choice of tenth district governor. Jehoshaphat has obviously met with some accident or impairment to think his daughter could fight in Israel's army."

A slow, wry smile crept across Solomon's lips. "Tell me, Prince Jehoshaphat, how will your daughter serve her nation?"

"I propose that my daughter fight for Israel's unity by becoming your treaty bride." The words were uttered quickly, quietly, matter-of-factly. The man never flinched. "As with the peace treaties you undertake by marrying foreign brides, my daughter will bring Israel peace."

At first Solomon wasn't sure he'd heard correctly, but Benaiah's wide smile and Ahishar's disgusted snort provided time to absorb the statement. "So, let me clarify," he said, noting the sparkle in Jehoshaphat's eyes. "You simply want me to marry your daughter."

"Yes, my lord. My only daughter."

Solomon's amusement was piqued. "Your tongue was looser when we talked about goat's milk and figs, my friend."

Jehoshaphat grinned but said nothing.

"Forgive me if this sounds rude, Jehoshaphat, but does your daughter have two noses or twelve toes so you hide her while you pursue a suitor?"

"No, my lord," Jehoshaphat said amiably. "She has but one nose and ten toes—at least, the last time I counted."

Solomon threw his head back and laughed. "Come now, you must tell me more! Does the girl have a name?"

"Her name is Arielah." Jehoshaphat resumed his silence and bounced his eyebrows.

"This is like watching a game of Hounds and Jackals!" Benaiah said with a delighted chuckle. "You must throw the knucklebones to advance your jackal, King Solomon. Give Jehoshaphat some information on your reforms to get information in return."

"Oh, this is utterly ridiculous!" Ahishar blurted, distinct red patches forming on his neck and cheeks. Turning his frustration on Jehoshaphat, he said, "Have you any idea how many kings and noblemen petition for their daughters to marry King Solomon? How dare you deceive your way into the king's chamber—"

"How dare you deceive the northern tribes and steal Abishag for King David's belly warmer!" Jehoshaphat's fury silenced the steward and startled Solomon. Benaiah was on his feet, ready to defend, but the king eased his commander with a glance. Benaiah resumed his place, and Solomon assessed his guests. Jehoshaphat's rage had been aimed at no one but Ahishar. That much was plain. *So the two must have quarreled when Ahishar visited Shunem last year.*

"My king," Ahishar gasped, "are you going to let him speak to me that way?" As if his fear rang the chamber servants' bell, their breakfast arrived on gold and silver platters.

Pausing while the bread, cheese, and fruit were served, Solomon studied the three men at his table. "I believe we will all speak plainly over our meal this morning." He pinned all three elders with an imposing stare. "And I suggest we speak respectfully to each other if we wish respect in return." Lingering on Ahishar, he noted the steward's pout. Benaiah nodded and remained alert since none of them knew yet if this judge from Shunem could be trusted.

Solomon spread some soft goat cheese on a piece of bread and handed it to Jehoshaphat. "Persuade me, prince of Shunem, that marriage to your daughter will assuage the northern tribes' anger. Prove to me that if I accept your treaty bride, northern Israel will cheerfully redistrict, pay taxes, and work as I command. In short, convince me that you come with honorable intentions and can aid my new government."

He reached for his own piece of bread, spread the pungent cheese, and took a leisurely bite, hoping the relaxed posture would mask his angst. *Lord, let Your promised wisdom be at work in me now.* Shunem's elder had been lauded as the wisest man in Israel. How would God's new gift of wisdom stand up to negotiations with him?

Jehoshaphat's expression was kind but intense. "By honoring a marriage contract with a Shulammite maiden, you will assuage the north's anger over Abishag. The gesture is a sign of goodwill, a step of respect toward your northern brothers that will at least open their hearts to discuss your reforms and taxation."

Solomon searched the man's expression. "You neglected

to mention the bride price, prince of Shunem. How much of the king's treasure will find its way into your pockets?"

Jehoshaphat's eyes penetrated Solomon's soul. "May I honor you, King Solomon, with the same candor you've shown me?"

"By all means," Solomon said. "It appears we have moved from Benaiah's game of Hounds and Jackals to treaty negotiations." Solomon's words were intentionally clipped, distant.

"I would rather offer my daughter to a Shulammite," Jehoshaphat said flatly. "I don't need your wealth, and quite frankly, I wish my grandchildren could grow up before my eyes in the solitude and safety of Shunem's hills."

"Ha!" Ahishar gave a reproving laugh. "Don't fall for his trickery, my lord."

But Solomon saw only sincerity in the eyes that glistened with tears. "I don't understand, Jehoshaphat. You are a man of great power in the north. Why have you allowed your constituents to proffer your daughter as the treaty bride?"

Instead of a direct answer, Jehoshaphat turned to Benaiah, who had grown quiet during the negotiations. "Did anyone force you or your son Ammizabad to fight for Israel?"

"Jehoshaphat!" Solomon was outraged. "Don't you dare compare—"

But Benaiah lifted his hand, settling the king's defense. And instead of indignation on the captain's face, Solomon saw respect. "Just as I gave my son for Israel's sake, my lord," he said, turning to Solomon, "the prince of Shunem is placing his daughter in a battle for her nation's unity."

"What?" Solomon felt as if he had taken a blow. "Have you both tipped too many wineskins?" He glanced at Ahishar, who rolled his eyes, showing the same cynicism he felt. "How could either of you suggest a wedding and a war are the same? Benaiah, your son gave his *life* in battle. Jehoshaphat's daughter would be a queen of Israel, living in the luxury of my harem!"

"And where did most of the threats to your abba's kingdom start?" Benaiah asked quietly, respectfully. Not waiting for the answer, he replied, "In King David's household, the very lifeblood of rebellion came from his harem."

No! Solomon rejected any such possibility. Solomon's firstborn, Rehoboam, would never rape one of his sisters as Abba's son Amnon had. One of Solomon's sons would not betray him as Absalom had betrayed Abba David. But even as the memories assaulted him, he knew Benaiah was right. The harem was both the lifeblood of and the deathblow to any kingdom.

"My king." Jehoshaphat's gentle voice shattered the painful revelation. Solomon looked up to meet kind eyes and an understanding tone. "Benaiah's son wore a leather breastplate to war. My Arielah's battle armor will be the robes of Israel's treaty bride." Pointing to the captain's dagger, he said, "Benaiah's son fought with a sword and spear, but my daughter will bring her own weapon to the palace."

"I'm sorry, Jehoshaphat," Ahishar said. "I must draw the line here. None of the king's wives are permitted to keep weapons in their private chambers." His voice raised in pitch, and Solomon stared in disbelief at his blathering steward. "Do you have any idea of the ensuing anarchy if the women of the harem had *weapons*? There is only one entrance at each of the kings' harems, and Judean watchmen guard the gates at all times, though no man is ever allowed inside the—"

"As I was saying, King Solomon," Jehoshaphat interrupted, ignoring the steward, "my daughter brings with her the most powerful weapon on earth—love."

Ahishar rolled his eyes, and Solomon couldn't contain a chuckle. "Ah, so you're a romantic man, given to shepherds' verses and psalms like my abba David, no doubt."

Shunem's judge inclined his head, agreeing but using few words—as was the practice of most wise men.

"So tell me, Prince Jehoshaphat, does love make marriage

a partnership, or is marriage a business arrangement between partners?" He hadn't planned on this conversation, but now he longed to hear what the wise elder of the north would say.

"Can a grapevine grow without pruning?" Jehoshaphat asked.

Solomon laughed. "Ah, a true teacher. One who asks questions and gives no answers."

Jehoshaphat nodded. Smiled.

"Yes, of course," Solomon replied. "A grapevine can grow without pruning, but its harvest is greatly reduced by wild growth."

"I have discovered marriage to be much the same, my lord," the older man said. "It can exist without love; however, our lives reap the greatest blessing if the relationship is pruned by love."

Pruned by love. Solomon's amusement faded. The idea of love was a fanciful thought, worthy of amiable discussion, but to consider its pruning, its cutting, its pain . . .

"My wife Jehosheba is as vital to me as the air I breathe," Jehoshaphat said, undoubtedly noticing Solomon's shifted mood. "A marriage filled with deep and abiding love is not only possible, my king, I believe it may be Yahweh's greatest gift." Jehoshaphat tossed a fig in his mouth and fixed his attention on the now uncomfortable king.

How had they arrived here, talking of abiding love, when this was simply a treaty negotiation? "A king's marriages are not his own, I'm afraid," Solomon said, reaching for a grape and trying to sound uninterested. "When Abba died, I inherited the responsibility of his twenty wives and concubines. I had ten wives of my own, and since returning from Gibeon, I've married . . ." He paused, looking to Ahishar for help.

"Five, my lord," the steward offered with renewed interest.

"Yes, five new women—all of them representing foreign nations that promise new trade agreements and treaties. The gift of Jehovah's wisdom has borne much fruit in my harem, my friend." Solomon leaned back, waiting for Jehoshaphat's congratulations. It didn't come. In fact, he saw . . . was that sympathy on the man's face?

"You cannot unlive your past or your abba's decisions, my lord," he said, placing his hand on Solomon's shoulder. "However, you can choose your *future* carefully, and I believe with all my heart that Arielah is to be your bride—perhaps your last wife."

Solomon felt a chill race through him. *My last wife?* The thought was absurd. A king in this political climate was forced to take many wives—not only to negotiate treaties and trade agreements but to build a lasting legacy.

Attempting to revive a more lighthearted conversation, Solomon countered, "Well, does that mean I'll be paying her bride price for the rest of my life?"

Jehoshaphat's expression was warm, but he didn't join in Solomon's light chuckle. Instead, he turned to Benaiah. "Captain, what price could the king offer to replace your son?"

"Jehoshaphat!" Solomon said.

But before he grew too annoyed, Benaiah leaned over and patted Jehoshaphat's shoulder. "Well played, my friend. Well played."

Solomon glanced between his two elders. It slowly dawned on him that his emotions had been masterfully maneuvered again.

Jehoshaphat's kind expression opened the king's heart. "As I said before, my lord, no amount of riches could compensate for my daughter. However, a fair bride price should be paid to continue building goodwill in the north." His eyes glistened. "The amount of that is between you and Jehovah."

Solomon marveled at Jehoshaphat's ability to bend an opponent's will and yet leave the rival's dignity intact. He was an incredible ally and an honorable man. *Who knows? Perhaps he'll even become a fine abba-in-law.* The thought amused him, and he extended his hand. "Well played indeed, my friend," he said, repeating Benaiah's words—and meaning them.

Jehoshaphat's combination of integrity and diplomacy was impressive and birthed a new concept in Solomon's transition for the northern tribes. "After falling victim to your treaty bride negotiations," he said, still shaking hands, "I have a request to make of you, my friend."

Shunem's prince nodded, relaxing again on his goatskin. "Make it, my lord. I am your willing servant."

Solomon raised an eyebrow, hoping he didn't have to remind him of that vow after asking the favor. "Each of my twelve new governors will have identical responsibilities. They will organize foreign labor and collaborate with our Israelite workforces on national projects, and each district will provide the supplies for my household one moon cycle of each year." Solomon waited for Jehoshaphat's nod before he continued. "But you, Jehoshaphat, have the wisdom and diplomacy to influence all the districts as my goodwill ambassador."

Jehoshaphat's expression was unreadable papyrus. "And what exactly does a 'goodwill ambassador' do, my lord?"

"Well," Solomon said, "you would travel among the northern districts, listening to concerns and shaping opinions on my reforms."

"Shaping opinions? Mm-hmm." Jehoshaphat's deeply furrowed brow created a V that seemed foreign on such a genial face. "May I ask how long it's been since you've visited a northern village, my lord?"

Solomon fought a moment of indignation. *Who is he to insinuate—*

"The king grieved for King David at Gibeon," Ahishar interjected, "which, of course, is the north's most holy high place."

But as Ahishar wore his smug expression, Solomon heard Jehoshaphat's message as if he'd sounded a shofar in his ear. "I haven't spent time among the northern tribes since I was a young boy and visited my abba's vineyards in Baal Hamon." Shame burned his cheeks. He'd grown accustomed to palace

140

life and forgotten that most of those in his kingdom had never seen a mosaic floor. "What is it you propose, Jehoshaphat?" Solomon heard nothing but his own heartbeat while he waited for Jehoshaphat's reaction.

When mischief played on the judge's lips, relief swept through Solomon. "I invite you to Shunem, King Solomon, to meet your treaty bride. During your journey north, talk with travelers along the way, reacquaint yourself with your northern brothers."

Solomon's heart jumped into his throat at the thought of leaving the safety of his guarded coach and mingling with those who might challenge his edicts. "But I—"

"You cannot possibly expect the king of Israel to meander about the hostile northern tribes!" Ahishar seemed indignant, and turning to Benaiah, he pleaded, "Tell him, Commander. Guarding the king's processional through the wilderness would be a nightmare. It's out of the question." Ahishar crossed his arms, lifted his chin, and leaned back as if the matter was settled.

King Solomon raised both eyebrows, a little surprised—and relieved—that his high steward had conveyed his concerns so vehemently. He too waited quietly for the new governor to address his steward's concerns.

With amazing calm, Jehoshaphat seemed eager to do so. "After you have arrived in Shunem, King Solomon, you will be introduced to my charming daughter. We will then sign a marriage agreement, and I will become your goodwill ambassador, traveling throughout the northern tribes, listening to their concerns, and explaining your national reforms." He leaned forward, his gaze seeming to reach into Solomon's soul. "We will both risk our lives to assure the people of Israel that the son of David is for them, not against them. And by Jehovah's wisdom and strength, Israel will live at peace." Pausing only a moment, he offered his hand in pledge. "You, my king, will win your nation's heart and discover my daughter's love."

Win my nation's heart. Solomon pondered such an ambitious dream. Could he dare hope that Israel might love him as they had once loved Abba David? Solomon grasped Jehoshaphat's hand. "I'll see you in Shunem, my friend."

"Ha-ha!" Benaiah clapped his hands and stood so quickly the table nearly toppled. "Israel has an ambassador, and the king will have a new wife!"

"The king has many new wives," Ahishar grumbled.

Solomon chuckled and patted his high steward's shoulder. "Don't worry, Ahishar. If Benaiah is this excited about the journey, you can wager three gold coins he'll take extra precautions to make the trip go smoothly."

Ahishar answered by withdrawing his clay tablet and scribbling notes. "We'll need to invite the Daughters of Jerusalem for the journey to Shunem. I'm sure Jehoshaphat's daughter has no idea what's required of a queen."

"My Arielah was born a queen," Jehoshaphat said to the steward, and Solomon noted renewed sparks between the two men.

The steward's eyes left his tablet and met the governor's in challenge. "If the unity of Israel rests on the success of this marriage, I must be certain Shiphrah and Sherah are ready to train your daughter in the ways of royalty."

"I'm sure if Arielah is half as enchanting as her abba is wise," the king intervened, "I am marrying quite a prize."

Jehoshaphat's gaze lingered on the steward, and Solomon cleared his throat, gathering the attention of all in the room. "I must have Jehoshaphat's oath on one matter before I can agree to sign the treaty." Silence fell and tension built. Solomon almost regretted his mischievous goad.

"Jehoshaphat, tell me truly—are you sure your daughter has only one nose and ten toes?"

All four men dissolved into laughter. Even Ahishar's rigid frown cracked into a smile as the morning meal fueled a new day for Israel.

PART 2

15

*If a man has a stubborn and rebellious son who does
not obey . . . his father and mother shall take hold of
him and bring him to the elders at the gate. . . . Then
all the men of his town shall stone him to death. . . .
All Israel will hear of it and be afraid.*

Arielah crouched to clear another clump of mud from
the hoe, the dirt now mingling with blood on her
hands. Her brothers had ordered her to dig trenches around
the base of the grapevines. Everyone knew it was too early to
tend the vines, but no one dared interfere. It was family business. A situation for Abba and Ima to address with the elders.

Arielah's heart was torn between mercy and justice. Ima
insisted she would reveal Kemmuel's cruelty when Abba returned. Arielah still hoped for her brothers' repentant hearts,
but pain and fear were chipping away at her faith. Tears
burned her cheeks, the salty drops stinging deep, sun-kissed
blisters. She set aside the hoe and inspected the palms of
her hands, now cracked and bleeding from the toil during
Abba's absence. Before he left for the Passover journey, he
had instructed his sons, "Continue your work with the hired

hands. Prepare for the barley harvest, and tend the flocks while I'm away."

They had done none of that. Instead, they ordered the servants to oversee the harvest and the flocks and allowed Arielah only two days in the shepherds' hills. The other mornings, they prodded her to the vineyard and pillaged Abba's wine stores. They then headed to the south side of town to mingle their wine with female delicacies.

"When we come back, you'd better be working, little sister." Kemmuel's threat kept Arielah's back bent all day.

Arielah looked down at her swollen hands, opening and closing them. They stung as if she'd grasped a hornets' nest. But she knew the pain in her ima's heart surpassed it when the well gossipers buzzed about Jehosheba's sons.

Stretching her arms to the sky, she arched her back for a moment's relief and then glanced quickly right and left. Listened. No signs of her drunken brothers. The sky was cloudless. The growing intensity of the spring sun would soon ripen the fruit of the vine, but for now it just blistered her face and arms. She pushed back the dark tendrils of hair from her forehead and looked south. *Abba, please come soon. Their cruelty lessens when you're here to shield me.*

She felt a light breeze touch her face, and she smiled with blistered lips. *Ah, the wind has come to greet me.* After looking once more to ensure Kemmuel and Igal were nowhere near, she dropped her hoe. Letting her arms float out and then down, she swayed slowly at first, dancing to an imaginary beat. The air began to stir. The wind had come to dance. The hem of her tunic flowed side to side, and some of her pain subsided.

A shepherd's song Abba had taught her came to mind, a song of David the shepherd king. "Praise be to the Lord, for he has heard my cry for mercy." She extended her arms high above her head, then plunged them toward the ground. Again and again she repeated the motion, dancing to the silent music, singing to the whispering wind. "The Lord is my strength and my shield; my heart trusts in Him, and I am helped. My heart leaps for joy, and I will give thanks to Him in song." The wind cooled her sunburned cheeks and tickled the loose tendrils of hair against her face. She was a child again, dancing for her abba, like when they used to sing the words together.

The muscles in her legs and arms cried out, but she didn't care. She took a quick sip from her water skin and grabbed the shepherd's flute lying beneath it. Inhaling deeply, she blew a gentle breath—life and joy emanated from the little wooden instrument. Her fingers moved slowly over the small holes, then quicker with more breath, more sound, more joy. Suddenly the trilling of the flute floated on the wind as she danced and swayed between the vines. Nothing else mattered. She played for Jehovah, and her heart lifted toward heaven. Time slipped away . . . until her worship was shattered by some inconsequential noise—a bleating sheep, a hired hand's cough. And the world intruded again.

She looked down at her flute. Blood stained it.

She reached for her water skin to rinse off the blood but was distracted by a commotion in the city. Abba's vineyard was positioned on the southwestern slope of Mount Moreh, just north of Shunem. She heard the watchmen on the city's walls shout, but she couldn't make out the words. Looking toward the southern horizon, she saw three camels descending from the crest of Gilboa, leading a caravan that displayed the king's standard. She rushed to the vineyard gate and peeked out to be sure her brothers were nowhere in sight. Leaving her hoe behind, she ran to the city as fast as her sore legs would carry her, just in time to hear . . .

"A caravan approaches," the watchman on Shunem's southern parapet cried. "It flies the king's flag, and—wait, yes, it's Jehoshaphat!"

Arielah's heart thrilled. She ran inside the city gate and

found her ima in their courtyard, making final preparations for the evening meal. "He's home, Ima! He's finally home!" she squealed as she had when she was younger.

"Yes, my lamb," Jehosheba said, eyes glistening with tears. "Perhaps now your brothers' cruelty will end."

Arielah gave her a quick peck on the cheek and ran past her to one of the water jars. "Ima, we must cover my blisters so that Abba doesn't see them right away. I don't want to ruin his homecoming." She splashed her face, allowing it to soothe the raw blisters from the sun's harsh rays.

Ima handed her a clean cloth. "Arielah."

Dabbing her face gently, Arielah chattered on. "He's accompanied by the king's men, Ima. That must mean he has good news."

Jehosheba stilled her hands, and when Arielah looked up, she saw tears on her ima's cheeks. "You cannot hide those blisters, my lamb. Your abba must know the extent of his sons' cruelty and disobedience."

Heart pounding, Arielah drew Ima into a fierce embrace. "Abba knows the hardness of his sons' hearts. The only way my brothers can truly harm me is if I allow bitterness to take root in me. Blisters will heal. Hatred will not." Releasing Jehosheba, she kissed Ima's cheek and used her damp cloth to wipe her tears. "Come now, let's at least cover my hands."

Working silently, they tore the cloth into long strips, wrapping each of Arielah's hands to cover some of her pain. "What courage fills your heart, my little lion of God," Ima said finally, gently tying the final knot in place.

"Our judge returns," another watchman cried to the gathering of city officials. "He comes with a small contingent, the king's own Mighty Men providing rear guard!"

Arielah and Ima Jehosheba exchanged an excited giggle and joined other Shulammites rushing out the city gates to await their beloved Jehoshaphat. The waiting crowd stirred with excitement as the procession marched across the valley floor. A young boy returned from the shepherds' fields, leading the shepherds he'd alerted to their judge's return.

Arielah searched every herder's face, but her brothers weren't among them. Were they sprawled under an olive tree, drunk in a far pasture? Her heart broke anew at the pain Abba would feel at their betrayal. Every Shulammite seemed anxious to hear Jehoshaphat's news—everyone except his own sons.

Just as she'd given up hope, she noticed two lone figures stumbling down from the tallest gray ridge of Mount Moreh. Her brothers' stuttered steps and weaving way confirmed her suspicions. Looking at her bandaged hands, she realized the shame her brothers cast on Abba was much crueler than blisters.

"I can't wait for you to meet my family," Jehoshaphat shouted at Benaiah over his camel's spitting protest. "And Reu can attest to the hospitality of Shunem. He was well fed and well cared for while staying with us for the grieving period after King David's passing."

The brief prompt sent Reu into a prolonged reminiscence of his days in Shunem and gave Jehoshaphat a few moments to contemplate his imminent homecoming. When he'd left Shunem before Passover, he was alone, carrying a single lamb for sacrifice. Now he returned as the governor of Solomon's tenth district, riding between his new royal assistant and Israel's army commander. *I hope the Shulammites hospitality extends to the king's new administration.*

King Solomon had insisted on sending Benaiah and his Mighty Men as escorts in order to keep his new governor safe from bandits as he traveled through the wilderness. But the king's wisdom reached further than wilderness bandits. Surely he wondered—as did Jehoshaphat—how the Shulammites would feel about Jehoshaphat's profitable bride price and his significant position of power in the new administration. Undoubtedly, some would accuse Jehoshaphat of betraying the northern tribes for personal gain, and the king's Mighty Men might be Jehoshaphat's only salvation.

"No wonder you were in such a hurry to come home," Benaiah said, interrupting the governor's thoughts. "And look at those fruit trees! I've never seen so many in one place!" He pointed to the hillside of groves where orange, lemon, pomegranate, fig, and olive trees boasted their springtime blooms and aromas. Jehoshaphat's chest swelled as he drank in the scent and felt the pride of home.

After descending Mt. Gilboa, the three men led their caravan across the Jezreel plain, clearing a path through riotous bursts of wildflowers.

"It looks like we've drawn a crowd!" Reu shouted, nodding toward the Shulammites gathered outside the southern gate. As their camels plodded infuriatingly slow, Jehoshaphat scanned the familiar faces of home, searching to quench the sudden thirst for his family.

"Welcome, Jehoshaphat!" one old woman cried, reaching up for his hand as his camel passed by.

"Greetings, Ruth," he replied. "Where is Jehosheba?" But the press of the crowd moved them toward the city gate before he could hear her response.

"Welcome to the king's captain," another man said, sidling up to Benaiah's mount. "I saw you when I attended King David's burial procession with Jehoshaphat. What brings you to our simple town?"

Benaiah exchanged a quick glance with Shunem's judge, his tone polite but not overly friendly. "I come at the bidding of the king."

Jehoshaphat's respect for Solomon's commander had grown during their three-day journey from Jerusalem. The instant rapport he'd sensed in the king's chamber had deepened to solid friendship.

The procession entered the city, the crowd swelling around each beast and rider. "What news? What news?" a few others chanted, reaching up to touch Jehoshaphat's extended hands.

He glanced back at Reu and watched with pride as the Shulammites welcomed the young courier like a lost son. "I had hoped you'd come back to sample more of my honeyed dates," the old widow Sarah said. Reu had listened for hours as she told of her husband's service in David's army.

The caravan stopped just outside the city gate. Jehoshaphat, Benaiah, and Reu clucked their tongues, and the camels knelt. Sliding from their mounts, the three men descended into the waiting throng.

Amid the confusion, Benaiah grasped Jehoshaphat's arm and guided him through the crowd. "I will accompany you, my lord." The commander nodded at the excited townspeople, bending low to speak. "I've seen this kind of emotion turn quickly from rejoicing to riot."

"Thank you, my friend," Jehoshaphat shouted above the noise. "Let's make our way to the well at the city's center." Carried along by the sea of bodies, Jehoshaphat almost forgot about his faithful young companion. "Wait! Reu!"

Jehoshaphat looked back to see the young man already instructing the caravan servants to refresh the tired animals. *A more competent aide I could never have hoped for.* Reu simply waved his hand when he saw the judge look his direction.

The droning of the crowd had become a nondescript roar, every voice asking the same question, each step toward the familiar well a fulfillment of the promise he'd secured in Jerusalem.

The crowd quieted as he stepped up on the well curb. Panning the sea of faces, he saw his sons, and he could barely breathe.

Kemmuel and Igal had tried to melt into the mob. But one look at their swaying stances, the way they tried to lean on those around them, and Jehoshaphat knew they had been drinking again. *Will I lose my daughter to duty and my sons to rebellion, Lord?* His heart broke at the thought. He had prepared himself for the prospect of Shunem's suspicion of his new title. He'd prepared himself for Arielah's fate as Israel's treaty bride. But he'd believed—he'd hoped—Kemmuel and Igal would change someday. Finally, he spotted his wife and daughter at the back of the crowd, standing almost as far as his family's courtyard gate.

"Arielah, come to me," he shouted with a smile. He hadn't planned to announce the treaty bride agreement publicly before talking with Arielah, but something in his spirit told him he must speak to her in this setting.

She hesitated.

Odd, he thought. *She seems almost frightened to come to me.* A sudden foreboding settled over him as he watched Jehosheba gently nudge her forward.

Arielah looked back at her ima and then turned to meet Jehoshaphat's gaze. Once begun, her course never wavered. She was obedient. The crowd parted as she approached.

"Look at her face, how blistered and red," Edna the matchmaker whispered.

"What is wrong with her hands, Ima? Why are they wrapped?" a little girl asked as Arielah passed by. The girl's ima clapped a hand over her mouth, but the little voice asked the righteous question that rumbled through the crowd.

At the sight of her, Jehoshaphat felt himself sway. *Oh, Lord Jehovah, no!*

The crowd's angry eyes cast daggers at Kemmuel and Igal. Kemmuel stared back in defiance. Igal looked away, too ashamed or afraid to face the truth.

Benaiah was stoic, his confusion evident. He reached out to steady Jehoshaphat. "What's happening, my friend?"

Jehoshaphat couldn't stem the tears rushing down his cheeks, and a low moan escaped.

Arielah knelt at his feet and bowed her head. "How may I serve you, Abba?"

He stepped down from the well curb and gently grasped her hands. She winced. He helped her stand and began unwrapping the bandages. Deep wounds on her palms and fingers testified against his sons. He lifted her chin with his finger to inspect the blisters on her face. The two stood for a moment in silence, Jehoshaphat lost in his daughter's beautiful eyes.

It was the first time Kemmuel and Igal had been so bold in their cruelty. They had mocked his discipline, disobeyed repeatedly. They had cursed both him and Jehosheba with word and deed, and all the mercy offered to them had been cast aside like filthy rags. The law was clear on the matter.

"God's will be done," Jehoshaphat whispered. He released Arielah's hands and turned toward Benaiah.

"Abba?" his daughter cried.

He could hear the confusion, the hurt, in Arielah's voice. The vision of her unveiled hands dangling at her sides would forever be etched on his memory. *I cannot do what I must if I stop to explain it to you, my lamb.* Jehoshaphat ignored the plea he knew she would make.

He stepped away from the well and approached Benaiah, who snapped to attention as though he were readying for battle. Motioning the big man to lean close, he whispered, "The men who inflicted these wounds on my daughter must be dealt with. I need you to ensure they do not leave the city."

Benaiah's features became hard as stone. He was a frightening fellow, head and shoulders taller than any man in Shunem. With his jaw set, he stepped away from the well and parted the crowd on his way to gather his guards. They stood waiting at the city gate.

The crowd had become so deathly quiet that a feather falling on dust would have resounded like a clatter. Jehoshaphat returned to Arielah and kissed her cheek. "It's all right, my lamb. Jehovah will make all things right."

Then, resuming his perch on the rim of the well, he said, "I recite for you, my brother Shulammites, the law of Moses: 'If

153

a man has a stubborn and rebellious son who does not obey his parents and will not listen to them when they discipline him, his abba and ima shall take hold of him and bring him to the elders at the gate of his town.'"

Nervous chatter rippled through the crowd like a boiling pot ready to overflow. Arielah looked wildly back at her ima, who was still standing at their courtyard gate.

Jehoshaphat's heart pounded and his stomach balled into knots, but he must finish this. He swallowed the rising emotion and continued, undaunted. "'They shall say to the elders, "This son of ours is stubborn and rebellious. He will not obey us. He is a prodigal and a drunkard." Then all the men of his town shall stone him to death. You must purge the evil from among you. All Israel will hear of it and be afraid.'"

Jehoshaphat gazed into the familiar faces of his friends and neighbors, those who would carry out judgment on his sons. Panic began a steady journey up from his stomach, and then it seized his throat. *Breathe! I must breathe!* he coached himself, bowing his head. *Lord Jehovah, give me strength to obey You and lead Your people in righteousness.* A few deep, heaving breaths escaped before he could regain a measure of control. When he finally felt the strength to lift his head, he searched the crowd of faces, gazed on his sons, and tore his robe.

"Kemmuel and Igal, you will be judged at the city gate."

16

Anyone who curses his father or mother must be put to death.

Jehoshaphat watched all color drain from his sons' faces. Kemmuel and Igal were standing at the back of the crowd near the southern city gate, surrounded by a clump of old men just under a market canopy. Shunem's judge stepped toward his wayward sons.

Kemmuel's eyes went wild. "Run, Igal!" He bolted toward the gate, but before he could take a second step, Benaiah's meaty hand seized the collar of his robe. Kemmuel swung a fist in the general direction of his captor and found it captured in the vice grip of Benaiah's mammoth paw.

Igal measured the commander from the top of his lofty head to the tip of his boat-sized sandals and crumpled into a whimpering heap.

Jehoshaphat arrived at the scene—as did Jehosheba and Arielah—just in time to see Benaiah's jaw flexing and his scar pulsating from lip to eyebrow. A pang of terror seized Jehoshaphat at the ferocity of his warrior friend.

Hoisting Igal to his feet like a ragdoll, Benaiah ground

out, "You will stand at the city gate like a man while your parents accuse you as the law requires." Two other Mighty Men righted Kemmuel to face him. "How dare you shame your abba like this."

A few in the crowd jeered and shouted, crying for justice—long overdue—against the sons of Jehoshaphat.

Jehosheba's head fell forward. She stood silently at her husband's side. Jehoshaphat took her hand and gently reached for the bandages that still dangled from Arielah's wrists. "My beloved wife, our sons have defied our discipline. We must now be Jehovah's obedient children and accuse them before the elders at the gate."

Jehosheba met her husband's gaze and nodded. This strong and silent woman loved her sons deeply, but Jehoshaphat knew by her eyes that she agreed with his judgment—God's judgment. Kemmuel and Igal had chosen their own destruction.

Jehoshaphat squared his shoulders and faced the king's commander. The eyes that moments ago blazed with battle fury were now the kind portals to the heart of his friend. Shunem's judge had no words for the big man, and Benaiah's affirming nod assured him none were needed.

"Where is the city's stoning platform, Jehoshaphat?" Benaiah asked.

Jehoshaphat's mind was a blank papyrus, and an eerie hush settled over the crowd as the reality of the impending judgment struck like a blow. He looked at the other six elders gathered around them. Two had never thrown a stone in judgment. Almost an entire generation had passed since Shunem had seen a stoning, and most of those crying for justice would likely falter if they had to hurl the final death stones.

"We . . . we don't have a platform. We use a natural ledge above the foothills of Mount Moreh. It is twice a man's height, as is required."

"Jehoshaphat," said Phaltiel, the leading elder in

Jehoshaphat's absence, "what grievance do you bring to the elders of Shunem?"

Lord Jehovah! Jehoshaphat squeezed his eyes shut. *He's beginning the proceedings.* With a frantic prayer for peace, he motioned for Arielah to take her place next to her ima so that all three stood opposite his sons. The two members of their household who would not heed discipline—or receive mercy—would look into the pained faces of those who would rather love them than judge them.

Jehoshaphat cleared his throat. "Elder Phaltiel, my sons, Kemmuel and Igal, are disobedient, stubborn, and rebellious. They have become prodigals and drunkards."

Phaltiel nodded gravely. "Jehosheba, what have you to say?"

Jehoshaphat felt her whole body trembling, their shoulders touching, their spirits bound in agony.

He closed his eyes, and tears dripped down his beard. Then suddenly, from deep within his soul, the emotions erupted in a piercing cry. "I love my sons! Ahhh!" Jehoshaphat fell to his knees before the elders.

The ever-silent Jehosheba released a mournful wail and collapsed into Arielah's arms. No other sound echoed among the Shulammites. Even the Mighty Men, hardened by years of battle, blinked back tears as the prince of Shunem's sobs ran their painful course.

Finally, when Jehoshaphat could stand, he gathered Jehosheba in his arms, and the two stood facing Elder Phaltiel. "Tell them, my wife. Tell them the words our son spoke to me the night of King David's death. The night our most recent attempt at discipline failed."

Lifting questioning eyes to her husband, she seemed hesitant to repeat such disrespect before the crowd. When Jehoshaphat affirmed his intentions with a nod, she spoke with a quivering voice. "Our son Kemmuel . . . Abba . . . weak . . . old man."

"Oh, say it so everyone can hear," Kemmuel shouted. "My

abba is a weak and foolish old man! He babbles on about love and mercy, but underneath it all, he's just a coward with fine words."

The back of Benaiah's hand nearly took off Kemmuel's head, and he fell to the ground motionless. The crowd gasped, and then an approving hum rippled over satisfied faces.

When Kemmuel finally stirred, he held out his hand for Igal's help. For the first time, Jehoshaphat watched the younger brother rebuff his older sibling.

"Kemmuel and Igal," Jehoshaphat said in a voice firm yet without malice, "though I love you, I must obey Jehovah, and by condemning you to death, all of Israel will hear and be afraid."

Kemmuel rose by his own power, though still blurry-eyed.

"I had hoped you could serve Israel with your lives," Jehoshaphat continued. "Instead, you will serve Israel by your deaths."

"Noooo!" Kemmuel screamed. "No! You will not make this a righteous cause, you broken-down banner bearer. And you . . ." Like a hawk pouncing on its prey, Kemmuel lunged at his sister. "This is all your doing!"

Benaiah's grasp tightened in time to restrain Kemmuel physically, but he continued to spew venom at Arielah. "You have brought this evil on Igal and me! If you hadn't stolen Abba's love, we would never—"

"Stop!" A male voice shattered the tirade—not Jehoshaphat or an elder. Not even Benaiah or one of the other soldiers. "Enough, Kemmuel! We've blamed our sister long enough." It was Igal. His words held a passion completely foreign to this shadow of a man. "She is not to blame for the blisters on her face or the wounds on her hands. She is not to blame for the scars under her headpiece and robe that others cannot even see."

Jehoshaphat's quiet young son had found his voice, and the crowd gasped. Benaiah's eyes narrowed to suspicious slits, and Jehoshaphat too wondered about his son's sincerity.

Only Kemmuel believed his brother—and his evil laughter made even their abba cringe. "You think you can escape judgment by turning on me, Igal? You have joined me in every deed. You'll find no mercy from the great judge of Shunem after harming his precious Arielah."

Igal was silent, his head bowed low. Finally, he looked up at Arielah, and for the first time, Jehoshaphat realized he truly *saw* her.

"I'm sorry for the pain I've caused you," he said. "You have always been kind to me, and I have repaid your kindness with cruelty. I don't deserve it, but I ask your forgiveness." He tried to kneel before her, but the soldiers on either side held him firmly in place.

Jehoshaphat watched in awe as Arielah stepped toward him. Benaiah held his hand up to stop her, but Arielah took the commander's large hand in hers, wincing when his calluses scraped her wounds. Their eyes locked, and something passed between them. Benaiah relented, and Arielah approached her penitent brother.

Igal knelt. Laying her hand on his head, Arielah spoke—not to the condemned, but to Jehoshaphat. "Abba," she began, "I believe your son Igal has truly repented of his sin. Look at the changes in his heart. Have you ever heard him speak against his brother or publicly declare his own opinion?" She removed her hand from Igal's head, leaving a small bloodstain there. Turning to face her parents, she continued, "Israel must hear of the evil purged from its borders, but perhaps mercy could also ring loud in its ears."

Already a queen, Jehoshaphat thought of his beautiful daughter. But before he could give his reply, Kemmuel's voice intruded.

"That's right, you witch! Have you come from Endor in a new form to beguile the whole town with your fine arguments?" Again his laugh was low, dark, otherworldly.

Before Kemmuel could bring further shame, Jehoshaphat

shouted over his ravings. "Elders of Shunem, because Jehovah shows mercy to a truly repentant heart, I forgive all right to reprisal against my son Igal. Instead, I bring only one rebellious son, Kemmuel, a prodigal and drunkard, who has refused all attempts at instruction and discipline." With unyielding determination, he concluded. "The law requires punishment to be carried out on the same day the verdict is rendered. The sun is past midday. My complaint is before you."

Igal's face contorted in an inexplicable mix of emotions as Arielah helped him to his feet and the two embraced. Jehoshaphat enfolded them both, enjoying the warmth of his middle child for the first time since Igal was a small boy.

Kemmuel roared, and this time Benaiah required the aid of two guards to control his outburst.

Jehoshaphat gathered Jehosheba, Arielah, and Igal under his protective wings while the elders deliberated.

As lead elder, Phaltiel announced the verdict. It hadn't taken long to reach. "We, the judges of Shunem, declare a unanimous decision. Kemmuel, son of Jehoshaphat, you are condemned to death by stoning, according to the law of Moses." No cheer of triumph. "Every man in the city is required to join the processional to the place of judgment."

Softening his voice to a whisper, Phaltiel turned to Jehoshaphat and his wife. "Jehosheba will be the only woman allowed in the procession. As the two witnesses against your son, one of you will cast Kemmuel from the stoning ledge of Mount Moreh, and the other will wait on the foothill below to hurl the death stone at his chest." Pausing at Jehosheba's shudder, Phaltiel lifted his voice again to the crowd. "If anyone can declare a reason for reprieve, he should declare it now or on the way to judgment."

Jehosheba began to tremble violently, and Jehoshaphat gathered her into his arms and kissed her forehead. "It will be over soon, my love," he whispered. Then he released her but kept an arm around her waist to catch her if she fell.

Noticing movement over one elder's shoulders, Jehoshaphat heard himself gasp. It was Reu. Fresh tears came as he sensed Jehovah's answer to a prayer he hadn't prayed. "Elder Phaltiel," he said, still uncertain of such a request, "the law requires that parents accuse a rebellious son before the elders, which we have done." Reu had pressed his way through the crowd and was standing just behind Arielah. The young man's tender compassion emboldened Jehoshaphat's heart to ask the unthinkable. "I humbly request that my wife be released from the task of second witness and another witness take her place."

Crowd whispers buzzed like a swarm of bees.

Jehosheba reached for her husband's hand and squeezed it. "Jehoshaphat?" A hopeful sob escaped.

Only her cry wrested his attention from Reu's startled gaze. "Yes, my love. Reu heard Kemmuel's curses and rebellion. It is my plea that the blood of your son will not stain your hands." When Jehoshaphat looked up, Reu's eyes were wide and his face the color of goat's milk.

Elder Phaltiel had observed in silence, but now he cleared his throat to draw the crowd's attention. Communicating to his peers with affirming glances and nods, Shunem's interim elder announced their hurried decision. "The royal courier, Reu, may serve as second witness if he confirms Kemmuel's guilt and willingly assumes the responsibility."

The elders stood aside as Jehoshaphat approached his young friend. "Do you affirm that Kemmuel has grievously and publicly defied my discipline and become a prodigal and a drunkard?"

Reu's eyes, focused on Jehoshaphat's face, swam in unshed tears. "I do affirm it," he said, looking neither to the right nor the left.

Holding out his hand, Jehoshaphat issued his final request, regret filling him. "Will you serve as second witness against my son Kemmuel?"

The jolly messenger boy from Jerusalem stood unable—or

unwilling—to move. Jehoshaphat's hand hung in midair as he waited for Reu's response. Moment lapsed into excruciating moment.

Finally, as if lifting the death stone already, Reu clasped Jehoshaphat's hand. "May Jehovah give me courage. I will."

Jehosheba's wail punctuated the moment, and Jehoshaphat nodded silent thanks to his young friend.

Thanks?

No. Thanks didn't describe the emotions roiling inside him. But perhaps relief would come to him with time, knowing he and Jehosheba had been obedient to their heavenly Abba.

Jehoshaphat watched Arielah gather her ima into consoling arms and noted Igal's hands shift awkwardly from his hips to his side. "Come, my son," Jehoshaphat said, embracing the young man and kissing both cheeks. "We will face this hardship together and then start anew."

Kemmuel let out another roar, but Benaiah's threatening glance quelled further attempts at violence.

As the law dictated, Jehoshaphat stepped forward to lead the procession as the first witness. Reu, as second, walked at his right side. Igal stepped in line with the elders, and Benaiah guided Kemmuel with a small detachment of his men for safety's sake. Kemmuel's hands were bound, his head held high in defiance but some of his bluster spent.

One of the elders removed Shunem's banner from the gatepost and held it aloft while another rehearsed word for word the commands Kemmuel had broken. The retinue of royal guards in Jehoshaphat's caravan who had watched the horrific proceedings now stood aside as the death march passed by. Words of support and hands of friendship eased Jehoshaphat's shame as he looked into the eyes of these strangers from the palace, people suddenly thrust into the most private pain of his life. They were strangers no longer. They were now friends, bound to him with the emotion he saw glistening on their cheeks.

Every Shulammite male twenty years and over joined the processional. The women followed from the southern gate to the western side of the city wall, where the men began the winding path up to Mount Moreh's stoning ledge. Jehoshaphat's ears ached to hear even one person speak in defense of his wayward son. The late afternoon air was as silent as the stones beneath their feet.

Jehoshaphat had climbed Mount Moreh many times, but it never seemed this far before. The procession stopped just below the natural gray precipice, and Phaltiel began his pronouncement. "Upon hearing no arguments in your favor, Kemmuel son of Jehoshaphat, you will face the punishment of death. You may now offer confession of your sins if you so wish."

Kemmuel's eyes registered nothing but disdain. He spit on the ground at his abba's feet. "I confess nothing."

Jehoshaphat's countenance remained unchanged.

Phaltiel recounted the procedure for those gathered. "You will be offered a mixture of wine and olibanum to ease your pain." Signaling one of the other elders to administer the potion, Phaltiel seemed pleased when Kemmuel refused it. "You will be disrobed and covered only on the front portion of your body. Then one of the witnesses will cast you from the ledge."

Jehoshaphat's eyes squeezed tightly at the words.

Phaltiel continued. "If the fall does not produce death, the second witness will hurl a heavy stone at your chest. In the instance that this too proves insufficient to end your misery, the Shulammites will throw stones until death. Do you understand?"

"I understand perfectly." Kemmuel's words were low, measured, but finally his head was bowed low.

Phaltiel turned to the two witnesses. "Who climbs the hill to cast Kemmuel from the ledge—Jehoshaphat or Reu?"

Every drop of blood drained from Reu's face as Jehoshaphat stepped forward. "I will climb the hill with my son. My hand will judge his sins."

17

[Beloved] Let him kiss me with the kisses of his mouth.

A mighty storm swept through Shunem. Black clouds, streaks of lightning, and peals of thunder revealed Jehovah's fury. Jehoshaphat was caught unaware while tending his flocks and quickly took shelter in a small cave on Mount Moreh. Watching the sky intently as the storm passed by, he heard a voice on the wind. *She is mine.* Lightning flashed in the sky and struck a nearby tree, splitting it in two. His head pounded with the rumbling of thunder. He covered his ears and looked up to the heavens. There it was. *Her life for Israel*, written in lightning across the sky.

Jehoshaphat bolted upright in his bed, sweat dripping into his eyes.

Jehosheba sat at his side, immediately soothing, caressing, calming. "The dream again?" she asked.

Jehoshaphat nodded, too breathless to speak. It had become more frequent since Kemmuel's death. He'd first experienced the dream on the day before Arielah's birth, and he'd hoped it was coincidence. But when it occurred every night for the first moon's cycle of her life, he realized Jehovah was speaking.

"You've told me the lightning doesn't say she will die," Jehosheba whispered in the predawn silence. "It simply says, *Her life for Israel.*"

Jehoshaphat lay back and drew his wife into his arms. "True."

"Today our daughter will meet the man she's loved all her life, Jehoshaphat. Igal is becoming an obedient and loving son. And our neighbors have accepted your new role as prince of Israel's tenth district." Lifting her head off his shoulder, she met his gaze through the morning shadows. "Jehovah has blessed us, my love. The dream is a promise from a loving God, not a threat from a vengeful deity." Her beautiful voice was a melody to his ears. She was a deep well of wisdom.

Tears flowed from the corners of his eyes and into both ears. "You know, I hate it when you make me cry in the morning." Jehoshaphat squeezed her tighter.

In the silence that followed, he recalled Phaltiel's reaction to Solomon's redistricting and Jehoshaphat's new responsibilities as prince of Shunem. "We are honored, Prince Jehoshaphat," the chief elder had said. "The king has seen in you what we have known for many years."

Jehoshaphat was humbled by his friend's confidence and trust. His fears that the Shulammites would think him a traitor to the tribes and resist his support of Solomon's reforms had been relieved in a most peculiar way. Many Shulammites confided that because he had championed God's law in the face of Kemmuel's rebellion, Jehoshaphat had been proven beyond reproach in their eyes. He had won their undying respect and deep sympathy. Those who might have questioned his motives before lost all doubts when Kemmuel was cast from that ledge on Mount Moreh.

Jehovah's ways are unfathomable, Jehoshaphat pondered

this morning. "Do you miss him?" he asked, finally breaking the silence. Two Sabbaths had passed since that awful day.

"I don't think we ever had him," Jehosheba said sadly, "but yes, I miss him. I miss hoping for him." Her tears moistened the bend of his elbow, where her head lay. "I hate it when you make me cry in the morning," she said, and they both tried to laugh a little. He felt her grip tighten around him. "Will Abishag's family be among the crowd that welcomes the king today?"

Jehoshaphat's heart squeezed a little. "I hope so. I've talked to her abba, and he assures me they're happy for Arielah, but . . ."

"But?"

"But he has warned me to be diligent and get every detail of the agreement in writing."

A long silence stretched between them.

"She loves him," Jehosheba said finally. "And we know Jehovah has chosen her for this purpose." Planting a kiss on his cheek, her eyes sparkled. "What other details do we need?"

He wrapped his arms around her and smothered her with kisses. She giggled like a maiden, and he gazed into the windows of her soul. "Are you ready to prepare our daughter to meet the king of Israel?"

The thunder of horses' hooves announced King Solomon's approach and shook the ground beneath Arielah's slippered feet. Lotioned and bejeweled, she felt a little silly in the blue linen robe and gemstone head covering the king's messenger had delivered at dawn.

She'd been awakened by an awful pounding on the door in the early glow of morning. "King Solomon sends a gift for the prince's daughter!" a royal servant had squawked louder than any rooster. Ima Jehosheba accepted the package kindly while Arielah peeked out from where her sleeping mat lay behind the cooking stones. Ima had rushed her into their bedchamber, removed Arielah's woolen tunic, and banished her worn sandals to a shelf in the corner.

"A whole day of primping is necessary for a newly betrothed bride," Ima had said.

"We're not *officially* betrothed," she reminded Ima, "until the king approves of me and signs the agreement." Ima waved away her words like a fly from rising dough and continued primping. When finally Ima Jehosheba placed the polished bronze mirror in Arielah's hands, the image was a stranger. Gone was the rugged shepherdess she'd seen reflected in the mountain streams. She saw herself, but better. Even her cheeks were almost healed of their blisters. She was a shepherdess dressed for a king.

Drawn back to the moment by the approaching chariots, Arielah watched the caravan race across Jezreel's lush green plain. A veiled carriage jostled on four golden orbs. "Abba! Look! It's as if four giant suns carry the coach across the valley!"

Jehoshaphat's easy laughter calmed her. "Yes, my lamb, that's Solomon's carriage." Leaning down, he spoke over the growing noise around them. "The king described it to me last week, but I must admit, my imagination fell short. He said it was acacia wood, and every detail—down to the last spoke—was covered by hammered gold."

"Oh, Abba! I've never seen anything so beautiful."

Jehoshaphat kissed the top of her head and tilted her chin. "I have." With a wink, he released her.

She giggled, looking right and left, and pecked a quick kiss on his cheek. The Shulammites graciously tolerated their affection, knowing abba and daughter shared a precious bond.

Jehoshaphat's family waited at the front of an entire village. Every man, woman, and child stood behind them—in physical presence and in heart—gathered outside the cactus hedges surrounding their city wall. North and east of the prickly and the pointed, however, grew lovely vineyards and groves of fruit trees. Shunem's landscape seemed as contradictory as her people's frayed emotions. Of course, they were honored that Arielah would become Israel's treaty bride, but Abishag's shame was not forgotten.

Glancing over her shoulder, Arielah glimpsed the expectant faces of Abishag's family. For the hundredth time, she wondered if a treaty wedding would heal their wounds or tear open half-healed scabs. Merchants' gossip had brought hope with Prince Adonijah's marriage proposal, but horror replaced it with word of his execution. Abishag was assumed to be in David's harem. *Assumed* to be. No one could attest to seeing her in the palace.

Focusing again on the procession, Arielah noticed the king's Mighty Men following Solomon's carriage. "Abba, is it normal for a betrothal procession to include such a large military presence?"

He patted her hand and gave a shrug. "What is normal for a king?" His attention returned to the procession, but Arielah thought she sensed unspoken concern in his reply.

The parade again stole her attention—this time the royal flocks and herds. Running and leaping behind the king's herdsmen, they left their aromatic contributions to the Jezreel Valley's rich soil. Arielah stole another glance at Abba. It was the responsibility—and privilege—of the host to provide meals for his guest. *So why did the king bring his own flocks?* Again, was this normal, or would Abba consider the king's flocks an insult to his hospitality?

"Look at that carriage!" Edna the matchmaker shouted, intruding on Arielah's thoughts.

Purple and blue veils flowed through golden rings around the outer framework. Arielah longed to run to the coach and fling open the door. *Solomon, you are mine!* A slight giggle escaped her lips. Abba smiled down at her, and she was glad he didn't know her thoughts.

Arielah had never experienced a man's kiss, but the tenderness she witnessed between her parents made her ache for it. She saw the way their eyes held each other, the way Abba took Ima's hand and gently closed their bedroom door each night. She allowed the giddiness of a young girl to consume her, tracing her lips with her finger. *Let him kiss me with the kisses of his mouth!* she thought with a playful grin.

This time she looked at Ima and discovered her looking back with a deeply furrowed brow. *Oh my.* Perhaps imas could read their daughters' minds.

Arielah ducked her head shyly as the royal stampede pounded closer. She reached for Abba's hand. Moments later, she felt the gentle touch of Ima's grasp wriggling into hers. Tightening her grip on both parents, Arielah felt her hands tremble—or were theirs shaking too?

Solomon was almost here.

The treaty bride agreement was really happening.

"Be at peace, my lamb," Abba whispered in her ear. "Your heart will win his devotion. Indeed, you were created for this moment in Israel's history." He squeezed her hand, and the trembling eased.

Finally the royal procession slowed, but a lone rider sped forward on his sleek stallion and skidded to a halt when he reached Arielah and her parents. He positioned his mount directly in front of the king's carriage, effectively blocking her view. After a quick dismount, he slapped the horse on its hindquarters, sending it in the general direction of a panicked stable boy. Clearing his throat, the herald crowed, "People of Shunem, the king of Israel, Solomon, son of David, has arrived!"

He paused. When no wild applause erupted, he issued a disgruntled huff. Another attendant placed a stool on the ground in front of the carriage, and the steward stepped up to open the door.

Finally! Arielah thrilled silently. Probing the cabin's interior, her eyes caught a momentary glimpse of pillows and fine linen just before she met the glaring disdain of one of the most beautiful women she'd ever seen. She heard herself gasp. She had expected Solomon's masculine features, but instead a second maiden emerged from the carriage! The two stepped out of the king's coach in a flurry of linen and pearls, their eyes hurling daggers at Arielah.

The Daughters of Jerusalem. Arielah should have expected them. Abba had warned about Ahishar's plan to "train" the Daughters of Jerusalem. Abba had understood the steward's sinister message. Not only would the twins accompany the king on this journey, but they'd also aid in Ahishar's quest to divide Israel.

Arielah returned the twins' stares and considered her enemy. They stood side by side as though one would topple over if the other moved. They wore identical purple robes with gold thread woven into delicate designs. Sheer linen scarves and belts accented their soft curves. The woman on the right looked at Arielah with a superior smirk, revealing a slightly crooked front tooth. The woman on the left boasted the only other distinguishable physical difference—a beauty mark just above her snide grin. Both wore gold necklaces, rings, and bangles, accenting vibrant eye paints and flowing veils. These maidens were stunning, and everything about them was calculated to intrigue a man.

Jehoshaphat leaned close so only Arielah could hear. "They are beautiful, my lamb, but do not fear them. We do not yet understand their game, but Jehovah will give us wisdom." Abba touched her cheek, and her heart warmed. She closed her eyes in silent gratitude. He knew her so well. In Abba's presence, her greatest fears were exposed and conquered, and his love enfolded her like a woolen blanket.

The Daughters of Jerusalem approached. The one on the right gasped. "This little goatherd cannot be the proposed bride!" Gliding like a willow in the breeze, she offered a condescending hand. "Greetings, little shepherdess."

Before Arielah could respond, the other twin sidled up to her sister. "My, how painful your face must have been to show such lasting scars."

Jehoshaphat stepped forward, tipping the sisters back on their heels.

"Forgive me," the first twin said, "we haven't been properly introduced." Issuing a scathing glance at the steward, she stepped back and bowed in unison with her sister.

Clearing his throat again, the steward obeyed the silent command. "I present the Daughters of Jerusalem. The fair maiden on the right is Shiphrah, and on the left is lovely Sherah."

Arielah felt utterly exposed and intolerably flawed. An antagonizing smile spread across Shiphrah's perfect face. "It is our duty to prepare you for the king's harem, little shepherdess." Lowering her voice to be heard by only Arielah and her family, she sneered. "I don't think we've ever had a more impossible task."

Fury creased Abba's brow. He leaned in and ground out the words, "You will speak to my daughter with respect. She will be your queen."

Fire lit in Shiphrah's eyes, and she stepped close to Jehoshaphat, whispering seductively, "So you say." Arielah heard garbled phrases, but the last words were clear. "Ahishar sends his regards, prince of goats." Shiphrah stepped back to rejoin her sister, bowing humbly as if offering Jehoshaphat total submission.

Rage bubbled up inside Arielah. How dare she speak to her abba that way! But the crowd's collective gasp drew her attention to the king's carriage. The Daughters of Jerusalem grudgingly turned from their verbal battle, relinquishing the attention they seemed to crave.

Arielah's heart pounded. She saw him. The face that dwelt in her dreams now appeared at the doorway of the resplendent carriage.

18

[Beloved] Your love is more delightful than wine. . . . No wonder the maidens love you! Take me away with you— let us hurry! Let the king bring me into his chambers.

[Friends] We rejoice and delight in you; we will praise your love more than wine. . . .

[Beloved] Dark am I, yet lovely, O daughters of Jerusalem. . . . My mother's sons were angry with me and made me take care of the vineyards.

Solomon waited in the carriage. He should have stepped out the moment he heard the herald's introduction, but fear bound him to the seat. Shiphrah and Sherah suggested he wait in the coach until they stepped out to prepare Jehoshaphat's daughter for the greeting. But they were just being kind. He hated to think that his fear might have been obvious.

He heard footsteps approaching the carriage door, and a swarm of bees stirred in his stomach.

Benaiah's face appeared in the doorway, and his warm,

confident eyes held no derision. "Come, my lord. Your friends are waiting to greet you."

Solomon nodded and let out a sigh. This journey into the heart of northern aggression had sounded so logical when Jehoshaphat had suggested it, but Ahishar had raised valid concerns after Shunem's judge left Jerusalem. His high steward had confided the hostilities King David's advisors had experienced while selecting Abishag as nursemaid. Solomon decided then to double his royal guard and remain in the carriage for the duration of his journey north—no mingling with northern travelers for the son of David.

Bending under the doorway, he faced the waiting Shulammites who stood three camel lengths away. Would they hold Abishag's fate against him? Stepping onto the footstool, he halted. Benaiah continued, but Solomon was in no hurry to follow.

Shiphrah and Sherah stood in front of the crowd, and Solomon silently thanked Ahishar for sending them as companions for the journey. On the second day of their jostling through the wilderness, Shiphrah had ventured an interesting question. "What if Jehoshaphat's daughter is as ugly as a frog?" she'd asked, wide-eyed. "You will have risked your life for nothing!"

Solomon smiled at the memory.

"King Solomon, I pre—" Benaiah began, but stopped when he realized Solomon remained at the carriage. Returning to the coach in six long strides, the commander appeared annoyed—and then his features softened. "Solomon," he whispered, "I would not escort you into an ambush. Jehoshaphat is our friend."

The king studied his top soldier. Had Benaiah become too friendly with Israel's district prince? Benaiah had seemed different since returning from Shunem. Though away from the palace only five days, his tolerance for Ahishar had plummeted. Whenever the high steward mentioned aggression from the northern districts, Benaiah accused him of agitation and bigotry. Perhaps Benaiah's defense was stirred by sympathy. He'd mentioned that during the single day he'd spent in Shunem, he'd witnessed Jehoshaphat's son stoned. Maybe both men having lost sons forged a deeper friendship than Solomon realized.

"Are you ready, my lord?" Benaiah's eyes held no censure, no lingering annoyance.

"Please order another guard to accompany us," Solomon whispered. "I wish to be flanked on both sides as I approach the single most hostile village in Israel." He hoped his commander perceived the mild censure. Solomon wasn't prepared to wager his life on a Sabbath-old friendship, even on Benaiah's good word. The commander bowed and signaled for a second guard to approach.

Walking between the double guard, Solomon stepped from the stool. Still glancing right and left, he remained alert for the slightest hint of attack and halted two paces before the crowd.

"King Solomon," Benaiah began again, "I present to you Prince Jehoshaphat, his son Igal, his daughter Arielah, and his wife Jehosheba." He motioned the northern family forward to meet their king.

As they drew near, Solomon for the first time allowed himself a moment of curiosity. *Ahh, the shepherdess.* Emboldened by the presence of his guards, he took a step closer but couldn't get a glimpse of the girl who stood behind her abba. "Shalom, Prince Jehoshaphat, governor of Israel's tenth district." A soft rumble fluttered through the crowd, and Solomon feared that he'd incited hostility with a simple greeting. He watched for the glint of a sword or an approaching rebel, but instead he heard a calm, kind voice.

"Shalom, my king." Jehoshaphat bowed and stood before him with a warm smile and a hand extended in friendship.

Focusing on the man he'd met just over two Sabbaths ago,

he saw genuine welcome in Jehoshaphat's eyes—no hostility or hidden motive, as Ahishar had warned. When Benaiah had returned with the terrible news of the stoning in Shunem, he'd offered no details—only that Jehoshaphat was a righteous abba who carried out judgment on a rebellious son. Glancing at the large young man behind Jehoshaphat, Solomon wondered if having a remaining heir was the reason for Jehoshaphat's enduring gentle spirit. Fine lines around the governor's eyes and mouth showed signs of sadness, but the subsequent changes in Benaiah's character seemed more pronounced than those of the man who had lost his son. The commander had returned to Jerusalem with no patience for Ahishar, causing a palace civil war between the king's top two advisors.

Stepping forward to grasp Jehoshaphat's offered hand, Solomon finally warmed to the idea of this northern visit, a short reprieve from palace chaos.

And just beyond her abba's shoulder . . . was Arielah.

"You've chosen . . . beautiful day . . . meet . . . beautiful betrothed." Jehoshaphat was speaking—quite loudly, actually, presumably for the benefit of the gathering. But Solomon heard little of it, so consumed was he with the young woman standing beside her abba.

This girl was quite different from Abishag. Abba David's Shulammite possessed a beauty rivaled only by the Daughters of Jerusalem. But this girl . . . *What has happened to her face?* He tried not to stare at the patches of skin peeling from her nose and cheeks. Yet underneath the damaged skin, there was a natural beauty that shone. This little shepherdess possessed an earthy stateliness.

Jehoshaphat was finishing a sentence. ". . . So honored to have you—"

"May I?" Solomon motioned toward Arielah.

Jehoshaphat's expression registered surprise, and Solomon cursed himself silently. He must be more polite.

Graciously, Jehoshaphat smiled and stepped away from his daughter. The girl's brow furrowed, and a spark lit her eyes. Solomon offered his most charming smile, and the spark kindled to a beautiful glow. *Those eyes! Beautiful dove's eyes.*

Clasping his hands behind his back, Solomon began a slow stroll around Arielah. From the top of her head to the tips of her slippers, he inspected his treaty bride. Adequate. *We'll give her my ima's chamber*, he thought. *That should provide sufficient honor to appease the northern tribes.* As a shepherdess, she would no doubt enjoy the private garden outside her door. He continued to consider other negotiations that might sweeten the agreement for his new friend Jehoshaphat.

He completed the circle and raised his eyes to assess her face once more. Instead of the quiet submission he expected, this girl boldly returned his gaze. In fact, she seemed to peer directly into his soul. It was unnerving. He suddenly felt as though he was the one being judged. When he tried to look away, her eyes held him. Something about her radiated a beauty unlike any he'd ever seen. *Say something—you're considering a wife, not a horse for your stable.* Solomon offered his hand and inclined his head, inviting her acceptance.

She smiled, took his hand, and chose that moment to speak her first words. "I believe loving you will be more delightful than wine." Her voice was soft yet clear, like a trickling stream. Her tone alluring, but not lewd or coarse. "Pleasing is the fragrance of your perfumes, and your name, Solomon"—she closed her eyes and spoke it slowly—"is like perfume poured out."

Her words enfolded him, creating warmth and security, eliciting peace in his innermost being.

Glancing over her shoulder at the Daughters of Jerusalem, she whispered playfully, "No wonder the maidens love you!"

Breathless at her boldness and delighted by her candor, Solomon gaped. And for just a moment, the king of Israel was speechless. Finally, absorbing the utter charm before him, he laughed with a freedom and joy that bubbled up from the depths of his soul.

And Arielah laughed with him.

He reached for her other hand and saw a lively sparkle in her eyes, matching his mischievous heart. She might not equal the beauty of Abishag or the splendor of the Daughters of Jerusalem, but this spirited Shulammite intrigued him. He was smitten. And for some reason, he thought of Ima Bathsheba. She would like this girl too.

"Say your name for me," he whispered.

"I am Arielah, lion of God."

"Indeed you are."

More words were unnecessary as the two locked eyes in a whimsical game of hide-and-seek. Totally captivated, they had entered a quiet place of their own amid the sea of dignitaries and townspeople. Never had Solomon met a woman so honest, so unpretentious, and so enchanting. Never had a woman spoken so little with her lips and so much with her eyes and heart. She was a refreshing change from the seriousness of the palace, and from just these few moments he knew his life had been forever changed.

Then, without warning, she looked away, casting a glance behind her at the crowd and the Daughters of Jerusalem waiting with them. When she met his eyes again, he noticed a change in her countenance. The mingling of sorrow in her smile squeezed his heart with emotions he didn't understand. Suddenly there were many things he didn't understand.

This afternoon's meeting was to be a political arrangement, not a matter of the heart. *Oh, but you . . .* He stared at her unabashedly. *You are so much more.* She was exquisite, breathtaking, and his heart was attracted to Arielah not because of the linen and jewels his messenger had delivered this morning. This girl possessed a loveliness rooted deep inside.

The mischief was returning to her eyes. "May I speak even more boldly, my lord?"

More boldly? Solomon's passions stirred, and he marveled at her audacity. "Of course, my Shulammite. You may speak as boldly as you like."

She touched his cheek, and the motion drew him close. "May I whisper?" she asked.

Solomon chuckled. This enchanting young creature was bold but bashful? "Of course, if you wish."

Arielah rose up on her toes and placed her delicate hands on his arms to steady herself. The warmth of her touch set his body aflame. "You are Solomon, king of Israel, son of David—correct?" She fell back on her heels with a grin and waited for his reply.

Hmmm. A game. "I am."

Then again on her toes with a whisper in his ear. "As king, you can marry when and whom you please—correct?" Back on her heels again to meet his gaze.

"I can." He smiled, hunger for her growing with each warm whisper.

She hesitated a moment before she rose again to breathe softly into his ear. "Then make me your bride today, my king. I have dreamed of becoming your wife since I was a child. Let the king unite God's people now, before the sun sets."

Solomon stood motionless, lost in her gaze, enthralled by her nearness, wrapped in the simplicity of her love. This was no game. He saw the sincerity of the request in her eyes. With every sensation that made him a man, he wanted to say yes. With every duty that made him a king, he must say no. He had given his word to Jehoshaphat, and this betrothal period was intended to provide time for Jehoshaphat to travel through the northern districts, unraveling the knotted tensions. After hostilities waned, Solomon would return to Shunem and lead the wedding processional back to Jerusalem, where he and

Arielah would be married. Surely Jehoshaphat had explained the conditions of the treaty to his daughter.

Gazing into Arielah's dove-like eyes, he wanted to forget he was king. *But wait. I am the king of Israel.* The realization stirred a new thought. *Why can't I marry her today?* His mind began to spin with possibilities. Perhaps he could be bold like his abba, take what he wanted when he wanted it.

Ima Bathsheba. He saw her face. *But God forgave Abba's impulsiveness, and David remained king even after he sinned.* Solomon wouldn't be breaking any laws by marrying Arielah now. Certainly he had promised to follow the betrothal traditions, but breaking his word was different than breaking the law of Moses.

"We've had such a long journey," Shiphrah said, her voice intruding on his thoughts, "and we need to prepare ourselves for tonight's banquet." Solomon stared into the vibrant brown eyes of his companions and was suddenly awakened from Arielah's dream world. Shiphrah and Sherah had wandered from the crowd and now stood beside him, brows furrowed, impatient red lips pouting.

Looking past Arielah's shoulder, Solomon focused on the Shulammites and realized how intently the whole town had been examining his every movement, expression, and word. He had almost given them a reason to revolt. He had almost let his emotions rule the nation. Returning his gaze to Arielah, he found her still awaiting his reply.

Her vulnerability left him speechless, but he couldn't do as she asked. So he did what seemed best.

He laughed.

"People of Shunem," he said grandly, reaching for Arielah's hand. "Jehoshaphat's daughter delights a king's heart." He led her toward the waiting crowd, choosing to face the Shulammites rather than deny her unmasked emotions. He'd taken the coward's way out by ignoring her request, but he couldn't simply marry a northern maiden without a betrothal period. Just because his foreign and Judean wives came to his harem that way didn't mean the conservative northern tribes would tolerate it. He and Jehoshaphat had reached an agreement, and tonight a wedding treaty would be signed. Solomon would keep his word and be remembered as a wise king—even if he wasn't a warrior like Abba David.

Arielah fought the tears that threatened to undo her. She saw a moment of decision flash in Solomon's eyes. And she saw the door of his heart slam shut at Shiphrah's precisely placed intrusion. Her wedding proposal had been an attempt to gain the upper hand on the Daughters of Jerusalem. If Solomon had agreed to marry her before leaving Shunem's soil, she might have been able to counter the women's conniving in the harem. Now she must pray Solomon would be wise enough to uncover whatever deception Ahishar had planned during their betrothal.

"Be patient, my little shepherdess." Solomon leaned close and whispered as a cheer arose from the Shulammites. "I will one day take you to the bridal chamber."

Arielah blushed, averting her eyes. He had interpreted her request as a lusty game of teasing. And why wouldn't he? The love Arielah longed to share was as foreign to Solomon as a beggar's mat. The only love he knew came from a crowded harem, where women whispered enticing phrases to win his favor. The reality of their differences staggered her.

Frozen by humiliation, she stood motionless and mute. Shiphrah must have glimpsed her awkwardness and stepped between the couple. "We rejoice and delight in you," she said, mimicking Arielah's initial greeting.

"And we will praise your love more than wine." Sherah joined the teasing, and both maidens dissolved into a fit of giggles.

"Truly, Arielah," Shiphrah said, stealing her hand away

from the king. "We must teach you more worthy phrases by which to woo a king."

Arielah's cheeks burned. They had treated the gemstones of her heart as if they were clumps of dirt on a farmer's plow.

"Shiphrah, Sherah, be quiet," Solomon whispered between clenched teeth, and Arielah's heart soared at the thought of his defense. But just as quickly her hopes sank when he nodded to the Shulammite crowd. "They'll hear you." His neck grew pink. "Prince Jehoshaphat, I apologize for the Daughters of Jerusalem. They have been commissioned to help acquaint all my wives with the ways of the court . . ." His voice trailed off, and tension grew as silence lingered.

The crowd, though they had not heard the interchange, must have sensed Jehoshaphat's anger. Restless whispers began to stir. Arielah watched fear shadow Solomon's expression, and she saw him glance at his commander.

"Of course, they are right to want what's best for you." Arielah had spoken the words before she realized it. Pushing past the flowing veils and perfumed bodies, she regained her place at Solomon's side. "They are right to adore you." Her words were meant to console, to reassure, but she saw him wince. A smudge of self-loathing rested beneath the gold crown on his furrowed brow. Everything within her screamed, *You are worthy of love, Solomon!* But it wasn't Solomon she should rebuke.

Turning to the Daughters of Jerusalem, she met their snide grins with a heated command. "Stop staring at me."

The words snapped the maidens to attention.

"My face may have been darkened by the sun," she continued, gaining fury with every breath, "but I possess a beauty you know nothing of. While you two soaked in your perfumes and lotions, my brothers' hatred sent me to work in the vineyards." Opening her hands, she presented her scabbed palms. "As you can see, my own vineyard has been neglected, but the fruit of my labor is a clear conscience and a loving heart. Without these wounds, I might be just as ugly as you."

Arielah heard the crowd gasp and felt Solomon's hands grab her wrists. The breeze seemed to hold its breath while the king inspected her hands. When he finally looked into her eyes, she no longer saw self-loathing. She saw rage.

19

[Beloved] Tell me, you whom I love, where you . . . rest your sheep at midday. Why should I be like a veiled woman beside the flocks of your friends?

[Friends] If you do not know, most beautiful of women . . . graze your young goats by the tents of the shepherds.

[Lover] I liken you, my darling, to a mare harnessed to one of the chariots of Pharaoh.

Trembling, Solomon looked into Arielah's pained expression. Assessing the nervous chatter among the Shulammites, he realized they were no longer the central fire of rebellion he feared. They would become spectators in his improvised courtroom. Someone would pay for Arielah's wounds.

Returning his attention to her dove-like eyes, he saw pain and then realized he was squeezing her wrists like a vice. "Oh!" He eased his grasp, cradled her hands. A hundred questions raced through his mind. Were the brothers of age to bear the punishment? Did Jehoshaphat know his sons mistreated her? Did they abuse Arielah in other ways?

"No one will ever harm you again," he whispered, tracing the peeling skin on her palms. With a gentle squeeze, he released her hands. Turning to his commander, Solomon kept his voice calm, though rage bubbled beneath the surface. "Benaiah!"

"Yes, my lord." The big man stepped forward, bowing before his king.

"Please take your place between Jehoshaphat and his wife." The commander seemed uncertain but obeyed. Solomon remembered Benaiah's loyal execution of General Joab at the altar and wondered if his loyalty extended beyond his friendship with Jehoshaphat. If Shunem's prince had contributed to Arielah's injuries—even by simply ignoring the abuse—Solomon would order his arrest.

Arielah cast a puzzled glance in his direction. Clearly unsettled, she lifted frightened eyes for reassurance.

"Please, Arielah," Solomon said, gently guiding her. "Step over here, on my right side." A protective fury had seized him unlike anything he'd ever known. Moving her tenderly, he separated Arielah a few more paces from her relatives. He knew from their recent bride negotiations that Jehoshaphat and his daughter were especially close. *Lord Jehovah, please let this man be innocent of all charges.*

The spontaneous courtroom now arranged, Solomon raised his voice for the crowd. "As king of Israel, I hear all manner of complaints. Today I will judge those responsible for Arielah's wounds, those who have harmed my treaty bride."

The crowd drew a collective breath, but Jehoshaphat's expression remained unchanged. A knot the size of Mount Hermon tightened in Solomon's gut. *Surely if he were innocent, he would say so now.* Hearing nothing, Solomon continued. "Arielah has accused her brothers of a crime, but ultimately the sins of a household rest on the abba." Fighting for control, he asked, "Jehoshaphat, prince of Shunem, did you know of the abuses committed against your daughter by those in your own household?"

An angry buzz spread through the crowd, heckles and jeers randomly shouted out. Like a little boy striking a beehive, Solomon had angered the swarm. A wave of fear swept over him, but he would not succumb to weakness when justice required a response.

"My lord, please." Benaiah stepped forward, his hand on the hilt of his sword.

Solomon whispered through clenched teeth, "If they condone this atrocity, they don't deserve to call themselves Israelites."

Benaiah released a heavy sigh, but to his credit, he prepared to defend without further argument. Solomon stepped in front of Arielah, completing the circle of guards around her.

The crowd began to swell, and Arielah grasped Solomon's robe. "Please, stop!"

"No!" Jehoshaphat shouted, his hands raised to the crowd. "No, my friends. There is no cause for anger." The Shulammites settled enough to hear their respected judge speak. "Today is intended to be a day of rejoicing, and our good king deserves an answer. How can he know if we do not tell him?" The crowd quieted further, and Jehoshaphat returned his gaze to Solomon. "Yes, my lord, I knew."

The knot in Solomon's stomach unraveled, as did his faith in this godly man. "Why, Jehoshaphat?" he asked, closing his eyes against the realization of what he must now do. "How could you allow Arielah to endure such pain from those who are supposed to love her?"

"Solomon . . ."

Startled at hearing his familiar name, the king looked into Jehoshaphat's tear-filled eyes.

"I did not know the *extent* of my sons' cruelty toward Arielah."

"You didn't know?" he asked. "But the wounds on her hands and face, Jehoshaphat. How could you not . . . ?" He allowed his skepticism to finish the question.

"By the time I returned from our meeting in Jerusalem, my sons' brutality had reached new depths." He paused, and the truth began to settle into Solomon's consciousness. "The law required that we punish our rebellious sons." A single blink sent rivers of tears into his beard. "We obeyed the law."

Finally absorbing the extent of this family's suffering, Solomon turned to Arielah and saw tears streaming down her cheeks. Like a dagger, the memory of Benaiah's report pierced him: Jehoshaphat's son had been stoned. Solomon had assumed the crime was murder. *Oh, Jehovah! What have I done?*

"Their son was stoned for his rebellion," Benaiah whispered, confirming the king's thoughts.

The crowd had grown utterly silent, and Solomon took a deep breath, lifted his shoulders, and spoke for all to hear. "Jehoshaphat, I have wrongly accused you. Can you ever forgive me?" When he turned to Jehoshaphat to offer his hand, the judge's hand was already waiting.

"You are already forgiven, my king." The warmth in the man's voice and expression instantly relieved Solomon's fears and almost as quickly drained the tension from the crowd and the king's guards. Cradling Solomon's hand in his, Jehoshaphat continued his public praise. "Your passion for my daughter's protection is a noble trait, King Solomon. You were her champion today. You defended her bravely, and I pray you never have to be her champion again."

Approving words rippled across the crowd, and even Benaiah's elite Cherethite and Pelethite guards ventured amiable grins.

Solomon was overwhelmed. "How can you forgive so freely, Jehoshaphat?" he whispered, drawing the man closer with the grip he held on his wrist.

"It was Arielah who taught me of forgiveness when she showed mercy to our younger son Igal on the day of judgment." Inclining his head, he directed Solomon's attention to a large man standing just behind Jehosheba. He resembled Jehoshaphat, but his eyes were downcast.

Solomon released his hand and struggled to keep a level tone. "One of your sons was spared?" He could feel the color of fury rising on his neck. "I do not see mercy as an option in the law, Jehoshaphat."

Igal's head snapped up, his face awash with fear.

"At some point, my king, we all need mercy," Jehoshaphat said. "Just as moments ago, you needed mine."

Solomon faltered. The words were true, but . . . "How can I know Arielah will be safe in your household?"

"How can I know she will be safe in yours?" Jehoshaphat's words weren't sharp or unkind, but they slapped Solomon like an offended maiden.

Remembering Jehoshaphat's concerns during their negotiations, Solomon placed a comforting hand on his shoulder. "Just because Benaiah lost his son at war doesn't mean your Arielah will be lost at the palace, my friend." An abba's satisfied smile confirmed the gathering calm, and Solomon lifted his voice to all Shulammites. "I am honored to receive Arielah, daughter of Jehoshaphat, as Israel's treaty bride! Tonight we sign the agreement!"

The crowd erupted in celebration, and Solomon thought the city walls might come tumbling down. Jehoshaphat, face beaming, slapped Igal on the back and extended his hand to Arielah, inviting her return to his side. She glanced at Solomon with a shy smile as she stepped away. He felt strangely lonely, somehow barren and cold on the side where she had stood. He wanted to reach out and gather her into his arms, but he'd given up that chance when he foolishly refused to marry her today.

❧⊱✠⊰❧

Arielah's heart was bursting—Solomon's tenderness and then his fury, his power and now the vulnerability splashed on his features. Could she ever love him more than at this moment? He turned and caught her staring. He winked, and her cheeks flamed.

"Jehoshaphat, my friend," Solomon shouted over the noisy celebration, "I have brought our agreed-upon mohar gifts for your lovely daughter."

The mention of the king's bride price settled the roar to a whisper. Everyone—including Arielah—seemed interested to know how much the king offered in payment for Jehoshaphat's only daughter. Craning her neck, Arielah noticed the heavy-laden camels for the first time.

"To which fields shall my herdsmen guide your new livestock? And in which home should my servants unload the pack animals?" The crowd's collective gasp affirmed their approval, and Arielah watched a slow, wide smile grace Solomon's handsome face.

The Shulammites came to life, scurrying to the tasks Abba and Ima had asked of them beforehand. "Igal will direct your herdsmen to my pastures," Abba Jehoshaphat said, his arm protectively placed around his son's shoulders.

Solomon glared at her tall, stocky brother, and she could see Igal wilting inside.

"He'll be an excellent manager one day," Abba said.

When Solomon's expression remained as hard as stone, Jehoshaphat released his son with a pat on the back. Arielah's heart ached that her report of abuse had caused a rift between the king and Igal, but Abba Jehoshaphat seemed undaunted, moving now to introduce Ima. "Jehosheba has arranged for some women to help unload the household supplies."

"Jehosheba." The king inclined his head, his demeanor tender now. "I see where your daughter gets her beauty."

Ima's cheeks colored, and she bowed before her king. No

words, simply her sweet smile and those sparkling eyes that embraced every heart.

Camels and donkeys paraded by until Shulammite whispers grew to applause. Lapis and linen, oil and spices, grindstones, spindles, and bolts of cloth—a bride price beyond Arielah's imagination. But then the bleating of sheep stole her attention.

On the plain, behind the king's escort, roamed more flocks and herds—fewer animals than the mohar gift and kept distinctly separate. The Daughters of Jerusalem must have noticed her unasked question because Shiphrah was quick to answer. "As you can see, little shepherdess, a king must make his own provision when traveling in a hostile land." Glancing in Abba Jehoshaphat's direction, she added, "Even a simple village judge can understand the wisdom of safe meat for the king's household while enduring a foreign land."

Arielah felt her abba tense, but when she searched his eyes, they were tender—and focused on the king. "I believe it is the responsibility and privilege of the bride's abba to provide for the betrothal feast, my lord." Solomon stared at his sandals while Jehoshaphat addressed the maidens. "And let me remind both of you—Shunem is neither hostile nor foreign to the king of Israel."

At the venom in Abba's tone, the king replied, "Please, my friend, don't be offended. I must be cautious. Ahishar made a valid point before we left Jerusalem."

Arielah's blood boiled at the mention of the steward's name.

"He insisted I protect not only myself but also my servants and guards by eating only palace provisions." He paused, glancing at Benaiah, exchanging some silent agreement. "My palace servants will mingle with the Shulammite servers at tonight's banquet, and no one will notice the separate provisions, my friend."

Arielah saw only compassion on Abba's face. "You look weary, my king."

The sudden observation seemed to startle Solomon. "Well, I . . . I mean, I suppose . . ."

"No one in Shunem wishes you harm. You are safe here, Solomon."

Hearing his familiar name seemed to give the king pause. Arielah wondered how often he heard it. *Does anyone call you Solomon anymore, or do you hear only 'my lord' and 'my king'?*

"Jehoshaphat, my friend," he said with a deep sigh, "I have learned in the past few weeks that betrayal hides behind every smile and lurks around every corner. So I have become cautious—extremely cautious."

"I understand." Jehoshaphat nodded toward the king's beautiful companions. "I hope you are as cautious about those you employ in your household."

Shiphrah stepped forward as if to defend herself, but Abba's heated stare pressed her and her sister back a few steps. Solomon ducked his head, hiding the almost imperceptible grin tipping the left corner of his lips.

"Take care, my king." Abba's tone was warm but insistent. "A constant stream of suspicion can strangle a heart in desperate need of peace. A king needs *godly* counselors, those who would remind him of Jehovah's plan for his nation, Israel—and God's love for Solomon, the man."

Arielah saw the king's cheeks shade pink. "Do you know my name?" he asked in a hushed voice. He glanced right and left, and his eyes grew round like a child who'd been found with the honey jar.

Abba's tender smile seemed perfectly at ease, but Arielah wanted to scream, *Your name? Your name is Solomon! Of course he knows your name!*

But before her confusion could root and grow, Abba whispered, "Nathan must have told you of the name Jehovah issued the night of your birth."

Arielah saw tears pool in the king's eyes. "How did you know?"

190

Abba placed a comforting hand on his shoulder. "Your abba and I met only a few times, but we shared deeply about our God and our sons." Pausing only a moment, he added, "He knew you were loved by God, Jedidiah."

Prickly flesh raised the hairs on Arielah's arm as a warm breeze anointed the moment. *Jedidiah*, she repeated silently while her Abba continued. "My Arielah's birth was surrounded by similar blessing, King Solomon. She is loved. She is chosen. And next year she will be yours." The two bowed, no doubt to Jehovah rather than each other. "You may choose any of the meadows of Shunem to graze your flocks," Abba said. "Our quiet pastures have much to offer a man seeking the peace of God's presence."

"Thank you, my friend," Solomon said. "I look forward to a little time of God's reassuring presence." Nodding to Jehoshaphat and Arielah, he said, "Until tonight's banquet then."

"Before you go . . ." Arielah's voice sounded small amid the lingering commotion of mohar camels and bustling servants. "May I ask one thing of the king before he retires to his camp?"

The warmth of his gaze enfolded her like a woolen blanket, giving her permission to speak.

"Will you send a messenger to tell me where you graze your flocks, so that I may join you tomorrow for a meal when you rest your sheep at midday?"

He laughed, and humiliation immediately colored her cheeks. She looked away, but he turned her chin with a gentle nudge. "Beautiful Arielah, I am not a shepherd king like my abba David. The royal shepherds tend my flocks, but I would be pleased to see you at midday." He released her chin, and his eyes grew distant. He signaled his servants toward a southern meadow, his mind obviously shifting to the tasks at hand. "I'm sure my tent won't be hard to find. You can ask any of my guards when you arrive tomorrow, and they'll direct you."

The Daughters of Jerusalem smiled triumphantly. "Yes, little shepherdess. You can just wander among the herders until you find us."

"I will *not* wander among your tents, my lord!" Arielah's venom snapped the king's head to attention. "I may not be jeweled and lotioned like a queen, but neither will I go from one tent to the next like a red-veiled woman on her nightly rounds."

Solomon appeared too shocked to answer, but Shiphrah spoke before he could. "If you can't find King Solomon's tent, oh *beautiful* Shulammite, why not bring your abba's goats and herding dogs? Surely they're smart enough to follow the tracks of King Solomon's flocks."

"Enough," Solomon said, casting disapproving frowns at all of them. "Shiphrah and Sherah, you will speak to Arielah respectfully, giving her the honor of a newly betrothed bride to the king." Casting a quick glance at Jehoshaphat, he said, "I'll say no more since I know better than to involve myself in women's issues. I saw verbal battles in Abba's harem deteriorate into nail-scratching, hair-pulling massacres."

The Daughters of Jerusalem lowered their heads, feigning repentance. But a silent threat cast at Arielah promised more trouble in days to come.

With a deep sigh, Solomon turned his full attention to Arielah. "I meant no disrespect, asking that you venture to my camp unescorted." He fell silent, seeming intent on her response. Could it be he actually cared that she might be offended? "I meant no disrespect, Arielah. Please, forgive me."

In the stillness of that moment, she could hear only her racing heart. "I forgive you, my king."

As he brushed her cheek with the back of his hand, she felt his warmth, saw tenderness in his deep brown eyes. Lifting his voice for the lingering Shulammites, he shouted, "Arielah is like a mare harnessed to one of the chariots of Pharaoh." Shiphrah and Sherah smugly crossed their arms, and Arielah wondered if she was about to be embarrassed again. "When Pharaoh gave me his prize mare with a battle chariot, he explained the brilliant war strategy of the combination. When the Egyptian mare led the chariot into battle, the enemy stallions broke into complete disarray." Stepping close, he whispered, "Just as it seems you've thrown my heart and household into a frenzy, beloved." The scent of saffron lingered when he stepped away.

"You called me *beloved*." She breathed the word reverently.

He laughed again, but this time she laughed with him. "I bring you all the treasures of a mohar, and yet you receive a simple word as more precious than gold." Turning to Jehoshaphat, he said, "Your daughter is the true treasure, Prince of Shunem." Playfully he swept his fingers through the chains dangling from her temples. The sound of rubies tinkled on the breeze. "You look beautiful in the head covering, Arielah, but it's nothing compared to the earrings of gold and silver I will give you. You will have sapphires, topaz, emeralds, and onyx—jewelry from every nation."

Words meant to thrill, or at least impress, left her cold after his warm touch. "I need no such bounty, my lord." She bowed dutifully, noting Solomon's puzzlement when she arose.

"What is this?" he asked Jehoshaphat, playfully annoyed. "I call her *beloved*, and she adores me. I offer her jewels, and she defers?"

"I warn you, King Solomon," Abba said with a glint in his eyes, "Arielah is like no woman you've ever known. My little lamb has a lion's heart."

Solomon captured her with his gaze. "I look forward to the challenge, Prince Jehoshaphat," he said wryly. "The women in my world are the spice that gives life flavor."

20

1:12; 2:2–3, 6–7

[Beloved] While the king was at his table, my perfume spread its fragrance. . . .

[Lover] Like a lily among thorns is my darling among the maidens.

[Beloved] Like an apple tree among the trees of the forest is my lover among the young men. . . . His left arm is under my head, and his right arm embraces me. Daughters of Jerusalem . . . do not arouse or awaken love until it so desires.

Arielah would remember last night for the rest of her life. This morning's sun cast golden rays on the papyrus document she held aloft. Those tiresome days of practicing words in clay tablets with Kemmuel and Igal were suddenly worth every excruciating moment. She gently caressed the scroll that her family would guard until her wedding day.

On this, the eighth day of the month of Iyar, in the city of Shunem, the honorable King Solomon—may Jehovah bless and protect him—enters into this wedding treaty with Arielah, the daughter of the worthy Jehoshaphat, elder of Shunem and prince of Israel's tenth district. Let Solomon the son of David, with the help of heaven, honor, support, and maintain her.

Let this treaty seal our betrothal, my promise to return to Shunem in no less than one year, when I will claim Arielah as my wife according to the law of Moses and Israel. In accordance with the custom of Israelite husbands, who fulfill the responsibilities of their position in truth, I will provide for her clothing, her ransom, and her burial. Furthermore, I, King Solomon, give flocks, fine linen, gold and silver jewelry, and every kind of precious stone as mohar in payment to the house of Jehoshaphat, the totals of which are listed below . . .

Arielah's eyes stung with tears at the memory. Happy tears. Frightened tears. She inspected the transparent drops and marveled that they looked the same—no matter the emotion. *Why don't I cry blue tears for sorrow and yellow ones for joy?* Why couldn't a wedding be as simple as tears? Unadorned, transparent. Why couldn't she and Solomon promise their love in a meadow? Instead, gold and jewels guaranteed a yearlong betrothal, and fine robes would bind them in a public wedding in Jerusalem. A deep sigh. Then a giggle. Delight quickly replaced her newly betrothed impatience, and she lingered on her sleeping mat way past the rooster's crow.

At dawn, Ima had peeked around the cooking stones to Arielah's private sleeping corner. "Rest a while longer, my lamb." Then the familiar sounds of clicking spoons and rattling pots began while Ima set about her daily tasks. The aroma of her efforts swirled into the memories of last night's banquet, wrapping Arielah in the familiar and the fanciful.

King Solomon! Arielah stifled a squeal. *I am going to marry King Solomon!* She remembered every angle and detail of his masculine face, his raven hair resting on the fox-fur collar of his royal robe.

"I stand before Prince Jehoshaphat and the people of Shunem to complete my vow and return to Shunem with my royal procession and claim Arielah as my bride." He'd called her his bride.

But the next words had nearly rendered her speechless, and even this morning sent prickles up her spine. "In the unlikely event of our divorce," he read from the treaty agreement, "I guarantee safe return to her abba's household with her bridal dowry intact." Solomon bowed, and the Shulammites' deafening cheer should have assured Arielah that the king's comment was simply a formality, included in all wedding arrangements. But the word still resounded in her ears. *Divorce*.

The morning sun shone through the window above her sleeping mat. She raised her hand, letting her new gold ring sparkle in the sun's rays. The simple symbol of Solomon's promise strengthened her heart. She hugged it to her chest and giggled, remembering poor Benaiah's expression when Solomon had chosen him as friend of the bridegroom. Shocked yet honored. The mountainous man stepped forward to affix his signature to the treaty. Reu's face had mirrored Benaiah's when Abba asked him to sign the document as witness for the bride's family.

Then she remembered Solomon's warm brown eyes and tender voice. "Jehoshaphat, I give this ring to your daughter as a testimony of our betrothal, our contract of marriage." Taking the simple gold band from a hidden pocket in his robe, he called her forward.

Finally, she remembered thinking, *something as simple as me*.

The king's luxurious black tent grew as quiet as a tomb. Holding the ring in the air, he said, "Arielah, my beloved, do you accept this ring and the mohar, thereby sealing our betrothal?"

"Oh yes!" she cried almost before he finished asking.

Solomon's rich, deep laughter filled the tent, and their

guests joined in. "For a simple gold band, you rejoice as though I've given you the world!" Then he brushed her cheek with the back of his hand and sent fire rushing through her body.

"If you keep daydreaming about last night, the king's meal will turn cold." Her ima's sweet face peeked over the cooking stones.

"But surely it's not midday already!" Arielah leapt from her mat, her cheeks burning. *Oh my!* She hoped Ima wasn't reading her mind again!

Jehosheba chuckled and held out a full basket of food. "Indeed, it is nearly midday, my lamb, and you've enjoyed dreams of your Solomon all morning—as a newly betrothed maiden should."

Giddy, she kissed Ima's cheek, splashed water on her face, and whispered her thanks. She scurried through their courtyard gate with the food basket over her arm, then passed the matchmaker and old Ruth just in time to hear their conversation.

"Did you see the lovely wedding garments the king brought for Jehoshaphat and Jehosheba, Edna?" Ruth's heart was as tender as a sun-ripened fig. "Appropriate gifts for good people."

"I wore a simple linen robe with an embroidered belt to my daughter's wedding," Edna groused. "And I had to stitch the embroidery on the belt myself!"

All of Shunem wondered at old Ruth's patience with the crabby matchmaker. Arielah listened with a half smile. She knew there would always be grumblers in the midst of celebrating. Inhaling deeply of Shunem's fresh air, she giggled at the mingling aroma of henna blossoms and sheep manure. *Like joy and jealousy, inseparable realities in my little town.* Her laughter earned a sideways glance from the old women as she hurried past.

The rolling green hills outside the city wall exploded with

wildflowers, and the men were well into their day of barley and flax harvest. As she skipped through the familiar meadows, her heart thrilled in anticipation of her quiet visit with the king. She couldn't wait to see his face light up at the contents of her basket—roast quail with curdled milk, fresh flatbread, warm raisin cakes, lentil stew, goat cheese, figs, and other country delicacies.

Making her way toward the royal encampment, Arielah spotted Solomon sitting beneath a fir tree, next to the eastern grazing hill. His eyes were focused in a distant stare, and her carefree thoughts gave way to deep concern. *He looks like a lost lamb.*

As though responding to her silent care, Solomon looked up and saw her. Arielah waved, and the joy she anticipated appeared. "Shall we simply float away on a cloud, my king?" she shouted across the meadow.

He stood to greet her, and—was it her imagination?—he seemed to drink in the sight of her. Did all soon-to-be brides think their men felt this way?

The Daughters of Jerusalem lounged just a camel's length behind him on a tapestry that looked tawdry on Shunem's lush meadow. Arielah offered a perfunctory nod to their chaperones. *They are like shadows, relentless and dark.* She turned and bowed to her betrothed. "Greetings from the house of Jehoshaphat. The prince of Shunem has sent delicacies for the king." Mischief escaped before she could capture it. "He also sent this basket of food."

Solomon's laughter rang through the hills. He swept his arms wide and returned her playful banter. "Please display your *delicacies* before me, daughter of Jehoshaphat." Their eyes met and danced—as was becoming their custom.

"Someday, King Solomon, my delicacies will fill every desire of your heart." Pausing, she lifted one eyebrow. "Until that day, my ima's cooking will have to suffice."

He clutched at his chest as though wounded. "Woman,

I feel like Moses. You've offered me the Promised Land but refused me entry!" He fell to his braided rug, feigning injury.

Arielah smiled as she knelt and began unpacking their midday meal, but the memory of his refusal to marry still pricked her heart. "It was not I who chose to wait, my king," she said, matching his playful grin. "Perhaps *I* am Moses and *you* are the Promised Land."

Once again she had shocked him. His eyes widened, and he laughed until tears rolled down his cheeks. "I suppose you're right, beloved, but you will be mine after your abba completes his goodwill tour among the northern tribes." His gaze grew more intense, probing, and Arielah felt her cheeks burn.

Glancing away, she noticed the disapproving stares of the Daughters of Jerusalem. She had undoubtedly broken every unwritten law of the women's court, and her momentary glimpse seemed to summon them from their chaperone's perch.

With three quick strides, Sherah was at Solomon's left side, kneeling over the freshly unpacked meal. "Although I'm sure your food is adequate, we must evidently remind you that our king trusts only the provisions of his own fields and flocks."

When Arielah ignored her intrusion, Shiphrah halted Arielah's hand from arranging the fruit. "We'll help you return the food to your basket, little shepherdess." The older twin spoke slowly as if Arielah were a dim-witted sheep, and then she reached for the wooden plates Arielah had arranged on the king's braided rug.

Solomon cleared his throat, and Shiphrah's hand froze.

Arielah held her breath. Would he refuse Ima's food or deter the Daughters' intrusion?

"Shiphrah, Sherah, I'm sure the bounty Arielah offers can satisfy me as well as any provisions from Jerusalem."

Arielah slowly lifted her gaze, struggling to speak past the lump in her throat. "What I offer can supply every desire of your heart, my king, if only you will promise me your whole heart in return." No games this time, no mischief or teasing. She would tell him from the start that she desired all of him, not just a harem wife's portion.

She watched his smile fade and his eyes grow cold. His voice was calm yet commanding when he spoke. "Shiphrah and Sherah, you will leave us now." Solomon's stare unnerved her while the Daughters of Jerusalem gathered their tapestry and moved a stone's throw away—further than the laws of chaperonage allowed.

Arielah looked down, unable to bear the intensity of his gaze.

"You want my whole heart," he said.

She glanced up, hopeful. But his expression remained chiseled stone.

"You offered to supply my every desire. Isn't that what you said?" He brushed her cheek with the back of his hand and continued down her neck. Yesterday the same gesture had warmed her heart, but today it filled her with fear. With one swift motion, he cradled her in one arm and cupped her face roughly with his hand. Their lips lingered dangerously close, and then his hand traveled down her neck, over her shoulder, down her arm.

Panic gripped her, sending a chill up her spine, and she whimpered.

His eyes narrowed and his grip tightened. Lifting her hand to his lips, he kissed her fingertips and smiled hungrily.

She was trembling uncontrollably, and a shadow of revulsion swept across his features. Suddenly the king gripped her shoulders and sat her upright. He leaned back as if having just concluded a routine ruling at court. "How can you imagine that one woman could quench my desires," he said flatly, "when no one knows what pleases a king?"

Arielah stared into the eyes of a stranger. With her simple statement, she had hoped to gain his loyalty. Instead, she'd awakened a callousness in Solomon that she never dreamed possible. Perhaps that was the problem. She had loved Solomon for as long as she could remember, but she hardly knew him. Had she been in love with merely a dream of him?

A simple statement had never had such an effect on Solomon—nor had a simple maiden. *If only you will promise me your whole heart in return.* Gooseflesh raised on his arms. How had their playful teasing turned to unreasonable demands? Jehoshaphat had made a similar comment during negotiations. "Perhaps Arielah could be your last wife," he'd said. Arielah and her abba seemed to have an unrealistic view of a king's obligations. If this girl believed the king of Israel could love her like a Shulammite shepherd boy would, she was sorely mistaken. His only defense against her innocent charm had been to feign the manners of a Philistine and paw at her as if she'd been a nameless woman in his bedchamber. Many maidens had whispered longingly in his ear, each having her own agenda for his affection. But he'd never feared he might yield to their wishes—until now.

Arielah sat trembling, those beautiful dove eyes waiting for him to speak.

Solomon's stomach churned, roiling emotions sapping his appetite. He shifted his attention to the food and reclined on one elbow. Distraction was often the best solution. "Is this quail? I love quail." He heard a soft sniff but couldn't bring himself to look at Arielah.

"Yes, my lord," she said quietly.

His chest ached at the distance in her voice. How could he restore her joy without raising false hopes for his commitment? He had to say something! "Shiphrah and Sherah aren't so bad. When you come to Jerusalem, they'll make sure you're pampered with all the lotions and perfumes of royalty." He heard another sniff and looked up to see new tears forming. "My ima doesn't like them either," he blurted out in desperation.

This tidbit won a slight giggle from the shepherdess. "Really?" she said. "Queen Bathsheba doesn't like the Daughters of Jerusalem?"

Relieved at the sparkle returning to her eyes, he said, "No, but we mustn't tell Shiphrah and Sherah. I'm sure Ima Bathsheba will inform them soon enough." Arielah smiled then, and he felt as if the sun's rays reached down to warm his heart. "I'm glad you brought the meal, Arielah."

She dipped a morsel of quail into the curdled milk and lifted it to his lips. "Pharaoh's chariots couldn't have kept me away from you today." The spark of mischief had returned.

He laughed aloud and received his meal from her hands, noting the bandages covering her palms. When only quail bones were left as evidence of their feast, Solomon leaned back against the fir tree and patted his rounded middle. "Arielah, that was perhaps the finest food I've ever eaten."

"I'll give my ima your compliments," she said wryly. "You might not have enjoyed *my* cooking so much."

He studied the scattered freckles on her sun-kissed face and examined the eyes that had captured his attention so thoroughly. A unique mixture of hazel with gray flecks, Arielah's eyes sparkled with life and passion. Reclining on his side, Solomon supported himself on his elbow and reached up to lightly brush her cheek. Relief washed over him when she didn't recoil, but it was more than relief. His heart ached in his chest, and he wondered if it was love or too much quail.

Arielah reveled in the warmth of Solomon's touch. No longer the lusty touch of a stranger, he had again become the gift of Jehovah she believed him to be. Heat rose in her cheeks as she memorized the contours of his muscular frame.

"Will you join me?" he asked, patting the grass beside him. "Here, I'll get the tapestry—"

"No thank you." Arielah stilled him with a hand on his arm. "I enjoy sitting in the grass. Remember, I'm a shepherdess." She ducked her head, tugging at her head covering to be sure her warm ears were covered. Surely they were as red as the roses in Ima's garden. "I don't need a tapestry, my lord."

He sat beside her again, picking at the blades of grass. "I must confess, I'm not sure what you need." She watched a small V form at the bridge of his nose as he pondered some deep thought. "Women are an important part of my life. They add color and flavor to an otherwise tedious existence." He paused, waiting for Arielah's response.

"You make us sound as if we're saffron flowers and cinnamon bark."

A wide smile creased his lips. "I suppose in some ways, that's an apt picture of women. Some are sweet, others pungent." He grew pensive. "I've known many women, Arielah, but never one like you. You seem uncomplicated yet complex. You are a shepherd girl but elegant like a queen." He cast aside the blade of grass he'd been inspecting and held her with his eyes. "You are more challenging to me than all the wise men of Persia."

"I am not so complicated," she whispered. "In fact, you understand me better than you realize."

"Well, you'll have to convince me of that." His eyes devoured every detail of her face. "Convince me, beloved. Prove that I understand you well."

Her heart stopped at the term. *Beloved*. "All right," she said. "Remember when I approached today with the basket of food? Did you smell the food or did you sense my presence?"

"I think I smelled your perfume."

"I don't wear perfume," she said, inspecting the blades of grass he'd abandoned.

"Ah, but you do. You have a natural scent, a mixture of lavender and henna blossoms."

She could feel her cheeks warm again. Should she keep the conversation light? "Shiphrah and Sherah would say I smell like old leather and sheep pens."

Solomon's deep laughter echoed against the hills. She watched him look over his shoulder and wave at the Daughters of Jerusalem. "It's just the way Judean women respond to other women."

Gently tilting his chin toward her, she regained his full attention and boldly held his gaze. "Well, this is the way a Shulammite shepherdess responds to a man." Heart pounding, mind whirling, she spoke in a shepherd's verse. "While the king lounged at his table, my perfume spread its fragrance." Arielah tugged on a leather string around her neck, lifting a packet of sweet fragrance from beneath her robe. "My lover is always with me, like a sachet of myrrh and henna blossoms from the vineyards of En Gedi."

She dare not tell him the truth—that he visited her dreams every night and took the place of that sachet between her breasts. A shepherd's verse was meant to be intimate, drawing on the senses using God's creative design, but she must use discretion until after their wedding in Jerusalem.

Solomon offered an intrigued smile. "Beautiful words. You tell me you are simple but then offer me a riddle. I said your scent was that of henna blossoms and lavender. Yet your shepherd's verse describes the fragrance of henna blossoms and myrrh—a burial spice?" Before she could answer, he added, "You see? You *are* as challenging as the Persians."

Delighted that he had caught her subtlety, she said, "How could I be anything other than challenging with a name like Arielah—lion of God?"

He reached out and traced the line of her jaw, and her heart skipped a beat. She must be careful this close. Even though servants mingled and the Daughters of Jerusalem lurked, he was still the king of Israel, and they were still only betrothed.

"Myrrh signifies pain, and henna blossoms embody joy." She watched the words slowly sink into his consciousness. "I'm learning that true love consists of both—pain and joy."

His hand stilled on her face, and his eyes narrowed. "Why? Why must love bring pain? Why can't love simply give pleasure?" He looked like a little boy arguing for extra sweets after dinner.

"The love that gives true pleasure is worth sacrifice," she said. In a whisper she added, "King Solomon, son of a shepherd king, speak to your shepherdess in the language of creation."

A moment of panic swept over his features before a hesitant smile settled into place. "You are beautiful, my beloved. Oh, how beautiful! Your eyes are doves."

She applauded lightly. "Israel's king has composed his first shepherd's verse! Now it's my turn again." Arielah stretched out on her right side, careful to leave plenty of space between them. She leaned on her elbow and mirrored his posture. His features brightened, and he reached over to touch her. She captured his hand and placed it back on the grass. He smiled coyly.

Arielah cleared her throat as if preparing for a long recitation, but with her eyes she massaged his soul. "How handsome you are, my king! Oh, how charming!" She swept her hand over the lush grass and gazed at the low-hanging branches that formed their overhanging canopy. "Our bed is lush and green, and the beams of our house are cedars. Our rafters are firs."

Solomon's reply was quick, and his eyes sparkled. "The beams of our house truly are cedars, beloved! And our rafters were built with firs!" Inching closer, he added in a husky voice, "My palace is filled with the aroma of your northern country. The cedars of Lebanon fill every room in your new home. You will have more gardens and gold than you can imagine in Jerusalem." Then, as if his next words were the most lavish promise he'd ever made, he said, "You will be my fairest flower and I your only gardener."

Arielah closed her eyes to hide the pain. *Oh, Solomon, I long to be your only flower, not just the fairest.* Her heart broke—for herself and for him. He knew nothing of love. One man and one woman devoted to each other for a lifetime. In the meadows of Shunem, she could almost forget about the harem, the battles waiting in Jerusalem. Almost.

"I am but a rose of Sharon," she said, her voice trembling. "I'm a lily of the valleys, the smallest flower among all the flowers in your gardens."

Like a trumpet blast in the peace of dawn, the king jolted from his repose to sit on his braided rug beside her.

"Solomon?"

His knees were bent, hands clutched tightly around them. Solomon's cold stare chilled her to the bone. "Like a lily among thorns are you among the other maidens, Arielah. And you are named well, lion of God. For you are as tenacious as a lioness on the hunt." He fixed his eyes on a faraway place and mumbled, "Evidently, the king of Israel is your prey, and gaining the rights of first wife is your chief goal."

The words pierced her. She had no desire for "rights," as he called it. Solomon interpreted her yearning for deeper commitment as a political play for power, and he'd responded by building an invisible yet impenetrable wall around his heart. But she was determined to teach him the wonders of a deep and abiding love. "Like an apple tree among the trees of the forest is my king among other men." When no comment came from the unyielding figure, she reached up to jostle his arm. Her playful nudge still gained no response, so she sat up and whispered in his ear, "I delight to sit in your shade, and your fruit is the sweetest of all delicacies."

An appreciative grin finally crept across Solomon's lips,

chipping away at his stony countenance. "What kind of non-sense is an apple tree in a forest?" he asked. "I'm a new student in this shepherd's language, but even I know apple trees don't belong in a forest."

"You are unique, King Solomon, and like an apple tree's presence is unusual but productive in a forest, you will bear unique fruit for Israel."

He smiled and joined Arielah again in their familiar pose, facing her on his side—this time just a handbreadth apart. "Explain about sitting in my shade and—"

"In order for me to sit in your shade, King Solomon," Arielah interrupted, "you must rest in one place!" She giggled and he reached for her, but she was able to capture his hand before he touched her. Once again she guided it to the lush green carpet between them and scooted a little farther away. "Now," she said, cheeks burning, "I was about to explain that your presence is the sweet fruit that delights my heart. We've enjoyed the noisy banquet hall, and you've given me extravagant gifts. Publicly you declared your banner of love over me." She reached up to trace the line where his cheek met his beard. "But it's in these quiet moments, my king, that our love and commitment can grow and bear fruit."

Solomon captured her hand, turned it over, and kissed her bandaged palm. Placing her hand gently on the grass between them, he traced her jawline and let his fingers begin a slow journey down her neck. She captured his hand and placed it back on the grass.

"Ahhh!" he said, rolling to his back. But this time a low, playful chuckle rumbled in his throat. "All this talk about love is making me hungry again."

Arielah's heart sang. *It's a good thing he's going back to Jerusalem*, she thought. *I'm not sure I could remain pure for a whole year if we lounged in the meadow every day.* Rolling on her back beside him, she dramatically rested her hand on her forehead. "Strengthen me with raisins. Refresh me with apples, for I am faint with love." Watching the clouds float by, she was lost in the sound of her own laughter until she realized the king had drawn closer.

"Arielah," he whispered to the melody of her laughter. In one fluid motion he covered her small form, his lips upon hers, his desire beyond reason. Did she not realize her touch would fan his embers into flames?

"No!" she said breathlessly. "Wait! We must wait!" She pushed against his chest, struggled, and turned her face away.

He rolled to the rug beside her. "No?" he gasped. "Wait?" His mind seemed incapable of more than one-word phrases.

"We are betrothed," she said, sitting up and straightening her robe and head covering.

"Betrothed?" Again, one word! Solomon shook his head to clear it.

"It is a stoning offense to lay with a betrothed woman, my lord." Arielah's eyes were pleading as she spoke. "If only you had listened yesterday, before the treaty was signed . . . when I asked you to take me to your chamber . . ."

"How dare you instruct me in matters of the law!" Solomon sprang to his feet. "I am the king of Israel, and I will take a maiden to my chamber when *I* choose. I will take a dozen wives if I wish it!"

Suddenly the little Shulammite was on her feet, fury on her stormy features. "I am not yet one of your wives!"

"Indeed you are not!" came Shiphrah's shrill voice. "And with a temperament like that, we can only assume you never will be!"

Sherah, quick as an Egyptian cat, appeared at Solomon's left side. "Come, my king, we'll leave these impudent goatherds to their mountain haunts."

Before Solomon could draw a breath, Arielah stepped to within a handbreadth of Sherah's face. "Listen to me,

Daughters of Jerusalem. I promise you by the gazelles and does of the field: I will come to Solomon as a pure and holy bride. True love is willing to sacrifice, willing to wait, willing to be blessed in Jehovah's time—and not before!"

"Enough!" Solomon shouted. "I've heard enough of your sacrificial love and shepherd's verse! You promise love, yet you deny me passion. Away from me, woman!" Arielah reached out for him, but Solomon pulled away. All her fine talk had brought nothing but frustration.

The Daughters of Jerusalem walked in stride beside him, glaring daggers back at Arielah. "Shall we send a messenger to tell Prince Jehoshaphat his treaty bride is unsuitable?" Shiphrah asked, brushing blades of grass from the king's robe.

"No." He ground out the word. He couldn't risk breaking the northern treaty—or the possibility of never seeing the girl again.

Shiphrah said no more.

Solomon rounded the corner of his tent and found Benaiah talking with a group of soldiers. "Prepare a detachment of men to accompany my carriage immediately!"

Benaiah's face registered confusion, concern. "My lord, the festivities tonight . . . will you return in time for the—"

"I may never return to this forsaken place!"

Benaiah glanced toward the meadow. Solomon followed his gaze.

Arielah was running toward home, their meal scraps a shambles on the rug beneath the fir tree. *Like this cursed treaty arrangement.* Solomon's heart twisted in his chest. "Prepare the whole caravan to return to Jerusalem!" he shouted. "The Daughters of Jerusalem and I will leave now in my carriage with a small escort!" Benaiah offered a curt bow, and Solomon issued the remainder of his instructions. "Make sure the rest of the caravan leaves Shunem before nightfall. My carriage and escort will travel slowly enough for the procession to catch up by morning."

Solomon didn't wait for Benaiah's response. He knew his commander would think it unwise to travel through the wilderness at night. *Perhaps God's gift of wisdom only applies to matters of nations, not matters of the heart.*

Solomon stalked away, using all his strength to hold his shoulders upright. Within moments, the king sat in his fine coach on a bench opposite the Daughters of Jerusalem, watching the fading image of Shunem's green meadow through the window.

"Well, at least you never have to return to this dusty little badger-hole town," Shiphrah said, fanning herself.

"Silence," Solomon growled. She obeyed. But his yearning was not so easily quieted. How did a simple shepherd girl reduce him to this jumble of emotions? Anger. Sorrow. Aching like he'd never known. She was supposed to have been an arrangement, a bargain. How dare she refuse him? And how dare she even suggest being his *only* woman. That's what she meant when she said she wanted his whole heart, wasn't it?

His deep sigh drew the Daughters' attention, but to their credit, they remained silent. Solomon's brooding continued on the long, bumpy journey to Jerusalem. *Perhaps a few new wives will help me forget the dove-gray eyes of Israel's treaty bride.*

21

King Solomon conscripted laborers from all Israel— thirty thousand men. He sent them off to Lebanon in shifts of ten thousand a month, so that they spent one month in Lebanon and two months at home. . . . Solomon had seventy thousand carriers and eighty thousand stonecutters in the hills, as well as thirty-three hundred foremen. . . . At the king's command they removed from the quarry large blocks of quality stone to provide a foundation of dressed stone for the temple. The craftsmen of Solomon and Hiram and the men of Gebal cut and prepared the timber and stone for the building of the temple.

I see it, my lord!" Reu shouted excitedly, bouncing on the center camel. "Jerusalem, like a crown on that hill! I can almost smell Ima's raisin cakes from here."

Jehoshaphat laughed. "After nine new moons, you've wasted away to a shadow of the man you were before." He leaned forward, straining to see Benaiah on the other side of Reu.

"If we let his ima feed him from the palace kitchens," the

commander joined the teasing, "he'll become three times the man he was before!"

Others in their procession joined the banter, and Jehoshaphat drank in the sound. It was a welcome relief from the panicked shouts they'd exchanged at Shiloh two days ago. Their relations with central Israel's wilderness towns had been deteriorating as families bore the burden of grain and livestock taxes while their men were away meeting the king's construction demands. Grumbling ignited from tension to violence in Shiloh, and one of Jehoshaphat's guards was injured. Word must have reached Jerusalem because Benaiah arrived the next day with his elite guard to escort Jehoshaphat and his retinue. The king wanted an update on the goodwill tour, and he wanted it from Jehoshaphat.

"Reu, my friend," Shunem's prince said, "your ima will need to fatten you up quickly. We'll stay in Jerusalem for tomorrow's Sabbath, but we must leave the next day if we hope to keep pace and reach all northern villages within the year's betrothal period." Smiling at Benaiah, he added, "I don't want Solomon to wait longer than necessary for Israel's treaty bride."

The commander's smile faded. His gaze wandered. Silence fell.

"What, Benaiah?" Jehoshaphat spoke quietly now. "What are you not telling me?"

Reu sat between them looking distinctly uncomfortable, trying to slow his cantankerous camel, Delilah, so the two elders could ride ahead and converse side by side. But the stubborn beast wouldn't slow down. She seemed as anxious to hear Benaiah's news as Jehoshaphat.

Something akin to guilt shadowed Benaiah's face. "Solomon has married over twenty royal wives since he left Shunem."

"What?" Jehoshaphat's stomach rolled. "How? No Israelite would allow his daughter to forego a betrothal period—"

"Judean families don't require a betrothal period in a royal match." Benaiah sighed. "But these are not Israelite *or* Judean wives." The joyful sounds of the guards ceased, and only the clop of camel hooves remained.

"King Solomon has taken twenty *foreign* wives?" Jehoshaphat's words were barely a whisper.

The commander nodded and rubbed his face with his massive paws.

"What about God's command that Israel's king refrain from taking many wives, Benaiah?"

The big man didn't respond.

"What about God's command that Israelites not intermarry with the surrounding nations lest their wives lead our men's hearts to worship other gods?"

Benaiah's head snapped to attention, fear streaking across his features.

Jehoshaphat's heart nearly stopped. "Tell me Solomon has not begun worshiping other gods."

"No." Benaiah's answer was quick and firm. He looked back at his Pelethite and Cherethite guards and spoke so all could hear. "No, King Solomon does not worship his wives' gods."

When Jehoshaphat drew a breath to press further, the commander gave an almost imperceptible warning glance. He obviously had more to say but didn't want to have the conversation here.

"Twenty wives?" Reu asked, seeming to have missed the significant interchange. "How could one man marry twenty women in less than nine new moons?"

Benaiah cleared his throat, ignoring the young messenger's valid question. "His marriages are the fruit of Solomon's growing fame. Kings and ambassadors, astronomers and physicians travel from places beyond our maps to seek his wisdom. When he astounds them with knowledge beyond any earthly revelation, they offer him their daughters as gifts."

Jehoshaphat squeezed the bridge of his nose, shook his head, and tried to process the dichotomy of this bright young king. "Forgive me if this sounds crude, but our king seems to be profiting from Yahweh's gift, and if that be true, I fear for him, my friend."

Benaiah began shaking his head before Jehoshaphat finished the thought. "No, no. Our king doesn't steal Jehovah's glory. He reveals knowledge that only El Shaddai could give and then speaks of the Creator of all things to these idolatrous nations. By the time the ambassadors leave, they know of Solomon's God and have agreed to allow their daughters to learn of Yahweh."

"So these women give up their pagan gods when they enter Solomon's household?" Jehoshaphat felt a glimmer of hope until he saw his question elicit another warning glance from Benaiah.

"I didn't say they gave up their native gods," he whispered—and then said no more. He didn't need to. Jehoshaphat saw the truth written on his face.

Arriving at Jerusalem's eastern gate, Benaiah tapped his camel into the lead, and a watchman saluted. "Greetings, Commander! The king is expecting you."

"Thank you, Oliab. Make sure Prince Jehoshaphat's men and pack animals are directed to the king's stables."

Benaiah continued through the gate, but Jehoshaphat heard the watchman mumble, "I'll not lift a hand to serve a northern Israelite dog." Reu's eyes rounded in disbelief, but it seemed no one else heard. Jehoshaphat ignored the rude watchman and followed Benaiah's mount toward the palace.

Casting a last glance over his shoulder, he noticed his capable young aide meeting with some resistance from the guard at the gate. Reu would undoubtedly employ his usual jovial manner to settle matters. *Jehovah, give me a gracious heart like Reu's to address my king with kinship.*

Arielah, like all Israelite maidens, hoped for an occasional endearing message from her bridegroom sent through his appointed friend. But too many Sabbaths passed and nine new moons came and went without a single word from Benaiah. Climbing the rugged rocks and hills of Mount Moreh, Arielah wondered if her betrothal had been a dream—ending with the nightmare in the meadow. The lush green carpet where she and Solomon had shared their meal had been parched by summer's sun and now lay wrapped in winter's colorless shroud. Rain chilled Arielah to the bone, and the gray, damp days before springtime mirrored her withered spirit.

She found that tending the family flocks soothed her hurting heart, and caring for living things sustained her. Leading Abba's sheep up the northern heights of Mount Moreh, Arielah scavenged the last green shoots of vegetation and rested on a hollowed-out boulder to examine her scraped arms and legs. Shepherding was demanding work, but the pain in her heart overshadowed all else.

"Solomon," she said to an especially stubborn ram named for her silent king, "will you return and honor the treaty bride agreement?" The animal replied with a blank stare. "Hmmm, funny. That's what King Solomon says."

Leading her flock to a small cluster of greenery, she sat on another smooth stone and directed her next question to the nearest ewe. "Was his heart truly stirred, or did I just imagine the emotion in his eyes?" This sheep bleated her response, and Arielah giggled. "I knew a woman would understand."

The sun was quickly melting behind the western horizon, so Arielah journeyed down the southern hills toward home. Leading her flock beside a mountain stream, she felt Jehovah's promise in the warming air. Oh, that a king could be as reliable as the seasons.

No doubt, some of her melancholy came from missing

Abba. He and Reu had begun their goodwill tour soon after Solomon left Shunem. They started their campaign in the heavily populated areas of Galilee, the nearness of those villages making it possible to visit home often. But four moons had passed since Abba and Reu ventured into the wilderness region of central Israel, and they hadn't returned home since. Abba sent occasional messengers with word that the harsh wilderness towns posed more resistance to Solomon's reforms. Traveling merchants brought reports of a riot in Shiloh a few days before last Sabbath. No word had come from Abba since, and each night after Ima's bedchamber door closed, Arielah heard her quiet whimpers.

Nudging the last woolen rump into the sheepfold, she glanced up to see Igal approaching. Studying the whistling, jovial young man before her, she marveled at the effects of mercy on one so willing to embrace it. She secured the gate's lock and was about to offer a greeting when Igal said, "Come quickly, little sister! Ima needs your help with the evening meal."

Odd, Arielah thought. *Ima usually takes care of all the cooking.* But she nodded with a sigh and assumed Ima must have had an unusually busy day. Grieving had slowed Ima Jehosheba's hands, and she hadn't quite caught up since their Sabbath rest three days ago. Igal nudged her toward home as if she were one of Abba's ewes. Shepherding her through their courtyard gate, he swung open their heavy front door.

"Hello, my lamb," Abba said, sitting on a goatskin by their leather table mat.

A gasp, and her mouth gaped. Overwhelmed. Overjoyed. She couldn't move or utter a sound. Finally, rushing to Abba's side, she fell to her knees and released the tears she'd held captive so long.

"Shhh, my lamb," he whispered. "Jehovah is at work even when we cannot see it."

"I haven't heard anything from Solomon or the friend of the bridegroom. Has he changed his mind? What about the treaty? I love him, Abba." He held her as she poured out her heart.

An unfamiliar sniff sounded from the corner behind the door, and Arielah darted to her feet. "Benaiah!" She cringed, her cheeks warming, wondering how much he'd heard. "What are you doing here?" Turning back to her abba, she questioned him with a glance.

"Arielah, come sit down. Benaiah and I need to talk with you."

Dread coiled around her legs, threatening to buckle her knees. She looked again at Benaiah, and this time he walked toward her, offering a kind smile and a strong hand to steady her.

She sat beside Abba as he explained, "Benaiah and a detachment of Mighty Men were dispatched to Shiloh, where our goodwill campaign met with hostility."

Arielah cast a fearful glance around the room and realized Reu wasn't there. "Reu!" Fear sliced through her like a dagger. When she saw her ima's red, swollen eyes, she asked, "Where's Reu?"

Abba spoke calmly, deliberately. "Only one guard was slightly injured during the riot, but Reu met with some mischief from a Judean watchman in Jerusalem. He's resting in our bedchamber." Motioning to Igal, Jehoshaphat excused his son from the room, and Arielah's brother gave a reassuring nod to his sister. Jehoshaphat touched her arm lightly to regain her attention. "Igal will tend to Reu, and you can see him in the morning. Right now I must ask you to listen as we tell you of some changes in Jerusalem."

She could hear her heartbeat in her ears, and the room darkened except for the men's faces before her. Abba looked weary, and Benaiah looked old. The distinguished-looking gray hair at their temples now devoured nearly half their heads, and both kind expressions were furrowed with deep lines of concern.

"Arielah, are you listening to me?" Abba was saying.

Tears sprang immediately to her eyes. "Yes, Abba, but before you begin, could you just answer one question?"

The men exchanged a troubled glance.

"Am I still to be Israel's treaty bride?"

Abba reached out to brush her cheek. "Only if you wish to be after hearing what I have to say."

"Abba!" She couldn't believe he would doubt her heart for even a moment. "Of course I want to marry Solomon. I love him!"

He winced as if she'd slapped him, his expression a mixture of sadness, anger, confusion.

"Tell me what's happening, Abba. You're frightening me."

Tears welled in his eyes, and his lips pressed into a tight, thin line.

"Solomon has taken many foreign wives since he left Shunem, Arielah." Benaiah spoke, his voice kind but without adornment. "Ahishar controls the flow of petitioners in King Solomon's court, ensuring that visiting dignitaries offering brides get priority audiences."

"*Foreign* brides?" Her voice sounded small.

Abba nodded. Benaiah continued. "Ahishar arranges the foreign marriages, and the Daughters of Jerusalem create dissension in the harems. The twins incite native-born wives to feel as though Solomon favors his foreign brides, and the northern Israelite wives complain to their already hostile families of favoritism shown to Judean brides. Of course, I have no proof of the Daughters' crimes that would stand in court, and the only harem news the king receives comes from Ahishar's carefully fashioned reports."

Arielah's head swam at the horror of the life awaiting her. Shunem's well gossip was like a stroll in the meadow compared to a harem. Gathering her courage, she asked the question that frightened her most. "How many new foreign wives has he married?"

The two men exchanged a troubled glance.

"Twenty," Ima said, emerging from her place by the cooking stones.

Arielah's hand instinctively flew to her mouth, muffling a gasp.

"Our daughter needs to know all the facts in order to make her decision, my love." Jehosheba spoke gently but firmly to her husband. "And we must tell her of Jehovah's commands."

Abba reached up for Ima's hand, inviting her to sit with the three of them around their leather table mat. Arielah tried desperately to push aside the thought of Solomon's twenty new wives.

Abba captured her attention by holding her gaze. "In the days of Moses, Yahweh instructed the Israelites not to marry Canaanites in the land He had promised them."

Arielah knew this was true, but she'd always wondered . . . "So did King David sin when he married Absalom's ima Maacah, since she was the daughter of a Geshurite king?"

Again Abba and Benaiah looked to each other for support, and this time it was Benaiah who explained. "Yahweh explicitly forbade Israelites to marry women from the seven Canaanite nations, but then He made a distinction that Ammonite and Moabite women were not to be brought into Israel's assembly until ten generations had passed, and Edomite women after three generations."

Arielah furrowed her brow. "Are you saying God approves of Solomon's foreign marriages—as long as he takes only Ammonite, Moabite, and Edomite women?"

"I'm saying Solomon has been cautious to follow the letter of the law," Benaiah said. "Like his abba David, he has not married a woman from any of the seven Canaanite tribes, but the *spirit* of the law was to keep Israel's men from being led to worship foreign gods."

Arielah began shaking her head. "Solomon would not

worship foreign gods. His godly wisdom would keep him from it."

Abba reached for her hand to reassure her; his eyes kind but his tone dire. "King Solomon is a man, my lamb, with a tender heart. He marries foreign brides while he teaches them about Jehovah."

Relief fluttered but fled the moment he spoke again.

"But they also worship their foreign gods in the palace while they learn of Jehovah. The God-fearing women have reported it to their families in Judah and in northern Israel, and the whole nation is in turmoil."

"Oh, Abba. No." Turning to Benaiah, she asked, "Can't you convince him to stop this? For the peace of Israel, he must stop his wives' pagan worship."

The commander swallowed hard. "Ahishar has displaced me as the king's favored advisor, and—" His voice broke, and he looked away, clearing his throat.

Abba Jehoshaphat continued like a second runner with a courier's scroll. "Ahishar has convinced King Solomon that if my efforts as goodwill ambassador fail, Judah's military should use force to silence any rebellion from the unskilled northern districts."

"No." Arielah barely breathed the word. The man she'd dreamed of would never do these things. "Benaiah, have you reasoned with him? Does he condone military force?"

"A king answers to no one, my lady." Benaiah bowed his head. Silent.

Her heart broke at the demonstration. This good and godly man was showing her what his life had become. Cool indifference with a dear friend.

When he looked up, Benaiah's lashes were wet with tears. "In regard to military force, King Solomon has said he hopes my friendship with your abba doesn't impair my ability to lead Judah's troops if the time comes to quash northern rebels. I assured him it will not."

A chill ran down Arielah's spine. No wonder these two men appeared weary and worn. They were carrying the weight of a nation on their shoulders.

"Arielah." Ima's gentle voice penetrated the sorrow and drew their attention. "You have heard these reports. And we leave the decision to you. Can you commit to Solomon for the rest of your life and live in a harem amid the worship of foreign gods?" The room fell silent, and Ima reached for her hand. "We do not doubt your love for Solomon. We simply ask you to listen to God in this moment and count the cost."

Count the cost. Arielah pondered Ima's words, measured the concern on her elders' faces. She had considered difficulties in Jerusalem, but never foreign gods. What other unexpected struggles would she face? Could she meet them and overcome? Or would she fail her family, her nation, and her God? Closing her eyes, she prayed, *Jehovah, what would You have me do?*

"I've been thinking." Reu burst from the bedchamber, shattering the silence. "We mustn't let word get out that a Judean watchman did this to my face. Ahishar would love to fan the flames of hostility between—"

Arielah gasped at the purple bruising around Reu's eyes and nose. The sight of her young friend and the mention of Ahishar's conniving stirred Arielah's commitment. She received the timing as Jehovah's affirmation that she must keep the treaty bride agreement. She offered a silent prayer of thanks.

Igal emerged from their parents' chamber too, his expression more quizzical with every moment of silence that passed.

Reu glanced from one face to another, his cheeks aflame. "I'm sorry. I must have interrupted . . ."

"Just the opposite, Reu. Your words were Jehovah's whisper." At his puzzled glance, Arielah motioned for him and Igal to take their places around the leather table mat. "I see the cost of my decision written on Reu's face, but I believe the value of obedience far outweighs it. I will make myself ready to be King Solomon's bride. Then it's up to him if—" Arielah's throat tightened, choking off more words.

Abba stroked her cheek, and she covered his hand with her own. His tender smile confirmed Jehovah's gentle whisper and gave Arielah the sense of security she needed to speak of her uncertain future. Turning to the one who knew the king best, she asked, "Benaiah, what if Solomon has acquired enough wives? What if he breaks the treaty bride agreement and doesn't return for me?"

Compassion shone from the commander's eyes. "I'm not sure Solomon will ever acquire *enough* wives." Then, with a wry grin, he added, "Fortunately, I don't think our king has had a moment's peace since he left Shunem. Whatever you did or said in the meadow that afternoon has rendered my young friend incapable of rest. I haven't seen him content since he looked into your eyes."

Arielah could barely speak past the lump in her throat. "Well, I plan to bring him contentment . . . if he'll receive it."

His face lit with a smile, and Israel's commander did something she would never forget. He winked. As if they were sealing a silent partnership, she knew he would forever be her advocate in Jerusalem.

"I guess we leave in the morning," Abba said, slapping his knees.

Arielah glanced between the two men, confused. "What do you mean you'll leave in the morning? Why must you leave so soon? And were you considering *not* going, Abba?"

Compassion shadowed Benaiah's features while Abba explained. "When we spoke with King Solomon in Jerusalem, he encouraged me to spend a few days at one of the northern fortress cities and consider suspending the goodwill campaign. He questioned the risks versus benefits of reasoning with these 'stubborn northerners,' as he called them, for the remaining three moons of our tour."

"He's begun using Ahishar's term, 'stubborn northerners,' a little too freely, and it has stirred the already boiling pot," Benaiah clarified.

"That's why Benaiah is here," Abba added. "The commander and a detachment of Mighty Men will accompany my caravan for the remainder of our goodwill tour. We were supposed to stop and ponder the decision at Jezreel, but we were too close to home to wait there."

Arielah's heart nearly burst. Wrapping her arms around the commander's wide neck, she hugged him tightly. "Thank you, Benaiah. Not many men would care about a silly shepherd girl's desires and escort her abba home."

Benaiah patted her awkwardly with one large paw. "Nor do I care about a *silly* shepherd girl."

Releasing him, she tilted her head in question.

His eyes filled with tenderness. "I care about the king's most precious bride who waits in Shunem."

Arielah lifted his huge hand and studied his scars. Suddenly aware of the danger these men faced, she felt emotion tighten her throat. "What if the northern cities riot? Three new moons is a long time to fend off their anger, and what if Judah turns against Solomon and Benaiah isn't there to—" She stopped, glancing at Abba and Benaiah, realizing the foolishness of her warnings.

Abba chuckled. "It seems we are all called to offer our lives for Israel, my lamb. I recall a very wise young woman saying, 'Only Jehovah can protect me now.' And she was right." He reached for Jehosheba's hand, and Arielah noticed her ima's tears for the first time. They would all face the fear of the unknown together. "Whether it is three moons or thirty," he said, "whether a small band of guards or an army, ultimately it is Jehovah who will guide us all."

22

SONG OF SOLOMON 2:8–9, 15–17

*[Beloved] Listen! My lover! Look! Here he comes. . . .
Look! There he stands behind our wall, gazing through
the windows, peering through the lattice. . . .*

*[Lover] Catch for us the foxes, the little foxes that ruin
the vineyards, our vineyards that are in bloom.*

*[Beloved] My lover is mine and I am his; he browses
among the lilies. Until the day breaks and the shadows
flee, turn, my lover, and be like a gazelle or like a young
stag on the rugged hills.*

Reu had proven remarkably resilient, his timely exit from the bedchamber a precursor to an enjoyable meal with Jehoshaphat, Benaiah, and Igal. Arielah helped Ima clear the food and dishes while the men continued their amiable conversation. Igal apprised Abba of the flocks and vineyard, as well as the status of their servants and hired hands. Though his mind wasn't as sharp as Kemmuel's had been, his integrity soon won the respect and loyalty of Abba's household. He'd become an effective manager while Abba was away.

Stealing a glance over her shoulder, Arielah whispered her concern. "Will Reu's wounds heal completely, Ima?" The large cut between his eyes looked as if it might leave a scar.

"Yes, my lamb. His bruises will turn every color of spring foliage while healing—purple, blue, green, and yellow. But he should be rosy-cheeked before Solomon arrives to collect his bride during the wheat harvest." She traced the delicate skin beneath Arielah's eyes. "But these dark circles aren't welcome in any season. They say you need rest, my lamb." She gently nudged Arielah toward the private space behind the half wall of cooking stones. It had no door or lock like her parents' chamber, but it was Arielah's place.

She rolled onto her sleeping mat, exhausted. Feeling cocooned in her little sanctuary, Arielah began counting stars through her high window. The evening sky sparkled, ebony and crystal. *Dawn always comes too soon,* she thought as a yawn tugged at her jaws. Repositioning on the mat, she felt her eyelids grow heavier, her breathing slower. The sounds of the household faded in that respite between sleep and wakefulness.

Suddenly the pounding of horses' hooves jolted Arielah awake. She sat up with a start, clearing the cobwebs from her mind. *Am I dreaming?* No. The hoofbeats drew near. She placed a small stool beneath the window and peeked through the lattice. Since Jehoshaphat's home was built within the city wall, she could see one strong steed with a single rider racing across the valley. Few travelers ventured through the Judean wilderness at night, and even fewer risked the journey alone. A horse could travel from only two cities at that speed, Jezreel in the south or Megiddo in the west. This rider approached from the south—Jezreel.

Perhaps it's a royal courier. She thrilled at the thought. *Maybe he came all the way from Jerusalem, trading for fresh horses at the three chariot cities along the way.*

Standing on her low stool, she saw the horse and rider slow

their pace. Arielah's heart nearly jumped from her chest when she realized the stranger was approaching her window! She looked around to find a weapon. She could wake Abba, but if the rider was a friend, she would seem like a silly, frightened child. Wondering if Benaiah slept in their common room, she considered waking the commander but decided to assess the danger first. Gathering her courage, she peered out the window once more.

The clouds cleared, and the moonlight revealed a man now on foot—tall, broad-shouldered, with a steady gait. Holding his horse's reins in one hand, he brushed the wall with the other as if searching for something. Arielah watched him bend over and pick up an abandoned crate. He continued walking, gazing at the wall, and dropped the reins in order to point at the windows one at a time. He was counting!

His path led under an olive tree, and when he emerged, Arielah finally saw his face. "King Solomon!" she squealed in a whisper. Her excitement unsettled her footing, tipping the stool. She slid down the wall, landing on her backside with a thud. Oh, she mustn't wake the whole household! Squeezing her eyes shut, she thrilled quietly, "He has come for me! Across the mountains, bounding over the hills!"

She reset the stool and peeked through the lattice more boldly now. "Oh, look at him, so sure and determined!" She could hardly believe it. She had prayed he would come for her, and now he stood near her window, having crossed the very meadow that had hosted their midday calamity so long ago.

Arielah followed Solomon's every move until a sudden realization robbed her of breath. Why did the king of Israel come alone—at night—to claim his bride? *He's breaking the treaty by coming three moons early. Why would he put the nation at risk? And why didn't he at least bring a royal escort?* But every question died when the next thought broke her heart. *Perhaps he is ashamed to claim me—a simple shepherdess.* She stared down at her bruised arms and calloused knees.

Torn between joy and sorrow, she peered into the shadows. He was only moments from her window now. Arielah waited breathlessly, confusion and disappointment wrestling with joy and desire.

How will he learn of love if I don't teach him? The thought staggered her. She remembered the way Abba and Ima silently mouthed the words "I love you" when they thought no one was watching. Had King David said those words to any of his wives? Had he ever said them to Solomon?

As she tenderly touched her bruises and calluses, they became precious reminders of good times spent with Abba tending flocks or with Ima grinding grain. How many moments had Solomon enjoyed alone with his parents? A royal upbringing had almost certainly robbed him of simple, loving moments, and she was determined to teach him of love.

No matter what his motives for this midnight desert ride, he showed a willing heart. She grinned at the thought of Israel's king peering through her lattice like a bandit in the night. Offering a silent prayer, *Jehovah, give him patience to wait one more time*, she pulled open her lattice and leaned into the window.

Solomon had ridden from Jezreel as if the witch of Endor nipped at his heels. He'd left Jerusalem soon after Jehoshaphat's caravan departed, remaining far enough behind to maintain secrecy. Ahishar had been the first to suggest the plot to retrieve his treaty bride, and after some consideration, Solomon had seen the wisdom in it. *Why wait three new moons to claim a woman who's already mine by contract?* Northern aggression was escalating, and if Solomon didn't act quickly, he might never see Arielah again.

And that was unacceptable.

This girl had cast some sort of spell over him. She haunted his dreams—day and night—her face, her voice, her scent.

227

No matter how many wives he'd taken, none of them could fill the emptiness left by Arielah.

"So here we are," he whispered to the trusty horse that had carried him through Gilboa's dense forest. "You're about to witness something incredibly romantic or utterly foolish." The animal bounced its head as if agreeing, nearly pulling off Solomon's arm. Steadying the creature, he glanced back at the crest of Gilboa where he'd left four royal guards.

When his entire company had reached Jezreel earlier that day, Solomon had chosen four men to trust with his secret. He wasn't really breaking the northern treaty agreement. He was simply collecting his prize before the agreed-upon time. None of the other soldiers were aware of the king's purpose, and when he confided his plan to his four trusted guards, they thought him insane to risk a nation's rebellion to steal a shepherd girl.

But they'd never met Arielah.

Shoving aside some of the cactus hedge lining the city wall, he placed a dilapidated crate under the fourth window in Shunem's wall. If he hoped to regain the peace he'd felt with Arielah before the meadow disaster, he must win her heart tonight. Stepping up on the wobbly crate, he steadied his hand on the window ledge and leaned toward the window.

A face gazed back.

"Ahhh!" Startled, he nearly fell into the cactus bushes. Regaining his balance, he watched Arielah stifle a giggle, seeing the moonlight dance in her eyes. The familiar ache deepened in his chest. *What is this feeling inside me?* He needed to understand her power over him. Why did he want her—no, *need* her so? Reaching through the window, he grasped her hand. "Come with me, Arielah. Come now, tonight, to Jezreel. And in the morning we'll hurry back to Jerusalem and announce our wedding before anyone even realizes you're gone."

Her dove-gray eyes spoke a language he couldn't yet

understand. "What are you doing here, my king? Why now? Where is your escort?"

He wasn't prepared for a conversation. Shiphrah and Sherah said any woman would be captivated by a moonlight visit. *I should have realized, Arielah isn't any woman.* "My escort is waiting for us on the other side of the valley," he said, trying to remember the other questions she asked. But the sadness in her eyes silenced him.

"I have longed to hear from you, my king." He heard the implied reproach.

"I know I should have sent a message with Benaiah, but I'm here now." He didn't want to admit that he and Benaiah had spoken very few kind words since returning from Shunem. Their relationship had waned to polite exchanges and official business. Solomon's chest ached again.

"Solomon," she said, interrupting his thoughts. Her smile, her eyes embraced him, and he was captured by the sound of her voice. "I won't break the treaty agreement we've made to unify Israel," she whispered, "and I won't break my abba's heart by sneaking away in the middle of the night."

"What?" The incongruity of her warm expression and cold words seeped slowly into his understanding. Solomon stood motionless. He had considered the danger of the northern districts but never the real possibility of Arielah's refusal. Disbelief turned to anger, warming his neck and cheeks. "You *won't*?" he asked incredulously. "You accuse the king of Israel of breaking a treaty?" His voice rose like a spoiled child. *Remember your emptiness without her, the desolation of the past nine moons. The nameless wives. The empty stares.*

"Solomon, please speak to Abba when the day breaks and honor him with your request."

"My request? A king does not request!" he said.

She grew quiet but didn't recoil. He wanted to reach through that window, throw her over his shoulder, and ride

229

back to Jerusalem tonight. *But I must speak with wisdom.* He tried to calm himself, remembering that part of wisdom included using phrases that the Daughters of Jerusalem assured him would woo a shepherd girl's heart.

Gathering his patience, he spoke in even tones. "My request is that you come to Jerusalem, Arielah. The winter has passed. The rains are over and flowers are budding. Doves are cooing. My city is a grand blanket of color awaiting your arrival. The fig tree forms its early fruit; the blossoming vines spread their fragrance. Come with me to my golden city, beautiful one." He bounced his eyebrows, hoping his carefully worded shepherd's verse would win her heart.

She reached out to push a strand of hair off his forehead, her eyes searching every detail of his face. "Exquisite words, my king," she said, cupping his cheek in her hand. "But many challenges await me in Jerusalem, more vivid to me than the beauty you describe."

So she's afraid. His chest ached, a passion so deep he could barely breathe. "But, my dove, my beautiful one," he whispered, "your mountain haunts and rugged hills are much more dangerous than my well-guarded palace."

Her eyes welled with tears, and she caressed his cheek, the tenderness of her touch different from any woman he'd known. Suddenly his planned speech was a filthy rag—exposed by her untainted honesty.

Before he could say more, her face vanished from the window, and she was gone.

Panic choked him. "Arielah!" She couldn't leave him! "My dove," he whispered, "please come back! Tell me what you fear in Jerusalem, or what makes you feel secure here in the clefts of Mount Moreh." When she did not reappear, he pleaded, "Say something, beloved. I need to hear your sweet voice and see your lovely face."

An excruciating moment passed. Finally she returned. "May I ask you a question, my lord?"

Solomon's heart pounded. He didn't want to talk anymore. Her questions probed too deeply. But it seemed talking was the only way to be near her right now. "Ask it," he said, reaching up to grasp the hand she had laid on the sill.

"When Jehovah hid Moses in the cleft of the rock, he placed limits on their relationship, didn't he?"

Solomon nodded.

"Was it because He loved Moses or hated him," she asked cautiously, "that God placed limits on him, allowing the man to see only His back?" She waited in silence. He could see her trembling.

Solomon too began trembling when her intention became clear. "How dare you presume to instruct me on love?" His voice rose. He expected her to cower in submission. Instead, she lifted her chin and gazed into his soul with those eyes, those dove's eyes. "Oh!" he cried. "You will come to Jerusalem with me, woman, willingly or not!"

She stood in the moonlight, looking almost—well, regal. Tears flowed down her angelic face and dripped onto the window ledge, her voice so soft Solomon had to lean in to hear it. "Indeed, my love, I will go to Jerusalem as your bride, but not tonight. I cannot face what awaits me there without my abba's blessing before we leave."

Her words assaulted his heart. Softening it. Squeezing it. Shaping it. The ache in his chest was now unbearable.

Solomon felt his shoulders slump, utterly surrendered. "Honestly, Arielah, I don't understand why you're so frightened to go to Jerusalem." Seeing the pain in her eyes, he ventured another shepherd's verse to please her. "Catch for us the foxes that would ruin our vineyard that's in bloom."

An approving smile graced her features, and Solomon's heart soared. She lifted her hand to his cheek, and his hope was reborn. *Perhaps she will come with me yet.*

"I look forward to the day I become your bride in Jerusalem," she whispered. Spinning the gold betrothal ring on her hand, she added, "Even now, I am already yours and you are mine, but . . ."

"But what, beloved?"

Lifting tear-filled eyes, she whispered, "Foxes ruin our vineyard because you browse among the lilies in your garden. Your heart and hands are full of other flowers."

Her words settled on his heart like a bit and bridle. "You fear Jerusalem because of my other women?" He pushed away her hand. "I thought I made myself clear in the meadow!" He stepped off his shaky perch, kicking the crate.

"Please, my king, let me speak!"

"No!" He caught his horse's reins and started to mount, but where would he go?

"Wait," Arielah half sobbed, half whispered from her window.

Solomon stopped and retraced his steps toward her. "No, *you* will wait, treaty bride." His words were a threat, not a promise. "I am the king of Israel, and I will build our nation with alliances and trade agreements! Would you have me refuse those women, Arielah? What about their love? Their desires? You demand too much of me, woman, and I'll not come begging at your window again!" He turned and led his horse toward the northern gate.

"Please, Solomon, listen to me!" Arielah now leaned out the window, her voice still a strained whisper. "Come and talk to my abba in the light of day. Do the honorable thing, Solomon. When the day breaks and the shadows flee, show your strength of character like a noble stag on the rugged mountains."

"Enough!" he shouted. "Your high-sounding words are like a thistle flower—beautiful but painful to grasp. I'll not return in the morning, shepherdess! I may never return."

A sob escaped Arielah's throat as the distance between them grew. "Please, Solomon, return for me at dawn. Talk to my abba." Her words dwindled as he approached the northern gate.

Arielah turned, letting her back slide down the wall, and crumpled to the floor. She glanced up and saw her parents standing by the cooking stones, offering their quiet comfort. "How much did you hear?" she asked as fresh tears came.

"Enough," Ima said.

"Abba, what should I do?"

Jehoshaphat entered her little sanctuary and knelt, kissing her hand before he spoke. "I believe you've already done what you should do, my lamb." Gazing into her eyes, he studied her for a long moment. "Do you want me to go find him? Tell him that he can take you to Jerusalem now, despite the treaty agreement?"

Another wave of sobs robbed her of her voice. Both Abba and Ima held her until she could speak again. Wiping her face with the skirt of her tunic, she said, "No, Abba. Solomon's visit at my window seems utterly foolish, but I have to believe Jehovah's wisdom is at work."

She watched approval light Abba Jehoshaphat's features. Brushing her cheek, he said, "Love grows like a dance, my lamb. It is a series of steps, a string of decisions both you and Solomon will make. Sometimes, when Solomon withdraws, you must pursue him, while other times you must step back and let him return to you." His tears glistened in the moonlight. "Remember, a man's character is defined by more than a single decision, and love is made of more than a single step. Keep listening to Jehovah. He will set the tempo of your dance."

23

*[Beloved] All night long on my bed . . . I looked for him
but did not find him. I will get up now and . . . search
for the one my heart loves.*

Small stones and twigs crunched underfoot as Solomon
marched around Shunem's western wall. Arielah's faint
cries faded behind him.

"Guard at Shunem's gate," he shouted, not caring who he
awakened, "I am King Solomon. Let me in!" He approached
a dilapidated double-cedar northern gate. "I will stay in this
village tonight!" He pounded the rotting panels, nearly shaking them from rusty hinges.

Instead of the polite welcome he expected, a grousing voice
sounded from the other side. "If you're King Solomon, I'm
the queen mother! Bathsheba's my na—" The gate opened
slightly. "Ohhh, royal master!" said a gritty old man with
teeth the color of camel's hair. "How can I hhhelllp you?"
He blew wine-saturated breath into Solomon's face, shoving
the gate open wide and falling to his knees. "Please accept
my hhhummmblest-est apologies. I hhhaaad no idea—"

Solomon stomped past, in no mood to be assaulted by

a blithering watchman. "Where can I find lodging for the night?"

Beads of sweat made muddy rivers down the man's forehead. "I'm sure Prince Jehoshaphat would be happy to offer lodging, my lord." Confusion—or was it hostility?—furrowed his brow. "His home is by the southern gate."

"Never mind! I'll find my own lodging, old man!" Leaving the man sputtering apologies, Solomon traipsed into the city, fairly dragging his stallion behind him. He'd bed down in the marketplace if he had to, find an empty merchant's stall.

The horse jerked its head, nearly lifting Solomon off his feet. "What is it, old friend?" Looking more closely at the creature, he noticed the heavy lather around its mouth and riding blanket. "All right. To the well first. I think we could both use a little cooling off before we go any further."

Shunem was a dark and lonely place at night. Not at all as he'd remembered it on his betrothal visit. Tonight the dusty streets and small stone houses looked menacing, the silence deafening. Surely his tirade had awakened most of the village, but no one stirred. In the eerie silence, he followed a narrow path toward the well at the center of town. In the marketplace, he heard footsteps approaching from behind. He whirled about, pulled the dagger from his belt, and braced for an attack.

The old guard from the northern gate wobbled and waved. "There's lodging and *entertainment* in the southeastern wall of the city—if you're interested, my lord."

The man turned abruptly and kicked a stone, wineskin in hand. Solomon watched him disappear into the darkness. *How does a man fall to such depths?* He sneered at the absurdity of a king in the bed of a filthy village harlot. He'd rather sleep with the rats in the market. Had his plan worked, he'd be sleeping with Arielah by now!

The silence nearly swallowed him. Shadows hid countless demons waiting to snatch Israel from his grasp. Nothing was simple. Arielah had said she was simple, but the "simple" thing she required was simply impossible! How could he be faithful to only one wife when the very currency of national politics was women?

Continuing toward the well, Solomon confided in his horse. "You're a lucky beast. You can have as many mares as you like and no one thinks the lesser of you." He chuckled at his own cleverness and then realized he was talking aloud to a horse in the middle of the night, unguarded, in hostile northern Israel. "Yes, Solomon, you're clever all right," he said aloud, wishing he'd asked the old man for a wineskin of his own. The well water would have to suffice.

Filling the trough twice for his horse, he curried the animal's coat with the wooden comb and checked his legs and hooves. All the while, he spoke to the stallion as though the beast was his best friend. "What would it be like to be a common Shulammite, to care for a flock and work the soil? Perhaps then I could take Arielah as my only wife and give her the life she desires. But I am a king, and I have a responsibility to lead God's people, to build this nation into a kingdom. Why can't she understand that?"

A hand touched his right shoulder.

Solomon dropped the currycomb and grabbed his dagger again. He swung around, crouched at the ready as Benaiah had taught him.

Standing there was a dainty maiden, one of the most alluring women he'd ever encountered. A lavender veil draped her head. Glossy black hair hung in soft waves over her shoulders. She wore a sheer garment with a purple sash fitted at the waist, the moonlight behind her illuminating soft curves.

"My name is Marah," she said, staring back at him with hungry eyes. "Were you the man asking for lodging at the gate?"

Solomon stood like a child, unable to form a sentence.

Marah held his gaze, moved his dagger aside, and bent

down to retrieve his currycomb. "I'd like to help you stable your horse, my lord." She began brushing the horse's coat, one hand combing as the other followed, traveling over the stallion's neck, back, and sides. Her hands gliding, veils flowing, hair shining in the moon's light.

Solomon watched as if witnessing a dream. Before he realized it, she was leading his horse away from the well. "Wait!" he said, breathless. "Where are you going?"

She turned, cradling the horse's neck to her cheek. "I'm leading your horse to my barn," she said, her eyes inviting him to follow.

"Your barn?" Solomon tried not to sound condescending, but how could a village prostitute afford her own barn? "You own a barn?"

A soft chuckle. "I have many friends in Shunem and the surrounding villages, my king." Marah stepped toward him. "There are many influential men—wealthy men—who offer me gifts and provide for my needs. They appreciate my soft bed and warm arms, and they need a barn to stable their animals during their visits." She paused, lifted an eyebrow. "Much like you are in need of a bed and a stable tonight, King Solomon."

His cheeks burned. He felt as awkward as he had at his first wedding chamber yichud. "I'm sorry, but I don't need your . . . um . . . *services*." She began a low chuckle, and anger fueled his candor. "The king of Israel will not indulge in a common prostitute!"

With two quick steps, she pressed her body against his frame. "I'm happy to hear it, my king, because I'm in no way common." She lingered there, allowing her warm breath and alluring fragrance to do their work. "My bed is covered with colored linens from Egypt and perfumed with aloes, cinnamon, and myrrh. The men who enjoy my companionship pay well for my pleasures."

Solomon was awed by her candor, stirred by her brazenness.

"Your stallion will pay for tonight's lodging," she whispered. Before he could reply, she kissed him deeply.

His passion soared, every conscious thought lost to delight. "Marah." Her name rolled off his lips. His eyes remained closed after the lingering kiss. She tasted sweet, not bitter as her name implied or her profession might warrant.

Marah took his hand, coaxed him, still tempting. "Come, great king, let's drink deeply of love until morning."

Drink deeply of love until morning . . . The words stopped him. Arielah had begged him to return for her in the morning, to speak with Jehoshaphat. *If I partake of Marah's pleasure tonight, I can never return to Arielah's purity.*

Marah was sensitive to his hesitancy. "Am I unworthy because I'm not a prince's daughter?" When Solomon looked surprised at her perception, she grinned. "All of Israel knows you're betrothed to Jehoshaphat's precious Arielah, and I would guess you're here instead of in her arms because of her righteousness."

Solomon turned away, ashamed.

Marah's eyes found him, a sinister smile creasing her lips. She chased his gaze. He looked down. She found it. Away. She sought his eyes again and laughed each time their eyes met. A silly game, but Solomon finally smiled.

Her gaze lingered, and the sparkle in her eyes dimmed. "There's no need for shame, my king. I once ate at Jehoshaphat's table, shared childhood secrets with Arielah. But I could not follow their rules or meet their expectations, so I was judged by the city elders and cast aside. I have learned to survive on my own."

Solomon turned away, uncomfortable with the woman's self-disclosure.

Drawing his chin up with a henna-dyed fingernail, she lightened her tone. "Now I live by *my* rules, and the same elders who once judged me now seek my favor with spices, wine, and perfumes." Her voice became as sharp as a Hittite sword. "Tell me, King Solomon. Who is more wicked—those who created the harlot or the one who must live as the harlot?"

Silence lingered while darkness seeped into Solomon's soul.

Leaning close, Marah whispered, "Let me love you without rules, without a treaty, without a wedding."

Solomon received her kiss, felt her tears on his cheek. This woman was not a harlot—at least, not like any harlot he'd imagined. She had a heart and a soul that had been broken by unreasonable people making unbearable demands. The same people who expected him to act like a Shulammite husband though he was a king. He could never be the man Arielah longed for—the man she deserved.

Stroking Marah's hair, he held her close. Was she really so different than he? She offered pleasure to wealthy men. He offered marriage to wealthy nations.

"Lead me to your chamber," he said. "We will indeed feast on love until . . ." He paused, thinking of Arielah's words. "We'll feast on love until the day breaks and the shadows flee."

Marah's smile lit her countenance. She led him and his stallion down a narrow street where red veils glowed in lamp-lit windows. "Oh, a shepherd's verse. How lovely."

Arielah waited long into the night for Solomon's return, but she heard nothing after his angry shouts subsided. She yearned to rush into Shunem's streets and declare her love, agreeing to whatever he demanded of her. But she knew Solomon must choose to return. He must step toward her in the dance of love Abba described.

When she finally drifted to sleep, Arielah experienced the fitful sleep of a lovers' quarrel. She dreamed of searching for Solomon in Shunem's southeastern district, calling for him, but to no avail. In the fog of dreamland, she passed two guards, opened a red-veiled door, and found Solomon watching Marah. She was dancing.

Arielah bolted upright in her bed, cold and clammy, shivering in the predawn darkness. Why had she dreamed of Marah? They'd been like sisters after Marah was orphaned at five years old. Abishag's family had adopted the girl, but when Marah became promiscuous, Abishag's abba accused her before the city elders. She was convicted of immoral acts worthy of stoning, but Jehoshaphat showed mercy and spared her life.

Arielah still remembered Marah's white-hot rage. "You elders are hypocrites," she screamed. "Whose sons made me this way?" In her twisted heart, she vowed vengeance on the judges and their families.

Arielah couldn't stop shaking, couldn't erase the memory of her dream—Marah dancing before Solomon. *Surely the king of Israel would not visit a common harlot.* But her self-assurances faded as she considered Marah's hatred of Jehoshaphat's family.

And Solomon's fury would make him vulnerable to her adept manipulation.

Arielah rose from her mat, slipped on her woolen robe, and picked up her sandals, then tiptoed around Igal and Reu as they slept in the family's main room. Abba's words echoed in her mind. *Love grows like a dance . . . sometimes pursue . . . other times step back.* When she saw Marah dancing in her dream, she knew it was time to pursue Solomon.

She glanced at her parents' bedchamber and offered a silent prayer. *Jehovah, give me the courage to forgive Solomon—no matter where I find him.* She continued rehearsing Abba's words as she hurried out the door and into the courtyard. *A man's character is defined by more than a single decision.* The words terrified her but propelled her toward the southeastern side of the city.

The predawn glow threatened her anonymity on the rough side of town. Marah's home stood separate from the other harlots' hovels. The common prostitutes barely survived in the crumbling, tattered section of Shunem's southeastern wall.

They received Marah's castoffs, men a respectable harlot—if there was such a woman—would never entertain. Marah's customers arrived by appointment, while the other women paraded through the streets after dark and concluded their business by dawn. All of them redefined love with dark and dangerous meanings, but Marah was most dangerous of all. In her arms, love meant exploitation and ultimately power. Marah was the champion of her trade.

Cold morning air enlivened Arielah's senses. Dew covered every surface, causing dust from the streets to cake her sandals. An old straw mat shifted on the path, and a furry creature scurried into a hole. She shivered but continued her march. Turning the corner, Arielah saw the glimmer of lamplight in the windows. Her heart pounded wildly when she saw Marah's red veil garishly displayed on the door. It was the prostitute's signal to other suitors. Marah still had a customer though it was almost dawn.

The dream flashed in her mind: Marah dancing, shedding her veils as Solomon watched hungrily. What if it were true? What if Arielah found Solomon in Marah's arms?

Suddenly two rough hands seized her and shoved her against the stone wall. Her head snapped back and hit hard, causing her vision to blur. A panicked scream escaped before she could stifle the cry.

"King Solomon does not need more company." The words were a growl, seething between clenched teeth.

Arielah's vision cleared, and through the shadows, she saw two men. One of them recognized her at the same moment her disbelieving tears began to flow. "Benaiah?" she breathed.

"Arielah! Please forgive me. What in heaven's name are you doing here?" His eyes shifted to the other guard standing beside him. "Hezro, go back to guard the door."

The man saluted his commander, right hand to heart, and Arielah spoke the moment he stepped away. "Have you seen him? Is he really in there—with her?"

Benaiah squeezed the back of his neck, releasing a long sigh. "I'm sorry."

She couldn't stop the tears. Trying to distract herself from the moment, she asked, "Did you hear Solomon at my window last night?"

His eyes were kind, patient. "Actually, I left for Megiddo after you went to bed. Solomon's escort from Jezreel came to Shunem and questioned the old guard at the north gate. One of the watchmen rode to Megiddo to alert me, and I arrived to discover Solomon had been approached by a woman at the well."

As if announced by his high steward, Israel's king emerged from the red-veiled door, light from Marah's clay lamps illuminating his weary face. "Hezro," the king said, clapping the guard on his shoulder, "so you've found me. Did Benaiah send you?"

"Solomon?" Arielah's voice sounded strange in her ears, like someone else spoke his name. Benaiah placed a hand on her arm. His strength and protection gave her courage.

Solomon's head snapped toward her. He seemed dazed for a moment, and then sheer horror registered on his face. "Benaiah, how could you bring Arielah here?"

The captain's hand tensed on her arm. "She found you, my lord, with no help from me."

Solomon's head fell forward. Unbearable silence. Benaiah was the first to shatter it. "Hezro, come. We'll wait for the king at the southern gate." Squeezing Arielah's arm, he added, "I'll make sure the city gates remain closed until after dawn."

She closed her eyes and nodded her understanding. The commander had just ensured their privacy until daylight. No one on this side of town would disturb them. They were all tucked in their beds alone after a long, busy night.

Arielah waited until the two soldiers disappeared around the corner, and then she looked at the disheveled robes of her betrothed while he scratched at the dirt with his toe. She felt rage. Humiliation. Defeat. "Why did you choose *her*?" Arielah's voice sliced through the morning air.

He didn't look up. "Because you refused me."

Arielah ran at him, her hand raised, aching to slap him. He lifted his chin, waiting for the blow.

A man's character is defined by more than a single decision. Abba's words echoed in her mind.

She stopped less than a handbreadth from Solomon's face. He winced. She let her hand fall to her side.

He opened his eyes, and disappointment shadowed his expression. "Hit me, Arielah." Unshed tears filled his eyes. "Jehovah knows I deserve it—and more."

"Yes, Jehovah knows!" she cried, and then glanced at the homes around them. Lowering her voice, she said, "He alone knows why you would crush my pure love and polish a cheap substitute."

"Because your love is impossible!" he shouted in a whisper. "It's unattainable, and I don't understand it!" Grabbing her shoulders, he drew her close, their lips nearly touching. She felt the warmth of his breath in the cool morning air. "Leave me alone, Arielah." He pushed her away. "Just go. I'll make restitution to your abba somehow. I'll find a way to appease the northern districts."

"The northern districts?" She could barely speak past her pain. "This"—she pointed to Marah's door—"is not about the northern districts. This is about a decision you made to intentionally hurt me!" She watched a war of emotions on Solomon's face, and then she stared at the dusty path between them. How many steps would it take to bridge the gap his betrayal had created? Glancing up again, she saw that Solomon's head was bowed. "You talk of 'restitution' to my abba, but what about me, Solomon? What will you do to restore my trust?"

Before she could brace herself, he rushed at her again. He closed the distance between them, grabbed her shoulders, and shook her. "I can never atone for what I've done. Don't you understand? I understood that embracing last night's darkness disqualified me to ever hold your light." He released her and stepped back. "You can't forgive this, Arielah."

She looked down at their feet, the gap between them gone. *Love grows like a dance, a series of steps, a string of decisions*, Abba had said.

"I can choose to forgive you, Solomon, and I can even love you still." She paused at the wonder on his face. "If you will let me." Her mouth spoke the words before her heart felt the emotion. He had hurt her deeply. This was not the Solomon of her dreams. This man was real, flawed, not easy to love. But Abba was right. In order to build the love she longed for, both she and Solomon must take steps to live it out.

"How could you ever love me after what I've done?" Tears dripped into his curly black beard. "I slept with a harlot, Arielah."

His confession nearly caused her to retch. *Lord Jehovah*, she prayed, *he's right. How can I love him? Give me Your love for him*. Seeing self-loathing in Solomon's eyes, she knew he was repentant, but for how long? Was it an enduring sorrow or a fleeting regret? "You said you chose a harlot because I refused you. I'm telling you now," she said firmly, "I have *never* refused you, Solomon. I have simply asked you to wait, to set aside your fleeting passion and choose a love that considers another before yourself."

Arielah watched tears erupt from the deepest places in Solomon's soul. His shoulders shook, and he covered his face. "This love you speak of does not exist!" Arielah reached up to comfort him, but he looked startled and stopped weeping as if remembering a long-forgotten dream. "Abishag." He whispered the name into the morning air and then met Arielah's gaze. "I saw that kind of love when Abishag cared for my abba." Sadness replaced the wonder in his voice. "I will never be that kind, Arielah. It's simply not in me." His hands fell limp at his side, his stare vacant. His lifeless bearing was more terrifying than his sobs.

Placing her arms around his shoulders, she guided him away from Marah's door, thankful the woman hadn't intruded. Solomon followed her direction, and the two found another quiet street and settled onto a bench at the weaver's back door.

Solomon regained a measure of awareness but still refused to look at her. "I'm the king of Israel," he said. "But I'm not like Abba David, Arielah. He was a warrior. I'm a negotiator. He built Israel, the nation, by winning battles. I am building Israel, the kingdom, through wise covenants." He swallowed hard. "You were right when you said last night was about you, but you must also understand, it was a decision that will affect my kingdom." Pressing both fists into his eyes, he rested his elbows on his knees and released a deep sigh. "With what shreds of honor I have left, I will go to your abba, confess my wrong, and seek his guidance to keep peace in the north." Finally, lifting tear-filled eyes, he gazed longingly at Arielah. "I release you from the treaty bride agreement. Your love would starve to death in my harem."

Arielah's heart stopped, and a sob escaped. "No!" She could say no more, her throat too tight, her emotions too raw. "No!"

Solomon held her, rocked her. "Beloved, I cannot bear the thought of hurting you again."

"But it was your choice to bed Marah that hurt me!" She controlled her whispered shout, hoping no one heard—yet realizing that the whole town would hear the well gossip by midday.

He traced the line of a tear down her cheek. "It's not just Marah, Arielah. You told me in the meadow and again at your window. You want all of me, my singular devotion." Gathering her again into his arms, he whispered, "A king can make no such promise, beloved."

As if they were adrift on the stormy Sea of Gennesaret, she clung to him, tossed and torn by the reality of his harem. She'd spent so much time dreaming of Solomon, she'd given little thought to lying in his arms moments after he'd held another. Could she commit to this life? Loving this man and saving her nation—even if she never received the love she longed for in return?

The eastern sky was brightening. Their time was slipping away. Sitting up, she tilted his chin to meet her gaze.

A sob escaped his lips. "Please, beloved, don't make me look into your eyes. I can't bear the thought of saying good-bye to those beautiful eyes." He laid his head on her shoulder like a child.

"From the first moment these eyes saw you," she said, "I loved you. I signed our wedding agreement because of that love." Lifting his head with a gentle nudge, she met his gaze once more. "You signed the treaty agreement because it will unite Israel. My prayer is that you will someday choose to love me as I love you. However, if that day never comes, I will live in your harem knowing with deep certainty that I am loved by God—Jedidiah."

He gasped. "My name. No one has ever called me by that name."

The wonder in his eyes assaulted the wall around her broken heart. "I overheard you and Abba talking about the name Jehovah gave you at birth through the prophet Nathan. God loved you at birth, before you'd established any goodness or worth." She looked at his lips and imagined them kissing Marah. Her stomach turned, and she squeezed her eyes shut. *Lord Jehovah, help me. I cannot forgive him in my own strength.* "I don't know what lies you believed that convinced you to settle for darkness when you could have waited for light, but I know this . . . Jedidiah. God's love always forgives—even when our love fails."

She watched understanding dawn in his eyes. "I believed

I could never equal your love," he said, wonder seeping into his voice.

A sprig of hope budded in her soul. "You see, it is not my love you should envy or imitate, but the sacred love of Jehovah to which we should both aspire."

With the same hand that had caressed Marah, he lightly touched her cheek. "With all my heart," he whispered, "I want to know this love, Arielah." His expression had changed, humility and hope seeming to nudge aside pride and self-loathing.

But has your heart truly changed?

The rooster crowed, and the weaver chose that moment to fling open his door and shake out a rug. "Oh my!" he sputtered. "King Solomon! Forgive me . . . Arielah . . . what?"

Arielah wiped the tears from her cheeks and took Solomon's hand, coaxing him to his feet. "Shalom, Dodo. The king and I appreciate the use of your bench this fine morning!"

The weaver stood gawking as Arielah led Solomon down a narrow street to Shunem's southern gate. Benaiah stood beside several watchmen and nodded approvingly when the couple passed him on their way to Jehoshaphat's home.

Solomon slowed when he realized their destination. "You want me to talk with your abba now?" His steps came to a halt at the courtyard gate. "Arielah, wait. How do I begin? What do I say?"

"Abba heard some of our conversation at my window last night."

"Oh no!" Solomon buried his face in his hands, crimson instantly consuming his neck. "I might as well ride back to Jerusalem right now. He'll never agree to let you be my bride after what I said—"

Arielah placed a quieting hand on Solomon's warm cheek. "He gave me this charge: a man's character is defined by more than a single decision, and love is made of more than a single step."

Solomon's eyes softened at the redemptive hope.

Arielah reached for his hand, opened the gate, and started walking toward the house. "Now follow me into my parents' bedchamber, where we can talk privately." Though her heart was still heavy as a millstone, she nearly giggled at the shock on Solomon's face.

"I am not barging into Jehoshaphat's bedchamber at dawn!" Solomon's voice echoed in the morning stillness just as the cedar door swung open on leather hinges.

"Good morning, King Solomon." The prince of Shunem stood somberly at his front door.

Solomon glanced behind him, wishing Benaiah had accompanied him to meet Arielah's abba. She tugged on his hand, urging him into the family's main room. He nodded his greeting. "Good morning, Jehoshaphat. I, uh . . . I . . ."

"Would you like some warm goat's milk and figs?" Jehosheba sat near the cooking stones, her tone kind but not overly inviting.

Perhaps they're poisoned. "Thank you, no." Solomon offered a half smile and nod, quickly surveying the room. The hulking brother, Igal, and the palace courier, Reu, were seated by a leather table mat in the center of the room. In the dim firelight and rising dawn, he could barely make out their faces, but everyone seemed more sad than angry.

"Why don't you join me in the bedchamber, my king?" he heard Jehoshaphat saying.

Startled at the invitation, he cast a questioning glance at Arielah, who said, "I told you, it's the only private room in our home, my lord."

Jehoshaphat ushered both Solomon and Arielah into the small chamber. Stacked wool-stuffed mattresses lay in the corner with a bedside table and lion-skin rug completing the modest furnishings. The prince did not offer any polite chatter or formalities. "Solomon, my son, I'd like to hear what's on your heart this morning. How do you feel about what has happened between you and my daughter?"

Solomon's initial apprehension grew to panic. How could he begin to describe his tangled feelings about Arielah? The meadow? Living without her in Jerusalem? The desert ride from Jezreel? Last night in Marah's arms? He winced at that thought. "I'm not sure, uh . . ." *Oh, Jehovah, give me wisdom!*

And then he remembered Abishag.

"I witnessed a pure and abiding love in the palace," he said, watching their puzzled expressions. "I was confused, like you are, because it came from an unlikely couple. You see, Abishag loved my abba, and he loved her with a tenderness I'd never seen before." Reaching over to brush Arielah's cheek, he said to Jehoshaphat, "I want to love your daughter like that. Deeply. Completely." He dropped his hand and cleared his throat. "Jehovah has given me wisdom to rule His nation, but it seems He requires me to learn of love the hard way."

The hint of a smile appeared on Prince Jehoshaphat's face. "Lessons of love are the hardest to learn," he said, resting his hand on Solomon's shoulder. The brief reprieve was swallowed by duty. "My son, I believe it's best to honor our original treaty agreement and wait three more full moons before marrying Arielah in Jerusalem. The wilderness districts might interpret any deviation from your vow as cause for further distrust."

The king squeezed his eyes shut. *Wait.* It seemed he must always wait! "All right, Jehoshaphat. I will bow to your wisdom on this decision."

The man nodded and turned to his daughter. "Arielah, I'd like to speak with the king alone. Would you please wait outside?"

Quietly slipping from the room, Arielah closed the bedchamber door behind her. Though her heart still ached from

Solomon's betrayal, she had new reason to hope. He had seen—and recognized—a pure example of love in Abishag and King David. This also meant that Abishag had not been abused by the old king but had received his truest affection. Inspired by the thought, she stepped into the main room and heard an ugly sound.

The shrill, dark cackles of twin Judean maidens.

"So, little shepherdess," Shiphrah said, "the guards at the gate told us our king found pleasure in the arms of a veiled woman." Her eyes traveled to the closed bedroom door. "But I see you too have finally given in to his charms."

Sherah's laughter sent a chill up Arielah's spine. "It's all right, little goatherd. A few royal wives should wash him clean."

Igal and Reu stood, but it was Ima Jehosheba who rushed forward, her whole body trembling. "Get out of my house!" she cried, shooing them with a dirty rag. "You harlots of Jerusalem are not welcome in my home!"

Arielah was as shocked as Shiphrah and Sherah. Never before had her ima spoken with such venom or zeal. Building on Jehosheba's anger, she added, "Before you leave this house, Daughters of Jerusalem, I will remind you of the words I spoke the last time we met. I vow by the gazelles and does of Shunem's meadow that I will come to Solomon as a pure and holy bride, and our love will *only* be awakened and blessed after we are married in Jerusalem."

When Igal stalked toward them, the women cowered. But they regained their bluster when he reached for the door. "You will leave this house *now*," he said.

Smiling wickedly, they turned to go, each one caressing Igal's face on her way out. He spit on the ground behind them and turned to Arielah. "They are dangerous, little sister. You must be on your guard in Jerusalem. I have seen this kind of darkness before."

24

✤ Song of Solomon 3:6–7, 11 ✤

*[Beloved] Who is this coming up from the desert?
... Look! It is Solomon's carriage, escorted by sixty
warriors. ... Come out, you daughters of Zion, and
look at King Solomon wearing the crown, the crown
with which his mother crowned him on the day of his
wedding.*

Arielah wiped the perspiration from her forehead. Already the morning sun beat down as she filled her
water jar at the city well. *Will I still be in Abba's house for the
harvest of the vines?* Five new moons had passed since King
Solomon's night visit. When he and Abba talked privately,
Solomon had confessed his betrayal with Marah and vowed to
cultivate integrity in the days ahead, starting with the treaty
bride agreement. He had promised to return in the month of
Iyar before the wheat harvest was complete. The wheat had
been cut, bound, and ground—almost two full moons ago.
Solomon was late, and the northern districts were outraged.

"Perhaps today is the day your bridegroom comes." Dear
old Ruth patted Arielah's cheek, interrupting her brooding.
"Keep your eyes on the southern horizon."

"Thank you, Ruth. I'll keep watching." The dry season descended like a thick, dusty blanket. No festivals, no rain—and thus far, no Solomon.

"He's not a noble king like his abba, that one," Edna the matchmaker said, wagging her stubby finger. She sloshed some precious water into the dust. "If he hasn't come by now, humph." She batted the air with her hand as though waving away all Arielah's dreams in an instant.

"Edna!" Ruth's cloudy eyes flashed. The matchmaker snapped to attention. "If King Solomon told this beautiful girl he would come, he'll come!"

Edna lifted all of her chins and walked away.

"Now, Arielah," Ruth's gentle voice soothed like balm, "don't let that grouchy friend of mine ruin your day." She patted Arielah's hand and sent her to the vineyards with a smile and a full jar of water.

Today all hired hands in Jehoshaphat's household were needed to tend the vines. Arielah joined the other women digging trenches and depositing water from the well, while the men built and raised trellises, exposing the leaves and grapes to the life-giving rays of the sun. Remembering when Kemmuel had ordered her to lonely days of labor, Arielah rejoiced with this community of workers in their stone-walled vineyard on the town's southwest side.

Needing a break from digging, Arielah lifted the hoe above her head, twisting left and right to stretch her back and arms. Her stomach growled, though the sun was barely past midday. She hadn't eaten much during their meal, choosing instead to doze in the shade under a rocky outcropping. Each day passed so painfully slow: working, praying, watching, waiting. A little nap seemed to speed the time along. Fixing her eyes on the southern horizon, she thought to her bridegroom, *Will you betray your nation—and me—again?*

As if answering her silent question, the watchman in the

vineyard tower cried, "I see a great cloud of dust rising in the south!"

Arielah's heart leapt to her throat, and she dropped the handle of her hoe on a woman's foot. After offering a quick apology, she raced to the vineyard gate. "Is it him?" she asked Abba. Ima joined them, and all three stood in silence, watching the cloud grow to a great column of dust just beyond the crest of Gilboa.

"It's him! It's him!" Arielah twirled around. "What else but a royal procession would raise such a column of dust in the desert?" She grabbed her ima's hands and danced in circles. "He is perfumed with myrrh and incense made from all the spices of the merchants. I can smell his sweet aroma from here. It is my king!" Joyous tears ran down her cheeks as she released Ima's hands and hugged Abba fiercely. "He's coming for me!"

The workers in the vineyard joined the celebration, and soon all of Shunem waited outside Jehoshaphat's vineyard to witness Solomon's arrival. The majestic escort spilled over Gilboa's rim and raced across the valley, shaking the ground violently.

Arielah's delight gave way to awe. "Look, Abba!" she whispered in almost reverent wonder. "I see a wedding carriage, but look at the *army* he brought this time." She counted silently, quickly. "Sixty of Israel's fiercest warriors, arrayed as if going into battle." Now awe fell to dismay. "They've poisoned him again, haven't they? Ahishar has terrified him, and he fears his northern brothers." She read the disappointment on Abba's face. The last days of his goodwill tour had soothed significant hostility between Israel and her king, but the two-moon's postponement of his treaty marriage had reversed much of the progress.

"Has the king come to wed or to war?" Arielah heard one old woman whisper to her husband. The scene was indeed an odd mingling of battle and repose.

Jehoshaphat turned Arielah's chin with one finger. "Look at me and remember my words. Jehovah's love for Solomon—shown through you—is mightier than all those warriors and will conquer the deception that binds him."

Abba and daughter joined hearts and hands, watching the procession draw near. Arielah set aside her fears and let her heart soar at the immense power and grandeur of the parade before her.

Not far behind the military stampede jostled the glistening bridal carriage, bumping along on uneven terrain. The golden wheels of the carriage shone like the betrothal coach, but this one was even more splendid. Gold, silver, and precious stones ornamented every curve and corner, and the canopy flowed with fine linen curtains. Even its horses were draped with blue, scarlet, and purple cloth, and a door of latticed ivory graced the side of the carriage.

Her gentle giant Benaiah occupied the lead chariot with another man at his side. "Abba, look! Solomon is with Benaiah in the lead chariot! They're almost here!"

The king stood regally, wearing the royal attire of a bridegroom. His chariot stallions pounded Shunem's dusty soil, their muscles glistening with perspiration, white foam beneath the leather harnesses that guided them.

"Isn't he beautiful?" she said breathlessly.

Abba rolled his eyes and chuckled. "I'll assume you're talking about the king's stallion." Ima squeezed her hand and shared an excited squeal.

Two horsemen with trumpets sounded the king's arrival, and Ahishar skidded his horse to a halt, throwing dust and gravel on Arielah and her parents. "The king of Israel has come to claim his bride!" the steward crowed.

Jehoshaphat wiped the dust from his robe and whispered, "Welcome back to Shunem, you bellowing she-goat."

Arielah giggled, and the king's steward issued an imperious glance.

The powerful army slowed behind the lead chariot, reining their horses to a stop at Benaiah's hand signal. Ahishar made a grand gesture toward the fierce-looking soldiers. "The king's Mighty Men will address any objection to the treaty bride agreement."

Arielah's heart pounded to the rhythm of the horses' heavy breaths. No other sounds. No objections. Who would dare?

Noting the silence with a smug expression, the steward unfurled a scarlet rug, connecting the king's chariot to the spot where Arielah and her parents stood. Ahishar stepped onto the carpet and walked toward Arielah, bowed, and arched one eyebrow. "Daughter of Jehoshaphat." He made no attempt to hide his perusal. It was the first time he'd seen Arielah, and his sneer readily revealed his opinion. "Your bridegroom, King Solomon, approaches."

Benaiah dismounted the chariot and bowed to prompt Solomon's descent. The king didn't move. Though his head was held high, his eyes darted back and forth from his Mighty Men to the Shulammites.

Ahishar has utterly paralyzed him with fear, Arielah thought. She took a step forward and heard the crowd gasp. Bold? Yes. But she was compelled to push the bounds of decorum to show Solomon he need not fear the Shulammites. Walking a few more steps toward the chariot, she bowed and said, "Greetings, my king. You are welcome here."

Solomon's eyes found her, and then Benaiah leaned in close, whispering something. And the king smiled and nodded. Arielah felt heat rise to her cheeks—yet another moment she hoped no one could read her thoughts. Solomon's handsome features glistened in the summer heat, his stature as sleek and strong as the stallions that drew his chariot. His most attractive quality, however, was the adoration in his eyes. She hadn't imagined it in the meadow. No longer did he lurk behind walls at midnight. Today he had come boldly to receive her as his bride.

Solomon addressed Jehoshaphat, but his gaze remained

on Arielah. "Greetings, Prince Jehoshaphat!" he shouted over her head as he walked toward her. He reached for her hands, raised them to his lips—

"Oh no!" She jerked her hands away.

Solomon jolted and looked to Benaiah for protection. "What?" he said breathlessly, his Mighty Men reaching for their swords.

She covered her cheeks with her dirty hands, looking down at her sweaty tunic and bare feet. "I've been working in the vineyard!" She was horrified.

Solomon dissolved into laughter and signaled his protectors to stand down. Settling his adoring gaze on her again, he moved her hands and traced lines down her cheeks. "Yes, and you have these adorable streaks running down your cheeks." He paused. "Tears of joy, I hope?"

Arielah gasped and covered her cheeks again. "Oh my!"

Solomon stood amazed at the simple beauty of his treaty bride. He hadn't overlooked her mussed appearance; he cherished it. *Who else in all of Israel greets me in such a fashion?* He chuckled at the thought.

She began frantically trying to wipe away the smudges with her head covering. He reached for her hands, but she pulled away. He reached for them again, but she pulled away a second time. His third attempt was gentle yet persistent, and he raised an eyebrow that said, *I will have my way.* This time she offered them willingly, and he gathered her hands to his chest like a precious gift.

But her palms felt—blistered!

Turning her hands over, he saw the sores and calluses. Rage bubbled up instantly. "Has someone—"

She pressed a finger to his lips.

"No, Arielah! If someone has—" He would not abide more abuse to this woman.

"Shhh, my love," she said, a mixture of peace and joy in her eyes. "It is the season of vinedressing. Everyone in Shunem works the vines. It is our livelihood—the way of your northern brothers."

He glanced at the crowd and noted each face tanned by the sun, shining with sweat. He had arrived in the midst of their tending season and on a workday. What would a king know of such things? He had much to learn of his northern districts in order to become a respected and beloved king. But who better to teach him? He lifted Arielah's hands and gently kissed her palms. When their eyes met again, the dove-gray windows to her soul revealed a little mischief.

Turning over his hands, she kissed his palms in return. "Your bride has made herself ready for your coming," she declared with an impish grin.

The gathered crowd gasped, Shulammites and Judeans alike. Kissing his palms was daring, but declaring her shoddy appearance as preparation for a king—that was . . . well, utterly Arielah.

A wide smile stretched across his face. Yes, he loved her. Whatever love was. "And I have made my house ready for my new bride," he said with a playful bow. Indeed, her bridal chamber was perfumed and polished, its entry through his chambers, beyond his private garden. He leaned close to whisper. "You will love our garden."

Just then, Ahishar's voice shattered their world. "Come all to see King Solomon's wedding carriage."

Solomon rolled his eyes and whispered, "My high steward is always on a schedule."

Arielah's laughter rang sweeter than a harpist's tune.

"King Solomon made for himself this carriage," the steward continued. "He made it of wood from Lebanon." Ahishar blathered on, and the crowd offered the appropriate oohs and aahs.

"Arielah," Solomon said quietly, "I had my carpenter

bring the carriage cedar from Lebanon so your journey to Jerusalem would smell like your northern hills." Her face lit with pleasure, and his heart skipped a beat. She turned to hear the rest of Ahishar's description, but Solomon couldn't take his eyes off the beautiful, dusty treasure standing beside him.

"Its posts Solomon made of silver, its base of gold. Its seat was upholstered with purple, its interior lovingly inlaid by the Daughters of Jerusalem."

At the proclamation of their part in the carriage preparation, Shiphrah and Sherah flung open its door, and Arielah looked as if she'd been robbed of breath.

"Are you all right, beloved?" Solomon had wondered if she might be upset that the Daughters of Jerusalem rode in the carriage. But where else would they ride? In a chariot?

The color quickly returned to her cheeks; in fact, she looked quite flushed all of a sudden. She stepped forward and bowed as if she were Shunem's official representative. "Welcome, Daughters of Zion." Solomon caught a glimpse of a precocious grin on her face. "Come, admire with me my bridegroom, King Solomon, with the crown of Israel on his head." When she rose from her bow, she continued the greeting, though Shiphrah and Sherah looked as though they'd been greeted sufficiently. "Traveling merchants brought word that Queen Bathsheba would present her son with a wedding crown—a diadem that was once King David's. They said the queen mother is pleased to have a woman of field and flocks grace the palace halls, that she eagerly awaits his new bride's arrival." Pointing to the jeweled halo atop her groom's head, she asked, "Could this be the crown we've heard described?"

Shiphrah sneered and Sherah stomped, proving Arielah's goad was finely fashioned. Solomon laughed, and the Shulammites celebrated their maiden's verbal victory. The twins stepped toward the couple, but Arielah redirected Solomon.

"Perhaps we should greet my parents." The Daughters' hurried footsteps shuffled behind them.

Arielah let out a frustrated growl, and Solomon chuckled. Life in the palace would be more interesting than ever.

"Shiphrah and Sherah are harmless, beloved, and they really did help their abba Bethuel upholster our wedding carriage." The fire in Arielah's eyes told him he'd misspoken. Tapping the tip of her nose, he winked, and her expression softened. He'd spend the rest of his life trying to understand this shepherdess. So far, he'd been as successful as a pigeon reading a scroll.

Jehoshaphat tiptoed into his bedchamber, soundlessly closing the door behind him. As abba of the bride, he'd been honored to host the grand celebration of Solomon's arrival, but rejoicing with strangers was second choice to spending time with his wife and daughter.

"Good evening, my love," came the familiar quiet voice on the night air.

His heart still raced at the thought of Jehosheba, the wife of his youth. "I believe it's almost 'good morning,'" he said, rolling onto the stuffed mattress. She snuggled into her customary place on his left side, and he drew her closer, hugging her so tightly that surely she could hear his heart. "I'm sorry I woke you, but since you're awake . . . I have news."

As usual, his quiet wife had no response. He waited a few moments, enjoying their familiar game of secrets and pauses. After so many years of marriage, he knew she was as eager to hear the news as he was to tell it.

He'd start with the difficult report first. "King Solomon has married ten more brides in the five new moons since he returned to Jerusalem. He now has sixty wives." The stillness throbbed. Jehosheba's breathing grew rapid, and he knew she was upset. "So I asked our future son-in-law to honor

Arielah with Shunem's traditional Days of Marriage. Since he's never celebrated more than Judah's seven-day wedding feast, I didn't think he'd agree to give Arielah thirty days." Jehoshaphat stopped talking, testing his wife's patience, enjoying their game.

The quiet became unbearable. "And?" she finally asked, jabbing his ribs.

"Ouch!" he said, chuckling and rubbing the tender place on his side. "The king agreed."

She sat up, staring at him in the moonlight. "King Solomon has agreed to thirty days *and nights* of wedding festivities with one bride? With our Arielah?"

"Ha-ha!" Jehoshaphat grabbed his wife, pulling her back onto the mattress amid a shower of kisses. "Yes, my love. King Solomon will be utterly and completely enthralled with our Arielah for an entire moon's cycle." Halting their play, he studied the beauty in his arms. "He may already have sixty wives, but I still believe Arielah could be his last bride. The queen mother seems to favor this marriage too. She's invited us to use her home on Jerusalem's western ridge as our own, the place Solomon will come to collect his bride on their wedding day."

Jehosheba covered her mouth, partially stifling an uncharacteristic squeal. "Our Shulammite relatives will accompany the wedding processional to Queen Bathsheba's home? Does she know how many people we've invited?"

Jehoshaphat laughed out loud and hugged her into the bend of his arm. "I don't know if she realizes the tribe of Issachar will be camping on her doorstep, but Solomon assures me his ima is extremely gracious." He kissed her forehead and drew her close again. "I've also heard Queen Bathsheba's abba was a farmer before he became one of David's Mighty Men. Perhaps this farmer's daughter turned queen will have some sage advice for our Arielah about life in the palace." He paused a moment, letting the events of the night settle into his soul. In a voice barely above a whisper, he added, "Benaiah has vowed to protect our little lamb, Jehosheba."

"And who will protect Benaiah?" she whispered.

He swallowed the sudden lump in his throat. "Only God, my love. Only God."

25

[Lover] How beautiful you are, my darling! Oh, how beautiful! Your eyes behind your veil are doves.

Arielah's eyelids rose to half-mast, wakened from an enchanting dream. A mighty king, accompanied by chariots and soldiers, had swept into Shunem and whisked her away in a glimmering bridal coach. Rolling to her side, she sighed and listened to the sounds of Shunem at dawn. Her dream was real, and today she would begin her journey to Jerusalem.

"Blessings, my beautiful girl." Ima peeked over the cooking stone wall.

"Good morning." It was all she could say before emotions tightened her throat. She sat up quickly and then looked down, allowing a tear to fall on the worn cover of her lumpy sleeping mat. She would miss this small space that embodied a lifetime of warmth.

"Come, little lamb." Jehosheba's open arms beckoned her, and Arielah rushed into her embrace. "Today you will leave this house, but our love stays with you forever." Ima held her as fiercely as a man grasps a battle shield.

Arielah's eyes were squeezed so tightly shut she didn't see Abba approach.

"Good morning, my lamb." His voice loosened Jehosheba's embrace, and Arielah wiped her tears, determined to cry no more on this day of celebration. Though leaving her parents' home, she dare not mourn and risk Solomon's misunderstanding.

She rushed to offer him a greeting hug, but he stepped back and fended off her attempt. "What's this?" she playfully demanded, hands on her hips. "No hug for your daughter on this special day?"

"Come to the mountain with your abba, little shepherdess." Before she could question further, he turned and was gone.

Slipping on her shepherd's robe and tattered sandals, she fairly flew to catch up with him. Excitement stirred Shunem's morning air as most of the residents awoke with the dawn. Cooking fires blazed, and women lingered at the well, sharing whispers and sly glances as the judge and the king's bride hurried toward the rocky hills of Mount Moreh.

"Where are we going, Abba?" Arielah asked, jogging backward up the hills she knew so well.

"You'll see, my lamb. You must be patient." His voice rang with that playful tone she loved.

Arriving at a rocky crevice halfway up the mountainside, abba and daughter nestled close at a familiar cluster of smooth boulders. "We have exchanged our hearts many times at this spot, haven't we, Abba?" She gazed at his large, calloused hands. Memories overwhelmed her.

He nodded but rushed on with words he seemed to have prepared for this moment. "I long to shelter you from the dangers in Jerusalem, my little lion of God, but I'm giving you to Solomon because I know it is Jehovah's will."

"I know, Abba." Arielah reached over to comfort him, but Jehoshaphat hushed her with a gentle finger to her lips.

Reaching beneath his robe, he drew out a richly ornamented golden headband. Chains hung down from an intricate gold weave, dangling coins, precious gems, and pearls, and creating a veil that fell just past her cheeks. "This is part of your dowry, one of the gifts in your shiluhim. It is my gift to you, my lamb, from abba to daughter, separate from the mohar paid by Solomon."

Arielah couldn't speak. Her mouth seemed capable of only gulps and quick breaths. She'd heard of daughters receiving a shiluhim, but she'd never seen a headpiece like this.

He fit the golden band around her forehead. "This gift will provide for your future. If Solomon ever . . ." Jehoshaphat paused as if weighing heavy words. "If he ever puts you away, Arielah—if he divorces you—"

"Abba, no! The treaty agreement—"

"I know the agreement provides for your return home, but . . ." His eyes betrayed his breaking heart. "My lamb, I have seen what happens to Solomon in Jerusalem when he succumbs to Ahishar's deception and the demands of his kingdom. I believe your love will ultimately win the war, but this is protection for the battles you may have to fight along the way."

Arielah bowed her head, and the coins jingled. When she looked up, she saw Jehoshaphat's face through the shimmering gold gift. "Abba, I know difficult days await me in Jerusalem, but I also know Solomon's heart. He desires Jehovah's best for Israel." She pulled the gold chains aside and looked intently into his eyes. With as much mettle as she could gather, she added, "And we both know Solomon's love for me is what's best for Israel."

Jehoshaphat hugged her ferociously. "Benaiah will help you as much as he is able, my lamb, but it will be Jehovah's hand that guides and protects you."

"Well, that's a relief," she said, leaning back to meet his gaze. "Jehovah is much bigger than Benaiah!" Abba and daughter chuckled together, enjoying a lighthearted ending to the difficult truth.

Removing the headpiece, she tucked it in her robe. She didn't want anyone to glimpse her wedding attire before she appeared for the processional.

"There's another special gift waiting for you when we return home."

"Really?" Arielah jumped to her feet, kissed his cheek, and nearly ran down the hills. Abba's laughter followed her down the rocky path and through the family's courtyard gate. When they arrived at the house, Jehoshaphat was gasping for air. Amid laughter and deep breaths, abba and daughter found their quiet home suddenly crowded with people.

"Ima, we're back!" Arielah said, weaving through the frenzied main room. Women were busy packing clothes, jewelry, and supplies as part of Arielah's shiluhim—the largest gift any Shulammite bride had ever received from her parents.

Arielah looked back at Abba Jehoshaphat. "You said I had another special gift?" She giggled with delight. "All of this looks special to me!" Tossing a corner of sheer blue linen into the air, she coiled herself in it as it floated down.

"Greetings, my lady." Hannah, a willowy girl from their village, approached her and bowed.

A little dizzy from twirling, Arielah looked behind her to see who the girl was addressing as "my lady."

Abba laid a steadying hand on her shoulder. "Arielah, Hannah will accompany you to Jerusalem as your handmaid and will serve you all the days of her life. *She* is the special gift I mentioned."

The young girl bowed again and waited.

Arielah stood motionless. "Abba, no. I . . ." Feeling awkward and utterly embarrassed before the young girl she'd met only a few times at the well, she struggled to show appreciation but decline her abba's unusual gift. "Thank you, Abba, but I have no need of a maidservant."

"Arielah." His voice was firm but kind. "Though Hannah is only thirteen, she has willingly indentured herself to serve you for a lifetime. Her parents have no other income, and I paid them well for Hannah's service." Then, almost pleading, he said, "Arielah—she is Abishag's sister."

Arielah's heart leapt to her throat. She knew one of Abishag's sisters had cared for their sick ima and seldom left their home, but she hadn't realized the connection with this girl she'd seen sporadically at the well. "But, Abba, who will take care of Hannah's ima if she comes to Jerusalem with me?"

The girl's eyes welled with tears. "My little sister will care for Ima, and I promise I will serve you well. I will not search for my sister." Her gaze quickly returned to the floor, and Arielah saw her wringing her hands.

Jehoshaphat spoke tenderly. "I explained to Hannah and her parents that King Solomon mentioned the love he witnessed between King David and Abishag; however, he didn't offer more details on the girl's current standing. I've explained that no one in the palace has been forthcoming about Abishag because of the tension surrounding Prince Adonijah's execution."

The girl looked up then. "I understand that even though I will live with you in the palace, I still may never see my sister again as long as I live."

Arielah's heart squeezed at the truth of the girl's words. Abba Jehoshaphat had seen many of David's women while at the palace, but never Abishag.

"The decision is yours, Arielah." Jehoshaphat spoke quietly. "But remember, you will be a queen and will receive a maidservant when you arrive at the palace—most likely Judean."

Lord Jehovah! Fear robbed Arielah's breath. Of course she would be assigned a Judean maidservant. Why had she never considered it? She was marrying the king of Israel! What if the Daughters of Jerusalem chose her servant?

As she studied the girl before her, a wave of compassion washed away her reservations. "I will take Hannah as my maidservant—and we will try to find Abishag."

Hannah flew into Arielah's arms.

Jehoshaphat's smile was warm as he placed an encouraging hand on Hannah's shoulder. "I would imagine the new bride of the king could request such a thing."

"You attend my daughter, and let the king find Abishag," Jehosheba interrupted, returning everyone's attention to the upcoming procession. "All the women, into my chambers to prepare the bride!"

Arielah was ushered away, submitting to the skillful hands of loving friends and servants. Hannah worked tirelessly, weaving pearls and strands of gold through Arielah's long black hair. Others toiled at the bride's hands and feet, rubbing in salt and scented oils, removing calluses formed by years of labor. Gone were the days of woolen tunics and leather belts, testified to by Ima's fine stitching on the elegant linen processional robe.

When the last thread was cut and the final pearl woven in place, Arielah lifted her polished bronze mirror. Gasping, she whispered, "Oh, Ima, who is this?" Arielah the shepherdess had become a king's bride.

A shofar sounded. Solomon was descending from his mountainside camp.

Arielah's heart pounded as hurried hands polished and primped. Bracelets and brooches were slipped into place, and her head covering formed a sparkling veil. A deep breath. The bedchamber door opened. Arielah stepped into her new world.

Abba met her there, eyes filled with tears. "Your outward beauty is still no match for your magnificent heart." Leaning close, he whispered, "But it certainly comes close today."

"Don't make me cry, or this kohl they've smeared around my eyes will run like the Nile in Egypt!"

His laughter helped stem her tide of emotions.

The sound of music drew nearer as the king's musicians led his procession to the southern city gate. Arielah stepped into the afternoon sun, her hand resting lightly on Abba's forearm. She bowed to the sounds of gasps and applause.

"I've always said she's the prettiest girl in Shunem," Edna the matchmaker said. Dear old Ruth offered her familiar wink as Arielah passed. More sentimental tears threatened.

The sounds of flute and lyre grew louder, and tambourines beat out a joyful rhythm. The gentle thud of horses' hooves declared King Solomon's imminent arrival. The bride-to-be stood with her family, just as she had more than a year earlier, to meet her king. But today the royal procession seemed to move in slow motion. The fierce Mighty Men on their magnificent stallions drew their swords and extended them like a glistening canopy under which the bridal carriage passed. The other members of the king's caravan waited near the foothills, ready with their camels and donkeys laden with tents and food for the journey to Jerusalem.

"I don't see Solomon or the Daughters of Jerusalem." Arielah couldn't help the venom in her voice as she whispered to Abba.

The door of the bridal carriage opened, and Solomon's muscular form unfolded from its center. He seemed thoroughly focused on descending the steps and didn't see her immediately. When he did, a small gasp escaped his lips. It was the reaction she'd hoped for.

Emanating strength and elegance, Arielah possessed an ethereal grace. The delicate hand of a queen rested on Prince Jehoshaphat's arm. Instead of satisfaction, however, Solomon felt deeply saddened. His little shepherdess, with her rumpled tunic and dust-streaked face, was gone. The simple manner and earthy beauty he loved had been sacrificed to royal pageantry.

His feet moved without command, and the space between them evaporated. "Greetings, prince of Shunem. May I collect my bride?"

Barely waiting for Jehoshaphat's nod, Arielah offered not one hand but both.

He enfolded them and stood silently for a moment, their eyes locked in the dance they loved. "How beautiful you are, my darling!" He brushed aside some of the tinkling coins that hung from her headpiece. "Oh, how beautiful! Your eyes behind your veil are doves." He caressed her cheek with the back of his hand and let his fingers brush through her glossy black hair.

She smiled. "You speak a shepherd's verse, my love."

He stared at her as if she were a dream, and then realizing how utterly mesmerized he must appear, he cleared his throat. "Prince Jehoshaphat, may I escort your daughter to her carriage and have a moment alone with her?"

A flutter of unrest rippled over the crowd. Solomon realized he'd misspoken, but how?

Jehoshaphat placed a hand on his shoulder. "In Shunem, as in most of your northern districts, a bridegroom does not spend a moment alone with his bride until after they are wed."

Realizing he had an opportunity to learn and comply with a northern custom, Solomon lifted his head and smiled, careful to speak in a voice all could clearly hear. "I would like to speak with Arielah under the chaperonage of the Daughters of Jerusalem."

The crowd quieted, though his bride seemed to tense.

"Please, beloved, will you accompany me to the carriage?" A wave of dread washed over him as he realized she might say no. She had a habit of doing so. He chuckled to himself when she bowed and proceeded to the waiting coach.

When they arrived, Solomon thrust his hand inside. "Come, Shiphrah and Sherah, out you go!"

Arielah made a miserable attempt at hiding her pleasure.

The twins pouted as they exited to stand outside the open door.

Arielah accepted Solomon's offered hand and stepped into her wedding carriage. "This is like one of my mountain caves." She giggled, ducking her head and curling into the small space. "Except for the soft pillows, of course."

He could hardly step up, he was laughing so hard. "Only you, beloved, would compare this wedding coach to a cave!" Securing her hands in his, he knelt before her in the cramped floor space. Words rushed out in an excited whisper. "Shiphrah and Sherah were furious when you knew that Ima Bathsheba had given me Abba's crown as a wedding gift. They seem a bit concerned that I might favor you over the other wives." He winked and noted her delight. "But Ima has given me another gift—a gift she helped compose for you. But you cannot laugh."

"All right." She touched the corner of his mouth. "But I cannot keep from smiling in your presence."

He gathered courage from her affection and took a deep breath. "Your hair is like a flock of goats descending from Mount Gilead. Your teeth are like a flock of sheep just shorn, coming up from the washing. Each has its twin; not one of them is alone."

Arielah giggled and cupped both hands over her mouth.

"No laughing!" he said, his own voice a gentle chuckle. "Ima helped me with the words, but my shepherd's verses are not as eloquent as Abba David's."

Arielah grasped both his hands. "Your words are more precious to me than a thousand of King David's songs."

All sound suddenly stilled. *More precious than my abba's songs.* No one had ever valued any of Solomon's skills more than King David. Her dove-gray eyes affirmed the truth in her heart.

"Your lips are like a scarlet ribbon, and your mouth is lovely. Your temples behind your veil are like the halves of a pomegranate." Reaching up to cup her cheek, he gently traced his thumb from her chin to the hollow of her neck—and felt her shudder. "Your neck is like the tower of David, built with elegance; on it hang a thousand shields, all of them shields of warriors." With a sly grin, he held both of her hands again and offered a mischievous wink. "Your breasts are like two fawns, like twin fawns of a gazelle." Arielah's eyes widened and she let out a prim gasp, but before she could utter her righteous protest, he added, "Gazelles that browse among the lilies."

Arielah's smile turned to wonder. "That night, at the window on our wall, I told you foxes ruin our vineyard because you browse among the lilies." She threw her arms around his neck. "You were listening!"

Solomon slipped his arms around her narrow waist. The warmth of her body made him dizzy. She drew back, seeming to realize what her embrace did to him. Her cheeks flushed, and he continued his verse. "Until the day breaks and the shadows flee . . ."

"Yes, I said that too." She giggled.

"I will go to the mountain of myrrh and to the hill of incense," he said, closing his eyes, drawing in the scent of her. Recapturing her gaze, he kissed her hands. "All beautiful you are, my darling; there is no flaw in you."

Arielah clasped her hands over her heart, and tears threatened the kohl around her lovely eyes.

"The Shulammites are becoming restless, my king." Shiphrah's voice threw a bucket of well water on their intimate moment. "Please hurry, I'm frightened."

Solomon offered an apologetic smile. "We must go now, beloved." He watched Arielah's radiance dim. "Please," he said tenderly, "leave your cedars of Lebanon, my bride. Come to Jerusalem, to my palace of cedars. Descend the crest of Amana, from the top of Senir, the summit of Mount Hermon. Leave your lions' dens and the mountain haunts of the leopards. This is a dangerous place. Come to Jerusalem, where you will be safe in my arms."

Arielah wiped away a tear, a smudge of kohl where the dirt had been yesterday. "I will gladly come to Jerusalem with you, my love, but have no doubts—Jerusalem will never be a safe place for me."

Shock and confusion wrestled with the ache inside him. *Arielah is still afraid?* He sensed her fears stemmed from more than just his other wives. But what? He would speak with Benaiah about increasing her personal guards. Gathering her in his arms, he called for those best suited to the immediate task. "Shiphrah, Sherah!" Their faces appeared in the doorway. "Arielah needs your care during our three-day journey to Jerusalem."

Both women nodded as Solomon descended the step. "Jehoshaphat!" he shouted. "Have you announced to your kindred the plans we finalized during last night's feasting?" Surely this news would lift his bride's spirits.

Jehoshaphat stepped forward, bowed, and could barely speak through the wide grin on his face. "No, my lord. I wanted you to have the privilege of telling your northern kinsmen of the decision."

Nervous chatter rippled from the front rows of finely dressed wedding travelers to the back row of the shabbiest town beggars. Solomon's booming voice silenced them all. "We will escort Prince Jehoshaphat and his family to the queen mother's home on Jerusalem's western ridge, where she has invited my bride, Arielah, to reside until I come with my attendants to bring her into my house of cedars as my wife."

Thunderous applause rose from the crowd, but Solomon raised his hands to quiet them. "And in honor of my beautiful bride and our northern kinsmen, we will celebrate the traditional Shulammite Days of Marriage rather than the seven-day Judean wedding feast—"

The rest of Solomon's announcement was lost in the

celebration. Men sent up cheers, and women rained down tears. Everyone congratulated each other on the fine maiden they'd raised in their midst.

Solomon raised his voice above the din. "Prince Jehoshaphat, would you like to speak blessing over your daughter before we begin our journey?"

Jehoshaphat nodded and joined Solomon beside the carriage, waiting for the Shulammites to quiet once more. "Today our beloved Arielah leaves my household to create her own home with the man Jehovah has chosen for her." Turning to her, Jehoshaphat recited the familiar abba's blessing: "Listen, O daughter, consider and give ear: forget your people and your abba's house. Your groom is enthralled by your beauty; honor him, for he is your lord. May you increase to thousands upon thousands, and may your offspring possess the gates of their enemies." Reaching for her hand, he touched it to his forehead, a sign of respect to Solomon's new queen.

Another cheer from the crowd, and Solomon joined the rejoicing. Stepping forward to close the carriage door, he found Arielah crying black rivers of kohl, while the twin beauties sat like statues across from her. He retrieved the linen cloth tucked in his belt and offered it to his bride. "Beloved, as tradition dictates, I will not see you again until I take you as my bride to the palace." She smiled and nodded, and he closed the door.

She will soon be mine! He marched triumphantly to his chariot and grasped the sidewalls. "Away, Benaiah!" His commander's skillful hands slapped the reins on the stallions' backs.

Solomon scanned the happy Shulammites as the chariot pulled away, when suddenly he felt as if one of the horses had kicked him in the stomach. There, in the back of the crowd by a donkey laden with supplies, stood Marah. Her head was uncovered, dark curls falling past her waist. Red and purple veils adorned her robe, wrapped tightly to reveal her soft curves. *Lord Jehovah, she can't be among the wedding guests traveling to Jerusalem.*

"Turn around." Benaiah chuckled, his huge paw steadying Solomon in the lead chariot. "You're sure to fall if you keep looking behind you."

The king set his gaze on the road to Jerusalem and marveled at his commander's unwitting insight.

26

⚜ 2 SAMUEL 11:3 ⚜

David sent someone to find out about her. The man
said, "Isn't this Bathsheba, the daughter of Eliam?"

Arielah's empty stomach complained loudly. "I may
starve by the time Solomon and his attendants come
for me tonight." Jehosheba and Hannah exchanged patient
grins as they continued working fragrant oils into the bride's
hands and feet.

The three had slept comfortably in a large chamber in
Queen Bathsheba's home—Arielah and Jehosheba sharing a
wool-stuffed mattress and Hannah enjoying her own smaller
mattress in the servants' quarters behind an embroidered
tapestry. Jehoshaphat and Igal had traveled with Solomon's
escort to the palace. They would spend today as Solomon's
guests, engaged in games of skill and competition, singing
and celebrating.

"Arielah, my lamb," Ima said, working an especially stubborn callus from her heel, "yours is not the only stomach
begging for bread this morning. I'm sure Solomon anxiously
awaits tonight's yichud meal."

Arielah's heart nearly leapt from her chest at the mention

275

of yichud. *Do all brides fear that portion of the wedding when the bride and groom consummate their union—and the guests celebrate a few rooms away?* No matter how many generations had practiced the tradition, she couldn't bear the thought of the most intimate act of her life occurring while the wedding audience awaited. A shiver worked its way from her head to her toes.

"Are you cold, Arielah?" Ima's brow furrowed in concern. She shook her head and avoided Ima's eyes. Her stomach rumbled again, and Hannah giggled. "Oh! Will my stomach make more noise than the wedding procession?"

Ima chuckled at her frazzled daughter, and Arielah knew she sounded like a spoiled child. But the three-day journey in the wedding coach with Shiphrah and Sherah had completely unraveled her already frayed nerves. The wedding fast, begun last night at sundown, simply added to her ill temper.

A soft knock sounded on the heavy cedar door, and Hannah's eyes rounded like the polished bronze wall mirror. "Perhaps it's Queen Bathsheba!"

Jehosheba continued massaging her daughter's feet, and Arielah arched her eyebrows at her inexperienced maid.

"Oh, forgive me!" Hannah said, receiving the silent command. She set aside the aromatic oils and lunged toward the door.

"Gently, Hannah," Jehosheba coached. "Greet the queen mother with dignity and grace." The maid nodded, wide-eyed, eager to please.

"Shalom." A regal woman entered, slender and beautiful—but unadorned in her loveliness. No black kohl outlined her eyes, no lapis powder shone blue around them. "I am Bathsheba, and you, my dear, are as exquisite as my son described you." She walked toward Arielah with the grace of a willow tree, barely stirring the air as she moved.

"My lady." Arielah stood and started to bow but felt a steadying hand on her shoulder.

"You need not bow, little one. You are about to become a queen in Israel." And then the willow tree bowed to Arielah.

"Oh, no!" She reached out to touch Solomon's beautiful ima but hesitated. How could she touch the queen mother of Israel? "Please, my lady—why would you bow to me?"

"Because, little shepherdess"—she searched Arielah's soul as she spoke—"I honor the woman who has touched my son's heart. I recognize the gleam of love in his eyes when he speaks of you—the spark I once saw in his abba's eyes." Sadness shadowed her countenance.

Just then a loud knock resounded on the chamber door. All eyes turned once again to Hannah, and Arielah teased, "Well, we know it can't be servants with the noonday meal!"

Bathsheba's melodic laughter captured Arielah. She marveled at the similarities between the grand lady and her son. The queen mother's smile dimmed when Hannah opened the door.

"My lady," a large, hairy guard said, "King Solomon sent the Daughters of Jerusalem to help with the bride's preparations."

For the first time that morning, Arielah was glad she hadn't eaten. The food wouldn't have stayed in her stomach.

Bathsheba stepped forward. "Shiphrah and Sherah," she said as the twins pushed their way past the guard, "you may remain here in Arielah's chamber. The bride and her ima were about to follow me to the mikvah for her purification bath."

Arielah's cheeks flamed. She glanced at Ima Jehosheba and saw the same stricken countenance she felt. A groom's ima could demand attendance at his bride's purification bath—and an examination by a physician—if she questioned the bride's purity. "My queen," she said, bowing to avoid the woman's gaze, "have I given any cause for you to doubt—" She felt a slight touch lifting her chin and looked up into kind eyes.

"Fear not, little one."

Swallowing hard, Arielah nodded and held out her hand to Ima Jehosheba. The Daughters of Jerusalem whispered and grinned as Bathsheba followed the hairy guard from the room. Arielah and Jehosheba exited, and two more watchmen provided rear guard, all now following the queen mother through cedar hallways and down a long stone staircase. Silence reigned. Arielah didn't want to venture more questions and be humiliated in front of the three men.

Upon reaching the bottom step, the first guard opened a heavy cedar door and peered inside. Seemingly satisfied by its state, he stood at the door and bowed as Queen Bathsheba entered the mikvah chamber. Sounds of trickling water drew Arielah, reminding her of her mountain streams. She and Ima stepped past the guard into an enchanting place. Every sight, sound, and smell tickled her senses. But what humiliation lay ahead?

"Thank you, Oliab," Bathsheba said icily. "You and your men may close the door when you leave." The guard inclined his head in a partial bow and was gone before Arielah could ponder the tension the watchman seemed to rouse. "Do you like my mikvah?" the queen mother asked gently.

Arielah's heart was pounding in her ears. "It's beautiful, my lady."

They were alone. No physician. Lamps in wall niches provided a lovely glow, and incense burned in braziers around the bath.

"Water from two cisterns and a small drain in the bottom make this mikvah living water," the queen explained, "always flowing, never stagnant." Arielah nodded but said nothing, hoping an explanation was soon to come.

Bathsheba wandered over to a bench and removed her outer robe. Dressed in her tunic alone, she stepped into the mikvah. "Please join me," she said, wrapping her hair into a knot atop her head.

Ima Jehosheba cast a questioning glance at her daughter.

Arielah shrugged. In keeping with the rules of hospitality, both women followed their hostess and removed only their robes, keeping their tunics, and knotted their long hair.

Bathsheba spoke as her guests readied for their bath. "When I saw Oliab and his henchmen at your door with the Daughters of Jerusalem, I knew you needed a rescue. Rumors from the palace tell me the twin daughters of Bethuel are causing havoc in my son's harem." She glanced at Arielah with a wry smile. "We won't have many opportunities to speak privately when you become a queen. We must make the most of our day."

Relief washed over the new bride like this warm bath. She'd descended the mikvah steps and now stood shoulder deep in the most refreshing, buoyant moment of her life. A giggle erupted before she could contain it. Both hands clapped over her mouth as if wild horses had tried to escape. Bathsheba's melodic laughter opened the floodgates, and even Ima Jehosheba laughed out loud, enjoying the utter freedom of three women relaxing in a mikvah.

Bathsheba relaxed against the side, resting her head against a hollowed-out stone, eyes closed. "Would you like me to send my maid Dalit to help with your preparations when we finish our bath?"

"Well . . ." Arielah shared a grin with Jehosheba. "My ima and Hannah applied my cosmetics for the procession, but I think they'd be relieved to have a more experienced hand paint my eyes and lips for the wedding." Ima nodded her silent assent.

Bathsheba lifted her head and asked gently, "Arielah, do you *want* to wear kohl and lapis around your eyes and those awful crushed carmine beetles to redden your lips?"

The thought and taste of it had sickened Arielah when she'd endured it for the wedding procession. "No." A wide smile began. She liked this woman more with every breath.

"The moment you walk into Solomon's palace, you are a

queen. The only person you must please is your king. Does my son wish you to wear these paints on your lovely face?"

"I believe he likes me better with dust in my hair and dirt under my nails."

Bathsheba laughed with the confident elegance of a woman who had fought and won her position. "Well, that might not be a good idea. But let him appreciate your true beauty." Touching Arielah's cheek, she grew thoughtful. Eyes glistening, Bathsheba cupped her chin and turned her face right and left. "Your natural beauty will set you apart from the others. It will serve you well in the days to come."

"Thank you for encouraging her, my lady," Jehosheba said.

Bathsheba released Arielah's chin and nodded in Ima's direction. "Your daughter's beauty radiates from within, like her ima's."

Ima Jehosheba's cheeks pinked. "I'm relieved my girl has found a friend in Jerusalem."

Arielah was surprised by Jehosheba's words—not that they were inappropriate or misplaced, but because she rarely entered a conversation.

"Indeed, you both have a friend in Jerusalem," Bathsheba said. Seemingly intrigued by this gentle woman, she asked Ima, "Where is your family from, Jehosheba?"

"My abba was a farmer in Nain."

The queen's smile grew distant, her brows knit together. Turning to Arielah, she asked, "Have you decided which blessing you'll recite to Solomon after your yichud meal?"

The question seemed an odd turn in the conversation, and Arielah's heart skipped at the mention of yichud. "No," she said, trying to keep her voice from shaking. "I thought I might compose my own shepherd's verse."

Bathsheba nodded, quiet, thoughtful.

"What is it, my lady?" Arielah asked with a grin. "I don't presume to know your thoughts, but your expression says you have more on your mind."

The lady winked and began humming a tune, her voice echoing in the rock-walled chamber. The water amplified the sound, and recognition lit on Ima Jehosheba's face. She joined the queen, haltingly at first, a few notes and then more, as she seemed to remember the song from her past. Their voices united and blended in haunting harmony, and then suddenly, abruptly, the music stopped. The two women stared at each other in wonder.

"I'd almost forgotten it," Ima Jehosheba said, grasping Bathsheba's hand. "I sang it to Jehoshaphat as my gift of blessing."

"I sang it to David," Bathsheba whispered almost reverently, "though our marriage didn't begin with the traditional yichud." A single tear escaped her bottom lash.

The matriarchs were sharing some holy moment, and Arielah felt completely lost. "Would one of you please tell me what just happened?"

Laughter echoed off the water and rock. "I believe this moment has been etched in eternity," Bathsheba said, cupping Arielah's face between her hands.

"My eternity with your son began years ago, my queen." At Bathsheba's puzzled expression, Arielah added, "From my birth, I was chosen. From age seven, I knew for whom."

Brushing Arielah's cheeks with her thumbs, she said, "Perhaps Jehovah was at work even before your birth, little one. Your ima and I have a common heritage as farmers' daughters, and the tune of the blessing we just shared was known in our day among village brides. The song of blessing you sing to your husband at yichud becomes as intimate as the act itself. It becomes your love's sacred song." Glancing at Jehosheba, she kissed Arielah's nose and released her. "I'm going to get out of this bath before I shrivel like a raisin, but you and your ima stay in this peaceful place to prepare your yichud blessing for Solomon." As she moved toward the mikvah steps, the water swirled around her. Suddenly she stopped, turned. "Every bride fears yichud, Arielah. But if your whole heart is focused on blessing your husband, the rest of the night becomes your blessing as well."

For the first time, Arielah heard the word *yichud* and didn't feel as if her skin would spontaneously peel off. "Thank you," she whispered, but Queen Bathsheba had already climbed the mikvah steps, donned her robe, and walked toward the door. "Wait!" Arielah said. "Shouldn't Ima and I return to my chamber for preparations?"

The queen lifted a single eyebrow. "The Daughters of Jerusalem are in your chamber at the king's command. He has chosen them as your virgin attendants to 'help' with your preparations."

Arielah's heart ached. She hadn't considered attendants. Her only friends were a ram named Samson and a ewe called Edna.

"But while the twins are in my home," the queen continued, "they will obey my command or be escorted back to the palace. Take your time learning the blessing. Then return to your chamber when you're ready. I'll send my servant Dalit to assist your handmaid."

"Thank you, my lady," Arielah said.

The queen mother fell silent, her eyes welling with tears.

"What is it?" Arielah asked.

Seeming to struggle for control, she said, "I wish my David could have met you. He would have loved you—and been proud of our son." She covered her face, turned, and was gone.

27

❧ SONG OF SOLOMON 4:9–11 ❧

[Lover] You have stolen my heart, my sister, my bride. . . . How much more pleasing is your love than wine, and . . . the fragrance of your garments is like that of Lebanon.

Arielah sat stiffly on a cushioned stool in the middle of her preparation chamber, polished, perfumed, and painted. Henna dyed her hands and feet, and a touch of red ochre tinged her cheeks. Her hair cascaded down her back, strands of gold thread woven intermittently through black curls. Ima, Dalit, and Hannah had worked tirelessly to make her the most beautiful shepherdess ever offered to a king. She giggled at God's peculiar plan.

Shiphrah and Sherah glanced in her direction, each raising an eyebrow. *Remarkable precision*, she marveled. The Daughters of Jerusalem had been Solomon's couriers, bringing more gifts for his bride. Her robe, woven with golden threads, and the exquisitely embroidered veil were purchased from Persian merchants. Her earrings, her armbands, and the ring for her nose—every bauble and bangle—Arielah would have traded for her woolen robe, a quiet meadow, and Solomon's presence.

The shofar's blast sounded in the distance, and Igal ran to the window. A smile creased Arielah's lips. He and Abba had spent most of the day with Solomon at the palace. Her brother was still wide-eyed from all the excitement, but Abba had been pacing since he'd returned to await the processional.

"I see them!" Igal reported from the window.

Abba continued pacing. "Solomon said he and his attendants would leave the palace just after dark."

"Yes, you've mentioned that, my love." Jehosheba's voice was gentle.

"They'll take the path across the Valley of Cheesemakers and climb the western ridge," Abba explained. He'd also shared those details repeatedly, but he seemed calmed by the repetition. "The wedding guests and people of the city should have plenty of time to fill their lamps and light the way for the bride's procession to the palace." His pacing came to an abrupt halt. "Hannah, did you remember to fill our lamps with oil?"

"Yes, my l—"

"Jehoshaphat," Ima interrupted gently, "all is ready for the bridegroom. Go back to your pacing."

Abba grinned. "Where was I?" He began another stroll around Arielah's stool. "Ah yes. When Solomon knocks on the door, Hannah will—"

The shofar sounded again, this time very near Bathsheba's house.

"Abba, they're almost here!" Arielah squealed. "Come stand by me! Ima, you too!" Igal and Hannah drifted to the shadows while the Daughters of Jerusalem stood directly in front of the door.

Jehosheba reached into the fold of her robe and pulled out an assortment of small seeds, emptying them into Arielah's trembling hand. "Chew these, my lamb. They'll make your breath sweet."

Arielah felt as if her heart might pound from her chest as

she listened for the song Solomon had promised. The deep baritone voices of the bridegroom and his attendants joined the music of shofar, timbrel, lyre, and harp. As the sounds echoed into the hallways of Bathsheba's home, every voice faded but one. Arielah's heart sang when she heard the soloist accompanied by the lilting notes of a shepherd's flute:

> You have stolen my heart, my bride,
> with one glance of your eyes,
> with one jewel of your necklace.
> How delightful is your love, my bride!
> How much more pleasing is your love than wine,
> and the fragrance of your garments is like that of
> Lebanon.

Her groom had penned the most beautiful shepherd's verse she'd ever heard. He'd even mentioned her lovely northern cedars. "I have come to claim my bride!" came his bold declaration outside the door.

Hannah stood frozen at the door, looking like a doe caught in a field at midday.

"Open it!" Shiphrah commanded.

In an instant, the door swung open. King Solomon stood framed in his luxurious purple linen robe, an ivory and gold belt cinched at his waist. Arielah heard herself gasp, her eyes traveling the length of him. King David's jeweled crown glistened atop raven hair. Precious stones graced the gold collar resting on broad shoulders, and soft leather sandals laced up his calves. Benaiah stood beside him, the friend of the bridegroom, his expression as proud as if he'd been King David himself.

Sweeping the embroidered veil from Hannah's hands, Solomon strode across the room and knelt before his bride. Mischief danced in his eyes. "This is not Rachel!" he cried, and the company of onlookers roared in laughter. Ima had described this tradition of bedeken, when Solomon would cover Arielah's face and lead her blindly throughout their wedding festivities.

"This is Arielah, daughter of Jehoshaphat, whom I willingly choose as my wife." Solomon's voice was tender, his eyes dark pools of love, and Arielah drank deeply from them. She basked in the nearness of her groom with a wistful sadness at bedeken's beginnings. Every Hebrew bride, since the patriarch Jacob's unintended marriage to the wrong sister, had been inspected before her wedding veil was lowered.

"Veil the poor girl, and take her to the palace before she faints from hunger." A man's deep laughter reverberated in the chamber.

"This, beloved, is my brother Nathan," Solomon said, nodding at the bold young man taking a bow. "The others are my brothers, friends, and counselors. All of whom you can meet later. Benaiah, do your work!"

The mighty friend of the bridegroom stepped forward. "Make way for the couple's family to witness bedeken before we begin the processional to the palace."

The groom's attendants parted, allowing Queen Bathsheba to approach the bride and her parents. Igal stayed hidden behind the king's attendants, seemingly more comfortable in the shadows.

Arielah focused on her bridegroom, the last time she would see his face until yichud.

"You are stunning, beloved." He breathed the words, and she ached at the thought of being separated—even just by sight—for the evening. "But I now veil your outward beauty to vow my love of your inner splendor of wisdom and godly character." Lifting the veil above her, he placed its golden crown on her head and unfurled the heavily embroidered linen over her face. "From this moment forward, let my bride trust her bridegroom to lead her, to care for her, to protect her in the tradition of an Israelite husband."

Arielah could see nothing now except the under knots of needlework and sandaled feet below the veil. The absence of sight, however, heightened her other senses, making sounds and smells even more vibrant.

Then Solomon touched her hand, and fire raced through her.

Lifting her to her feet, he said, "Benaiah, please make your announcements." Others in the room began to clap and cheer. The sudden noise made her jump.

Solomon leaned close, pressing his body against her. His hand held the curve of her back, his lips whispered warmth on her ear. "You are mine," he said softly. "I can hold you. I can kiss you. I can love you as I've longed to love you since the moment we first met."

Arielah released the breath she hadn't realized she'd been holding. She couldn't think or move with him so near. *Oh, Lord Jehovah*, her heart cried, *how far is the palace?* Her breaths came in quick, short gasps.

"Come, beloved," he said, releasing her. "It is time." Circling her waist, he pulled her to his side, their hips moving together in step. "It's all right. I've got you." She took her first blind stride, hesitant, timid. Instinctively she reached out, making sure there was no obstacle. She felt him stop, press her arm to her side, and then completely enfold her in an embrace.

"Solomon!" she whispered. "What are you doing?" He'd trapped her arms, and she couldn't wiggle out of his grasp. "How many people are watching?" she asked, becoming frustrated. Benaiah's voice resounded in the distance, shouting instructions to the attendants about oil for their lamps and parched grain for the children along the way. "Solomon, let me go. People will see us!"

"Arielah." His arms tightened around her. He waited and she stilled.

"Yes?"

She heard his low chuckle, and her heart melted. His alluring whispers turned to amused questioning. "Do you need someone to lead you since you can't see through that veil?"

"Yes." Begrudging yet playful.

"Would you like that someone to be your husband?"

It was her turn to chuckle. "Yes."

His hands traveled over her back, traced a line down both arms, and then lifted her hands to his lips for a kiss. "Then give yourself to me, beloved. Trust me to lead you, care for you, and protect you as I have promised." He pushed the veil aside and nuzzled the bend of her neck. "And don't swat the air like a blind woman." His nuzzling turned to a quick tickle and laughter, but only for a moment before he held her in the safety of strong arms. "Let's try this again," he said, arranging the veil and squeezing her elbow. She nodded, relaxing into his touch.

She heard him pause and felt his body lift and sway, as if his tall stature were searching over the heads of a crowd. "Oh, there they are," he said. "Shiphrah, Sherah! Are the bride's attendants ready to lead the procession?" Benaiah too was shouting instructions, and soon the whole company was ready to proceed.

Arielah heard the approach of clicking sandals on the marble tiles. Two sets of dainty feet appeared below her veil, halting in front of Solomon. "Thank you, my king, for choosing us as your bride's attendants," one of the twins said. Arielah couldn't distinguish the voice.

"I'm sure you'll serve my bride well, Sherah." Solomon leaned close and whispered against Arielah's veiled ear, "I thought it important that Shiphrah and Sherah understood from the start how valuable you are to me. I want them to treat you differently than the other wives in the harem." He punctuated his explanation with a kiss, and she sensed triumph in his voice—as if he'd bestowed on her a great gift.

The processional instruments began to play, and Solomon

led her in their first step. Releasing herself into his care, she considered perhaps the true reason for a bride's veil—the underlying root of the bedeken tradition. *Perhaps every bride must hide a few tears.*

Ahishar waited at the palace entrance. Perched on the slope of Mount Moriah, he watched the lamps emerge from the belly of Mount Zion, Bathsheba's home and hiding place. The procession throbbed and swelled like a living thing, spectators joining the celebration along the northern path through the valley.

"Oliab!" Ahishar shouted, and in moments, the hairy, odorous watchman stood too close.

"Yes, my lord."

"Are you sure the Shulammite Marah knew the parade route?" He spoke softly, though all the guards on duty were loyal to the cause.

"Yes. I saw her this afternoon, and she'll make sure the bride knows she's among the celebrants."

"Good. Good."

The watchman chuckled. "I followed Jehoshaphat's fat messenger boy when I returned from meeting Marah. I taunted him but didn't touch him—as you commanded." Ahishar grinned, imagining young Reu adequately frightened. "I've also placed Sons of Judah as guards on the palace perimeter for the celebration," Oliab said. "But as I'm sure you've guessed, Commander Benaiah has ordered only Pelethite and Cherethite guards inside the palace for the wedding feast."

Raucous singing, music, and dancing interrupted the report. Ahishar waved the guard away just in time to see Benaiah leading the massive procession. The commander had refused Ahishar's suggestion to lead the parade through the City of David, convincing Solomon that too many important northern officials would be vulnerable to Judean zealots on the south side of the fortress. *And you were right, my mighty friend.* The safer path Benaiah chose simply challenged Ahishar to find new ways to intimidate the northern Israelites.

Benaiah arrived at Ahishar's side on the steps of the palace entrance. Raising his hands, he shouted, "Quiet, friends! Quiet!" Dancing and singing continued on the plot of land north of the palace, bells and drums outplaying trumpets and rams' horns. Wine had already raised everyone's spirits. "Please, I'd like to—"

Ahishar nudged aside the friend of the bridegroom. Pressing both hands to his stomach, he said, "Use the gut, Commander. The gut." Turning to the procession, his deep voice boomed. "King Solomon, royal attendants, honored guests, and loyal witnesses . . ." The crowded square stilled, and he cast a condescending glance at Benaiah. "Those of you having received an invitation and dressed in the proper attire may enter the palace for the wedding feast." A shout arose, and Ahishar quieted them with upraised hands. "For those of you waiting to seek justice from our king, he has declared a thirty-day wedding feast to honor the tradition of his northern bride." Ahishar nearly choked on the words but hurried on, hoping to hide his distaste. "Let the wedding supper begin!"

Another roar of the crowd and the procession swelled toward the door, but Benaiah grabbed Ahishar and roughly shoved him into the corner of the entryway. "I will remind you, steward"—he ground out the words, grasping Ahishar's robe in his fist—"that *I* am the friend of the bridegroom, and *I* will make the announcements at this wedding."

Ahishar met his gaze, unflinching. "When *you* can wield your words as well as you wield your sword, I will let you address the crowd."

Benaiah stepped back and shoved him away. "You will *let* me?" He laughed mirthlessly. "Well, let me remind you that for the next thirty days, you have no responsibilities in Solomon's palace."

The big man stormed away, leaving Ahishar shaking with rage. "I have many responsibilities, Commander," he mumbled, resolutely weaving through the procession entering the palace. He found the king's brother Nathan. "My lord, excuse me," he said, interrupting the prince's long pull on a wineskin.

A sideways glance and a sneer. "What is it, Ahishar?" Solomon's younger brother had never liked him.

"I'm concerned about Benaiah, my lord. He seems nervous in front of such a large and prestigious crowd." Pausing, he measured the prince's response, but who could tell if he was even listening? He was poking one of the other princes. "My lord, did you hear me?"

"Benaiah is fine, Ahishar. Next question."

With every shred of control he had left, Ahishar swallowed the bile in his throat. "I simply offer my voice, my lord, should it prove necessary that an expert address the crowd."

With a bow, he allowed the prince and the processional to proceed. Prowling the borders of the celebration, he watched Solomon and the shepherdess arrive in the courtyard. The royal couple ascended a dais and faced the audience, the king's attendants lining one side while the shepherdess, her family, and her attendants stood on the other. Ahishar noticed Prince Nathan lean over and whisper something to the king. *Could it be?* The steward held his breath while Solomon listened intently to his brother. After a short exchange, the king patted Nathan on the shoulder—and shook his head. No. The answer was no.

Benaiah stepped forward and began reading the treaty agreement aloud. The festive guests were utterly silent, seemingly enthralled by the romance of the moment. Ahishar fell silent as well—except for the outraged grinding of his teeth.

28

[Lover] You are a garden locked up, my sister, my bride; you are a spring enclosed, a sealed fountain. . . .

[Beloved] Let my lover come into his garden and taste its choice fruits.

[Lover] I have come into my garden, my sister, my bride.

Solomon studied every detail of his bride's petite form while Benaiah continued reading their betrothal agreement.

"I will betroth you to me forever. I will betroth you in righteousness and justice, in love and compassion. I will betroth you in faithfulness . . ."

Solomon listened to the words and pondered the depth of their meaning. He loved Arielah today immeasurably more than he had when he signed that scroll more than a year ago. *Is it possible to love her more a year from now?* The thought intrigued him, challenged him, delighted him.

"These are the words of the agreement," Benaiah's voice boomed, "as it was signed in Shunem on the eighth day of

Iyar. I, Benaiah ben Jehoiada, commander of Israel's hosts, testify as friend of the bridegroom to its authenticity." Turning to Solomon, he bowed and offered up the scroll.

Receiving it, the king handed it to Jehoshaphat. "Arielah is my wife, and I am her husband from this day forward."

The men bowed to each other as the scroll was exchanged, and a whoop of celebration nearly rattled the shields hanging on the courtyard walls. Jehoshaphat embraced Solomon in an abba's hug and then gave the scroll to Arielah as her lifelong treasure. Benaiah raised his hands for quiet, but the guests would not be stilled. Solomon recognized his friend's distress, and knowing Benaiah's aversion to public speaking, he thought it a good time to employ Nathan's suggestion.

"Ahishar!" Solomon shouted, scanning the courtyard for his high steward. He spotted the man racing toward the dais. Patting Benaiah's shoulder, Solomon chuckled and said, "Don't worry, old friend, help is on the way." It was at that moment that he actually saw Benaiah's face—his stricken countenance, a shroud of pain. "Benai—"

"Yes, my lord?" Ahishar appeared, cheerful and eager.

Solomon had no intention of replacing Benaiah as friend of the bridegroom. He could read the accusation on his commander's face. "Ahishar, I'd like you to quiet the crowd whenever Benaiah has an announcement to make as friend of the bridegroom."

Benaiah's eyes squeezed shut; his scar throbbed.

"My commander remains the host of these wedding festivities. I simply ask that you act as *his* high steward for the wedding, similar to the way you serve me at court."

"I think that's a splendid idea, my lord!" Ahishar's enthusiasm would undoubtedly be a pebble in Benaiah's sandal for the next thirty days.

Turning to his friend and commander, Solomon extended his hand and spoke quietly while Ahishar silenced the guests. "I meant no disrespect, Benaiah."

The man's expression softened, his giant paw grasping Solomon's wrist.

"Now, make sure you move through the blessings and riddles quickly so my bride and I can enjoy our yichud." The king winked and received a welcome smile from his friend.

Arielah fought panic, watching her feet and the mosaic tiles in the hallway where Solomon was leading her.

"Just a little longer, beloved." His voice was laced with concern. "I'll take the veil off as soon as we enter my chamber."

She couldn't stop shaking. How did any bride survive a wedding day? The frightening mikvah had turned into a joy, but the Daughters' dark presence during preparations had clouded Arielah's happy day. Solomon's nearness during bedeken had nearly driven her mad with desire, but then to be blindly led among tittering maidens as they giggled and danced for a king's pleasure—well, the already soaring summer temperatures made Arielah's hot temper even more stifling under the veil.

But it was the child with the cloth that had frightened her.

Clutching the small red square of fabric, she lifted her hands beneath her veil and inspected the stitching again. Marah's needlework. She and Arielah had sewn the same designs as girls a hundred times. Tears rolled down her cheeks. How could Marah be in Jerusalem? How dare she rejoice with the crowd at her wedding?

They halted, and Arielah saw the sandals of two large guards, warriors' sandals laced to the knee. "Thank you, Ima," Solomon was saying to Bathsheba.

She felt Jehoshaphat's hands grasp her shoulders and draw her close to kiss her veiled forehead. "Abba," she whispered, holding out her hand, revealing the traitor's cloth.

"Where did you get this?" He fairly shook her.

"Shhh!" she said, certain Shiphrah and Sherah were

watching and listening. "A little boy placed it in my hand during the processional. I thought he was giving me a gift like some of the other children, but when I saw what it was, I . . ."

Abba pulled her into a ferocious embrace and spoke in a strained whisper. "I'm so sorry, my lamb. Today is to be a day of rejoicing." He swayed with her slightly—soothing, infusing her with peace. "Do not let your enemy triumph by robbing you of this moment. You have waited to become Solomon's bride all your life, and you are about to experience God's greatest gift." Pausing, he squeezed her once more and then added, "Remember, my precious girl, yichud is your gift to each other. Let no one spoil it with distractions."

His words soaked through the veil, penetrated her soul. When he released her, she took his hand and pressed Marah's cloth into his palm. "I won't need this, Abba. You can burn it." No one could see the slight smile on her face, but it didn't matter. Jehovah was lifting her spirit.

Arielah felt another embrace, the scent of saffron. "Remember the blessing, my lamb." Ima's tone was light, reassuring. Arielah was thankful she hadn't heard the ugly truth of Marah's presence.

A kiss on her cheek, and she heard Bathsheba's voice. "I count you as my first daughter."

Arielah's breath caught, and tears welled in her eyes. Yes, this was a joyous day.

"Now, if you'll excuse us," Solomon said, cradling her elbow, "my bride and I will say good night and good-bye. Please make our guests feel welcome while we enjoy our seven days of yichud. And, Benaiah . . ." He paused. Arielah felt a slight jolt as if he'd grasped his friend's shoulder. "When we rejoin you for the remaining Days of Marriage celebration, you'd better plan some contests I can win. I need to impress my bride, you know."

"You've always been good at puzzles, my king." The commander's voice held as much pride as any loving abba.

"We look forward to welcoming your bride to the harem."

Arielah's heart skipped a beat. That giddy voice ground her nerves like a stone grinds wheat.

The other Daughter of Jerusalem added her wicked taunt. "Your yichud meal awaits, young lovers! Eat and drink your fill!"

"Thank you, friends." Nudging Arielah forward, Solomon added, "Benaiah, please wait here. I'll have Hannah deliver the purity cloth for you to display to our guests."

Arielah's heart leapt to her throat. The shaking returned.

Solomon must have sensed her distress and gently encircled her waist. Leaning close as he'd done during bedeken, he whispered, "Forget about everything else, beloved. Think only of my love for you."

No distractions. Different words but the same advice as Abba had given. *Thank you, Jehovah, for wise men in my life.* She leaned into her husband's guidance, hearing the clicking of retreating sandals behind her.

Solomon led her forward and then stood before her. She held her breath. He lifted her veil.

Finally! The air had never smelled so sweet or felt so refreshing. And when she saw her surroundings . . . "Ohhh!" she said, twirling in a circle, trying to take in the splendor. "Is this the bridal chamber?"

Solomon chuckled softly. "No, beloved. This is my meeting room, part of my private chambers."

She ran to the giant table, felt the smooth finish of its surface. Then to the couches, the tapestries—she even knelt down to inspect the rugs.

"What do you think?" he asked, clearly amused.

"I think we could fit half of Shunem in here!" she said, delighted.

"Would you like to see our garden?"

"We have a garden?" she squealed.

Arielah rushed in the general direction of Solomon's

pointed finger and discovered a veritable Eden. Standing in silent wonder, she examined the beauty and aroma of Solomon's spring-fed plants and trees. An almond tree stood central in the garden with a lovers' bench tucked beneath it. "I smell dill and cinnamon, and those are the most beautiful mandrakes and henna blossoms I've ever seen."

He snuggled in behind her, and she turned to wrap her arms around his neck. "Thank you, my love."

Solomon lifted her into his arms. "Now, let's explore our bridal chamber." He bounced his eyebrows and spun her in a full circle of delight. Solomon pushed open a door just beyond the last rosebush, and the aroma of their union meal overpowered the flowers.

"Oh, Solomon," Arielah whispered, "I've never seen such beauty." Breathless at the ambiance of paradise, she and her groom fell silent. A riotous blend of flower petals covered the floor, and rose petals decorated the white sheet on their bed. Lamplight and braziers cast an ethereal glow through the multicolored sashes draped through golden rings on the bedposts.

Hannah waited in the corner.

"How did you do all this?" Arielah wriggled out of her groom's arms and rushed to embrace her maid.

"Well, I . . . uh . . ." the girl stammered, awkwardly patting her mistress's back.

Arielah released her. "You have served us beyond my imagination. Thank you."

A timid smile curved her lips. "Your abba's aide, Reu, spent most of the evening helping me." She smiled up at Arielah, a twinkle of romance lighting her eyes. "He offered to acquaint me with the palace too, but then his ima Elisheba arrived and put a stop to that." Her face clouded slightly, but she bowed to address Solomon. "I beg your pardon, my king, but Elisheba, your palace cook, was rather offended when I insisted on making your yichud meal according to our Shulammite recipes. She made me promise to confess that the lentil stew is all my doing and she had no part in it." Hannah peered at Arielah from beneath a furrowed brow, and the new bride bit back a giggle.

Solomon chuckled outright. "I'm sure your lentil stew will be quite tasty, Hannah." Clearing his throat, he motioned to the small adjoining chamber in the corner.

"Oh!" The young maid's eyes registered understanding, and Arielah felt her cheeks flame. "Mistress, I'll retire to my room now, but I've tied these bells on a string so you can ring them during your days of yichud when you need nourishment." Holding out a strand of five gold bells, the maid cast a final shy glance at Solomon.

"Thank you, Hannah." The king nodded. "I believe we have all we need for the moment."

She bowed, turned, and left the chamber before Arielah could even say good-bye.

Arielah giggled. "I think my maid was afraid of being a nuisance."

"I think your maid was very perceptive." He slipped one arm around her waist and drew her close. "Are you hungry?" he asked, leaning over her, crushing her to his chest. He brushed her cheek with his beard, inhaled the perfume at the curve of her neck.

She felt light-headed, closed her eyes, let her head fall backward. "I . . ." She couldn't think. What had he asked her?

Before she could speak again, he covered her mouth with his—just for a moment. A full but gentle kiss. "I said, are you hungry?"

The kiss left her breathless. "Yes. Hungry, yes, but I want the blessing." He raised an eyebrow, and she realized her mistake. "I mean, I want to sing my blessing for you."

He smiled, looking pleased. Taking her hand, he led her to the bed. He drew back the beautifully draped sashes and cleared away the scattered rose petals. He sat down and patted a place beside him on the soft woolen mattress.

Arielah paused. Instead of sitting down as he expected, she knelt and touched his hand to her forehead—obeisance to her lord. Then she began the song Ima had taught her with the tune Bathsheba had sung in the mikvah.

My heart is stirred by a noble theme
as I recite my verses for the king;
my tongue is the pen of a skillful writer.
You are the most excellent of men,
and your lips have been anointed with grace,
since God has blessed you forever.
Gird your sword upon your side, O mighty one;
clothe yourself with splendor and majesty.
In your majesty ride forth victoriously
in behalf of truth, humility, and righteousness;
let your right hand display awesome deeds.
Let your sharp arrows pierce the hearts of the king's
enemies;
let the nations fall beneath your feet.
Your throne, O God, will last for ever and ever;
a scepter of justice will be the scepter of Your
kingdom.
You love righteousness and hate wickedness;
therefore God, your God, has set you above your
companions
by anointing you with the oil of joy.
All your robes are fragrant with myrrh and aloes and
cassia;
from palaces adorned with ivory
the music of the strings makes you glad.
Your sons will take the place of your fathers;
you will make them princes throughout the land.
I will perpetuate your memory through all generations;
therefore the nations will praise you for ever and
ever.

Arielah finished the song as Ima and Bathsheba had ended it. Precisely. Abruptly. She waited for his response.

Silence.

The chamber was full of shadows cast by lamplight, so she couldn't see his expression. But he said nothing. Did nothing. She had offered him her blessing, but she feared that somehow she'd offended him. Rising from her knees, she stepped over to take her place on the bed, and the shadow cleared from his face.

She saw his tears.

Jaw flexing, he was fighting for control. "Beloved, I've never heard anything so beautiful in my life." He buried his face in her neck and sobbed. Then in one fluid motion, she was in his arms, and he covered her like a blanket. His kiss was gentle, his love the culmination of every breath she'd ever taken. He caressed her cheek, searched her eyes. "Did you write the song, or is it a northern tune?" His eyes held an awed delight she'd never seen. "I've never heard it before."

Brushing his hair from his forehead, she engraved his expression on her heart. She would remember this moment forever. "It is our sacred song, my love." She began her story of the mikvah and their imas' shared tune. They laughed in wonder at Jehovah's dominion.

His eyes danced. "I've been working on another shepherd's verse for you." Tracing his finger down her neck, her shoulder, her arm, he leaned over her. "You are a garden locked up, my bride, a spring enclosed, a sealed fountain. You are a bountiful orchard of pomegranates with choice fruits, with henna . . ." He kissed one finger. "With nard . . ." Kissed another fingertip. "Saffron." A kiss. "Calamus." A kiss. "And cinnamon."

Each kiss sent fire racing through her.

"With every kind of incense tree, with myrrh and aloes and all the finest spices. You are a garden fountain, a well of flowing water streaming down from Lebanon." He turned her hand over and began a string of kisses at her palm, working up her arm. "I long to be washed by your fountain."

Without pause, she said, "Awake, north wind, and come, south wind! Blow on my garden, and let its fragrance fill your heart. You've given me your garden, Solomon. Now I give you mine. Come and taste its choice fruits."

Tenderly, joyfully, they shared the firstfruits of the marriage bed.

Arielah lay beside Solomon, gazing at the ceiling of their bridal chamber in the afterglow of dawn's ecstasy. Solomon's voice was a gentle whisper. "I have enjoyed my garden, my bride. I have gathered my myrrh with my spice. I have eaten my honeycomb and my honey. I have drunk my wine and my milk. You, beloved, have quenched every desire of my heart."

Tears formed, but she had determined not to cry. "Our seven days of yichud are over, my love. We must return to our wedding guests, but part of lasting love is creating yichud within our daily lives."

Solomon placed a finger at the corner of her eye, tracing a path for the escape of her tear. He'd become sensitive to her slightest change in emotion. "Let's just stay here. Our guests won't miss us."

She gathered his hand, kissed his palm. "We must join the musicians and dancers in entertaining our guests, but we can return to yichud every night." She sounded so brave, but her heart was breaking. Fear threatened to rob her of breath. Would she have to leave the bridal chamber after their thirty days of marriage were over? Would he assign her a place among the other wives in his harem?

"I have never known a love like this," Solomon said, looking more like a boy than a king. His tousled hair and short linen tunic showed his comfort in her presence. "Never have I trusted anyone so completely, Arielah. You have great power, my wife—power to break my heart if you so desire."

"My only desire is Jehovah's best for you." Cautiously but determinedly, she ventured the truth once more. "I still desire your whole heart, and I'll never settle for less."

To her surprise—and delight—he didn't refuse. But neither did he commit. Instead, he seemed lost in thought, his eyes distant. Arielah snuggled into his chest to enjoy their last few moments alone before rejoining their guests.

"Arielah," he said, rolling over, coiling the linen sheets around them. He paused, lying on his back, and she looked down into his clear, content gaze. All worry, all burdens of his kingdom seemed far away. "For the first time in my life," he said, "I understand how a man can be thoroughly satis-fied by one woman. We will share this chamber from this day forward, Arielah. I need not 'browse among the lilies' any longer. You will be my only flower."

Speechless, she searched his expression for some sign of mischief. If he was teasing, she would torture him slowly and let Benaiah help her! "You're certain?" she asked, joyful tears dripping down on his cheeks.

"I've never been more certain of anything—except perhaps Jehovah's wisdom," he said.

She buried her head in his chest. "I love you. I love you," she whispered.

He kissed her deeply and then held her face gently. "And I love you." His eyes answered any lingering doubts his kiss left behind. "Now, let's hurry and greet our guests so we can return to this chamber tonight!"

She giggled and slid off the mattress, then donned the linen robe Hannah had provided for her first walk to her private preparation chamber in the harem. Though she dreaded the experience, the promise of forever soothed the sting.

Solomon took her hand, and they emerged from their pro-tective cocoon of yichud. A few steps into the king's garden, and already Arielah's joy wrestled with fear. He had promised her the desire of her heart—but was his commitment strong enough to withstand the weight of responsibility and Ahishar's deception? *Lord Jehovah, only You can protect both of us now.*

The sounds of celebration swelled. Stepping into Solomon's private suites, they were greeted by Benaiah's warm smile and the calculated grins of the Daughters of Jerusalem. Both women bowed.

"Shalom, Shiphrah and Sherah!" Solomon said, a little more joyfully than Arielah would have liked. He seemed to genuinely esteem them, trust them, and she dreaded the battles ahead.

"Shalom, dear king," Shiphrah answered, stepping between the bride and groom. "Arielah's beauty treatments begin today," she shouted, whisking Arielah away. "We've already sent word for her little maid to join us in the harem. Sherah and I will make sure your bride returns to the festivities in gowns and jewels befitting a queen."

Solomon's chamber well behind them, Sherah spoke quietly as the three climbed a secluded stairway. "One of your guests left a message before returning to her new home in the City of David." Exchanging a wicked grin with her sister, she said, "I've forgotten her name, but she said she was a childhood friend from Shunem."

"Oh, I think her name was Marah," Shiphrah said.

The twins laughed all the way to the harem, but Arielah refused to be baited. She would fix her thoughts on yichud and take comfort in Hannah's faithful service.

PART 3

29

Solomon brought Pharaoh's daughter up from the City
of David to the palace he had built for her.

Every day for eight full cycles of the moon, the Daughters of Jerusalem had escorted Arielah to the harem, and every night Solomon had remained faithful to his promise. No more browsing in the lilies for Israel's king. Their love had grown during evening meals and garden strolls. Occasionally they chatted about a court ruling or foreign policy, but most often they simply enjoyed the comfort of each other's presence.

"Perhaps your maid should use the honey treatment on your cheeks," Shiphrah said, wrinkling her nose. She seemed especially surly this morning. "I think I still see some damage from those awful freckles and peeling you suffered from your brothers' abuse." Sherah sniggered as she always did, and their march continued up the southeast stairs to Solomon's second-story harem.

"I don't see any freckles or scars, my lady," Hannah whispered. "Why don't you tell the king how they treat you?"

Arielah covered her mouth, keeping her voice low. "We

need not burden the king with the bawling of twin Judean heifers." She crossed her eyes and twisted her face.

Hannah giggled, eliciting a scowl from Shiphrah and Sherah. The moment Arielah made the childish gesture, she regretted her pettiness. Arielah had become like Hannah's older sister when they were told to cease their questions about Abishag. Arielah took the role seriously and chided herself for reacting to wicked words with a spiteful act.

Arriving at the marble-arched harem entrance, Shiphrah addressed the Judean guards on the right. "Would one of you send word that we need to speak with Oliab?"

The rough-looking watchmen leered at the twins, and one ventured an answer. "Yes, my lady. Is there anything else we can help you with?" Sherah stepped forward, motioning for the guard to lean down to hear her whisper. He did so, and his eyes sparked. "Yes, my lady."

Shiphrah and Sherah walked through the gate, the watchmen's eyes on them. Sekhet's Nubian soldiers, on the left side of the entrance, never moved, blinked—or even seemed to breathe.

Arielah and Hannah followed, entering a different world—the world of women. Since men were strictly forbidden in the harem, these walls possessed a unique feminine evil. Few rules applied. No one escaped unharmed. Each of the wives had a personal couch, some separated only by a curtain, others within private walled chambers. Arielah kept her head bowed, avoiding any provocation.

"Ima, it's the goat queen!" a little voice shouted. "Nahaha! Nahaha!" Solomon's firstborn son, Rehoboam, was only three years old, but his ima Naamah had taught him to make goat sounds when Arielah arrived for her daily anointing.

No wonder King David built a private home for Ima Bathsheba. The queen mother, like Arielah, had been singled out for ridicule among the harem, and her private home had been her salvation. She'd visited Arielah a few times since the wedding feast; however, as she'd predicted, the Daughters' control of the harem made her visits almost impossible.

"Here she comes," one of the Edomite wives shouted. "Let's all bow to the queen of goats."

Arielah received the ridicule from other queens, but poor Hannah endured a double portion. Queens *and* their maids heaped insults on the quiet Shulammite behind her mistress. The daily processional never changed: the Daughters of Jerusalem, followed by Arielah and then Hannah. Like prisoners marched to their execution.

"Oh!" Hannah cried out, and Arielah turned in time to see a small pillowed image of Molech bounce off her maid's head.

Fire rose in Arielah's cheeks. "Who threw this?" she shouted, pointing at the doll, and the whole assembly roared with laughter. Even the ox-headed image of a man seemed to mock her from where it lay on the floor.

The harem was clearly segregated, each cluster defined by its gods. Those loyal to Molech had little patience for Chemosh followers, and those devoted to Asherah were scantily clad in sheer veils and little else. Solomon's native wives—both northern and Judean—had grown accustomed to the foreign wives' gods and were now simply angry that their son of David spent too much time with Jehoshaphat's daughter. Despising Arielah seemed the only subject on which all wives could agree.

"Would you like to know what he whispered in my ear, little goatherd?" The sultry Moabitess taunted her with intimate details of past encounters with the king. Though Solomon had been faithful to Arielah alone since their wedding, she still ached at the thought of these women in her husband's arms. Tears stung her eyes.

"What's the matter, little shepherdess?" Sherah asked as they entered the stark chamber set aside for Arielah's daily cleansing. "Are the other wives unkind to Jehoshaphat's daughter?" She bit her bottom lip in a mocking pout.

Shiphrah pressed Arielah's shoulders down, forcing her onto a waiting bench. "Why don't we call for a scribe who can send a message to your abba, explaining that Judeans are simply unbearable? Jehoshaphat can rally northern farmers and field hands to war." Her eyes became slits. "They'll need to gather their best fish nets and winnowing forks for the battle." The Daughters giggled with delight as Hannah poured perfumed oils into a bowl to begin the treatments.

Arielah stiffened her spine and her resolve. "The only message I will send to my abba is the joyous report when King Solomon finally discovers Ahishar's scheme and executes *all* the Judeans plotting against our nation." She heard Hannah gasp but didn't temper her threats. "Someday Benaiah will gain the proof he needs to expose the Sons of Judah."

A slow, wry smile crept across Shiphrah's face. "Now, now, little shepherdess," she said, exchanging a knowing grin with her twin, "keep your voice down. Someone might hear your threats and do you harm."

Solomon waited in his private meeting chamber, summoned from the crowded throne hall like a naughty child at the whim of an angry ima. Hearing the clicking of sandals on the tiles outside his door, he glared at Ahishar. "This had better be important, steward! I can't believe you've canceled the rest of today's petitioners to deal with this . . . this . . ."

"Now, my lord," Ahishar soothed before his guests arrived, "remember our alliance . . ."

The cedar double doors opened, and Queen Sekhet marched in, followed by her entourage of priestesses and Nubian guards. In the almost two years since he'd married Pharaoh's daughter, he'd spoken with her three times, lain with her twice. She was cold, calculating, and the most terrifying woman he'd ever met.

"I demand my own palace," she said without preface, her

orange lion-mane wig emphasizing the dark sheen of her Egyptian skin.

"We've just started stonecutting and preparations for the temple," Solomon said, trying to be reasonable. "We haven't even laid a foundation for Jehovah's palace, and you want me to stop and build you one instead?" She didn't flinch, not a single eyelash quivered. "I'm not going to delay King David's lifelong dream to bow to the silly demands of Pharaoh's daughter!" His temper was rising, but he couldn't help himself. Her indifference was infuriating. "And furthermore, why would I build a palace for *one* of my sixty queens?" He stepped closer, attempting to gain some advantage over this robust woman who almost matched his height—and probably his strength.

She straightened her back, lifted her chin, and took a step toward him, matching his posture.

He was awed by her composure. She was magnificent, and Solomon found himself suddenly more intrigued than annoyed. A grin worked at the corner of his mouth. *You are daunting!* He examined her high cheekbones and fathomless black eyes. Was that amusement he glimpsed?

Speaking before a smile dared break her icy calm, she said, "You will build a palace for one queen because you have only one Egyptian among your herd of bellowing cows."

He laughed aloud, and her defenses showed serious cracks. But as he let his laughter dwindle, he saw her expression change again. "You show your Shulammite wife too much favor," she said. "She has stayed too long in your bridal chamber." The hint of her merriment vanished as quickly as it had come, and a shadow of sadness crept over her chiseled features. "I will have the respect a daughter of Pharaoh deserves." She lifted her chin again, and any vulnerability was lost to the impenetrable walls of Sekhet, the powerful one.

Studying her, Solomon considered this exotic, fascinating woman. What was her life like in the harem? Her Nubian

311

protectors were banned from the harem and could stand only at the entrance. She had her priestesses to attend her, but the Daughters of Jerusalem had reported Sekhet spoke with no other women. She hadn't conceived a child in the two times they'd been together—as was the case with many of his queens. His silent contemplations must have roused her further.

"You must at least fulfill your responsibility to give me an heir!" she said, tears like diamonds suddenly falling down her dark cheeks. He didn't even have time to explain before her words became almost desperate. "I will be the disgrace of Egypt if I do not produce an heir. Pharaoh Psusennes sends couriers to inquire of my success, and each time I must report my failure."

He tried to hold her, but she pushed him away. He couldn't bear watching her weep alone. Overpowering her in a firm embrace, he saw her Nubian guards advance to protect her, but Solomon's Mighty Men held them at bay. "Shhh, Sekhet. Shhh." Finally she relaxed into his arms, like a wild horse relenting to its first master. He whispered, soothing her. "You don't always have to be the powerful one."

Solomon caught Ahishar's attention and silently signaled him to clear the chamber. This woman had suffered alone long enough. It was time for him to comfort his wife and fulfill the duties of a husband to which he had agreed when he accepted her in pledge from Egypt. *It is the way of kings, Arielah*, he grieved silently. And then he kissed away the salty drops from Sekhet's cheeks. "You will have your palace—after I've finished God's temple." Kissing her tenderly, he said, "And you will have your heir—if Jehovah wills it."

Arielah sat in her assigned chamber of Solomon's harem, confused, trembling, and alone. It was as if the whole world continued with their day, but life stopped the moment the Daughters of Jerusalem whisked Hannah away without explanation. Arielah had no idea how long she waited alone. Without a window in this chamber, she couldn't measure time, but the rumbling of her stomach told her midday had passed, and it was surely almost evening. *Lord Jehovah*, she prayed, *what do I do now?* Hopefully Solomon would miss her soon and send someone to find her.

She heard the incessant rumble of the harem change to an eerie quiet, and then the faint slapping of sandals approaching. The Daughters' ominous words rang in her memory: *Someone might hear your threats and do you harm.* Trembling, she glanced around. What could she use for a weapon? The footsteps neared, and she held her breath.

"My lady?" Hannah's round face appeared, and Arielah released a sigh. But her relief was short-lived when she saw the tray of food in her hands. "You must eat something, my lady. Elisheba sent some broth."

"I don't want broth, Hannah," she said more sharply than intended. "I want to share my evening meal with my husband—as I always do. I want to know why you were taken from me, and I want to know why I've been kept a prisoner in this room all day!" She could hear the panic in her voice and hated it.

Hannah's eyes swam with tears. She kept her head bowed and placed the tray on a table, offering no answer. Instead, a vaguely familiar voice spoke from the doorway. "I suppose I have been chosen to answer your questions, my queen."

Arielah turned toward the voice. Gasped. "Abishag." She whispered the name, not entirely certain the woman before her was real. Dressed in a plain blue linen gown bearing the embroidered symbol of David's concubines, Abishag looked worn and weary, though she was only a year older than Arielah. Still, her beauty and grace radiated across the room.

"Yes, Queen Arielah, it is I, and I'm happy to see you again." She paused. "Though not under these circumstances." She offered a deep bow.

313

"Please don't bow." Arielah tried to stand, but Hannah fell at her feet and clung to her waist. "Hannah, what is it?" She cast a questioning glance at her maid's older sister. "Abishag, let me explain why we haven't come looking for you." She reached out, but Abishag drew back, seemingly frightened—or at least suspicious. Her trust had been spent like a pauper's last shekel. Arielah dropped her hand and began smoothing Hannah's hair instead. "Please, Abishag. Sit with us."

The beautiful Shulammite sat on the floor beside her sister and offered her attention to Arielah.

"Well, I hardly know where to begin," Arielah said, considering the sisters before her. "I asked Solomon to reunite you with Hannah as soon as we came to the palace, but he said it was best that you remain separate. He never explained why."

Hannah reached out to her older sister.

"I'm sorry, Abishag," Arielah said, emotion tightening her throat.

"It's all right, my lady," she said. "King Solomon was right. It was best that I not leave King David's harem—until now." Arielah watched Abishag squeeze her sister's hand and release it, seeming to give strength and gain it. "My queen, I'm sorry to come to you this way—with the message I have to bring."

A cold chill raced up Arielah's spine, and her palms grew sweaty. It was her shepherd's warning—a familiar sign from Jehovah of impending danger, most often coming right before a lion or bear appeared to threaten her flock. It had been so long since she'd felt Jehovah's presence, but He seemed especially close in these unsettling moments.

Abishag must have sensed her fear. This time it was she who reached for Arielah's hands, gently cradling them in her own. "I've been told to move you to Bathsheba's chamber."

The words struck Arielah like a blow. The room spun, the moment suspended in time. Surely she was lying in her bed, and Solomon would reach over and wake her from a terrible nightmare.

"I'm sorry, Arie—my queen. It is widely known that you love him. Such is not always the case of a treaty bride." Abishag rubbed her thumbs over the backs of Arielah's hands, gently reassuring. "Bathsheba's chamber is the finest in the palace. It's attached to the beautiful private garden of King David's women."

"What?" A second blow. Arielah jerked her hands away. "I'm not even to be included in the courts of *Solomon's* wives? He's banishing me to the other side of the palace?"

Abishag and Hannah reached for her simultaneously, hugging her so tightly Arielah felt their hearts beat as one. "The ways of kings are beyond reason, Arielah," Abishag whispered. "But listen well to my warning. I've heard the Daughters of Jerusalem laughing with some of the guards at the harem entrance about moving you to that chamber because it is more secluded than others."

Hannah gasped and drew away. Abishag sat back and directed her next words to her sister. "Now is not the time for fear, little sister. You must be strong for your mistress." Softening her tone, she once again spoke to Arielah. "It was the Daughters of Jerusalem who suggested that King Solomon move you to Bathsheba's chamber. They convinced him of its special meaning to you as a shepherdess, its nearness to Bathsheba's garden, but . . ." Abishag leaned close and looked intently into Arielah's eyes. "Take care, my queen, for many are the dangers in these palace walls."

For a moment there was silence. Hannah's breaths were shallow and quick.

Arielah studied David's beautiful concubine. "I do not know you well, Abishag," she said, "but I need another friend. I'm afraid the only ones I can trust in this place are your sister, Reu, and Benaiah."

"It's good to keep a short list of trust, my lady." The Shulammite beauty knew well the betrayal of supposedly noble men.

"Perhaps you can teach me about palace politics," she said, measuring her next words carefully. "What other secrets lurk in these halls, Abishag?"

Looking right and left as though they were the old gossips at Shunem's well, the older girl said, "I sometimes linger near the flowerbeds and fountains near the harem entrance, listening while the guards speak lewdly of the Daughters of Jerusalem." She furrowed her brow. "I suppose they think a concubine is deaf because she couldn't coax a king to marry her."

Arielah gasped at the mischief of this once prim beauty. Hannah clamped both hands over her mouth, and all three grinned in spite of their circumstances.

Abishag continued. "Sometimes it pays to have the guards *think* you're deaf," she said, her eyes sparkling. "They talked about the Daughters' plan to move you into Bathsheba's chamber and also described another Shulammite in our midst."

Arielah's stomach twisted at the possibility. *Lord Jehovah, please no . . .*

"It's that awful Marah," Abishag said. "She's moved her 'business' to the City of David. Judean men may hate their northern brothers, but they certainly enjoy northern women."

Arielah tried to hold her breath so the others wouldn't notice her panic.

"But here's the worst of it," Abishag continued. "I heard the Daughters of Jerusalem making arrangements with a detachment of guards to escort someone from the palace to visit Marah tonight." She let out a disgusted huff.

Hannah's eyes went wide. "Who from the palace would visit a common prostitute?"

30

[Beloved] I slept but my heart was awake. Listen! My lover is knocking.

I will claim Arielah as my wife according to the law of Moses and Israel . . .

Her eyes burned with angry tears, the moon's shadows casting long black daggers across the treaty agreement in Bathsheba's chamber—Arielah's chamber now. The agreement hung on the northern wall in a beautifully engraved silver frame, mocking her.

"Hannah," she called into the girl's adjoining chamber. "Could you come in here for a moment?" She removed the frame from its hook on the wall.

"Yes, my lady?" The girl emerged, drying her hands after clearing away their evening meal.

"Please pack this with the rest of the shiluhim gifts we brought from Shunem." Arielah ran her finger over the words on the papyrus. *In accordance with the custom of Israelite husbands, who fulfill the responsibilities of their position in truth . . .*

Hannah remained silent, seemingly hesitant to take the

317

frame. "Queen Arielah, shouldn't you keep the agreement on the wall so the king will see it—if he comes to your chamber?" A little anger flared in her voice. "Perhaps he will read it and remember his vows."

A knock interrupted their decision. "Who could it be?" Hannah asked. "After our scare in the City of David this afternoon, I can't imagine Benaiah's guards letting anyone near your door."

Arielah lifted an eyebrow and grinned. Hannah remained a far better companion than servant. "Perhaps you should open the door and see."

"Oh yes!" she said, rushing to open the door.

Arielah gasped. The silhouette of Queen Bathsheba's regal form glowed in the lamplight.

"Good evening, little one. I hope I haven't intruded on your evening."

"Oh no . . ." Her words were choked by tears, and she rushed into her arms.

"I know, little one. I know."

When Arielah could speak again, she stepped back, still holding the framed wedding agreement. "Hannah and I were debating if a king can ever truly be considered a husband." Another sob. "One morning I left his bed, and I haven't seen him, heard his voice—or even received an explanation for my changed position—in three Sabbaths! Why, Ima Bathsheba? Why?" Hysterical now, she felt as if her heart was being ripped from her chest.

Bathsheba guided her toward the bed and rocked her like a child. Silently. Arielah didn't know how long.

When the tears slowed again, the queen mother lifted Arielah's chin and captured her gaze. "I am here to answer your questions and to give you some advice, but first I must fulfill my vow to a friend." With a sad smile, she explained, "I must be a nagging ima since Jehosheba isn't here. Benaiah sent one of his Cherethite guards with news of the trouble you experienced today in the City of David."

"It was my fault," Hannah whispered. "I begged her to take me to the merchants' shops on the south side of the fortress." The maid's cheeks flamed at the confession. "I asked if the messenger, Reu, could accompany the guards. I wanted to spend time with him. It was foolish."

Bathsheba's expression was stern but her voice gentle. "I'm sorry you saw the ugly side of Judean loyalty in the City of David. The zealots flinging rotten vegetables at Israel's treaty bride do *not* speak for all Judeans." She reached out to Hannah, squeezing the girl's hand. "I'm thankful Benaiah's soldiers whisked you and your mistress back to the palace unharmed. He's placed double guards at Arielah's door."

"Does Solomon know what happened?" Arielah spoke barely above a whisper.

Silence. Awkward silence.

"I have spoken to you as an ima," Bathsheba said, "and now I will speak to you as a queen." She removed the framed treaty from Arielah's hand and gave it to Hannah, then grasped the young queen's shoulders and squared her own. "Most likely, Solomon has not yet been told about the near riot in the City of David. He will be briefed on today's business by the high steward tomorrow morning."

A knot the size of a melon coiled in Arielah's stomach. "I am *business* now?"

Bathsheba continued, ignoring the question. "The king has reinstated *relations* with his other wives." She paused momentarily to recapture Arielah's gaze when she turned away. "The day he moved you to this chamber was the first time he bedded one of his other wives. I know my son, little Shulammite. His heart is too tender to hurt a woman and then observe the wound he's inflicted. He has not seen you or spoken to you because he doesn't want to witness the pain he's inflicted."

"He's a coward." Arielah's rash statement caused the queen mother to wince. *I'm not sorry I said it*, she thought. *Only sorry you heard it.*

"As a king," Bathsheba said quietly, "Solomon must fulfill responsibilities to his God, to his nation, and to his wives." Her countenance softened. "And as a queen, Arielah, you are responsible to your God, your husband, and yourself. Though it may seem you have no alternative in many matters, you have more choices than you may realize."

Arielah sat in tortured silence. Confusion wrestled with pain. Loyalty struggled with justice. Modeling Bathsheba's royal grace, she swallowed her tears. "Wise words, my queen, but I see no choice to be made when my husband abandons me without explanation."

"You speak of only one area of your life, little one. Your choices are vast in your relationship with Jehovah and the ways you choose to conduct yourself."

Arielah had no answer. Reaching for the framed papyrus, she shook it in front of the queen's face. "A king who doesn't keep his vows cannot be trusted to rule a nation!"

"The king has kept every one of these vows," Bathsheba said calmly. "He's provided generously for his wife. Just look at this beautiful chamber."

"But what of love, Ima Bathsheba?" She hugged the treaty against her heart. "What of love?"

The queen's regal air crumbled, and tears finally escaped Bathsheba's long lashes. "A treaty agreement mentions nothing of love or loneliness or piercing disappointment." Pausing, she searched Arielah's face as if seeking lost treasure. "Did you marry a king and expect a shepherd boy? Solomon is deeply flawed—as was his abba, as are we all. But if your marriage is truly ordained by Jehovah, as you told me in the mikvah, you must learn to love Solomon by Jehovah's wisdom and power."

Like a stroll through a market, Arielah's mind replayed

God's wonders in her life. Abba's dream the day of her birth. The moment she first saw Solomon. Then she remembered Marah, Solomon's betrayal in Shunem. She had promised to love him even if he never returned her love. "I didn't know love could hurt so much," she whispered, leaning into Bathsheba's embrace.

"But it's like birthing a child," she said, stroking Arielah's hair. "It's an exquisite pain because of the results it brings. Solomon loves you, Arielah. He won't stay away forever. And when he comes back, you have a choice to make." Kissing her gently, she stood. "Benaiah's men are escorting me home tonight. From now on, if you want to leave the palace, visit me—not the City of David."

Hannah opened the door, and the gracious lady departed. Arielah gazed at the moon through her latticed window, exhausted after their harrowing day. Hannah carefully placed the treaty agreement in the shiluhim basket near Arielah's bed and then waited awkwardly, seemingly frightened to retreat more than a camel-length from her mistress.

"Hannah, did you lock my chamber door?"

The girl nodded but didn't look up.

"Were there two extra guards as Ima Bathsheba reported?"

Another nod and then a whisper. "Could we leave the door between our chambers open—just for tonight?"

Arielah nudged her shoulder and coaxed a smile. "Of course."

Hannah's countenance brightened immediately, and she reached for an ivory comb, seemingly ready for their nighttime routine. After both women were washed, dressed, and ready for bed, Hannah retired to her sleeping couch, but Arielah gazed through her window at the sky of ebony and crystal.

Hannah's steady breathing proved she had finally relaxed into sleep, but for Arielah, sleep was as much a stranger as her husband had become. In the three Sabbaths since she'd moved into this chamber, Abishag's warning of the Daughters' dark purpose had become a constant shadow. Her last conscious thought was of the cold metal dagger she kept hidden under her pillow. Finally she slept, but her heart was awake, mourning the absence of a love she believed Jehovah had promised. The deep, contented sleep of a newlywed gone, she now drifted in fitful half consciousness, neither fully aware nor fully at rest.

In the land between darkness and dawn, Arielah heard the rustling of footsteps outside her door. Someone tried to lift the latch and then jiggled the lock furiously. She bolted upright in her bed.

Hannah heard it too. She whimpered and scampered into Arielah's bed. The girl sucked in a roomful of air when Arielah produced the dagger from beneath her pillow. "Where did you get that?"

"Shhh! Benaiah gave it to me," Arielah said, waiting for the intruder to make another sound.

Solomon stood trembling outside Ima Bathsheba's bedchamber. *No, Arielah's bedchamber now.* The dew was forming in the darkness before dawn, and the chilled damp air shrouded his withering soul. How long had it been since he'd seen her? Arielah, his life and breath.

Guilt had nearly gutted him.

But why should he feel guilty? He could rationalize his marital visits to Sekhet and other wives as duty. The prickly truth of his rendezvous with Marah wasn't so easily dismissed. *Arielah need not know I visited the wayward Shulammite that night.* He'd been out of his mind with guilt over bedding Sekhet and moving Arielah to Ima's chamber. He'd had too much wine, and when Ahishar mentioned the Daughters of Jerusalem had returned from visiting a Shulammite friend named Marah in the City of David, he thought his luck too good to be ignored. When he questioned Shiphrah about her friend, his blood was stirred and the tryst was planned. *At least it was only one night.*

Pressing both fists against his eyes, he tried to clear his throbbing head. He'd had too much wine again, started visiting his wives too early tonight. But he must face Arielah and explain a king's duty to produce heirs for many wives. *She'll understand. She must understand.* He couldn't live without his Shulammite queen.

Stepping between the two guards, he knocked lightly on her door. Leaning close, he heard her voice. "Hannah, it must be Solomon!"

She sounded pleased. Or was it fear? Hard to discern while his head throbbed. He belched and staggered. Marah's full curves flashed in his mind unbidden, the lurid temptress he couldn't resist. He mustn't allow himself to think of her and be with Arielah.

Turning to Benaiah's Cherethite guards, he mustered his most commanding voice. "You are dismissed." Both men instantly bowed, turned, and obeyed.

When they were out of earshot, he pounded the door harder. No reply. Perhaps Arielah required a shepherd's verse to open her door. Trying to remember all those flowery phrases he'd attempted—and failed—to compose as brilliantly as Abba David, he began to recite, "Open to me, my sister, my darling, my dove, my flawless one." His voice grew louder, his patience waning. "And hurry. My head is covered with dew, and it's cold out here."

"The dew itself testifies against you, King Solomon. Do you intend to make my pillow the last of many tonight?"

Fury, white-hot, roiled inside him. *How dare she refuse me?* This stubborn she-goat wasn't even going to let him offer his well-rehearsed explanation! "I am not some lovesick boy in your meadow now, woman. I am your husband! Let me in!" A swift kick on the door jarred the cedar panel.

A woman's voice cried out, and he waited to hear the hurried unlatching of the lock.

Nothing.

"It's late, Solomon," came Arielah's controlled reply. "I've taken off my robe, and it's too chilly to get out of bed. Hannah has already washed my feet, and I don't want her to rewash them."

"Wh—I—you—" Anger gripped him by the throat. He couldn't speak. She refused to answer her door because she didn't want to trouble her maid? "Ahhh!" Solomon's shout introduced his shoulder to the door, shaking the thick cedar panel on its hinges. Only the lock held it fast. He thrust his hand through the opening, grasping at the iron clasp, but his hands were shaking too wildly to free the lock.

He heard a hysterical cry and a chastising command. "Hannah, stop your tears! He won't hurt me."

The words pierced him. He *had* hurt Arielah already— many times. *You will be the only lily in King Solomon's garden from this day forward*, he had promised her. His hand stilled on the lock. What was he doing here? The door barely hung on its hinges, and he could see a petite figure stirring inside. His anger rekindled, his heart wrung dry. He ground out the words, "I'll find a northern maiden willing to soil her feet." He left the memory of love behind a broken door—to find a way to forget his broken promise.

Arielah trembled. Her heart began to pound, and she ran toward the door. "Solomon?"

Hannah was shaking wildly. "Come back. What are you doing?"

Arielah turned, determination in her voice. "I would rather address his anger than suffer his indifference."

"Solomon?" But when Arielah reached the door, his hand no longer probed the lock. She heard footsteps. Running. Retreating. Her heart sank. She tried to open the door quickly, but the lock was bent. Her fingers slippery, hands wet with perspiration, she looked down at her palms, and a familiar chill ran up her spine. She recognized the sensation. It was her shepherd's warning, this time accompanied by a gentle inner voice. *My hands drip with myrrh*. She examined her fingers and pondered the meaning. "Myrrh, the death spice," she whispered. *Oh, Jehovah, what danger lies ahead?*

Arielah turned back to Hannah. "Open the shiluhim basket." Doe eyes registered only questions, and the girl seemed rooted to the bed. Arielah fairly flew to the basket at the foot of her sleeping couch and dug to the bottom. "You must send Reu to Shunem right away. He must bring Abba to Jerusalem as soon as possible."

Hannah sat as still as the graven images on Jerusalem's eastern hill. "Why, my lady? What are you doing?"

"I'm finding something to wear so I can follow Solomon."

"But he must summon you first. You cannot go to the king unbidden."

Arielah issued a sideways glance, trying not to laugh at the irony of such a statement. "Hannah, if anyone questions the king's intent, we can show them my broken door."

The girl's cheeks reddened, and she climbed from the bed to help. "How will you find him?"

Arielah tried to swallow the lump in her throat. She remembered Abishag's report about the palace official's escort to Marah. "I believe he has gone to find Marah."

The look in the girl's eyes was almost as painful as Solomon's betrayal. All innocence shattered. "No! The king would not do such a thing!"

Ignoring the girl's protests, Arielah lifted out her old shepherd's garb and sandals. She'd hidden these tattered treasures in her dowry chest against Ima's wishes. "Yes, Hannah, my faithful friend. I believe he is the palace guest the guards escorted that night."

Hannah gasped and tried to cover the sound with both hands.

"The Daughters of Jerusalem are part of a conspiracy to divide our nation," she explained quickly, "but Marah threatens Solomon's heart. I must try to save Solomon and then trust him to save Israel."

"But, my lady." Tears rolled down Hannah's round cheeks. "You cannot go to Marah's house. Abishag said it was in the City of David. We witnessed their hatred today in the market!"

"I'm going to find my husband, and you must do as I asked. Send Reu to Shunem. He must bring Abba to Jerusalem." Arielah kissed the girl's cheek. "Now, help me dress."

Arielah donned a one-piece tunic Ima Jehosheba had woven and a dark brown cloak that shadowed her face. Her well-worn shepherd's sandals felt as natural as bare feet, and a gentle sigh escaped as the queen became a shepherd boy who could wander unnoticed in Marah's part of town. Hannah's protests continued as Arielah hurried toward the door.

She left the girl standing in the middle of the chamber shivering—from fear or cold, Arielah wasn't sure. But the surety of her purpose grew with every determined stride. Wiping sweaty palms on the thick woolen robe, she prayed, *Jehovah, guide me in the shadow of Your wings.*

31

*[Beloved] I looked for him but did not find him. . . .
The watchmen found me as they made their rounds in
the city. . . . I am my lover's and my lover is mine; he
browses among the lilies.*

Slipping silently out of her chamber, Arielah left the hall of David's women and padded down the hallway into the deserted courtyard. The guards at Solomon's harem entrance were absent. Strange. The waning moon cast haunting shadows, and every leaf and branch threatened to reach out and grab her. She turned into the throne hall and hugged the wall, remaining under the balcony.

She noticed all the palace guards were either dozing or away from their posts. *Thank You, Jehovah!* The ease with which she was making her way past the guards seemed to confirm Jehovah's blessing. He would lead her to Solomon.

Silently making her way along the northwest wall of the courtroom, she had only to clear the entrance hall. She peeked around the corner. *Praise Jehovah!* Nahum, the one-eyed guard, was on duty tonight. Arielah would flank the entrance hall on the man's blind side. Her worn leather sandals made no sound on the stone walkway, and the cool night air slapped her cheeks. She rounded the corner of the fortress of Zion and prayed, *Lord, shield the eyes of the guards in the tower.*

When no clatter of suspicion arose, Arielah slipped quietly into the untamed streets of the City of David. Her heart pounded so loudly she was certain she'd wake every sleeping Judean. The tall stone buildings and narrow passageways blocked much of the moonlight, and she turned her ankle more than once on the uneven cobblestones.

"Solomon? Solomon, are you here?" she called out in a whisper, uncertain how to find Marah's home. Did they display their talents with red veils and lamps like the harlots of Shunem? Her wondering soon ceased when on the extreme southeast edge of the city, she heard the bawdy voices of women calling out and men's coarse laughter.

Staying low, her head and face shaded by the oversized cloak, she caught a glimpse of a man guarded by several attendants rounding a corner up ahead. "Solomon!" Her voice pierced the darkness before she could restrain it. But no one answered.

Arielah hurried to catch them. Again in her strangled cry, she called, "Solomon, is that you?" Finally, turning the corner, she ran headlong into two watchmen. She drew in a quick breath. "Oh, I'm sorry." Remembering her shepherd's disguise, she kept her eyes downcast and her face shadowed.

"Let us see your face, Queen Arielah." A deep voice laughed, and the shepherd's warning skittered up her spine.

Arielah looked into cold, black eyes. The guard didn't blink, and one side of his lips curved into a wicked grin. "Oliab, the queen has come to visit us." Another watchman offered a low, sickening chuckle.

She recognized the hairy guard from Ima Bathsheba's house on the day of her wedding processional. "Yes, I am Queen Arielah," she said, straightening her posture, "and I can see by your uniforms that you are city watchmen making rounds." She was just about to expound on their duty to protect her when Shiphrah and Sherah stepped out of the shadows. All breath left her.

"So, Arielah." Shiphrah emerged from a dark corner with two more guards. "You guessed correctly the king's destination after you foolishly refused him."

The Daughters of Jerusalem had finally captured Jehoshaphat's lion of God. Before she could utter a reply, the four guards surrounded her, and Shiphrah taunted, "Didn't you think it odd that the palace guards weren't at their posts tonight?"

Sherah joined the mocking. "Tell us, queen of goats, have you come to join Marah in her trade? It's the only use a Judean has for a Shulammite."

Arielah was silent before her attackers.

"Say something!" Shiphrah's voice became an otherworldly screech.

Arielah saw a scourge in one of the guards' hands. It was a rebel's weapon, illegal in the land of Israel. Those who used it intended more than punishment, they intended torture.

The other guards began to jab at the hem of Arielah's cloak with the tips of their spears, shredding it, nicking her legs. "This doesn't look like a queen's robe."

One guard grabbed her by the collar and ripped the cloak from her arms. He swung it over his head, sending up a victory whoop as he whirled her robe into the darkness. Arielah covered herself, now wearing only the seamless woven tunic in the night chill. *Protect me, Jehovah.* Her mind whirled, but she made no sound.

"Who gets the tunic when we're done?" the guard called Oliab asked. "I'd eat roast lamb for a full moon if I took that home to my wife." The guards bickered and bartered.

"Enough!" Sherah's voice was shrill. "You can cast lots for the queen's robe, but her tunic remains. I've paid you to kill her, not grope her. Now get on with it."

Arielah's eyes were pleading, but Shiphrah nodded, and the watchmen began their feast of fury. The blinding pain of the scourge hit its mark. Her mind reeled. *Oh, Lord Jehovah, help me!* Arielah waited silently for the next blow. Her quiet confidence enraged her attackers. One guard kicked her, and another brought his fists down, striking her face.

Almost like a dream, she saw sheep in a shearer's grasp and heard the wind whisper, *Like a lamb led to the slaughter, don't breathe a word*. She remembered the many times she'd silently endured her brothers' torture. She remembered the quiet pastures of Shunem.

Crouching on her knees, she curled into a ball and tried to shield her head from the blows. The rod and then a kick. The strikes became indefinable. Then white-hot pain, one overpowering surge. In agony of spirit, Arielah cried out for the first time, "Jehovah, help me!"

"Let her cry out to God! If God is for her, let Him rescue her!" Shiphrah screeched.

Arielah continued the words Abba had taught her in the shepherds' fields. "In You our abbas put their trust; they trusted and You delivered them." Her voice became gravelly. "They cried to You and were saved; in You they trusted and were not disappointed." She could feel herself slipping away.

The beating stopped. The night fell silent. Was she dead?

"I wash my hands of this woman, Sherah. I am innocent of her blood." The man Oliab spoke. Arielah looked through swollen eyes. The others gazed at her as though she were an apparition. "She just recited one of King David's songs. I know that song, Shiphrah. We're acting out every verse."

"What do you mean?" Shiphrah ripped the rod from one guard's hand and brought it down across Arielah's back. "Finish her!"

Arielah gasped. Sherah knelt and rolled her over. Shiphrah threw the rod aside and leaned over to hear her final plea.

"Daughters of Jerusalem . . ." Arielah tried to swallow but couldn't. "When you see Solomon . . ."

Shiphrah shook her shoulders. "Arielah, what do you want us to say to Solomon?"

Solomon. The name still thrilled her. "Tell him I am faint with love." She smiled, then winced at the sting of it. Peering through the small slits her eyes had become, she saw the twins exchange unbelieving glances.

"How can you say that?" The awe in Sherah's voice was unmistakable. "How can you still love him after bringing you to this?"

One of the guards stepped forward. "Leave her. We can send other Sons of Judah to collect her body later."

Arielah felt as though she spoke in a dream. "My lover outshines ten thousand men," she said. "His head is purest gold, his hair wavy and black as a raven." Her passion fueled her, but her breath was leaving. "His eyes . . . doves by streams . . . washed in milk . . . like jewels. His cheeks . . . spice yielding perfume . . . lips . . . lilies dripping . . . myrrh."

She saw the look of utter fury on Shiphrah's face and was determined to make praise for Solomon her dying words. "His arms . . . rods of gold . . . chrysolite . . . His body . . . polished ivory . . . with sapphires . . . legs are pillars of marble . . . pure gold." She gasped for more air—and suddenly it came. Her voice was still weak but clear. "His appearance is like Lebanon's cedars. His mouth is sweetness itself."

"No! I will not hear any more of this!" Sherah stood, her face twisted with anger. She tried to kick Arielah, but one of the guards stopped her. "You are dying, and Solomon is to blame!" Sherah shrieked. "He betrayed you!"

With strength only Jehovah could have given, Arielah focused on the two women, the dream gone, the pain diminished, her mind clear. "Solomon is altogether lovely. He is both my lover and my friend."

Silence reigned for only a moment before evil found its

voice. "Where has your lover gone?" Shiphrah asked, scourging Arielah with words. "Sherah and I will help you look for him. Where do you think we'll find him?"

Arielah looked up and saw the gloating faces of her darkest nightmares. The pain in her heart now surpassed that of her body. "My lover has gone down to his garden to gather lilies."

"Yes, shepherdess, I'm not sure you can call tonight's Shulammite harlot a lily, but he's certainly gathered more than his share of lilies in the last two years." Sherah's low laughter spat salt in Arielah's wounds. "Did you really think a little shepherdess could satisfy a king?" Silence hung heavily in the air.

Shiphrah shoved Arielah's shoulder. "Is she dead?"

"I am my lover's and my lover is mine—even if he browses among the lilies." Arielah remembered the first time she'd spoken those words to Solomon—that night at Shunem's wall. He'd refused to stop his browsing, and tonight she gave her life for it.

"He may belong to you, Shulammite, but he still *wants* the lilies." Sherah spit in her face, and the gentle wind carried her into unconsciousness.

The ground shuddered beneath Benaiah's pounding feet, but he was too late. A few paces ahead, he saw his worst nightmare lived out. Four large figures scattered, and two elegant silhouettes loomed over a small bundle in the street. "Hezro, Eleazar, don't let those men escape!"

"We'll get them, Commander." Benaiah's two best men began the chase.

The Daughters of Jerusalem gasped at his arrival, instant tears and feigned concern. "We found her lying here as we were on our way back to the palace." Shiphrah's eyes gloated as they wept. "Those four watchmen were the king's escort to Marah's home." Nodding in the direction of the escaping guards, she said, "We told them to rush to the palace to secure help for King Solomon's northern queen."

Benaiah shook with pent-up fury. He dare not lift his hand against them without two male witnesses. Solomon had become completely ensnared by their web of lies. "Just tell me this," he said between clenched teeth. "Did Ahishar plan this, or should I give the Daughters of Jerusalem full credit?"

"I resent your implication," Shiphrah said, warning in her voice. "Arielah made open threats against Judeans while in the harem, and the foreign wives hate her with equal passion. Anyone could have done this."

"Now, if you'll excuse us," Sherah added, "we should return to Marah's house to inform King Solomon that one of his wives has been injured." Without waiting on a reply, the two turned and stalked away.

Using every measure of restraint he possessed, Benaiah let them go and knelt beside Arielah. If he'd not recognized the simple gold band she wore on her finger, he wouldn't have identified her broken body. Wrenching sobs shook his massive shoulders. "My lady?" He placed his hand near her face. She was still breathing. "Don't try to move, Arielah. I'll take you home. You're safe now." She groaned when he slid his hands under her legs and shoulders. He'd tended men on the battlefield and could see by her injuries that she would be dead by morning.

"Benaiah?" Her whisper was full of death's rattle.

"I'm here, Arie—my lady. I'll take you home now to see Hannah. She's very worried about you." Hannah and Reu had arrived at his chamber moments ago telling of Arielah's foolish pursuit of Solomon.

"Abba?"

"Yes." Tears streamed down his face. "Yes, Reu has gone to get your abba." How would he ever face Jehoshaphat? The man had asked him to protect Arielah while she was in Jerusalem.

"Solomon? Find Solo . . ." Arielah drifted in and out of consciousness, and with each glimmer of awareness, she uttered his name.

"Yes, little Arielah, I will find your Solomon." Benaiah's fury grew with every step. "And by everything Jehovah holds sacred, he will judge whoever did this to you."

32

*On the testimony of two or three witnesses a man shall
be put to death, but no one shall be put to death on the
testimony of only one witness.*

Ahishar swirled the last dregs of sweet wine in his cup
before downing the last drop. It was too early for wine,
but he was celebrating. Goat's milk and figs hardly seemed
an adequate breakfast for such an auspicious victory over
Jehoshaphat's daughter.

"My lord!" A frantic knock sounded on his door.

*Hmmm, probably Solomon's chamber servant summon-
ing me to convene a council meeting.* The king had no doubt
heard of Arielah's plight by now. Imagining the shame Solomon felt, Ahishar smiled.

"My lord, the king's secretary Elihoreph requests a word."
Another knock, and Ahishar signaled his servant to open
the door.

The chief secretary looked as if his tunic had shrunk three
sizes. The poor man always resembled a deer in the woods.
His eyes bulged, and his ears stuck up like two silver platters on his head. But this morning, his rumpled robe and

bloodshot eyes announced his distress before the man ever opened his mouth.

"Good morning, Elihoreph. Would you care for a cup of wine?" Ahishar tried to put him at ease.

"Clear the chamber, Ahishar," he demanded, his voice wavering. When Ahishar started to explain that his servants were loyal to the point of death, Elihoreph shouted, "Now! Clear it now!"

"As you wish, my friend," the steward said, nodding silent orders. His guards understood to wait close by.

When the door clicked shut, the secretary's words spilled out like an overturned inkhorn. "You never mentioned violence against a queen," Elihoreph seethed. "The Sons of Judah are men who fight battles against Israelite *men*, Ahishar. We do not attack defenseless women a few paces away from where the king lies with his harlot!"

"It was obvious that the shepherdess would not be coaxed to rally her abba and his northern tribesmen to rebellion. We tried humiliation, isolation, but none of it pressed the girl to incite Jehoshaphat. So we had to take more serious measures." He paused for effect. "And it worked! She sent that fat courier Reu to Shunem last night!"

Elihoreph's eyes became slits. "Who is this *we* you keep referring to, Ahishar?" Suspicion laced his tone, but his expression became a forced and friendly mask. "Has that frightening Egyptian queen taught you the folly of Pharaoh's court, to create puppets and then make them do your work?"

Ahishar chuckled warmly, recognizing his own manipulative tactics being used by the chief secretary. Perhaps the chief secretary could be trusted with more responsibility in the Sons of Judah, but Ahishar would never divulge his well-thought-out secrets and strategies. What would stop Elihoreph from making a play for sole leadership—especially if he learned of the Daughters of Jerusalem's crucial role?

"Ah, my friend," he said, guiding the chief secretary toward the door, "it is best that you don't know all the details." Hesitating before he opened the door, he added, "If there should be an investigation into Arielah's beating, it's best you don't know all the hounds and jackals on the board."

"My son, you must eat something." Bathsheba stood over Solomon with a bowl of broth and an ima's worried expression while he sat, head in hands, on a cushioned couch in his private chamber.

"I can't eat, Ima." And he couldn't stop shaking. When Shiphrah and Sherah appeared at Marah's door just before dawn and told him of Arielah's attack, he had retched in the street. *If only I'd tried harder to unlock her door. If only . . .* With every regret he replayed in his mind, he had vomited again. "Please, Ima. Go home. Or go see Arielah. You can't help me here." He didn't wish to sound unkind, but he didn't need to worry about Ima Bathsheba's worry!

"Solomon, *you* should go see Arielah." Her words pierced him, and he cast daggers back with a glance. She set aside the broth and straightened her spine.

Oh no. I know that posture. He was about to get a full-blown lecture. "No!" he said before she could speak. "No, Ima. Not another word . . ." His voice broke into a sob, and he shouted, "Out! Guards. Servants. Out, all of you!"

Sandals shuffled and doors clicked shut. Ima melted onto the cushions beside him, cradling him as she had when he'd skinned his knee or tangled with a hornets' nest. This time, however, they cried together, both feeling the pain of one they loved so dearly.

"I can't," Solomon whispered when he could trust his voice. "I can't go to her. It's my fault. All of it." He grabbed Bathsheba's face between his hands. Anger. Frustration. Guilt. He shook her and ground out the words, "I was killing her before the beating, Ima. Arielah was created for a better man

337

than me. I can't love her enough." Releasing her, he fairly leapt from the couch. His head swam, and he reached out to steady himself.

Bathsheba stood and embraced him. Held him upright. "I love you, my son," she whispered, "and I will honor you by remaining silent on the matter."

Solomon squeezed his eyes shut and then pulled his ima close. "I love you too." A new wave of tears attacked him. "Whatever love is."

When Solomon called the council meeting, he was so wobbly he had to use one of Abba David's shepherd's crooks to steady himself as he climbed the dais to his throne.

He heard one council member whisper, "See how he honors his dying Shulammite by carrying a shepherd's crook."

Curse my supposed honor. His stomach rolled again, and he almost emptied its contents on the counselor's lap. But his stomach was empty—almost as empty as his soul.

The shofar blared, and Ahishar shouted, "King Solomon calls his counselors to order—"

"Enough!" Solomon barked. The throne hall echoed, empty but for his council members and a few Mighty Men. "Dispense with the pomp, Ahishar. We have two matters of business to discuss before we begin our day at court."

Puzzled glances ricocheted between his advisors, but no one dared challenge him.

"Yes," he said, answering the unasked question. "We are going to proceed with petitioners and other business as planned." Raised eyebrows shouted their disapproval. "It won't help Queen Arielah if the nation of Israel falls apart while she's—" A sob leapt from his throat, but he covered his mouth before another could escape. *You must get control of yourself!* Taking several deep breaths, he regained composure. "As I was saying, we have two items of business. First, I don't know what rumors you've heard, but I will tell you plainly. Queen Arielah is not dead. She was brutally beaten while in the southern city early this morning, and my physicians are attending her now. Your prayers are much appreciated."

The old priest Zadok lifted a gnarled hand to interject. "My king, might I ask why she was wandering alone in the southern city so early?"

Solomon's heart stopped beating. The high priest—the man who had anointed Solomon as king of Israel—had asked a fair question. "No, you may not ask," he said flatly. He felt crimson rise on his neck as he watched the high priest's gaze grow hard. Would he rebuke the king as the prophet Nathan had rebuked David when he sinned and took Ima Bathsheba from her first husband Uriah?

"The second reason I've called this meeting," he said, hoping not to be interrupted by a fiery and holy rebuke, "is to report on Commander Benaiah's progress in apprehending Queen Arielah's attackers—"

As if speaking his name had introduced him to the court, Benaiah burst through the rear entrance, bloodlust on his face. With long strides, he reached the platform and immediately ascended to the throne without hesitating for permission. Kneeling beside Solomon, he lifted his giant hand to shield whispered words. "My men caught one of the attackers," he said, his voice quaking with unspent fury. "He's willing to testify against the leader of a secret group of Judean zealots called the Sons of Judah. These men have been plotting a rebellion to incite civil war and divide Israel."

Solomon gazed into his commander's eyes directly, searching for confirmation of such an incredible tale. Benaiah nodded and continued. "Our dilemma is this: he is only one witness, and we need two witnesses to convict the men who beat Arielah and the man who planned her attack. My prisoner swears under oath that if I bring him before you and let him testify against the leader, there is a man on your council who will verify his story and become that necessary second witness."

"What?" Solomon said loudly, causing his council members to chatter with confusion.

"Shhh," Benaiah said in his ear. "I know it sounds odd. I asked why he wouldn't simply tell *me* who this second witness advisor was so we could secure his testimony beforehand, but the man made a valid point. He doesn't know which of your officials and guards to trust, so he doesn't even trust me. These zealots have infiltrated the highest ranks of Judean society. He will only reveal the leader's name to you, and he swears the second witness—one of your council members—will verify his testimony against the leader of the zealots at the moment our prisoner stands before you." Benaiah stood, crossing his arms over his leather breastplate. His left eyebrow arched, and that long pink scar danced with every flex of his jaw.

Solomon scanned the faces of his trusted advisors. One— or more—of them was a betrayer. One might confirm the prisoner's testimony to convict Arielah's attacker. It was a risk . . . a risk he must take. "Bring in the prisoner!" he shouted, and the whole room seemed to gasp for air.

"My lord," Ahishar said, "what's happening? We aren't ready for the court proceedings to—"

"This has just been added to our list, Ahishar."

Every eye turned toward the rear entrance, where a bruised and bloodied man was being led between two Cherethite guards. "My lord," Ahishar sputtered, "this is most irregular. I have not seen any record of this prisoner, and his case has not been registered with the—"

Solomon silenced his steward with a glare.

Benaiah addressed the guard standing on the prisoner's right. "Eleazar, is the witness ready to make his statement?"

Solomon watched Benaiah's second-in-command shove the watchman forward.

"State your name," Benaiah said.

"I am Oliab," the man said through swollen lips.

"And what is your testimony?"

"I am here, Commander, to confess my role in the attack on Queen Arielah—"

A collective gasp begged him to continue. Solomon watched each advisor carefully to measure their expression.

"And to name Ahishar as the man who commissioned the attack."

"This is ludicrous!" The high steward's nasally pitch echoed off the cedar walls.

Solomon had been so busy watching those seated on the council couches, he hadn't considered the man standing at his right hand.

"Look at his bruises," Ahishar continued. "He's been coerced into this ridiculous story!" Stepping around Solomon, he pointed a crooked finger at Benaiah. "Him, he's the commander. He's hated me from the moment we first disagreed, and he hates me for taking his place as friend of the bridegroom at your wedding, my king."

Solomon's anger flared. "You have *never* taken Benaiah's place in anything, steward!"

"Of course not. No," he said, his defenses winding down like a spinning top. "But, my lord, why would I wish Queen Arielah harm? What benefit would I gain?"

"Perhaps you hope her abba Jehoshaphat will stir the boiling pot of unrest in the north." Solomon was startled to hear Elihoreph rise as second witness. "You rejoiced when the royal courier was sent to Jehoshaphat last night with word of his daughter's injuries. I heard the words with my own ears."

Solomon's relief was joined momentarily by humor as he wondered if the man with platter-sized ears knew how comical that sounded.

"I testify as second witness against Ahishar," the chief secretary continued. "Your high steward is the leading Son of Judah and is responsible for Queen Arielah's attack."

Solomon couldn't decide which urge was stronger—to kiss Elihoreph or to kill Ahishar. The first urge was fleeting, the second was law. "Ahishar, stand before me to be judged."

Benaiah caught the steward before his knees gave way and dragged him off the dais to stand beside Oliab, the watchman. Solomon studied the two men. Oliab was burly and obviously humbled, honest and dubiously helpful. His palace high steward was weaselly and proud, deceptive and immeasurably destructive. These two men, utterly opposite, had worked together toward a common purpose—to destroy the nation and the woman he loved. How many more lurked in the shadows of Judah? Men in the spectrum between Ahishar and Oliab—family men, merchants, shepherds, the king's own relatives and friends?

"Elihoreph!" the king shouted, and everyone in the courtroom jumped. "I will speak with you privately after this hearing to discover your methods of uncovering Ahishar's guilt." The chief secretary nodded regally, seeming too confident for a man who might be tried next. How had the secretary heard with his own ears, Solomon wondered? In what context had Ahishar confided such treason to Elihoreph?

"Oliab." Solomon began his judgments. The watchman lifted his head, seemingly weary of life itself. "You have confessed in our hearing of your participation in attacking my queen." Fresh rage bubbled up as he said the words, and the king almost reconsidered his planned ruling. Taking a deep breath, he reminded himself of God's wisdom and spoke evenly. "Because you seem to show some level of repentance in your testimony and aid at uncovering this band of zealots, I do not sentence you to death."

The man closed his eyes, releasing two small tears down his round cheeks.

"You will, however, remain in the palace dungeon until Benaiah and his guards have squeezed every detail out of you concerning these Sons of Judah."

"I will tell them all I know, my lord," he said, his voice gravelly. "But I'm afraid I know very little. I received orders only from Ahishar and—"

Ahishar struck the man before Benaiah could restrain him, shocking everyone in the courtroom. "You will tell them nothing of our cause, you coward!"

"Commander! Shackle that prisoner!" Solomon shouted, leaping from his throne. "May the Lord deal with me severely if Ahishar doesn't pay with his life for his treachery against Israel and Queen Arielah! Benaiah, find out what Ahishar knows of the Sons of Judah and then take him to the southeast side of the city. Strike him down beside the dung gate, where his soul can meet its end with the other refuse of our city!"

"Hello, my lamb." Arielah could hear Abba's voice, but she couldn't make her lips respond. She couldn't open her eyes. Frustration gripped her. Like bedeken during her wedding, she must use other senses to interpret her world.

"I can't believe she's lived a full day." Hannah's voice. "It's only by Jehovah's kindness that you arrived from Shunem in time to say good-bye."

"When do you expect Jehosheba to arrive?" It was Queen Bathsheba. What was she doing here?

"Reu will arrive shortly with Jehosheba. My wife has never ridden a galloping camel before."

"We will pray that Jehovah smiles a little longer on you, little one." A light kiss on her forehead. The scent of henna and nard. The queen mother again.

Arielah heard the door open, and the scent of fresh bread and saffron entered the room. Ima Jehosheba. "Oh, Jehovah, help us!" she cried.

"Come now, Jehosheba. You must be strong for our girl." Bathsheba's voice gently soothed Ima.

Quiet sniffs and then footsteps. "Hannah, have you used

the poultices of aloes wrapped in grape leaves?" Arielah could feel Ima's ministering hands on her wounds.

"Yes, I knew how to prepare them because I used them on my ima when she was ill."

"Hello, my lamb. Ima is here." Arielah could feel Ima's soothing touch on her head. "Jehovah smiled on us when he gave you to Arielah as her handmaid, Hannah. What other herbs have you used?"

There was a slight sniff. "The king's physician won't let me touch her anymore. He has taken charge of her care."

Arielah could feel weight on the other side of her bed, and Abba spoke. "Jehosheba, my love, the physician said he could find no broken bones. However, there is little hope that she'll survive because of the bleeding inside her. See?"

Someone pulled away her blankets, and she heard Ima cry out. *Oh, Ima, it's all right. It doesn't hurt badly.*

Jehoshaphat continued speaking quietly. "The king's physician said the blood from her ears is a sign of severe head injury, and the lacerations on her face will be—well, disfiguring. If she lives, he gives little hope for a normal life."

Arielah could hear Ima crying softly. Oh, how she ached to comfort the woman who had cradled her when she was a child. Instead, Jehoshaphat gently gathered Arielah into his arms and rocked her like she was a babe. "Oh, my precious lamb, we knew the battle would come, but we had no idea the cost." Though the pain of his embrace was excruciating, the love he poured out was soothing.

Again she heard the door open, and Abba tensed. The strong scent of frankincense filled the room, and Ima's breathing quickened. Bathsheba's voice was stern. "Why have you come?"

Jehoshaphat eased Arielah back onto her sleeping couch and stood, jiggling the bed and causing her to inwardly wince. "We've never met," he said, his voice harsh and clipped, "but as you can see, our daughter is badly hurt. We don't need you here. Please go."

Arielah tried so hard to open her eyes, to see who her abba would address with such disdain.

"I come with remedies," said the voice with a thick Egyptian accent. "Among my people, I represent the goddess Sekhmet. She is the patron goddess of physicians and healers."

"The physician won't let us touch her." Arielah heard Hannah's small voice.

"The physicians do not command a queen, little mouse." The woman's sneer was evident without seeing her face. "To my enemies, I am the lady of terror," she said, "and to my friends, the lady of life."

Arielah heard shuffling, footsteps. The room bloomed with the scent of spices and unguents she'd never smelled before. She felt Sekhet's strong presence.

"Prince Jehoshaphat, I have come with Egyptian remedies beyond your Hebrew scope of knowledge."

"If you are here to offer friendship and medicine," Abba said, his voice growing kinder, "we welcome you, Sekhet. But we worship only one God, the living God, El Shaddai. It is He who will give life or take it."

The room fell silent, and when Arielah became aware of those around her, she sensed that the light in the room had shifted. Had she dozed?

"Don't eat it, silly girl!" She heard the coarse Egyptian accent and recognized Hannah's timid sniff. "We won't have enough left to treat your lady's swollen eyes."

"I was just cleaning off my finger." Arielah felt her maid's gentle touch and then a cool, wet paste smoothed over her eyes.

Ima's reassuring touch cradled her hand. "Queen Sekhet, I've never heard of ground carob mixed with fermented honey." A faint swipe across the concoction and Ima smacked her lips. "It really does taste quite good." Ima's gentle laughter soothed the tension in the room as always, and Arielah felt the warmth of her family enfolding even the imposing Egyptian queen.

"Jehosheba," she heard Abba say, "I believe our girl is going to live through this." A tear fell on her hand, and she wondered whose it was. "Now that Ahishar has been executed, perhaps the rest of the Sons of Judah will be discovered too."

Ahishar executed? Arielah tried to move again. Nothing. Tried to speak. Her voice would not cooperate.

"Perhaps Jehovah will somehow use Arielah's pain to bring peace and healing to Israel," Abba said, his voice weary.

There was a long silence, and Arielah's frustration mounted. How many days had she been like this, lingering between death and life? Where was Solomon? Did he know of her injuries? Though her eyes were covered with carob and honey, she could feel a tear escape down her cheek.

"Shalom, my lamb." Jehoshaphat's voice was filled with wonder as he brushed away her tear. "Hold on. God's light will shine in your eyes again soon."

She heard Ima begin to hum a familiar tune, the song she always sang as she ground the wheat. Arielah gained strength basking in their love. Love, she well understood, was the strongest of all medicines. Suddenly she felt a gust of wind and heard her ivory-latticed shutters bang against the wall. Hannah's sandals rushed across the floor.

No, don't shut the window! The wind has come to visit me, wash me, heal me.

Awareness came that she might be able to speak if she rallied all her strength. Her mouth was as dry as chaff, but she formed the words. "Forgive him, Abba, he didn't know . . . his betrayal would . . . do this."

Jehoshaphat cried out, a guttural moan. Relief. Joy. Pain. He cradled her face in his hands, hovering over her. Ima Jehosheba showered her hands with kisses.

"My precious lamb, my lion of God," Jehoshaphat said. "Even after the evil you've suffered, your heart remains loving." His tears now bathed her face. "May your strength grow to complete the work your heart has begun."

Arielah saw a shadow move toward the window. "Window," she said.

"Hannah, keep that window open," Jehosheba said, understanding as only an ima can. The breeze wafted over her, and God's Spirit breathed life into her.

Arielah heard distant cries, sobbing that grew louder. Abba's hands left her face, and she heard him walk a short distance. "Queen Sekhet, are you all right?" she heard him ask.

"Prince Jehoshaphat," she hiccuped between her tears, "my remedies did not do this. I have never seen a force equal to this thing your family calls love. It is a most exquisite and frightful power."

Arielah's lips curved into a hesitant smile, careful not to split open her wounds. Sensing Ima's hand still holding her own, she gave a weak squeeze. "Wish Solomon could see so clearly," Arielah said. Wearied by the thought, she gave herself to the slumber that beckoned, letting the balm of love do its work.

33

*[Lover] You are beautiful, my darling. . . . Turn your
eyes from me; they overwhelm me. Your hair is like a
flock of goats descending from Gilead. Your teeth are
like a flock of sheep coming up from the washing.*

Solomon hadn't slept in days. Every bone in his body ached
for rest, but his mind still whirled, always in the direction
of Arielah.

"She won't make it through the day," the palace physician
had reported the morning after her attack. But when she regained consciousness three days later, the same man shook
his head in wonder. "Her injuries are grave, but it appears
Jehovah will spare her life." Every day the physician reported
her progress, and every day Solomon found a reason *not* to
visit her chamber. Duty had been his most ready excuse. Sitting in judgment from dawn till dark, Solomon scanned the
sea of hopeful faces in his throne hall and wondered how
many of them were betrayers. Ahishar had taken the Sons
of Judah's secrets to the dung pile with his soul.

"Such are the rulings of Israel's wise king on this second day of Nisan, the third year of King Solomon's reign,"

announced Elihoreph, Solomon's new high steward. "You may return tomorrow to seek justice." The petitioners stirred and became a knot at the back entrance.

"Well, my king," Elihoreph said, casually perusing the crowd, "only a few more days and we'll be choosing our Passover lamb." He patted the king's shoulders as if they were two shepherds appraising a flock.

Solomon stared at the hand on his shoulder, and the steward quickly removed it. Solomon was in no mood to build a relationship with this bowl-eared man. Though his one-time chief secretary had been cleared of conspiracy charges before last Sabbath, Solomon still replayed the scene of the man's interrogation in his mind.

Solomon had ordered the throne hall emptied, leaving only himself, Benaiah, and Elihoreph in the imposing courtroom.

"How did you discover Ahishar was a traitor?" Benaiah began, standing over Elihoreph, who knelt before the king.

The chief secretary's hands were cupped before him as if holding the answers to the king's quest for truth. "I overheard Mahlon and Elisheba talking about Ahishar's involvement with the Sons of Judah."

"So you lied in my courtroom," Solomon said. "You said you heard Ahishar with your own ears!"

"I beg your pardon, my lord, but no," Elihoreph said all too calmly. "Remember my exact phrase. I testified that I heard the *words* with my own ears. I didn't say I heard *Ahishar* speak them."

Solomon tried to recall the man's exact testimony. Since Elihoreph was chief recording secretary, the written transcript would no doubt reflect whatever words best served him. So Solomon asked a question to which there was no written record. "So tell me, Elihoreph, if you knew of Ahishar's involvement in the conspiracy, why did you wait until your queen was beaten before alerting Benaiah to the danger?"

The man's calm exterior cracked slightly. "When Mahlon and Elisheba realized I'd heard them talking, Mahlon begged me not to tell anyone for fear that Ahishar would make good on his threats to torture Elisheba's son, Reu." Elihoreph sniffed back some emotion. "What was I to do, my lord? I wasn't sure whom I could trust among your leaders."

The man seemed convincing, but Solomon wasn't satisfied. "Bring Mahlon to my courtroom. I want to hear his version of the story."

Elihoreph cast his first uneasy glance at Benaiah. "I . . . well, our friend Mahlon . . . he . . ."

"What?" Solomon thought surely he had caught the secretary in deceit.

"Despite my protective silence, Ahishar discovered that Mahlon had confided secrets to Elisheba, and . . ."

"And what?"

"Ahishar tortured Mahlon and had his tongue removed." The secretary swallowed hard, and Solomon's sense of shrewdness turned to regret. How could he proclaim the presence of God's wisdom when his own high steward mutilated a scribe, attacked a queen, and only Jehovah knew what else—all without a hint of suspicion from Solomon?

"We can summon Mahlon to this courtroom," Elihoreph offered, "but I'm afraid he'll only nod when asked to testify."

The king had no stomach for more interrogations. Benaiah brought in other witnesses who testified to Elihoreph's unyielding loyalty to the king, so the chief secretary was cleared of involvement in Ahishar's deceit and promoted to the high steward's position. However, both Benaiah and Solomon remained cautious in his presence. They remained cautious in *everyone's* presence.

Benaiah burst through the courtroom doors, startling Solomon back to the moment. His resolute march up the center aisle made Solomon groan. "What, Benaiah? I can tell by your face it's bad news."

The big man glared at Elihoreph. "I'd like to talk in your private chamber—alone."

"All right, my friend," Solomon said, hoisting himself off the throne. "Elihoreph, go to bed. Dream of beautiful women who love you dearly and give you fat babies that grow up to take care of you in your old age."

The steward was utterly speechless. Precisely the point. Solomon followed Benaiah toward the hidden door behind his throne, bowing under the tapestries when the big man shoved them aside. His private meeting chamber was a bevy of activity, but a single nod ordered a cup of wine and cleared the chamber for the king and his commander.

"So what makes you pout like one of my wives, Benaiah?" Solomon asked, folding his legs beneath him on the goatskin rug by their customary ivory table.

Benaiah wasn't amused. "I can't find a second witness willing to testify against the others involved in Arielah's assault."

Solomon felt anger warming his neck and cheeks. "How hard can it be, Commander?" He tried to control his venom, but his voice began to quake. "You have Oliab, and he's told you the names of the other watchmen that helped him. Get one of them to testify against the others. Make a deal. Promise one of them I'll be lenient. Lie! I don't care what you have to do to get them into my throne hall, but do your job, Benaiah!" He slammed his hand on the table, upsetting the cup of wine that a servant had placed in front of him. The red liquid dripped from his face, beard, robe, and hands.

Benaiah handed him a cloth he had tucked in his belt. With utter calm, he said, "The other attackers have vanished. We've searched their homes, asked their neighbors and families where they might be, but they're gone. Oliab has testified that he knows of only two others involved in the plan . . ." He hesitated. "You're not going to like what I have to say. Are you sure you want to hear it right now?" He motioned to the wine staining the king's robe.

351

Wiping his face and hands, Solomon said, "Yes. Tell me." Offering the wine-soaked cloth back to his friend, he met his gaze and dared him to distress him.

"Oliab swears it was the Daughters of Jerusalem who ordered him and his partners to attack Arielah." The commander's scar throbbed, and Solomon swallowed the bile rising in his throat.

"That is ridiculous." He kept his voice subdued, emotionless. "They are young maidens who have lived and socialized in the palace most of their lives. How would they ever have occasion to communicate with men like Oliab and his friends?"

"They are beautiful young women surrounded by hungry Judean guards, men who would willingly carry messages for maidens trained in seduction by their ima Miriam." Benaiah lifted an eyebrow, and Solomon recalled the questionable reputation of the girls' ima. He'd heard some of Abba David's advisors joke coarsely about the tailor Bethuel's wife.

"But you have no proof—and no second witness against Shiphrah and Sherah either." His voice sounded more hopeful than unbiased.

"No . . . and no."

"My lord." Elihoreph knocked but didn't wait for an invitation before he fairly ran into the room.

"A door was intended to make people knock!" Solomon shouted. "Guard! Who let this fool walk into my chamber without permission?"

But before he could chew anyone's ear off, Queen Sekhet appeared with only a single Nubian guard at her side. "I must see you now." She stood feet apart, arms crossed—a warrior's stance.

Solomon squeezed the bridge of his nose, closed his eyes. Breathing deeply, he addressed Queen Sekhet first. "You will not barge into my chamber and command me. Leave now and knock on my door, waiting *outside* for permission to enter." He matched her stare, waiting for her to yield. Finally, with a menacing scowl, she turned and walked out the door, slamming it behind her.

"And you!" Solomon said to Elihoreph. "Your fear of my Egyptian queen does not excuse your impertinent entry to my chamber. You too must knock to gain permission." When the steward started to speak, the king silenced him with a raised hand. "Permission is denied, Elihoreph. I dismissed you earlier. I do not want to see you again until sunrise unless the ark itself is on fire! Understood?"

Duly repentant, the steward bowed just as a loud pounding was heard on Solomon's door. Elihoreph's eyes bulged. "Do I have to walk past her to leave your chamber, my lord?" Terror was etched on his features. Solomon almost said yes just to watch him squirm.

"No, Elihoreph. You may leave through the throne hall door this time." Glancing in Benaiah's direction, he saw the stifled grin. As the steward left, Solomon waved aside his chamber servants. No doubt Sekhet would take off their arms if they opened the door too slowly. Hesitating with his hand on the lock, he threatened his commander, "You stop your laughing or I'll aim her fury at you!"

Benaiah held up hands of surrender as Solomon opened the door.

Sekhet entered alone, her Nubian guard evidently dismissed for the night. "All your servants may leave. The commander may stay." She walked directly to the table where Benaiah sat and lowered herself on the goatskin rug beside him.

Solomon's weariness fled, as did his servants and guards. Shaking his head, he joined his friend and the Egyptian queen at the table. "Sekhet, my bride, we really must discuss the boundaries of your authority."

Benaiah laughed out loud, but the lion-wigged woman appeared confused. "I am a queen, you are king, and they are servants. I see no problem with this."

The commander scratched his beard and tilted his head as if to say, *Yes, Solomon, explain the problem to us.*

"Is there a particular reason you barged into my chamber, Queen Sekhet?" Solomon's weariness returned, sapping any patience for his Egyptian wife's etiquette lesson.

"Why haven't you visited Queen Arielah since her beating?"

The air suddenly grew tense, all amusement gone.

Solomon stared at his sandals. "Benaiah, you may go."

"No," Sekhet said. "He may stay."

"Your boldness grows tiresome, *Queen Sekhet*." Solomon pinned her with a stare. "I do not wish to discuss Arielah with both of you in the room."

"And why is that?" Benaiah spoke softly, but the eyes that met Solomon's were determined to have an answer.

"She has asked for you," Sekhet added, placing her hand over his. Her sudden tenderness startled him.

"What is this? Did you two plan to ambush me?"

Sekhet glanced at Benaiah and offered a comrade's nod. "Your commander and I have become acquainted in the time we've spent with Arielah and her family." Returning her gaze to Solomon, she said, "I have seen love work a miracle in your queen's life, my husband. You should see what your God has done."

Shocked, he couldn't speak. He'd avoided seeing Arielah for over two Sabbaths by staying busy, reassuring his other wives, making grand pronouncements about catching the offenders. All the while his guilty heart screamed, *You are to blame.* How could he face Arielah when the last time he'd seen her was through a broken door of anger and neglect? The two faces before him pleaded silently, but they didn't know, didn't understand the depths of his shame. How could he ever look into Arielah's dove eyes when all he would see there was the reflection of his broken promises?

"Please leave, both of you." He rose from the table and walked toward his sleeping chamber.

"Solo—" Benaiah stopped his familiar address. "My lord, she has already forgiven you. Just go to her."

He stopped but didn't face them.

"Be a man." Sekhet's voice was filled with venom. "Be a king."

He didn't answer. He stood alone, cold and unmoving, until he heard their retreating footsteps. And then the door clicked shut.

Swallowing his third fig, Solomon washed it down with goat's milk and watched the Daughters of Jerusalem fairly float into his private chamber. Their flowing veils created an ethereal presence, and he wondered for the millionth time if he was making a mistake. "Welcome to my breakfast table," he said brightly. "Please join me." He motioned them to the two goatskin rugs beside his ivory table.

The twins bowed in unison, precision being one of their strengths. "We are honored," Shiphrah said, daintily descending to her knees. "What service have we rendered that we should deserve the privilege of breaking the fast with our king?" A slight quiver niggled at the corner of her forced smile. Sherah knelt on her goatskin, eyes darting from her sister to the king, seeming equally unnerved.

"I have reached a decision that will affect my harem, thereby affecting you two." He watched their reactions carefully, this invitation a test of their motives. "I have delayed my court proceedings until after midday in order to visit Arielah."

The twins exchanged concerned glances. "My king." Sherah spoke first. "Do you think it wise to see your poor wife in her current state?"

"And what state is that?" he asked, challenging the slow-witted twin.

"My sister simply asks," Shiphrah intervened, "that you

consider the shepherdess and her feelings before you go. She might be embarrassed by her disheveled appearance."

Solomon could feel his anger rising. "She is a *shepherdess* no longer, Shiphrah. She is my wife and your queen."

Color drained from both women's faces. "Of course, my lord," Sherah conceded. "The queen might feel inadequate before you." Something flashed in her eyes, and then she smiled sweetly.

"Arielah has never been inadequate." He held her gaze and signaled the end of his meal. A chamber servant poured water on his hands as he held them over a silver bowl. "I'd like you to accompany me to her chamber," he said casually and then watched uncertainty color their cheeks. "I plan to give her divorce papers, and you two will serve as my witnesses."

The hint of a smile crossed Sherah's expression before she tucked it into wide-eyed concern. "Oh, my king, I'm so sorry. I didn't realize she displeased you so thoroughly."

"She doesn't *displease* me, Sherah, but I cannot ensure her safety in Jerusalem until we completely destroy the nest of vipers called the Sons of Judah." He leaned over the small table, grinding out the words. "And we will destroy everyone conspiring with the Sons of Judah." He relaxed onto his rug, wiping his hands dry.

"Well, I should hope so!" Shiphrah huffed, coaxing Sherah to nod affirmatively. "None of your wives are safe. If these traitors are bold enough to attack one queen, they could surely attack any of the others."

"They do not want the others." Solomon's throat tightened with emotion. "They want the one I love." The Daughters lowered their eyes and fiddled with their veils. He didn't dare confide that it was love that prompted his divorce, love that was about to alienate the only woman who had ever captured his heart. "Elihoreph!" he shouted, causing the twins to jump. "Where is that divorce scroll?"

"You may enter, King Solomon," Hannah said, opening her newly repaired chamber door. Arielah watched the girl cast daggers with her eyes.

But it was Solomon who captured her attention. She was seeing him for the first time in almost two full moons. "Solomon," she whispered too softly for anyone to hear. His eyes were downcast, seemingly afraid to look her way. He searched the room, nodded at Abba and Ima, and hesitated when he saw Queen Sekhet. Then finally—almost painfully—his gaze wandered to Arielah's bed.

He didn't gasp. It was more of a blow, as if someone had landed a fist in his gut. His complexion grayed; his shoulders sagged.

Would he turn and go? The thought seized her with fear. She lifted her hand, beckoning him to come, but he stood rooted to the floor.

"Welcome, my king." Ima Jehosheba stepped forward, lacing her hand inside his elbow, directing him toward Arielah's bed. Nudging ever so gently, she spoke softly as they walked. "We are grateful you have come."

As he drew nearer, his resistance grew until he pulled his arm from Ima's grasp. He was a single pace from Arielah's bedside. Close enough to speak, far enough out of her reach. The silence became awkward, and finally he spoke. "You are beautiful, my darling," he said in a raspy voice. Clearing his throat seemed to strengthen his resolve. "You are as lovely as Jerusalem, when her troops are arrayed with banners."

She watched him wince. Surely he must realize how ridiculous that sounded. She was not beautiful. She had asked to see her reflection in a mirror and had seen her emaciated face covered with half-healed green and yellow bruises around her eyes. Half-healed lips and new patches of hair testified to the scourge that had been used on her head. "Jerusalem's troops are not majestic to me, my love," she whispered. "It was troops such as those who did this to me."

His face twisted in sorrow, tears immediate. "Turn your eyes from me, beloved." His voice broke in a sob. "They overwhelm me."

He stepped away, and Arielah tried to reach out. But the pain was still too great.

"Poor dear." Shiphrah pushed past the king and stood by Arielah's bed. "You've been through a terrible ordeal."

Sherah followed her sister's lead, blocking Arielah's view of her husband. "Yes, but you've emerged the victor!"

Solomon loudly cleared his throat and returned to Arielah's bedside, still out of reach. He had wiped his eyes and affixed a regal bearing. "Your hair is like a flock of goats descending from Gilead," he said. "Your teeth are like a flock of sheep coming up from the washing. Each has its twin, not one of them is alone." With the cold repetition of his tired shepherd's verse, her heart shattered into smaller pieces. "Your temples behind your veil are like the halves of a pomegranate . . ." His voice trailed off. Did he realize the indifference on his features cut her more deeply than the scourge had?

"Is your heart so completely shallow that it holds only old shepherds' verses from our wedding procession, Solomon?" Her whisper drew him a step nearer, and he leaned over her to listen. The scent of him, aloe and frankincense, overwhelmed her. Through tears, she pleaded, "Is there no life-giving spring of new words for me, my love?"

He drew a breath and held it. Standing over her, he looked up and slowly exhaled. The eyes that gazed at her again were cold, unfeeling. "I have sixty queens and eighty concubines—and have had virgins beyond number—but you, Arielah, my dove, my perfect one, have always been unique."

The words sliced her heart in two. Unique? "A lily among thorns" he'd called her in Shunem's meadow that awful day when he'd become a stranger. Now he was her husband—but he'd become a stranger again.

His words stole her breath, but he didn't seem to notice—or care. With icy calm, he drove the words deeper. "You are surely your ima's favored child for a reason, and you've even won the favor of many queens. Some even praise you while they lie in my arms."

"That's enough!" Abba Jehoshaphat grabbed Solomon's arm and shoved him away from her bed. "Get out!"

The Daughters of Jerusalem continued Solomon's verbal lashing. "Yes, and you are as lovely as the dawn, Queen Arielah, fair as the moon, bright as the sun, majestic as the—"

Queen Sekhet rushed at the Daughters, sending them scurrying past Solomon and toward the door. Arielah curled into a tight ball, stretching her wounds and muscles excruciatingly. She couldn't breathe. The pain of the position paled in comparison to the agony of her soul.

"Go!" she heard Abba shout as he followed the king out of her chamber. Ima stroked her hair, soothed her, as darkness mercifully consumed her.

34

*[Lover] I went down to the grove of nut trees to look
at the new growth in the valley.*

Bring him to my chamber!" Solomon commanded the Cherethite guards waiting outside Arielah's door. "Prince Jehoshaphat needs a lesson in respect for his king." He could feel Jehoshaphat's rage burning a hole in his back, but he marched on, feeling as though he might retch any moment. *Jehovah, please . . . please . . .* But he didn't even know what to pray anymore. How had his life become such a mess?

Entering his chamber through the throne hall's hidden door, he began shouting orders. "Everyone out! Servants. Guards. Everyone!" Jehoshaphat halted, as did the Cherethites, and Solomon dismissed his elite protectors as well. The guards' hesitation was uncharacteristic. They'd been trained to act immediately on command. "Yes," Solomon said through clenched teeth. "I wish to be *alone* with Prince Jehoshaphat."

Both guards saluted—fist to heart, a warrior's honor. Jehoshaphat's crimson fury seemed to fade to confusion by the time the double doors closed. All those who could protect their king or testify on his behalf had been ordered from the room. Jehoshaphat's curiosity appeared to temper his rage.

They stood in silence for a long moment, the two wise men of Israel, neither willing to yield the advantage by speaking first. Finally Solomon walked toward the ivory table where they had first struck the treaty bride agreement. Extending his hand, he directed Shunem's prince to be seated on his customary goatskin. Accepting at least the first effort to be civil, Jehoshaphat sat.

"I am divorcing your daughter," Solomon said plainly, watching the prince's eyes flame. "Because I love her," he added tearfully, sniffing back emotions that threatened further explanation.

Jehoshaphat seemed unconvinced, his protective instincts undiminished. "After the words I heard you speak to her in there, I cannot believe you love her," he said, arms crossed, brow furrowed. He offered no sign of the mercy he'd once given so freely.

Why would he? Solomon sighed and began, "I hope she was as convinced as you are." He paused, watching confusion reign again on Jehoshaphat's face. "If she knew of my love, she would stay in Jerusalem, and it's obvious that I can't protect her here. I have no idea how deeply these Sons of Judah have infiltrated my palace officials and the Judean military. She'll be much safer if she returns to Shunem with you and Jehosheba."

Jehoshaphat's probing gaze was unsettling, searching every corner of Solomon's soul. "Why divorce her?" he asked, suspicion still lacing his tone. "Why not simply send her to Shunem until Benaiah roots out the Sons of Judah and the conspiracy is ended?"

Solomon had dreaded the question, knowing that wise Jehoshaphat would cut to the bone eventually. "I love Arielah as I've never loved anyone in my life," he said, unable to contain his tears any longer. "But her love was not created for a harem wife." His voice broke into a sob, and he buried his face in his hands. "Her love will shrivel and die in my harem, Jehoshaphat, and I cannot bear Jehovah's judgment for destroying Arielah's pure heart." Rocking back and forth, Solomon released days—even years—of sorrow, grieving with a mourner's wail.

He felt two strong arms embrace him, an abba's comfort like he'd never felt before. Time passed. His tears ebbed. Jehoshaphat remained at his side.

Finally his stomach growled and broke the silence. Shunem's prince patted his shoulder. "You must eat something, my king, before you begin the day's court proceedings."

Solomon nodded but laid a hand on Jehoshaphat's arm when he tried to rise. "So what is your answer?" he asked. "About the divorce papers? I've had Elihoreph draw them up. Will you serve as witness when Arielah signs them?"

His eyes were kind but determined. "Let's wait, my son. Give Jehovah time to work in both of your hearts separately. If after sufficient time you still believe divorce to be the answer, I will witness my daughter's acceptance and grant it."

The bumpy wilderness roads between Jerusalem and Gibeon jarred Arielah's bones like a hand mill grinding wheat. Hannah had added more pillows inside the faded wedding carriage, but the jolts to her slow-healing wounds were still excruciating. "We're almost there, my lady," Hannah whispered, peering out the ivory-latticed window. "I see the Tent of Meeting on the high place ahead."

Ima reached for Arielah's hand, lips moving, eyes closed in silent prayer. The Shulammite queen gritted her teeth against the pain, trying to decide which hurt worse: her broken body or a potentially broken marriage. *A year*, she thought. *Abba said Solomon would send divorce papers in a year.*

Benaiah led Jehoshaphat's procession with Mighty Men

forming the front and rear guard. Abba's camel plodded beside her carriage, but he shouted directions nonetheless. "We'll make camp near the main pool, as close to the tabernacle as we can get."

She heard Benaiah shout back, "Why beside the pool?"

"We'll need the water to carry our voices across the crowd," Abba answered. "Many northerners will arrive at Gibeon's Passover ready for war."

Arielah squeezed her eyes tightly shut. Would the violence never end?

Jehoshaphat's caravan arrived well before twilight on the fourteenth day, plenty of time to set up their tents and get everyone settled. Ima Jehosheba coaxed Arielah to enjoy a short nap before Benaiah carried her to the sacrifice. He'd become her personal chariot, his strong arms her safest and gentlest means of transport. Hannah had placed a slice of cucumber over each eye and a warm cloth to hold them in place, and then settled down beside her to hum a tune.

"Prince Jehoshaphat!" Arielah heard the familiar voice outside their tent and swept the cucumbers to the floor. Shunem's chief elder, Phaltiel, greeted Abba across Gibeon's crowded hillside. "Thanks be to Jehovah, I finally found you!" Though the man had rendered the guilty verdict in Arielah's brother's execution, he remained a beloved family friend.

Abba rose from his stool at the open tent flap. "Phaltiel! Welcome!" He peeked his head inside the tent. "Jehosheba, Benaiah, come greet our friend."

Though Arielah couldn't see Phaltiel's countenance, she felt his warmth grow cold in silence. She saw Ima bow her head and reenter the tent, her eyes subtly saying, *Pray, Arielah. This is not good.*

When Phaltiel broke the silence, his words were clipped and harsh. "What brings the commander of Israel's army to our northern Passover celebration? Has the war begun and I'm the last to know?"

"No war, my lord," Benaiah said, and Arielah saw through the tent opening that the commander offered Phaltiel his hand in friendship. "I have come to guard Prince Jehoshaphat and his family on their return to Shunem. It is an honor to see you again."

No reply. Arielah held her breath, watching Benaiah's hand hang in lonely silence.

When Shunem's new chief elder finally grasped the big man's hand, Arielah sighed her relief. "Welcome, Benaiah," Phaltiel said, some kindness returning. "I'm sorry to have been abrupt, but word of Arielah's abuse has reached northern ears. And we will not abide it."

"Nor will I," Benaiah said, fire in his voice.

Abba Jehoshaphat embraced both men's shoulders. "My friends, it's almost twilight. Let's celebrate the Lord's Passover together and speak of Israel's unity after we remember our great deliverance." As he spoke, a sound like rushing water reached Arielah. The ground beneath her stacked tapestries began to quake.

"What's happening?" She turned to Ima Jehosheba, who ran to the tent opening.

Covering her mouth, Ima gasped, and tears immediately shone in her eyes. "Oh, Arielah," she whispered.

"What, Ima? What is it?"

Ima pulled back the tent flap to reveal a mob of several hundred men approaching their camp, carrying torches. Some even carried winnowing forks and scythes.

"Prince of Shunem," one man called out, "our northern tribes stand ready to fight. All of Israel will gather to avenge your daughter's betrayal and set Judah in its place. You need only issue the command."

Benaiah pressed Jehoshaphat into the tent behind him. "Stay in the tent, my friend. My men will protect you."

Jehoshaphat stepped around his mountainous friend, reaching up to pat his shoulder. "No, Benaiah. This time I believe it is you who needs my protection. Go back inside the tent and wait for me there."

"Oh no, my friend. I have never run from a battle, and I will not start today."

Jehoshaphat squeezed Benaiah's shoulder. "There will be no battle here. There will be a Passover Feast. Now, go into the tent and bring Arielah out to the crowd."

Arielah's heart leapt to her throat, and Ima cried, "Jehoshaphat!"

Benaiah's confusion seemed to root his feet to Gibeon's soil.

Jehoshaphat turned to address his wife. "Jehosheba, my love, what was written in the sky of my dream?"

"What?" Arielah asked instinctively, but understanding dawned before the word died on the breeze.

Ima's face showed the same radiant awareness. "Yes, husband, in lightning across the sky—'her life for Israel.'" Jehosheba stepped aside and said to Benaiah, "Take her outside. Israel must see their lamb."

Though Arielah's fresh wounds amplified her fear of violence, she trusted the resolve in Abba's voice and nodded her willingness. The commander, though seemingly still confused, must have also trusted Abba's confidence. He ducked inside the tent to retrieve her.

The crowd began to jeer. "That's right, big man, run!"

Another man called out, "Judah has ruined its last northern maiden!"

Gently cradling Arielah, Benaiah lifted her from the stacked tapestries and emerged from the tent. All noise ceased. They must have made quite the spectacle. Arielah, frail and broken in the arms of Israel's top soldier. Benaiah, his leather breastplate and wristbands glistening in the twilight, his sword, dagger, and bow attesting to his warrior skills. Israel's revered elder trusted this gentle giant with his daughter, and Abba trusted her resolve to be as strong as the man who carried her. But how did he want her to show it?

"Abba?" Her single word prompted his explanation.

"These men want to fight for your honor," Jehoshaphat explained in a loud, clear voice, "because your blood was spilled." More people were gathering now, hearing his voice amplified across the great pool. With a tender smile and meaningful wink, Abba said, "Tell the Israelites why the Passover lamb spilled its blood so others could be saved."

Arielah's heart swelled, her throat tight with the realization of Abba's intention. Dare she suggest such a thing, that *she* be similar to the Passover lamb, sacrificed so the death angel would pass over their nation and bring unity instead of civil war?

In her hesitation, she felt herself trembling—but quickly realized it wasn't her shaking. Hearing soft weeping, she looked up at the fierce soldier who held her. Benaiah's beard dripped with tears. "Tell them, Arielah. Tell them," he said.

"Men of Israel, I am your treaty bride." Her weak voice rose, and even the crickets seemed to still. "As you can see by my wounds, we are already engaged in a great battle."

A great roar swelled, and men shook their coarse weapons. Jehoshaphat motioned for silence so she could continue.

"But you must understand. Our battle is not against flesh and blood. It is a battle against the enemy within the hearts of men—and women."

Confusion and dissension rippled across the sea of men.

"Please listen. You know only a vague tribe called Judah and a lofty king named Solomon, but I see Judean friends I've come to love." She touched Benaiah's cheek. "And my husband is a wise and godly king who seeks to unite Israel and make her strong."

"What of your wounds, Queen Arielah? Does your blood mean nothing?" one man in the crowd cried out.

"Oh, I pray that my blood means everything," she shouted,

then coughed. The crowd quieted again, seemingly aware of the price her body paid for raising her voice. "I pray that because my blood was spilled, no other Israelite need be wounded. Let *me* be the Passover lamb, brethren. Let the death angel pass over Israel. I know my husband's heart." At this, her voice faltered. A sob escaped. Did she know his heart? What about the divorce papers?

He is Jedidiah. A voice seemed to echo in her spirit, and she gained strength to go on.

"He will return for me someday. I believe he will honor the treaty bride agreement. Jehovah has a plan for Israel, but he also loves Solomon the man. Let Jehovah do His work in both the nation and the man."

Silence.

Uneasy glances changed to furtive whispers, and one by one, the mob turned away. Benaiah stood with Arielah in his arms until the last man had gone.

Twilight came, and the Passover lambs were slaughtered. The whimpering questions of the first-time shepherds could be heard. "Abba, why must the lamb die?"

And the faithful abbas in Israel continued teaching their children. "It is the Passover sacrifice to the Lord, who passed over the houses of the Israelites in Egypt and spared our homes when he struck down the Egyptians' firstborn sons. We will commemorate God's faithfulness for all the generations to come."

"Will the Israelites allow God to prove faithful once again, Abba?" Arielah asked.

"Only Jehovah knows, my lamb."

Though three full moons had passed since Passover, Solomon still reveled in the glow of its joy. He had required all his wives to attend the sacrifice at twilight and to celebrate the seven-day Feast of Unleavened Bread. Even the foreign wives had been forced to enjoy themselves, and it seemed all but one did. A wry smile creased his lips at the memory of Naamah's face when he threw Rehoboam's Molech doll into the sacrificial fire. It had been a grand celebration.

"Why do you smile?" Sekhet's long, brown finger poked at his cheek.

Her brusque manner had become rather endearing since she'd witnessed the love of Jehoshaphat's family. Her sharp mind provided worthy exercise for his thoughts. "I'm remembering all the times I've beaten you at this game," he said, throwing the knucklebones across the game board. "Ha! And I've won again!" He advanced his jackal to its final position, but before he removed his hand, Sekhet wiped the board clean—sending hounds and jackals bouncing across the tiled floor. He laughed and pointed at her with the piece remaining in his hand. "You, Queen Sekhet, are a terrible loser."

Her only reply was a half smile, which for Solomon was a victory greater than the game. In the days since Arielah's departure, he'd had little female companionship—a decision of his own choosing, and one that had thrown his harem into anarchy. The Daughters of Jerusalem had bravely tried to appease his angry wives with added beauty treatments and overnight journeys to the springs of En Gedi. Shiphrah and Sherah had been worth their weight in temple gold. And after refusing any further visits with Marah, Solomon heard she had left the City of David—destination unknown—which was for the best.

"You seem distracted," Sekhet said, reaching over to touch his hand, a rare display of tender concern. Solomon wondered if the child in her womb was already softening her heart.

He noticed shadows under her eyes. "Are you getting enough sleep, Sekhet? Does the babe keep you awake at night?"

She tilted her head, and the lion-mane wig caught the lamplight glow.

"Perhaps you should return to your chamber to rest."

Her expression grew rigid, all tenderness gone. The hand she'd extended drew back, placed precisely in her lap. "If you wish me to go, I will leave. But I will not return to my chamber where those sisters of Set rule the underworld of your harem."

Solomon's shock at her flood of words must have been evident.

"Close your mouth," she said. "You gape like a hippo."

Leaving his goatskin rug, he pulled her into an embrace. His warrior wife was trembling. "Should I assume these 'sisters of Set' you mentioned are the other wives? Have they been mistreating you?"

She remained silent, stoic. Though he never interfered in the harem's world of women, he would not sit idly by and allow Sekhet to be terrorized.

"Sekhet, I cannot protect you if I do not know the trouble." Even as he said the words, the image of Arielah's broken body flashed in his mind. He squeezed his eyes closed against the memory.

"I master your other wives," she said, a hint of "the powerful one" returning.

Solomon waited for her to explain further, but she remained silent. Who but his wives would represent Set, the Egyptian god of chaos, destruction, and evil? "Sekhet . . ."

"I will go." She struggled to her feet.

"No, wait," he said, catching her hand before she could walk away. "I'm thinking of taking a stroll in my garden. Would you join me?" Obviously his Egyptian queen had said all she was going to say on the matter. Probably for the best. Sekhet was Pharaoh's daughter. She probably realized that he couldn't go meddling in harem politics for one wife without being drawn into all the women's quarrels.

He stood and kissed Sekhet's hand. They ambled toward his garden, the blossoming almond tree ushering them into his private sanctuary. Solomon breathed deeply, letting the soul healing begin. It had become his nightly retreat, where he contemplated the moon and stars. Perhaps his garden would refresh Sekhet more deeply than sleep.

"What is your favorite flower, Sekhet?" he asked after a little while.

"Blue lotus," she said, her gaze growing distant. "It's not grown in Israel."

He would have his gardener send merchants to Egypt to retrieve some starter plants. "That will change," he said softly. He pretended to study the rosebuds lining the path beside them, but Solomon pondered his Egyptian queen instead. He'd come to care for her, respect her, even enjoy her. They'd become close friends, sharing the marriage bed in order to produce the child she now carried. But their hearts were forever separate because she refused to fully embrace El Shaddai.

He sighed, and she gave him a sideways glance. Smiling, he squeezed her hand and continued their stroll, rounding the corner where the henna bushes met the budding mandrakes. Solomon considered his new garden project in the Kidron Valley. Arielah would be pleased. He had checked it yesterday to see if the vines had budded or if the pomegranates were yet in bloom. Pomegranates were Arielah's favorite.

"Do you like pomegranates, Sekhet?"

"I like pistachios," she said, rewarding him with another coy smile. "Why do you ask?"

"Just wondering," he said, not willing to share his heart. "The first pistachios will be ready for harvest soon." She nodded and seemed content to continue in silence. It pleased him.

The excitement of the throne hall had once been like daily bread to him, and he'd thought Arielah's need for Shunem's meadows an unusual shepherd's trait. But like the spinning of wool and spindle, his heart had learned the rhythm of solitude and peace. Now he craved it like sweet wine. "I'm going to have Benaiah escort me to my best vineyard."

"Where is it?" Her eyes brightened. "Close to Egypt?"

Squeezing her hand, he was reminded again of the loneliness a foreign wife suffered. "No, Sekhet," he said, rubbing his thumb over her soft, dark skin. "My abba's best vineyards are in Baal Hamon, in the very northernmost part of my kingdom . . ." His heart began to race. He lifted her hand to his lips. "Just past the Jezreel Valley and Mount Moreh, near the cedars of Lebanon. Very near our old friend Prince Jehoshaphat."

She smiled—this time a smile that reached her eyes and bore her soul. "Tell Queen Arielah I said 'shalom.'"

35

[Lover] Before I realized it, my desire set me among the royal chariots of my people.

[Friends] Come back, come back, O Shulammite; come back, come back, that we may gaze on you!

Have I lost her, Benaiah?" Solomon finally asked. They'd left Jerusalem three days ago, and the question had nearly burned a hole in his heart. Swaying silently on a plodding camel, he was content to let his friend form a profound response. Moments passed, and then more moments. "Benaiah!" he shouted when the man remained silent.

"What?" the commander shouted back.

Both camels spit and squawked, conveying exactly how Solomon felt about his friend's indifference. "Did you hear me?"

"Hear what?"

"Ahhh!" Solomon roared, the sound vaguely similar to his wives' complaints when he didn't feel like conversing. "Did you hear my question about Arielah?"

"No, I suppose I was a little distracted by the scorching

372

heat, the lurking bandits, and our dwindling water supply."
The big man's scar began to throb, and Solomon considered
that the final straw.

"Commander, you may take your camel and join Hezro
at the head of the procession. I'm weary of your company."
Holding the big man's gaze, he saw the slightest glimmer of
amusement.

"Before I 'take my camel' . . ." Benaiah said, wobbling his
head like an old woman. Both men chuckled at their bicker-
ing. "Can you clarify again why you insisted on these plodding
Bactrian camels instead of couriers' dromedaries? We could
have been to your vineyard and back by now."

"I've already told you—"

Benaiah held up a hand to interrupt. "And if you could also
explain why we took the eastern route around the mountains
and why you chose the vineyard in the farthest reaches of
hostile northern Israel—I would appreciate those clarifica-
tions as well."

In that moment, inexplicably, Solomon missed his abba
more than ever. Only Benaiah would dare goad him this way,
and he had earned the right because he was as close to an
earthly abba as Solomon would ever have again. Emotion
nearly strangled him, and he turned away.

"My lord, I'm . . ." Benaiah's voice grew tender. "Solomon,
I'm sorry."

Wiping away the unexpected tears, he roared, "Well, you
should be, you old goat!" He laughed away the moment,
and the two rode awhile longer before Solomon explained.
"I miss Abba, my friend," he said, his throat still tight with
emotion. "I have so many questions . . ."

Benaiah nodded but remained silent. What could he say?
No one could bring Abba David back. Death was a part of
life. Knowing these things, however, didn't make Solomon's
void less painful. "So, you see, my friend," he said, trying to
lighten the mood, "that's why I chose Bactrian camels and

the northeastern route." When Benaiah lifted a questioning brow, Solomon chuckled. "To torture you while I contemplate life's deeper questions."

"But why must you *contemplate* this far north?" Benaiah almost growled. "I know Baal Hamon is legendary, and the best palace wine comes from those vines. But, Solomon . . . you must realize the former tribe of Asher is almost as dangerous as Shunem itself."

Solomon's heart skipped at the mention of Shunem. "I know it's dangerous, Benaiah, but the vinedresser at Baal Hamon is like an abba to me. Perhaps when I see old Shimei, he can answer some of my questions. He's always known how to speak to my heart, and he helps me listen to my heart as well."

Benaiah was silent, distracted. "We're entering the forest. Stay alert!" he shouted to his guards. He turned back to Solomon, his voice mingling frustration, regret, and concern. "You could have at least let me bring more than ten Mighty Men. Now stay close."

"I'm done being afraid, Benaiah," Solomon said, his words sounding far braver than his wildly pounding heart. "If the northern districts see that I roam among them as a brother, perhaps they'll trust me again."

But Benaiah had already ridden ahead of him, the other guards forming a single line before and behind. The dense Gilboa forest required concentration from both rider and beast to trudge through the underbrush and juniper trees.

When finally they emerged from the shadowy woodland, the Jezreel Valley stretched before them. The little village of Shunem shone in the afternoon heat, drawing Solomon with a radiance brighter than the sun.

Benaiah issued a sideways glance, his previous intensity eased. "I miss your abba too," he said, "but I think you've forgotten the most important instruction King David ever gave you."

Solomon felt the blood drain from his face. Had he failed his abba so completely? "What, Benaiah? What have I neglected?"

"On the day David prophesied God's blessing over you, he said Jehovah told him that you would build the temple—"

"And I'm doing that—"

"Let me finish, Solomon."

The king felt like a boy being scolded. "I'm sorry. Go ahead."

Benaiah smiled, his eyes kind. "The Lord said to David," he began, reciting the words as if they were written on his heart, "'Solomon is the one who will build My house and My courts, for I have chosen him to be My son, and I, the Lord, will be his Abba.'"

Solomon's heart pounded as the words ignited his soul. "How could I have forgotten?"

"Jehovah is the Abba you desire," Benaiah said. "He will answer the questions of your heart. What you need, my friend, is a wife who will teach you to truly love." Benaiah pointed to the little village across the valley. "I believe your Abba Jehovah has placed her within your grasp."

"A small caravan approaches, and it bears the king's banner!" a watchman in Jehoshaphat's vineyard tower cried.

Every worker in the vineyard halted their labor and stared at Jehoshaphat. A wide smile graced his lips. "We shall go welcome our king!"

The Shulammites exchanged cautious glances, leaving their hoes in the dirt and their clay jars in the trenches. Gathering outside the vineyard, they'd let the vinedressing wait.

Reu and Igal met Jehoshaphat, uncertainty etched on their faces. "I think it's Benaiah on the camel beside the king," Jehoshaphat said, shading his eyes from the afternoon sun.

Reu's face was pinched and red. "Perhaps the king comes to

ensure we haven't bartered the chariots he sent for our second goodwill campaign." Casting a sour glance at Jehoshaphat, he added, "We could trade those chariots to supply many weapons for a northern stand against Judah."

"Enough, Reu," Jehoshaphat said, fire in his voice. "There will be no northern stand. You should be ashamed speaking against your brother Judeans, my friend."

"I may be Judean by blood," Reu mumbled, "but I want nothing to do with the Sons of Judah."

Ignoring his young friend's petulance, Jehoshaphat continued toward the city gate. The king's small entourage moved slowly on their camels, giving Shunem time to gather. "Phaltiel, my friend!" Jehoshaphat greeted the leading judge at the southern city gate. "It seems the king comes to pay a visit."

The man ducked his head and spoke so only Jehoshaphat could hear. "And it seems the Shulammites are less than pleased." Phaltiel nodded at the crowd gathering inside the city walls. They were carrying rough-hewn weapons— winnowing forks and plowshares strapped to sticks.

Jehoshaphat's head fell forward. *Lord Jehovah, I need You now.* When he looked up, Solomon had drawn near with Benaiah and only ten Mighty Men. For the first time since he'd been named prince of Shunem, Jehoshaphat wished Solomon had brought his army.

He quickly walked toward the small retinue of royal guests. "Greetings, King Solomon. What brings you to the fertile lands of your nation?"

Solomon scanned the sea of faces in the crowd, seemingly oblivious to the danger. "We were on our way to my vineyard in Baal Hamon, but before I realized it, my heart drew me to your gates." Giving up his search, he met Jehoshaphat's gaze. "I must speak with you—and with Arielah."

"We've heard too many words," one Shulammite shouted from amid the crowd, stealing Solomon's attention again. "What about Arielah's broken heart? What about her broken body?" Protests began to rumble like the slow boil of lamb stew.

Solomon clucked his tongue, and his camel knelt to dismount its rider. Benaiah did the same, but leapt from the beast when he saw Solomon step to the ground ahead of him.

Jehoshaphat blocked the king's path. "No, my son. You must not walk into that crowd."

"Jehoshaphat, I will not live in fear of my northern brothers." Raising his voice, Solomon proclaimed his intentions. "Listen, fellow Israelites. I intend to walk through those gates and beg for my wife's forgiveness. I failed to love and protect her. I have wronged her."

"What about us? What about the wrongs you've committed against Israel?" The crowd swelled toward the king, and a man ran at him. Benaiah jumped in front of Solomon with his sword drawn, but when he saw the man's face, he froze.

It was Igal. Jehoshaphat's lone son planted himself between the angry Shulammites and King Solomon. "Listen to me! Stop! Listen!" Slowly the mob quieted. "You all witnessed my sister's mercy when I deserved stoning. Because of her mercy, I learned to love and now live at peace with my family." Stepping aside and placing his hand on Solomon's shoulder, he said, "Israel enjoys peace on every border, and the foundations of God's temple will soon be laid! Should we show any less mercy to our king who seeks Israel's good?"

The crowd remained silent. Jehoshaphat's chest swelled with pride at the fruit of Jehovah's mercy in his son's life.

Solomon turned to Igal. "Thank you, brother." Then, raising his voice to the crowd, the king said, "I am a man like all of you, susceptible to deceit, desire, and distraction. But I am the son of David, chosen and anointed by God to rule this nation. The decisions I make for Israel are born of love for my God and His people. Jehovah has given me wisdom to rule. Now let me do it." Receiving their silence as a truce, he resolutely marched toward the gate, parting the crowd.

While Igal and Reu directed his caravan to the stables, Solomon nearly ran toward Jehoshaphat's home, but Shunem's prince reached his courtyard gate first. "My son, why did you send them?" His hand rested atop the gate, stalling Solomon in the dusty street.

Wishing to be sensitive but anxious to see his wife, Solomon prayed for patience. "Please, Jehoshaphat. I realize you wish to speak about the chariots for the second goodwill tour, but can't we talk after I see Arielah?" Solomon pushed through the gate, and Jehoshaphat followed closely behind.

"That's not exactly what I meant—"

Solomon reached the front door in a few long strides and flung it open—and wished he'd listened to his abba-in-law.

"Come back to Jerusalem, little Shulammite," Shiphrah said, hovering over Arielah. "We're planning a lovely feast to celebrate, and you can dance the Mahanaim."

Sherah's kohl-rimmed eyes met Solomon's. Her lips parted in a painted smile. "Oh, King Solomon! We're surprised our escort arrived before yours!"

Jehoshaphat placed his hand on the king's shoulder to steady him. "I meant, why did you send the Daughters of Jerusalem?"

"What are you doing here?" Solomon asked the twins. "How did you even know I would come to Shunem?"

"When we heard you'd decided to visit your vineyard in Baal Hamon, we thought you might collect your wayward queen." Shiphrah smiled down at Arielah, placed a possessive hand on her shoulder. "We've come to escort her back to Jerusalem. We certainly wouldn't want any more harm to come her way."

Solomon glimpsed terror in Arielah's eyes, and Jehoshaphat fairly ran to her side. Pushing away Shiphrah's hand, the protective abba stood over his daughter. "I should have known the king would never send you to my home. Now get out."

"They said I sent them?" Solomon felt the blood drain from his face and realized he'd seriously misjudged the Daughters of Jerusalem.

"We simply said . . ." Shiphrah began an embellished tale that he might have believed—yesterday.

Suddenly it all made sense. "Sisters of Set," Sekhet had called them. These women had ruled his household and very nearly ruined his nation. He'd dismissed Benaiah's warning of the twins' involvement because no witnesses were ever found. *Lord Jehovah, what have I done?*

"You!" he shouted, abruptly ceasing Shiphrah's drivel. "Get away from her!" He rushed at them, grasping their arms and flinging them toward the door.

Fear etched their faces. "My king, we simply came to welcome your wife back into our company." Shiphrah's eyes brimmed with tears, but he would not be drawn into their deceit again.

Instead, he studied them, allowing his perusal to unsettle them and God's wisdom to instruct him. Noting their dusty and disheveled appearance, Solomon concluded they'd ridden swifter dromedary camels along the western sea route. They might have left a day—even two—after the king's departure, depending on when they realized his destination. Everyone in the palace knew he was traveling to Baal Hamon, but news of Arielah's welcome feast was fresh, revealed to him only moments ago.

He'd heard enough of the twins' lies.

Turning to his wife for answers, Solomon knelt beside her. "Beloved, what did they tell you about this so-called feast they're planning?"

"We simply told her—" Sherah began.

"Silence, woman!" Solomon roared at her interruption. He gently lifted Arielah's crooked hand to his lips. "Please, beloved. What did they say?"

The room fell silent. His bride looked to her abba and then

back at him. Jehoshaphat had protected her, loved her, rescued her when Solomon had abandoned her to these women. Would she trust him? "Arielah," he said, touching her cheek, "these women will never harm you again."

Jehoshaphat stepped toward her. "Tell him, my lamb. Tell your husband what the Daughters of Jerusalem asked of you."

Seeming still hesitant, Arielah answered quietly, "They asked me to dance the Mahanaim at the celebration they were planning." Her gaze fell to her misshapen left leg. "They said since Mahanaim means 'two camps,' and since the dance commemorated your abba's flight from Jerusalem when Absalom tried to steal the throne, well . . ." She looked up then, a single tear falling over her lashes. "They thought it appropriate for the wife who fled Jerusalem to dance among your other wives."

A low, guttural moan started in Solomon's belly and exploded into a roar. Like a flaming arrow shot from a bow, he propelled himself at the twins. Grasping their arms, he nearly lifted them off their feet. "Ahhh! How can you say these things? Do these things?"

Shiphrah and Sherah whimpered but didn't speak.

Drawing them close, he spit as he ground out the words, "It is both of *you* who dance in two camps! You speak honeyed words to me but drive a dagger into Arielah's back." Releasing his hold, he cast them aside like filthy rags. "You will leave this house immediately and return to Jerusalem. I will deal with you when I return."

The two women stumbled and cowered, taking their first few steps toward the door. Shiphrah turned as if to plead.

"No!" Solomon screamed. "You will not speak! Out of my sight, both of you!"

Just then Benaiah arrived at Jehoshaphat's doorway, panting, his sword drawn, ready for a fight. Glancing at the scene before him, he braced his hands against his knees, relief evident as he explained. "My men have just arrested ten Judean soldiers. When they said they escorted the Daughters of Jerusalem, I knew where I would find them."

"You were right, Benaiah." Solomon's voice trembled with pent-up fury. "I'm certain the Daughters of Jerusalem were complicit in Arielah's beating."

The twins' eyes bulged. "My lord, no!"

"I said silence!" Solomon shouted. Turning back to Benaiah, he asked, "Do you trust the ten Mighty Men who accompanied us from Jerusalem? Could any of them be Sons of Judah?"

"I trust those Cherethite guards with my life," he said, fist to heart.

"Do you trust them with Arielah's life?" Solomon asked, and Benaiah's scar began to dance.

A single nod preceded the words. "What are you thinking, my king?"

"I think it's time we found witnesses against the Daughters of Jerusalem." Solomon watched a smug grin form on Shiphrah face. He shoved the two women into Benaiah's arms. "Take the sisters of Set and their ten Judean soldiers back to Jerusalem with nine of your Mighty Men." Solomon pinned Benaiah with a determined look. "Leave Hezro here with me, and make sure you and your Cherethites don't fall under these women's power."

"I will not leave you with only one guard in Shunem!"

Solomon exchanged a glance with Jehoshaphat. "I have three guards in this house alone, my friend." He chuckled when Jehosheba proudly thrust her shoulders back and her chin out. The women in Jehoshaphat's home were small but held a mighty sway among the Shulammites. Igal and Reu suddenly appeared at the doorway, and Solomon's amusement peaked. "Make that five guards, Benaiah—six if you include our soldier friend Hezro! I'll be safe in Shunem until you send an escort to retrieve me."

"But, my lord . . ." Benaiah's protests faded when Solomon turned toward Arielah.

In two long strides, Solomon was at his wife's side, kneeling again. "I suppose I should first ask if I am welcome to remain. Beloved?"

A slow nod and raining tears answered him.

Jehoshaphat placed a hand on Solomon's shoulder. "You are welcome in our home—and in Shunem—my king."

36

[Lover] How beautiful your sandaled feet, O prince's daughter! . . .

[Beloved] The mandrakes send out their fragrance, and at our door is every delicacy, both new and old, that I have stored up for you.

Arielah combed her fingers through Solomon's hair as he and Abba watched Benaiah escort Shiphrah and Sherah through the courtyard gate. "I'm glad you came," she whispered, drawing Solomon's attention.

She caught only a momentary glimpse of the victory he must have felt, and then his eyes immediately grew dim. "Oh, beloved." He buried his head in her lap, immediate sobs shaking his shoulders.

"Shhh, my love." She caressed his back, stroked his hair, let his sorrow flow.

"I did not love or protect you as I promised at our wedding, as an Israelite husband should."

Abba and Ima knelt beside him, placing supportive hands on his shoulders. "My son," Abba said, "we are proud of you

383

for coming. You've shown great courage and integrity amid daunting circumstances."

"But I—" Solomon started to protest, but Ima interrupted.

"There will be time for us to talk later. Now is the time for you to share your heart with your wife . . . alone." With a voice that left no room for argument, she said, "Off to our bedchamber where you can speak the things a husband and wife need to hear. Come, Arielah, on your feet."

Abba and Ima stood on each side and braced her so she could stand. As always, that first press of weight on her legs sent a stab of pain and stole her breath.

"What?" Solomon cried. "What can I do?" Tears filled his eyes again. "I did this to you, beloved." He stood alone, dejected, forlorn—and Arielah's heart broke.

Taking a step toward him, she fell into his arms. He swept her up, cradling her like a child. "I love you," he said, burying his head in the curve of her neck. "I love you. Can you ever forgive me?"

Cupping his cheek, she said, "I have already forgiven you in the midst of the pain. It's the reason I know the forgiveness is not my own. It's born from above, and I am as grateful to give it as you can be to receive it." She kissed him gently. "Now take me to my ima's chamber, where we can speak of our future."

She watched his cheeks pink as he exchanged a nod with Abba Jehoshaphat and then carried her through the bedchamber door. Setting her gently on the edge of her parents' stacked mattresses, his eyes traveled over her, devouring her from the top of her head to the tips of her sandaled feet. "You are the most beautiful sight I've ever seen." His voice was full of wonder.

Instinctively she drew the sheer linen veil over her deeply scarred face, but he pulled it away. His eyes ravenous, he leaned over to kiss her. She relaxed into the moment, ready for the first sweet taste of his lips in five full moons, but—nothing. She opened her eyes and watched him lift the washbasin from the bedside table. He knelt at her feet and removed her worn sandals.

Cringing at the thought of his regal hands on her twisted foot, she cried, "No! Wait! What are you doing?"

His only answer was the tenderness with which he splashed water on her dusty feet, and her misgivings dried up as her tears rained down.

"How beautiful are your feet, oh prince's daughter," he said, drying her feet and massaging her calves. "Your graceful legs are like jewels, the work of a craftsman's hands." He rose up and eased her back onto the bed. Her robe lay flat against her stomach. His hands stopped their caressing, and his eyes grew as round as Abraham's well. "Arielah! You are with child!" He pulled his hand away as though the small babe within her might reach out and grab him. "How can this be?" he said, propping himself on one elbow, careful to keep his weight off her rounded middle.

Arielah smiled at his boyish wonder. "Solomon, you are an abba many times over. Do I really need to explain it?"

The delight on his face matched the awe in his voice. "How could the child have survived the beating? How could you have conceived when we . . . when I . . ."

Arielah's sorrow mingled with the joy of this moment. "We slept in the bridal chamber until the day I moved to your ima Bathsheba's room." She touched her rounding belly. "I remember curling into a ball as they were beating me. This baby is strong, my love, and seems quite determined to know its abba."

Solomon's eyes filled with wonder. He kissed her stomach and moved his hand across the contours of her shape. "Your navel is a rounded goblet that never lacks blended wine. Your waist is a mound of wheat encircled by lilies. Your breasts are like two fawns, twins of a gazelle."

Arielah giggled. "Your shepherd's verse was unique and new to my ears until you reached my breasts, King Solomon."

Solomon bounced his eyebrows. "It's because that phrasing—like your breasts—cannot be improved upon. Now be silent while I finish."

She covered her mouth, enjoying each moment of his renewed familiarity.

"Your neck is like an ivory tower. Your eyes are the pools of Heshbon by the gate of Bath Rabbim. Your nose is like the tower of Lebanon looking toward Damascus. Your head crowns you like Mount Carmel. Your hair is like royal tapestry; the king is held captive by its tresses."

She laid her head back on the pillow and let the deep baritone sound of his voice wash over her.

"How beautiful you are, and how pleasing, oh love, with your delights!" Stroking her cheek, he kissed her softly.

Her body responded, wanting, needing to be loved. But she had to know his heart. "What is your name?" she whispered. He had been both lover and liar, kind and cruel. Was he the king who had cast her aside, the stranger who had ruthlessly stood over her broken body and later demanded divorce? Or was he the loving son of David, anointed by Jehovah and given to her as a precious gift? "What is your name?" she asked again. She must refuse his kisses until she knew his heart.

Eyes that at first registered confusion began scanning some point outside the window. She wondered if he would storm away in a rage as he'd done before, but he lingered, deep in thought. "I've learned much in the hours of contemplation in my garden."

"Your garden?" Arielah asked, her heart growing hopeful.

A glint of mischief shone in his eye. "Someone once told me an apple tree could grow in a forest, so I had to investigate some of Jehovah's handiwork for myself." Tracing the line of her jaw, he spoke softly. "In my nights of contemplation, I determined to use God's wisdom for better purposes than pleasure and folly. So I employed an army of scribes to record my reflections on life and its meaning, the pursuit of pleasure and its fruitlessness." He kissed the end of her nose. "We'll certainly learn more as we grow old together, but I thought it wise to begin the record now and expand as Jehovah gives greater understanding."

She smiled at the thought of gray hair at his temples. What a distinguished-looking king he would be.

"You have changed me, beloved. You've shown me the value of solitude." He searched her expression, probed the windows of her soul. "My name is Jedidiah."

Arielah cupped his cheeks, showering his face with kisses. "Yes! Yes, it is, my love." She rejoiced with him. "You are changed, but I have not changed you. I was in Shunem while Jehovah tended your heart."

Solomon held her head between his hands, studying her anew. "You are amazing, my little shepherdess. What new verse shall I create to describe you?" he asked, his eyes suddenly alight. "You are like a palm tree!"

"A palm tree?" Arielah laughed. Leaning up to capture his lips, she teased, "I think we've heard enough shepherd's verse, my love."

He pulled her into the curve of his frame, holding her so tight she felt as if they breathed the same breath and shared one heartbeat. "You have weathered a storm that would have snapped a mighty oak," he whispered into her ear. "You are a palm tree, beloved, and I plan to climb my palm tree and take hold of its fruit!" He nuzzled the nape of her neck with his beard, and she squealed. "Shhh!" he said. "Your parents are right outside!"

She reveled in the ease with which he teased and loved her. Gazing into his eyes, she saw her reflection there. Her scars were washed away in the glistening of his tears. A light kiss. A brush of his nose against her cheek.

"Your breasts now bear the fruit of a child, like clusters of fruit on the vine," he whispered. "The fragrance of your breath is like apples, and your mouth like the best wine."

"Why don't you taste that wine, my love? Let it flow gently over your lips." Arielah closed her eyes to wait for the kiss she knew would come. His mouth covered hers, and with the fullness of God's blessing, they enjoyed the fruit of their union.

Solomon awoke to the sound of a rooster's crow and felt the reassuring warmth of Arielah's small frame in the bend of his arm. Were it not for the cramped space of their tiny wedding carriage and his aching back, this would be the perfect Shulammite sunrise. Deep hues of purple and orange glowed through the ivory-latticed window, and the sounds of Shunem's waking helped him understand Arielah's homesickness when she had first arrived in Jerusalem.

"Good morning, beloved." He kissed her awake.

"Mmm." She stretched and purred like Sekhet's Egyptian cat.

"I have a surprise for you this morning," he said and watched her eyes instantly go wide.

"What?"

"I talked with your abba last night, and he believes we can travel safely if I dress in shepherds' garb."

She tried to turn on her side but winced.

"Lie still," he said. Soothing her, he rose on his side to hover over his beloved girl.

A tentative smile touched her lips, a hint of fear at its edges. "Travel? Are we going back to Jerusalem before Benaiah arrives with our escort?"

His heart ached at her resolve to accept the inevitable return to the city of her pain. "No, beloved. We're traveling north." He watched her surprise.

"But there is nothing to the north—except Tyre. Are you going to visit King Hiram?"

"Actually, I considered that," he said, stroking her cheek. "But no. This trip will be strictly pleasure." The adorable tilt of her head made him chuckle. "We're going to my vineyard at Baal Hamon."

"Oh!" she squealed and grabbed his neck, nearly tumbling his full weight down on her. "I've always wanted to see your famous vineyard! Oh, can we leave early? Can we go right now?"

He laughed at his impatient bride. "First we must gather some Shulammites to accompany us as guards, just in case there's trouble along the way." Dawn's light cast an ethereal glow on his shepherdess queen. "Do you know how much I love you?"

A shadow of sadness passed over her features. She grew utterly silent, her smile dim. "I know that I've belonged to you since our betrothal," she said, stroking his cheek. "And your journey to Shunem despite the danger shows your desire for me. But love . . ."

His chest felt like a wineskin being squeezed of every drop. "Arielah, what are you saying?" She had turned away. He captured her chin and saw tears beneath tightly closed eyes. "What else must I do to prove that I love you?"

"Ohhh," she moaned as if her heart were breaking. "Please, Solomon, listen to my heart, not just my words."

She paused, opened her eyes. Searching his gaze, she waited until he nodded before she spoke. But he wasn't sure he could hear anything except his wounded feelings.

"The only love I know," she began quietly, "I learned from my abba and ima in the warmth of Shunem's vineyards and meadows. You learned of love in King David's harem filled with wives and children." She laid her hand on her rounded middle, cradling the child within. "Somehow we must live a love that will nurture our child in Jehovah's care."

Solomon's heart pounded. How could he teach a child of love when he himself didn't know how to explain the emotion?

"Take me to Baal Hamon," Arielah whispered. "During our journey, I'll give you my love in the fields of mandrakes amid their fragrance. We'll study the old lessons of love and the new pathways of our hearts."

He fell silent, wishing he could be angry with her. He was King Solomon, granted divine wisdom from El Shaddai. Yet somehow he knew she was right. Love was not understood by the mind of wisdom. It was learned through the scars of a Shulammite shepherdess, and Jehovah was guiding their journey.

Brushing her forehead with a kiss, he said, "All right, beloved. We will learn of this mysterious love together, and we'll find a way to love each other in Jerusalem."

37

[Friends] Who is this coming up from the desert lean-
ing on her lover?

[Beloved] Under the apple tree I roused you; there your
mother conceived you, there she who was in labor gave
you birth.

Jehoshaphat and Reu led the Baal Hamon procession on dromedaries. Shepherd-robed Solomon and Hezro followed on their camels with Arielah and Hannah in the wedding carriage, bouncing along the coastal highway by the Great Sea. The little coach, stripped of its gold and veils, appeared as any other wealthy merchant's transport. Igal and his choice of nine capable Shulammites provided rear guard.

"I'd like to ride by Jehoshaphat for a while, Reu," Solomon said on the third and final day of their journey. "I have something to discuss with him, and I don't want to shout." Jehoshaphat's young aide said nothing, simply halted his camel, allowing Solomon to take his place. The young man maintained the same sullen expression that had been chiseled on his face since Solomon arrived in Shunem. "Thank you, Reu," he said as his camel moved into position.

A curt nod was Reu's only reply.

Solomon lifted his eyebrow when he arrived at Jehoshaphat's side. Keeping his voice low, he asked, "Do you think he'll accept my offer when he still holds this kind of resentment toward me?"

"All we can do is offer it. I'll take him aside while we're here at Baal Hamon and tell him what you and Arielah have decided." With a shrug, he added, "If the Lord has laid it on your heart, Solomon, you must offer."

The reality of Israel's conflict had never been more real to Solomon. "Is Reu's bitterness shared by everyone in the northern districts? Is war in Israel inevitable?"

Jehoshaphat's eyes grew kind. "Only Jehovah's plan is inevitable, my king." His smile opened Solomon's heart to receive hope. "The Lord promised you a reign characterized by peace, *Shalom-on.* You must offer to your nation—like you must offer to Reu—the gifts and wisdom God lays on your heart, and then it's up to them to accept it." Jehoshaphat pressed his lips into a thin line. "Reu must learn not only to admire forgiveness but to realize he can—and should—implement it in his own life. Israel must learn the same. They must not simply talk of peace, but they must also work to live it."

The words struck a harmonic chord in Solomon. Forgiveness, peace, love—they were similar. Solomon had admired the love he saw in Jehoshaphat's family, but he must embrace it for himself, work to give and receive that same love in his own life.

"I've never thought of you as a man of the soil," Jehoshaphat said, interrupting Solomon's pondering. "This is the first I've known the son of David to visit a vineyard."

The man's smile was warm, his interest genuine. Solomon might have bristled in weeks past at the implication that he didn't appreciate nature as Abba David had. "When I was young," he began, "Abba David took me to Baal Hamon to learn of vineyards. While Abba traveled further north for business with King Hiram, I stayed with the vinedresser, Shimei, who taught me of the vines." Glancing ahead, Solomon caught a glimpse of the vineyard tower and . . .

Leaning forward, shading his eyes from the setting sun, he saw a lone figure standing in the vineyard watchtower, frail and bent. "I think that's him, Jehoshaphat!" Turning to alert the caravan, he shouted, "Baal Hamon is ahead!" Excitement brimming, he felt his heart nearly burst with memories. "Abba David put Shimei in charge of Baal Hamon over twenty years ago, and his faithful service has kept the palace wine stores overflowing. I spent many summers under his guidance, learning to tend the vines."

"So why did you stop coming?" Jehoshaphat's question was innocent, but it dampened Solomon's enthusiasm.

"Duty stopped my visits," he said sadly. "As Israel prospered, Abba spent less time in Tyre, and I spent less time at Baal Hamon. As I got older, my responsibilities grew, and our view of Baal Hamon changed. Instead of it being our family's vineyard on the way to Tyre, it became the vineyard too far into northern Israel to visit." The confession made his camel's plodding seem even slower.

"Go!" Jehoshaphat said.

"What?" Solomon turned to find the prince smiling. He must have noticed Solomon's impatience.

"I said *go!* We'll catch up."

"Ha-ha!" Solomon swatted his camel's backside, and all four hooves flew.

Solomon heard another camel beside him and found Hezro gaining ground. He should have known Benaiah's Cherethite wouldn't let him too far out of reach. As they neared the vineyard, Solomon noticed the stooped old man had arrived at the narrowly opened gate. Solomon and Hezro halted their camels directly in front of a beaming Shimei.

Peering from beneath wiry gray eyebrows, Shimei shouted, "Shalom, young Solomon!" His unkempt beard looked as if a family of doves nested in it.

"Shalom, good Shimei! Your young prince has returned."

"Ah, can it be the little prince has returned a king, or has the king become a shepherd?" His pink gums gleamed from his wide smile.

Solomon remembered his shepherd's disguise and marveled that the old man had recognized him from the tower. "I come to inspect your work, old man!" Solomon tapped his camel's shoulder, and the beast rocked to its knees. Hezro mirrored the king's descent, and both joined the vinedresser at the gate.

Though the old man's eyes were cloudy, they saw into Solomon's soul. "Surely my work is least on your list of pressing national issues, my lord."

"You're right as usual, good Shimei. I bring a woman for your approval. She has pressed my heart like a winepress squeezes grapes."

The old man's weak shout sounded like wind through sackcloth. "The son of David comes to visit his vineyard. Sound the shofar, for today we celebrate!"

The heavy wooden gate swung open at the hands of two burly Judean guards. They stared at Solomon with interest.

"King Solomon, my lord." Shimei ceremoniously bowed.

"Stand up, old friend." Solomon chuckled. "I'm afraid you'll topple over if you bow any lower."

The old man stood, and his laughter ended in a fit of coughing. Solomon held him until he quieted. "So what *really* brings you to your northern vineyard, Solomon?"

No more games. No more trifling words. Solomon pointed to the little wedding carriage approaching. "The woman in that coach, Shimei. She is my wife and says we must learn how to love before we return to Jerusalem."

The old man nodded. "She seems wiser than you already," Shimei said, mischief in his eyes. "Your abba tended the royal flocks when he needed to listen to Jehovah, but you, young prince, have always listened best amid the vines." They entered the vineyard, Solomon with his arm around the old man's waist to steady him.

When they reached the vinedresser's home, Solomon said, "Wait here. I'll escort Arielah and her abba Jehoshaphat and introduce them as soon as the caravan is settled inside the vineyard gate."

"I'll have Cook prepare the evening meal for our special guests," Shimei shouted over his shoulder, setting off another coughing bout. "I see love has bitten you hard, young prince. We have much to celebrate."

By the time Solomon returned with Jehoshaphat and Arielah, the meal was waiting, but Cook was wringing her hands. "I'm sorry, my king," she said hesitantly, "but Shimei has gone out to your old meeting place and asks that you bring your bride to greet him. I'll serve our other guests while you and your bride find Shimei."

A bit embarrassed by his friend's eccentricity, he apologized to Jehoshaphat and the others, asking Cook to make them feel welcome. Handing a lamp to Arielah, he gathered her into his arms. "The paths are too uneven for you to maneuver in the dark, beloved." She nodded and relaxed into his arms, and he noticed Hezro following close behind. "I'm sorry, my friend, but you're not invited." When the guard started to protest, Solomon interrupted. "Hezro, think about it. We're in *my* vineyard, guarded by Judean soldiers, and I'm meeting an old man who can barely stand." He paused for the length of a heartbeat. "I'm safe. Go eat your meal."

The Cherethite barely blinked. "I will stand at a distance, far enough to give you privacy, but close enough to see the flame of my queen's lamp." He then turned and addressed Arielah. "Please, my lady, make sure you hold your lamp so that I can see it at all times, or you will call down my wrath on whoever is standing near you."

Arielah nodded, her eyes wide.

Solomon's heart warmed at the guard's care. He turned and found the path he'd walked a hundred times with the old vinedresser. Hezro was true to his word, his presence felt but not seen or heard. Finally Solomon saw the faint glimmer of Shimei's lamp under the lush green canopy where they'd shared so many secrets.

"Welcome, young prince!" he said, coughing again with the greeting. He pounded his chest and rocked on the boulder where he sat.

Solomon eased Arielah onto a smooth rock, dented in its middle as though hewn to receive her.

Solomon turned over a watering jug and sat on it. "Don't die out here, you old raisin," he teased when Shimei's coughing subsided. "I can only carry one of you, and my wife is much prettier."

"Indeed she is," the old man said, a sparkle in his eyes.

"Now why did you call us out here and leave your guests to be entertained by Cook?" Solomon tried to sound gruff, but the vinedresser knew him too well.

"I wanted to meet the woman who bruised your gizzard."

"Excuse me?" Solomon laughed, and Arielah joined him. This old man loved riddles, and Solomon loved this old man. "I've come to believe myself a man of some knowledge," Solomon said, "and I've never beheld a gizzard." He glanced at Arielah and found her rapt attention on the old vinedresser.

"Well, whether you've heard of it or not," Shimei said, grinning ear to ear, "yours has been bruised. Love is a funny thing—shakes like a lizard, runs around your heart, and grabs at your gizzard."

As they enjoyed the old man's sage wisdom, their laughter wound down like the last clump of wool on a spindle. Solomon left his place and knelt by Arielah. "Shimei, this is my beloved, Arielah. Our union was born of duty, a treaty agreement between the house of David and the northern tribes."

His throat constricted as he contemplated how to relay the rest of their story. "Because my heart became so thoroughly satisfied by her during yichud, I promised her a singleness of commitment as if she were my only wife, my only marital responsibility." He saw Arielah's head bow, watched a tear drop to her folded hands. "Shimei, I broke my promise to her. I betrayed her, not just with my other wives but with—" He hesitated, shame strangling him.

"Does your wife know the details of your betrayal?" Shimei asked.

"Yes."

The old man pointed to the moon and shimmering stars. "Have you confessed your sin to Jehovah, Solomon?"

"Yes."

"Then I have no need to hear the details of such a betrayal," the old vinedresser said. "Go on with your story."

Solomon gathered his composure. "It was my betrayal that caused her scars," he said through a tight throat. "Yet she has forgiven me." He lifted her crooked hand and kissed it. "I love her as I've never loved anyone before. I would give my life for her, but—"

"But what?" Shimei asked abruptly, startling the two lovers. "So give your life for her!"

Solomon glanced at Arielah and back at Shimei. Arielah appeared to be as confused as he felt. "I'm not sure I know what you mean."

"Change your life for her," he said as if Solomon were the dumbest sheep in the flock. "Remain faithful to God's calling as king, honor all your promises, and change anything else that needs changing."

Arielah ventured a word for the first time. "Good Shimei," she said hesitantly, "how can Israel's king honor his promise to me—to love me with his whole heart—and yet faithfully fulfill his duty to the other treaty wives? I'm afraid the agreement that sealed our beginning necessarily requires our end.

He cannot remain faithful to me and still honor the other treaties he's made."

"The beginning of a relationship has little to do with its end," Shimei said. "David and Bathsheba are testimony to that." Like an old gossip, he bent low and whispered from behind a raised hand, "Solomon, did I ever tell you that you were conceived under an apple tree?"

"Shimei!" he gasped while Arielah stifled a giggle. "How in the name of pomegranates do you know that?"

"Hee-hee!" The old man chuckled. "Because when your abba brought you to this vineyard, he realized Jehovah shouts to you among these vines. King David said, 'Perhaps since Solomon was conceived under an apple tree, he will always be more attuned to God's voice amid His creation.'"

The old man paused and grew serious. "You have both come with heavy hearts. Baal Hamon is far from Jerusalem, but I have heard of Arielah—the lion of God." Turning to her, he said, "When you return to Jerusalem, your enemies will say, 'Look how she leans on her lover,' and they will think you weak, little lioness." He leaned forward, his eyes holding the couple in a firm grip. "But you must look at your husband and remind him, 'Amid God's creation we will renew our love. In the quiet places of creation where your ima conceived you and gave you birth, we will listen to Jehovah together.'"

Solomon massaged his forehead. "Shimei, you say I hear Jehovah in creation, but so far all I've heard are riddles about a gizzard." Trying to keep the frustration from his voice, he pleaded with his old friend. "If the lesson of love is in this vineyard, I'm missing it. This is important, my friend. No more riddles. I've failed Arielah once; I don't want to fail her again."

"Oh, young Solomon, everyone fails. But not everyone truly loves." Shimei reached up and plucked a cluster of nearly ripe grapes from the vine. "Love is like these grapes. It must be allowed to grow and ripen in its time." The old man threw the cluster at Solomon, and the king caught them by sheer reflex. "That's how you love, young prince." His pink gums shone in the lamplight. "You simply catch it as it comes at you."

Solomon inspected the cluster in his hands.

"Now take one. Eat it," Shimei said.

"No!" Solomon chuckled. "They're not ripe."

Shimei pointed at the cluster. "Look at them carefully, young prince. Some are ripe. Some are not." Piercing Solomon with his gaze, he said, "As I have been given wisdom from Jehovah to work the vines, He gave you wisdom to create trade routes, peace agreements, and labor contracts through marriage to foreign brides. Choose to bed those wives as carefully as I tend the vines. Couple only with those who are ripe, giving them heirs, fulfilling their purpose and your responsibility." He nodded at Arielah. "Though the lion of God came to you as a treaty bride, she's become the apple of your eye, the beating of your heart. To your other wives you owe a debt, an oath, a promise. To Arielah, your gift from Jehovah, you owe your life."

Solomon looked with renewed wonder at the cluster of grapes in his hand and then turned to his wife. "Your abba once told me that I couldn't unlive my past, but I could choose my future carefully. I cannot unmarry the women in Abba's harem or my own, but I can deal with them shrewdly."

Tears streamed down her cheeks. "My love," she said, her voice whispered awe. "I have always asked you to give me your whole heart, but because my experience has been in a Shulammite household, I wanted to be your only wife." Pushing a stray lock of hair from his forehead, she said, "I realize now that you have signed treaties and agreements with nations, binding you in marriages with other women. I cannot expect you to break your oaths to them in order to keep a promise to me." Glancing at Shimei, she winked and received a delighted laugh from the old vinedresser.

Solomon threw a grape at the old man. "Stop flirting with

my wife!" he said, gaining another chuckle. Looking into Arielah's eyes, he saw peace there. "It seems the vines have spoken to us both, beloved, teaching these lessons of love."

"You need only signal your coach driver, and he'll get word to me that we must rest awhile." Solomon closed the door of their wedding carriage and offered a silent prayer. *Jehovah, keep Arielah strong for the long journeys ahead.* He'd seen her weakened by the three-day trip from Shunem to Baal Hamon, and he knew that the three-day return and then three days more to Jerusalem would exhaust her. *What else can we do?*

"King Solomon!" Reu's anxious shout interrupted the king's fretting. "May I have a word with you before we leave for Shunem?" He looked as if he'd swallowed a bad fig. Pale and puckered, Jehoshaphat's aide marched toward the coach with purpose.

Sighing deeply, Solomon could think of nothing he'd like less than debating a bitter young man. "Of course, Reu." He motioned to a private area near the sheepfolds.

Once they were away from curious eyes and ears, Reu began in a controlled voice. "First, my lord, let me thank you for your kind offer."

"Before you go any further . . ." Solomon held up his hand, interrupting the young man. "I'm thankful Jehoshaphat explained Arielah's and my desire to help pay for Hannah's bride price, but since we've visited Baal Hamon, I have a second offer for you to consider." Solomon noticed crimson splotches forming on Reu's neck but assumed he was overcome with gratitude. "I'd like you to consider returning to Baal Hamon and becoming Shimei's apprentice."

"My lord, I—"

Again Solomon stopped Reu's reply. "Please, let me explain. Shimei is a dear friend, and I see him growing weak. He loves the vines and would enjoy having a young man like yourself to train to love them as he does. I know you've been learning to tend the vines with Igal in Jehoshaphat's vineyards."

Reu simply nodded, his eyes round and filling with tears.

"Good. Good." Solomon laid a hand on the young man's shoulder. "So is that a yes, then? Will you accept the mohar for Hannah and return to Baal Hamon to begin your life here with her?" He smiled. "After a proper betrothal period, of course."

The splotches on Reu's neck had grown into a deep crimson, more the color of ripened grapes. "Why?" he asked.

"What?"

He shrugged off Solomon's hand, fire lighting his eyes. "Why would you do all this? I mean, I know why a man like Jehoshaphat would do it—he has integrity and character." He sputtered as if sorry for the misspeak but not repentant. "What I mean is . . . well, why would you offer to pay the groom's mohar for your wife's own serving maid? And why on earth would you offer to make me the caretaker of Baal Hamon, the most beautiful and productive vineyard in Israel, when I've never tended vines in my life?" His breath escaped in short, angry spurts.

Solomon allowed a little silence to cushion his words. "Reu, I'm offering to pay Hannah's bride price because Arielah has told me of the love she's witnessed between you two, and I want to reward you for the friendship you showed Arielah in Jerusalem—when I betrayed her." Reu's eyes flamed, and Solomon knew. "That's what this is really about, isn't it? I know you feel like a part of their family, Reu, but even Igal has forgiven me." Solomon waited for his reply but heard nothing except the bleating of sheep and the restless sounds of the waiting caravan. "You don't have to forgive me, but you should still take the mohar for Hannah's sake. It's your only hope for the life of love you desire with her."

Solomon took a step to go, but Reu touched his arm. "I

want to hate you for what you did to Arielah, but the love I see in Jehoshaphat's family is too big to let any of us hold on to the past." Before Solomon could respond, Reu knelt and bowed before him. "My lord, I choose to forgive you, and I ask you to forgive me for speaking to you so harshly."

Solomon placed his hand on the man's shoulder. "Thank you, my friend. And yes, you are forgiven as well."

When the king lifted his hand, Reu grasped it and placed his forehead on the back of it. "May I ask one more favor?"

"Ask it, Reu."

He looked up, and the words came out in a flurry. "Will you serve as friend of the bridegroom and negotiate with Hannah's abba on my behalf?" He stopped as if unable to believe he'd said it. His final words were spoken with an impish grin. "I believe Hannah and her abba will agree, but it wouldn't hurt to have the king of Israel negotiate for me."

38

[Beloved] If only you were to me like a brother ... I
would kiss you, and no one would despise me. ... Place
me like a seal over your heart, like a seal on your arm.

Arielah watched Mount Moreh grow larger in the window, and a tangle of emotions knotted inside her. "Thank you for our visit to Baal Hamon," she said as their wedding carriage jostled toward Shunem. "And you were right. I love old Shimei."

The coach dipped into a rut, but she barely noticed, cuddled against Solomon's strong chest. Hannah had begged to ride a camel alongside Reu for the final leg of their journey, and Arielah was thankful that Solomon had joined her in the coach. They would linger one night in Shunem and be on their way to Jerusalem at dawn. She needed to be near him now.

"Solomon?"

He didn't respond, just drew her tighter. She could feel his breathing grow ragged, his chest heave in uneven gasps.

A lump formed in Arielah's throat. "What are you thinking?" she asked. It seemed both their hearts had become weighted as they crossed the Jezreel plain.

Solomon drew a ragged breath. "I know I must be king in Jerusalem, and I know we have determined a plan by which I can fulfill my obligations to the other wives but still guard my heart for you alone." He paused, sighed, and then laid his cheek on top of her head. "But now my concern is guarding you from further attacks from the Sons of Judah. I pray Benaiah brings us good news of plentiful witnesses when he arrives with our escort."

She felt tears wet her hair. He lifted his head. She looked up, and he kissed the curve of her neck. Neither spoke again. They kissed away each other's tears.

When Arielah glanced out the window again, she saw Benaiah waiting at Shunem's southern gate. "It appears we'll hear news of witnesses sooner than we realized, my love." Pointing toward the window, she saw panic in Solomon's eyes.

Seventy-three, seventy-four, seventy-five. Solomon counted the royal guards waiting at Shunem's gates. Why would Benaiah bring so many guards? Unless . . .

Arielah scooted closer to the window. "Why did Benaiah bring so many men?" she asked. "You came to Shunem with only ten guards."

Determined to remain calm, he leaned over and kissed her again. "Because there are bandits in the wilderness, beloved. And now I carry my greatest treasure in her wedding carriage." She smiled, and her wide, innocent eyes pierced him. She had no idea how much loving her had changed him. Perhaps Benaiah brought the large company of guards as a show of power, a deterrent for random bandits. *Jehovah, let it be so. I pray it's simple bandits, and not to guard against an enemy so bold they would attack on our way to Jerusalem.*

Their carriage halted by Shunem's gate, and as usual a crowd gathered to greet the royal guests. Benaiah was first to meet them, opening the carriage door like a concerned ima. "Are you all right? Did you run into any trouble?"

Solomon smiled, refusing to borrow trouble. "Hello, Commander. It's nice to see you too." The comment won a grin from the big man.

Jehoshaphat had already dismounted his camel and led his wife to the carriage. "I believe we have an anxious ima here to greet her daughter." Solomon stepped out of the carriage, lifted Arielah into his arms, and placed her feet on Shunem's soil.

"Shalom, my lamb," Ima Jehosheba said as she wrapped her daughter in loving arms.

Arielah closed her eyes, receiving comfort like a parched desert wanderer's first drink. "Shalom, Ima. It's good to be home."

While Igal and Reu led the rest of the caravan to Jehoshaphat's barns, Benaiah's expression turned grim. "My king," he said, lowering his voice for only Solomon and Jehoshaphat to hear, "the news is not good from Jerusalem."

Solomon's heart fell to his toes.

Exchanging a glance with Jehoshaphat, Benaiah confirmed the king's worst fears. "I could find no second witness to corroborate Oliab's testimony against the Daughters of Jerusalem." Looking over his shoulder, he said, "Please, both of you, follow me to the meadow where we can talk in private."

Solomon's heart pounded with every step. The silence of the three men's march was broken only by the swoosh of their sandals through Shunem's green grass. When they reached a cluster of fir trees, Benaiah resumed his story. "Plenty of women in the harem would testify that they heard Shiphrah and Sherah bribe the palace guards to ignore Arielah when she ventured into the city unescorted." Turning to Jehoshaphat, he lifted his hands, pleading. "I had no idea the Daughters of Jerusalem held sway over watchmen in the city, my friend." His eyes swam with tears. "Abishag even testified that she heard the guards speak of the plan to beat Arielah, and I've used every means possible to *persuade* the harem guards to talk, but—" A sob robbed his speech. He shook his head.

"All right, my friend," Jehoshaphat said, placing his hand on the commander's shoulder. "Have you announced a general plea to the public, asking for a witness to come forward?"

Anger seemed to fuel his tears as much as his remorse did. "I even tried knocking on doors, asking individual men, heads of their households. But the whole city fears retribution from the Sons of Judah. And Shiphrah or Sherah seem to wield the power. One word from them, and traitors are beaten or their homes are burned. I've never seen men so committed to a cause. It's infuriating!"

"They're not protecting a cause," Solomon said flatly, and both men's brows furrowed in question. "The guards. They're not protecting a cause. Men wouldn't endure Benaiah's torture for a simple cause." He watched as understanding dawned on their features. "These men are protecting Shiphrah and Sherah because the Daughters of Jerusalem have become the idols of Judah's worship." He scratched his beard, and a thought began to take root and grow. "You said the harem guards talked openly about their bribes?"

"Yes," Benaiah said, hope seeming to calm his frustration. "And from your foreign wives' reports, the Daughters of Jerusalem paid the guards outside the harem gate."

A slow, determined smile creased Solomon's lips. He began a victorious nod.

"Have you thought of a way to let a woman's testimony stand in your court?" Jehoshaphat asked.

"But you can't have your wives testify," Benaiah said, his frustration returning. "Though I'd like nothing more, your council members would never support your ruling if you allowed females to testify." He grew quiet. "I'm sorry, Solomon. I've tried every method I know to get those harem guards to talk. They simply will not testify against the Daughters of Jerusalem."

The king reached out to touch his commander's shoulder. "You have served me well, Benaiah. I know you have done everything humanly possible to find a witness. But with *Jehovah's* help, there is a way." He winked at both men, bent to pick a wildflower for his wife, and left them staring. Twirling the flower between his fingers, he whistled and returned to the city with a lighter step. *Thank You, Jehovah*, he prayed silently. *Your wisdom is truly amazing.*

As the royal caravan reached Jerusalem's gates, the midday sun glinted off trumpets, their joyful blast announcing Israel's returning king. Arielah's heart pounded wildly at the sound. Every sight, sound, and smell of this city reminded her of the beating, and panic began to set in as well-wishers crowded around the coach to welcome home their king and his treaty bride.

"Beloved." Solomon's rich, deep voice intruded on her fear, and she realized her eyes were closed. When she opened them, his loving gaze held her. Leaving his side of the coach, he snuggled beside her, gathering her close. "When you entered these gates the first time, you had to fight the battles alone. Now we will fight them together."

Resting in his nearness, she said, "Yes, but I'm tired of fighting, my love."

He kissed her forehead and asked, "Do you not have one happy memory in Jerusalem?"

The thought intrigued her. She turned to face him and smiled, and a memory came immediately. "This may not be what you were hoping for, but during my very first journey to Jerusalem, Kemmuel and Igal were young and playful, not old enough to show their jealousy. The three of us danced and skipped through the streets of Jerusalem." She let a little mischief leak out. "If only you were like a brother to me," she said, twirling a stray lock of his hair, "I could love you and kiss your cheek and no one would care. Perhaps we wouldn't have all these battles."

Solomon captured her hand, kissed it, and then brushed her cheek with his lips. "If I were your brother, we wouldn't be enjoying this wedding carriage."

Arielah smiled, and she tried to console herself with the plan Solomon had confided to her during their last night in Shunem. Surely this time the Daughters of Jerusalem would be exposed. But what about the Sons of Judah? Would their conspiracy dissolve when Shiphrah and Sherah were condemned? Jerusalem seemed to be a fox chasing its own tail, a constantly boiling pot.

She sighed deeply, and he lifted her chin to search her eyes. "If you were my brother," she said, "we could have stayed at my ima's house. We could learn more of love before it was tested again so soon." Seeing the pain in his eyes, she prayed for strength and lightened her tone. When he turned away, she caught his chin and recaptured his gaze. "I would give you my spiced wine and the nectar of my pomegranates."

He kissed her soundly. "Mmm, I love your spiced wine and pomegranates."

She tried to grin, tried so hard to hide her mounting anxiety, but a sudden rush of tears defeated her.

"Oh, beloved," he said, hugging her tightly. "What? Are you this frightened? I'll have a hundred Cherethite and Pelethite guards outside our door every moment."

"Our door?" she squeaked, sounding utterly pitiful.

He was silent for a long moment, stroking her cheek. "You can move back into the bridal chamber if you like, but I must have a place to be with the other wives." He paused. "Are we not agreed?"

Again she fought for control and for the reasonable facts

she needed to accept—for her peace and Solomon's integrity. "I understand that as a man of honor, you must be a king to your other wives." She sniffed back tears. "But it is still difficult for me to think of you lying in another woman's arms—even when I know I possess your heart."

She felt the rise and fall of his chest, a deep sigh. "Indeed, you have my heart, beloved. You and you alone." Grasping her shoulders, he pulled her away in order to search her gaze. "How can I assure you of my love, that it is faithful and true? How can I remind myself?" His eyes welled with tears, and his voice broke. "I don't want to fail you again. I don't want to allow my heart to wander, so I need your help. How can we protect our love in Jerusalem?"

Arielah's heart ached at his sincerity. He looked so vulnerable, like a young soldier preparing for his first battle. Reaching up to push that stubborn lock of hair from his forehead, she let her hand brush his cheek and his neck, then rest on the slight impression at the base of his throat.

He reached up, cradled her crooked hand, and squeezed it too tightly. She winced.

"Oh, beloved, I'm sorry." His face looked stricken as it always did when he saw the lingering effects of her beating.

In that awkward moment of pain and pleasure, she realized how to portray their love. "Solomon!" The excitement in her voice must have confused him. She reached for the leather cord he wore around his neck, and he looked as if he might call a guard to protect him. Giggling now, she lifted the metal bauble suspended on the cord, pulling it from beneath his robe. He watched her with rapt interest, his brow furrowed, his grin intrigued.

"Is this the seal you press into wax on official documents?" she asked. Already knowing the answer, she kissed his cheek as a silent request for his patience.

"Yes . . ." He smiled, evidently a willing student.

She rolled the decorative cylinder between her fingers. "Just as you press this symbol of ownership into beeswax, so I want you to place me like a seal on your heart."

"Ah," he said softly and returned a quick kiss. "A very apt comparison."

She snuggled close. "But there's more," she said. Growing quiet, she hoped his heart would receive the next lesson as readily. "At first I hated the thought of my scars and crippled leg," she said. "But now I see that my lasting wounds make me like this seal. I'm always leaning on your arm as the seal is constantly around your neck. Wherever we go, I'm sort of a permanent attachment, like this leather necklace and your seal."

He pulled her closer, resting his chin on her head. She heard a sob, felt his chest heave. "Oh, beloved. Yes. This is a picture of our love that I can carry with me always. I hate that you bear these scars, but it is with deep honor that I will forever be at your side."

She kissed him and held his gaze. "How would you feel if someone stole your seal or offered you great treasure for it?"

He smiled a forbearing smile as if to say, *Our lesson isn't over?* "I would never relinquish my seal. It is mine and only mine until the day I die."

Settling into his side, she said, "The love of which we speak is like your seal—as strong and lasting as death, and my jealousy is as unyielding as the grave. Even a river can't wash away the blazing fire of love in my soul." She lifted her head and cupped his cheek. "I will never joyfully share you with other wives. But I can accept my place in your heart if I know I am forever sealed with your love."

He gazed at her for a long moment, the crowd outside growing in noise and number. Too soon the carriage stopped at the palace entrance, jostling back and forth, while the stallions jittered at the crowd noise. Kissing her forehead, he whispered, "Always with me," and then he returned to the bench on the opposite side of the coach, awaiting Benaiah's arrival.

The rest of the royal procession continued to the stables and storehouses, and finally the commander opened the carriage door. "The people await your greeting, my lord."

Arielah wiped her eyes. Solomon leaned over and brushed her cheek, inhaled deeply, and affixed his regal smile. When he emerged from their canopy of serenity, a cheer rose, sounding as if all of Jerusalem had gathered to celebrate the long-awaited arrival of its wandering king.

Arielah heard only their incoherent rumblings, her attention completely captured by her strong yet tender husband. Solomon whisked her into his arms and twirled her around, sheer linen veils encircling them. "Solomon, put me down!" She giggled, and his laughter boomed over the jubilant crowd.

She could feel her cheeks grow pink. Solomon must have noticed too, because he set her down gently and asked, "Ready for our first battle, beloved?" She nodded, and he lifted his voice above the noise. "People of Jerusalem, your treaty bride has returned." Another cheer, and Solomon lifted his hands to quiet the crowd. "As most of you know, Queen Arielah was brutally attacked in the City of David. We have found only one man willing to testify against those responsible for planning and carrying out the assault. But we must have two male witnesses in Israel's court to condemn a criminal to death." Chatter fluttered across the crowd, and the Mighty Men formed a barrier between the audience and the royal couple. Solomon stepped between them, focusing on a few men in the front rows and some guards near the entrance hall. "If any man here is willing to serve as second witness, please register with my palace steward in order to testify at the public hearing in the throne hall after midday."

Arielah's heart thundered as Solomon returned and brushed her cheek. "May I carry you, beloved? I need to feel you in my arms."

She nodded her quick approval, and he swept her up as if she weighed nothing at all. Stirred by his wisdom and

strength, she whispered, "It would appear you're quite a warrior, my love. Perhaps you should assign yourself Benaiah's
job."

He chuckled softly. "My love is a sharp sword," he said
with a playful wink. Solomon kissed her forehead and turned
to enter the palace.

"Long live King Solomon!" someone cried, and the crowd
erupted in applause.

Solomon turned back to their audience, and Arielah saw a
young woman shout, "And blessed be Queen Arielah!"

Her heart was overwhelmed. The dark prospects of sharing
her husband and the political battles with the Sons of Judah
had almost snuffed out her hope.

"Wave to your people, my treaty bride," Solomon said.
"They are Judean, but perhaps there are many who remain
true Israelites."

She waved and warmed to the people of Jerusalem, feeling like their queen for the first time. Solomon resumed his
march up the stairs while Benaiah followed closely behind
them. When Solomon reached the palace entrance, Arielah
noticed the one-eyed guard she'd slipped past on the night
of her beating. He stood beside a scribe, a pleasant-looking
man with ink-stained fingers. Both men were startled from
a traditional bow when King Solomon stopped beside them.

"Mahlon, please rise," the king said, still holding Arielah
like a roll of tethered wheat.

Arielah pondered the name. *Mahlon . . . where have I heard
that?* Suddenly she remembered. Mahlon was the scribe Ahishar had tortured—Elisheba's friend who had been like an
abba to Reu!

She watched a terrified glance pass between the scribe and
the one-eyed guard. Mahlon raised an eyebrow, and the guard
spoke. "How may we serve you, my king?"

Solomon chuckled, no doubt as amazed as Arielah that
two men could communicate as one. "Mahlon, I've been told

of the terrible wrong Ahishar did to you, and I'm sorry you suffered at the hands of someone I trusted."

The scribe stared wide-eyed and then uttered some unintelligible sounds to the guard. "Mahlon says, 'Thank you, my lord. Your kindness is enough of a gift.'" Both the guard and Mahlon bowed as one.

"The small honor I give you now cannot atone for the wrong, but I hope it brings you—and Elisheba—great joy." Arielah's heart skipped a beat, and she could barely contain a squeal. Solomon grinned in her direction before sharing the news with the waiting scribe. "You, Mahlon, will be the bearer of happy news to Reu's ima. Please tell her that Reu has served his king well and will soon marry Queen Arielah's young maid. Furthermore, I have entrusted Reu with the position of vinedresser at my vineyard in Baal Hamon. Elisheba and her guests will travel by royal escort to her son's wedding in Shunem after the next Passover."

Arielah had never seen a mute man rejoice, but the sight was one of the happiest she'd ever witnessed. Solomon's laughter echoed in the hallways of the palace as they resumed their journey toward his private chambers. Arielah breathed a contented sigh and nestled her head against his shoulder, enjoying these few moments of calm before the battle turned to war.

39

✤ Song of Solomon 8:8 ✤

*[Friends] We have a young sister, and her breasts are
not yet grown. What shall we do for our sister?*

Solomon stopped outside his chambers, examining the
soldiers stationed at his double doors. Though their
training dictated unflinching posture, their furrowed brows
revealed curiosity. "You are members of Benaiah's Pelethite
guard, are you not?" Solomon asked, though Benaiah stood
directly behind him, leading a number of other Mighty Men.

The men saluted, fist to heart. "Yes, my king," they said
in unison.

"And you are lifetime warriors, having protected my abba
before me?"

"Yes, my king."

Nodding to Arielah, who lay with her head on his shoulder, he said, "You will now guard Queen Arielah with the
same loyalty that you showed my abba and with which you
protect me."

They hesitated, glancing to their commander for direction. No king's guard had ever been asked to guard a queen.
Benaiah issued an almost imperceptible nod.

"Understood?" Solomon shouted.

"Yes, my king!"

Benaiah leaned down to whisper, "You are a wise man, King Solomon. These are two of my best men." The approval in his friend's voice bolstered his confidence.

"I hold you two personally responsible for Queen Arielah's safety. One of you is to be aware of her presence at every moment of every day. Only your commander or myself may gain an audience alone with her, and she is to be escorted any time she leaves my chamber. Questions?"

The Pelethites exchanged a glance, and one man ventured a grin. "May I say"—he offered a quick bow—"we are pleased to welcome the queen and guard her with our lives." Both guards returned to their solemnity, saluted their king, and opened the double doors.

"Welcome home, my king." Sekhet's wry grin would normally have lightened his mood, but at the moment his concern was Arielah. She seemed to be wilting like a flower without water.

Lifting her head off his shoulder, Arielah greeted the Egyptian. "Shalom, Sekhet."

"What has happened to her?" Sekhet asked, nearly leaping off the couch where she'd been sitting. "Lay her on the bed." Gently Solomon placed Arielah on his sleeping couch. "What did you do to her?" Sekhet glared at him and swatted his arm.

He was too amazed to be offended. The Egyptian's tender care for Arielah was endearing, and he watched in wonder as his wives enjoyed their reunion. He had no idea of the depth of their friendship forged during Arielah's recovery. *Jehovah, Your ways are unfathomable.*

"I'm all right, Sekhet," Arielah said. "Just tired from our wonderful trip to Baal Hamon."

"Yes, Solomon said you were—"

"Excuse me," Solomon said. Both women glared as if begrudging the interruption. He chuckled. "Could you two catch up after we . . . ?" Turning to Benaiah, he nodded his silent command, and his top soldier began selectively clearing the chamber.

When the chamber door clicked shut, Sekhet's Nubian guards surrounded Solomon and Benaiah. The king's heart nearly pounded from his chest, anticipating the answer upon which all their hopes rested. Inspecting the massive black warriors, Solomon asked Sekhet, "Do your Nubians understand only Egyptian, or do they also speak Hebrew?"

The king sat silently on his throne, his expression cool, his gaze fixed. Arielah glanced at him, trying to appear as strong as her husband, when inwardly she longed for nothing more than a quiet nap in a sunny meadow. Appraising the throne hall's exclusively female audience, she leaned over to whisper, "This may be the first time the aroma of cedar has been overpowered by lotions and perfumes." Shiphrah and Sherah had fallen into Solomon's trap. His plea for public *male* witnesses had prompted them to fill the throne hall with both royal harems.

Solomon stifled a grin, maintaining his regal bearing. "It seems the only royal wife missing from Abba's harem or mine is Ima Bathsheba. So far, it's the only move in our real-life Hounds and Jackals that I didn't anticipate." The rest of the wives and concubines were present—David's harem lined the left side of the aisle, and Solomon's women waited on the right.

Elihoreph's shrill voice interrupted Arielah's observations. "Seeking justice from King Solomon's court, Shiphrah and Sherah, the Daughters of Jerusalem." All eyes turned to the entryway between the courtyard and the throne hall, the portal through which royalty entered.

Solomon's eyes narrowed, and he gripped Arielah's left hand too tightly. "Gently, my love," she said, grimacing. His expression showed a moment's panic. "Remember God's wisdom. Remember your plan."

"But this isn't part of—"

Looking into his eyes, she said, "The Daughters may have surprised us, but they didn't surprise the Lord. He is the source of your wisdom." She watched peace return to his features, like a feather settles after a slight breeze.

While the Daughters of Jerusalem entered, Solomon challenged his steward privately. "I declared only one matter to judge in court today. By allowing the Daughters of Jerusalem to add to your list of petitioners"—he looked directly into the man's wide eyes—"you have placed yourself at the top of my new investigation list, steward."

Elihoreph stuttered, hesitated, gulped, and tried to explain. "But Shiphrah and Sherah said—"

Solomon held up a hand to silence him. "I will deal with you later."

Shiphrah and Sherah floated toward the throne, their fine linen robes of better quality than any queen. Each offered a perfunctory bow at King Solomon's throne before Shiphrah spoke. "We bring a matter of national importance, my lord."

Solomon's face was like stone, but Arielah noticed his cheeks flush. "Get on with it, Shiphrah."

Shiphrah smiled coldly. "We represent the wives who stand before you, each of them lodging the same complaint. Before this shepherdess came into the palace," she said, casting a disparaging glance at Arielah, "you followed the wise custom of King David and other powerful kings by establishing your household with a growing harem."

When she took a breath to continue, Sherah forged ahead with the complaint. "My sister and I have been pleased to manage the king's household, aiding your foreign alliances by embracing your foreign wives."

"However . . ." Shiphrah wrenched the attention from her sister. "It has come to our attention that the woman seated on your right intends to reclaim her position as your only wife." A ripple of discontent spread through the royal women.

Solomon's expression remained dismissive. "Is anything else bothering you, Shiphrah? Is your chamber too small or the mikvah baths too cool?" His condescension stoked her ire.

"Yes, now that you offer me a hearing," she said, her voice rising, "we have young Judean maidens that are as flat as walls right now, not as round as your Shulammite wife has become." She raised an eyebrow, pointing at Arielah's stomach. "You've married plenty of foreign women, but what should we tell Judean girls who dream of someday being the king's wife?"

Solomon began to laugh, further fueling her tirade.

"If our Judean women lack beauty, we'll cover them with silver and jewels. We'll even enclose them in cedar panels if you want them to *smell* like your northern shepherdess."

Solomon slammed his hand down on the lion's-head armrest, his laughter ceasing.

Arielah reached for his hand, calming him. She leaned close. "This is not our battle, my love. May I address her complaint?"

He looked into her eyes, a nod his only response, his lips pressed tightly in barely contained fury.

Arielah was filled with a calm like she'd never known. "Shiphrah, *I* am a wall, strong and enduring. And I've become 'round,' as you call it, because I will soon bear the king's child."

The crowd hummed at the news that her loose-fitting robe had evidently hidden.

"Some kings strive endlessly to rule a nation and gain power. Solomon's heart now rests in the contentment of my love and Jehovah's power." Turning toward David's wives and concubines, she raised her voice to be heard. "Do you remember the difference in the days of King David's peace and the days of his striving?"

Some of the older women nodded their affirmation.

The grand doors of the entrance hall burst open, and Bathsheba stood at the threshold. Utter silence ushered her forward, and the crowd parted as she approached the Daughters of Jerusalem. "When a king's heart is marred by sin, he cannot rule his nation well." Taking her place among David's other wives, she added, "But when a king is at peace with Jehovah and finds contentment in the arms of a woman he loves, Israel flourishes under his reign."

Sherah's voice crescendoed. "But we were chosen to manage the harem! We were to determine whom he favored!" Her tantrum was interrupted by Benaiah's sudden appearance at the entrance hall doors. He and Hezro led Oliab between them.

Solomon waved away the Daughters of Jerusalem. "Shiphrah and Sherah, I find your complaints tiresome and without merit. Queen Arielah is one of my treaty brides, and I will honor the vows I have made to her." Then looking across the anxious faces of his other wives, he added, "And I will fulfill my vow to produce an heir for each of my other treaty brides—as God allows."

Whispers rippled over the audience, and Arielah would have found Solomon's disclosure utterly humiliating had the courtroom been filled with men. But as she looked into the grateful tears of other women, those who undoubtedly longed for a child, she placed a protective hand on her belly and thanked Jehovah for an honorable king.

Two Cherethite guards reached for the Daughters of Jerusalem to escort them aside, but both women issued deadly stares and stepped nobly to the right of the platform.

Benaiah reached the dais with his prisoner, and Arielah could barely breathe. She knew this moment was coming. Solomon had reviewed the plan with her, and Oliab would admit his crime before the throne. She had been coached to act terrified. How could she have guessed the terror would be real?

Her whole body trembled uncontrollably. "It's him. It's one of the men who beat me that night." Tears sprang to her eyes.

Benaiah exchanged a concerned glance with Solomon. "I bring before you Oliab, a watchman of Israel," Benaiah said, his voice echoing off the walls. "He comes to confess his crimes against Queen Arielah."

She felt Solomon's hand begin to tremble beside hers. His anger, like her fear, did not seem rehearsed. "Look at my wife," he growled at the man who bowed before them. "Lift your head and look at what you've done."

Arielah felt every eye in the courtroom examining her scars.

When Oliab lifted his head, he appeared broken, his words seeming sincere and humble. "The Daughters of Jerusalem paid me and three other watchmen to punish . . . to beat . . . Queen Arielah." His voice broke.

Then he turned to Arielah, startling her. She wanted to flee, to run, but his eyes—they were different. Sad. Defeated.

"I can't forget how your face glowed with peace," he said. "Even when Sherah spit on you, my lady." His face twisted with emotion. "I hate what I have done to you, but I'm thankful for seeing Jehovah in your eyes, my lady." A sob escaped, and he raised his shackled hands to hide his shame.

"This is ridiculous!" Shiphrah cried. "He is trying to discredit us before the king and the women of his harem, whom we hold dear." Sherah, chin held high, nodded her agreement.

Solomon, maintaining a semblance of calm, appealed to the audience. "Who in this courtroom will testify to the truth of this man's actions?"

"No one can testify," Sherah interrupted. "Even if we were guilty, which we're not"—she received a leering reprimand from her sister—"there are no men present to testify."

"Yes, I see that somehow only women—royal women—have found their way into my courtroom," Solomon said, pointing to the crowd. He gasped, and then with mock surprise, he said, "But wait! Who is that in back?"

Holding back a grin at his poorly feigned shock, Arielah watched the twins' heads snap to attention. "Who? No one." Shiphrah answered her rhetorical question. "Only royal women and harem guards are present." She undoubtedly knew best whom she and Sherah had invited to the hearing.

Solomon signaled Sekhet to begin her slow march up the center aisle. The six Nubian guards trailed behind her. And indignation bloomed in the Daughters of Jerusalem.

"That Egyptian queen cannot testify!" Sherah stomped her foot.

Sekhet glanced in her direction and said something in Egyptian—no doubt delightfully evil. Solomon added to the moment by saying, "I have no idea what Queen Sekhet said, but I would imagine her Nubian warriors could translate for us."

All color drained from the twins' faces. "How can they translate?" Shiphrah asked. "They don't speak Hebrew."

Solomon's only reply was a victorious smile.

"I will not repeat the words of my queen," one Nubian said, his voice deep and rich, his words perfect Hebrew.

"I believe Israelite law says a foreigner cannot testify against an Israelite woman," Shiphrah said flatly.

Solomon laughed out loud. "Shiphrah, there is no such law. Your lies and tricks have been dried up like a wadi in summer's heat. We can choose any of these Nubian guards to serve as second witness—a male witness—against you and Sherah. Would you like to pick which man will condemn you?"

"Nooooo!" Shiphrah lunged at Solomon, but Benaiah swept her into his grasp. "You cannot do this!" she said, kicking and fighting his restraint. Sherah merely sobbed, melting into a puddle on the floor.

Solomon stood, walked to the edge of the platform, and glared at the twins. "Silence them," he said, giving Benaiah permission to use whatever means necessary to gain control.

Turning to Sekhet's guards, he said, "Tell me in Hebrew words how the Daughters were involved in Queen Arielah's attack."

The Nubian guards used the Israelite language to condemn the Judean women and described the atrocities they'd witnessed.

Only one question came from Solomon's lips. "Why didn't you tell someone before Arielah was attacked?"

Without malice, the Nubian answered with a question of his own. "Who would you have believed, King Solomon—six Egyptian guards or your two Judean maidens?"

The truth of his words pierced the king. Before Arielah's beating, Solomon had viewed Sekhet as a nuisance, so he never would have listened to her guards. "I believe you now," Solomon said. The Nubian inclined his head, and the king thought he noted a hint of promise in the man's arched brow. "Are you aware of more information on other traitors among us?"

A slow, wry smile stretched across the Nubian's lips. "I had hoped you would let your commander . . . what is the Hebrew word . . . *extract* names from the Daughters of Jerusalem."

Solomon realized the sad irony in what he was about to say. "Unfortunately, using any statements from Shiphrah and Sherah would be prohibited for the same reason they couldn't be condemned earlier. A woman's testimony is inadmissible in my courtroom."

"My Nubian brothers and I have more to say on the matter, King Solomon." He bowed and backed away, honoring the most important task at hand—the judgment of those present.

"My lord," Benaiah said, still holding Shiphrah's rigid form, "those guilty of crimes against Queen Arielah await your verdict."

Solomon stood at the edge of the dais, his back to Arielah. The crowd was utterly silent. "Solomon, my love," he heard Arielah whisper.

No. *She wouldn't.*

"Solomon," she said a little louder.

He knew what she was going to suggest. He wouldn't. He couldn't. Someone must pay for her scars.

Whispers from the crowd. Women covering their mouths and pointing. He turned and found Arielah standing unaided by his throne.

"What are you doing?" He rushed at her, grasping her waist before she fell. He held her but looked away when he felt her eyes on him. "Do not ask it of me, Arielah. I cannot."

"Solomon, my love. Look at me."

Slowly, almost painfully, he lifted his gaze.

"Jehovah asks that we act justly," she said. "But he also loves mercy."

He could feel his composure slipping. "Arielah, this watchman admits to the crime, and we finally have two witnesses against the Daughters of Jerusalem. The law supports a death sentence for all three. Why offer mercy when they have offered you nothing but pain?"

"I keep thinking of my brothers, Solomon. Abba offered them mercy repeatedly."

"And they hurt you repeatedly!" His shout echoed in the courtroom.

She let the echo die before she answered. "But Igal repented, and now his life is rich and full of love. Oliab reminds me of Igal's changed heart. Couldn't we offer all three of them an *opportunity* to repent?"

Solomon shook his head, closing his eyes and his heart. "I won't forgive them, Arielah. Not after what they've done. If they repent, I'll be expected to forgive, and I can't. I *won't*."

She lifted her hand to his cheek and said the words gently. "Mercy and forgiveness are like water, my love. When they flow *to* us, they must be allowed to flow *through* us, or they become stagnant and putrid in our souls."

The words stung his freshly forgiven heart. Jehoshaphat's wisdom, Reu's forgiveness, Arielah's love—all these had tilled the soil so her words could take root in his soul.

A little mischief crept into her voice. "Perhaps you could show the same mercy to the Daughters of Jerusalem that I've heard you offered the old priest Abiathar."

Solomon's furrowed brow begged an explanation.

"Give them the opportunity to live in solitude—away from Jerusalem—in the northern districts. If they refuse your mercy, then like Kemmuel, their blood will be on their own heads."

He studied her and stroked her cheek. She was tenacious, this lion of God. Turning to announce his verdict, he said, "Oliab, stand before me."

The man's face lost all color.

"Have you ever dressed a grapevine?" He heard Arielah's soft gasp. Solomon looked at her with a grin, raised an eyebrow. She nodded her silent approval, and the king turned to Benaiah. "Captain, if Oliab agrees to testify against the remaining Sons of Judah, I will offer him mercy and a position in one of my vineyards."

Arielah placed a hand on Solomon's shoulder, pulling him close. "Look at his face, my love. I saw the same expression of repentance and redemption on Igal's face the day of his judgment."

"Thank you, my lord." The prisoner choked out the words. "I accept your mercy gladly."

Solomon cast an adoring glance at his wife. "You should thank Queen Arielah. Were it not for her mercy, we would all be lost." Nodding at the guards to move Oliab aside, Solomon fixed his gaze on the traitors. "Daughters of Jerusalem, stand before me."

Benaiah brought them forward, Shiphrah like stone, Sherah a ragdoll.

"The law of Moses says by the testimony of two witnesses, these women shall die."

Sherah let out an otherworldly wail.

"Is there no mercy for the Daughters of Jerusalem?" Shiphrah's voice held as little hope as her verdict.

Solomon smiled, and a panic deeper than Sherah's wail flashed in Shiphrah's eyes. "Yes. In fact, the woman you plotted to kill has shown you mercy."

The audience chattered with excitement.

"You will live under guard in Dothan—in the quiet grazing meadows where our patriarch Joseph was betrayed by his jealous brothers." Solomon paused and spoke to the crowd. "A fitting location for jealous deceivers, don't you think?"

Nervous laughter almost equaled Sherah's moans.

"Perhaps while herding young goats, you two will discover Jehovah's creation and learn the value of peace." Solomon hesitated, and the courtroom grew quiet. "However, should your hearts remain hard, Daughters of Jerusalem, should you refuse this gift of mercy I extend to you now, you—will—die."

Shiphrah and Sherah were dragged from the throne hall in utter defeat. A slow but mounting applause rippled through the crowd and grew to a thunderous celebration.

Arielah turned to celebrate with her husband. "Oh, Solomon . . ."

But as he leaned down to embrace her, the haunting expression of a woman came into view. Abishag.

40

[Beloved] Solomon had a vineyard in Baal Hamon. . . .
But my own vineyard is mine to give.

Solomon hadn't seen Abishag since she'd been placed with Abba's concubines. She looked weary of life, but worse—she seemed utterly alone. His heart broke. Suddenly Abishag looked up, and he was staring into the liquid brown eyes that had mesmerized him at Abba's bedside.

"Oh, my love." Arielah hugged him tightly. "You did it! Jehovah's wisdom made us victorious!"

His wife's warm embrace drew him back to the moment. He kissed the top of her head, and Abishag averted her eyes. "Yes, beloved," he said, still gazing at Abba David's Shulammite. "Jehovah is victorious." Holding his wife, he continued to appraise Abishag. However, to his surprise—and profound relief—no passion stirred. Only concern for this lonely young woman.

Arielah must have noticed his distraction. Lifting her head from his chest, she searched the object of his interest. "Abishag!" she whispered. "Solomon, she looks so alone." His wife's tender heart had broken as immediately as his own.

Kissing her forehead and settling her at his right side, Solomon quieted the crowd with upraised hands. "Abishag, caretaker of King David in his final days!" he shouted, and Abishag flinched. "Please approach the throne."

Her eyes, so soft and tender moments before, were now as round and frightened as a deer in a hunter's sight. She didn't move. Perhaps she couldn't.

Guards started their foreboding journey toward her, but Solomon motioned them away and said tenderly, "Abishag, come to me."

She moved with the grace of a breeze toward the throne. "Yes, my king?" Her head bowed.

"You served my abba well, yet you were never taken as his wife. I release you, Abishag, from David's harem."

The crowd gasped and then reveled in the grandest gossip of their generation. Solomon's advisors shouted their objections in a dissonant chorus.

"But, King Solomon, the Shulammite lay with your abba," the royal secretary said. "Though King David never took her as a *true* wife, she has been considered his concubine."

Zadok the priest offered his two shekels. "She has been tainted, my king. No man will have her. It would be cruel to expel her from the palace without a husband to support her."

Solomon raised his hand for silence. Abishag stood tall, a regal presence amid the unsettled souls around her.

"I offer you freedom," Solomon said, quieting the last murmurs. "But it is my intention that freedom brings you joy, not pain. Therefore, I offer you the ability to choose your future."

A slight smile graced her face, and her voice was quiet but clear. "May I ask the king a question before I decide?"

Solomon chuckled. He'd seldom heard this timid girl speak above a whisper. "Yes, you may ask."

"Is it true my sister is no longer Queen Arielah's serving maid, that she is now betrothed to the new caretaker of your vineyard in Baal Hamon?"

"Yes, it is true. I myself am serving as friend of the bridegroom."

A collective gasp added more fodder for merchants' tales.

A slight smile curved Abishag's lips. "Then, if I am truly free to choose a future, I offer my service to Queen Arielah."

The tittering crowd was like a nest of eagles stirred.

"Silence!" Solomon's wisdom obviously fell short when women were involved. He was thoroughly baffled by the Shulammite's request. "Abishag, though you are a concubine, you are not a servant. Why would you place yourself below your current station?"

"Oh, my king, I care nothing of my *station*. Your counselors have said I am tainted. Perhaps in their eyes I have been, but I know I would be welcomed in my abba's loving household at Shunem." She turned to Arielah, her lips quivering as she spoke. "But Queen Arielah once spoke of me as her friend, and since my sister will soon become a bride, the queen will need a friend to care for her. It would be my honor, my pleasure, to serve her for a lifetime."

Solomon was speechless. What could he say to such a request?

"Solomon." He turned to see tears streaming down Arielah's face. "May I speak and offer Abishag a gift—as a gesture of appreciation for her offer?"

He laughed aloud, cupped his wife's cheeks, and wiped her tears with his thumbs. "I wish you would," he said so only she could hear. "I have no idea how to respond to the extravagant grace of you women from Shunem." He chuckled and placed his lips by her ear. "This woman has pledged her life to you in service. Make her gift extravagant, beloved. She'll be tending my most precious treasure."

Arielah nodded, eyes sparkling. "Will you help me walk to the edge of the platform?"

Encircling her waist, Solomon stood beside her while she addressed King David's Shulammite.

"Hello, my friend," Arielah said, and then she turned to the gathering. "As many of you know, King Solomon's vineyard in Baal Hamon is quite lucrative, and tenants pay a thousand shekels of silver for its fruit. The only vineyard I own stands before you—broken," she said, motioning to her still-mending body. "But it's mine to give. I give myself freely to my husband, and he gives his love in return." As she turned to Abishag, Solomon heard wonder in his wife's voice. "My friend, if you are willing to serve me—to tend my vineyard—the king offers you two hundred shekels of silver."

Abishag gasped and cupped both hands over her mouth, fresh tears coursing down her cheeks. The crowd exploded in celebration, and Solomon laughed. Gathering his wife into his arms, he kissed her cheek and said, "Well, Queen Arielah, giving your serving maid twenty times a warrior's reward is indeed extravagant, but I approve!" Her giggling filled his heart with joy.

Suddenly, she pulled away. "Solomon, look at her." Abishag stood alone, smiling awkwardly at the foot of the platform while everyone celebrated around her. Arielah looked pleadingly into his eyes. He nodded, granting permission before she asked.

"Abishag, please come to me." Arielah opened her arms wide to receive her friend.

The girl's face lit up as she ascended the dais steps. Abishag tried to bow, but Arielah reached for her, nearly falling into the Shulammite's warm embrace.

Solomon watched and marveled at Jehovah's mystery. The woman who selflessly served his abba in death would now tend the woman he loved more than life. Abishag had begun his quest for love, but Arielah had defined its sacred passion. If old Shimei was right, and love, like a vineyard, grew better with time, then surely their love would outshine even the vines of Baal Hamon.

EPILOGUE

*You who dwell in the gardens with friends in atten-
dance, let me hear your voice! Come away, my lover,
and be like a gazelle or like a young stag on the spice-
laden mountains.*

Thirty-Seven Years Later

King Solomon's breathing grew labored, and he realized his
aging body was beginning its slow, deliberate march toward
eternity's gates. "Abishag, my friend, it seems you will comfort two dying kings."

Abba David's Shulammite sat quietly at his bedside, her
silver-streaked hair falling in soft waves under her fine linen
head covering. She was as lovely as the first day he'd seen
her peer from beneath Abba's blankets. She glanced at him,
smiled, and then returned her attention to the wool and
spindle in her hands.

"I want to talk about *her*," he said.

Abishag's hands stilled at his declaration. When she finally
met his gaze, he searched the cloudy brown eyes that had once
mesmerized him. "I need to speak of her with someone who
knew her as you did."

Abishag laid the spindle aside and placed her hand on his forearm. "Say her name, my king."

"I want to talk about what she taught me." He tried to sit up, but he couldn't lift himself.

"Wait, let us help you." Abishag signaled to the palace physician. Several other servants were immediately at the king's bedside, fluffing the doeskin pillows, arranging his lion-fur blankets. Solomon's chamber was every bit a man's room though women filled his world until just a few weeks ago.

"Abishag." Solomon captured her hand as she gathered his robe around his neck. Their eyes met again, his stinging with tears. "Remember when I used to finish my day in court and return to her in our private garden? I would say, 'You who dwell in the garden with your friend, let me hear your sweet voice!' And you would sit with her on that bench under the almond tree." Solomon labored to lift his hand and point to the little limestone bench he had moved from Abba David's old palace. The suite in Solomon's opulent palace now boasted an extravagant garden, making the little bench appear stark. But it had been *their* bench, the place they shared their joys and secrets. "And then she would giggle. Abishag, do you remember her giggle?"

Tears made their way into every crease around Abishag's beautiful eyes. "Yes. It sounded like summer rain on palm fronds."

"Ah, a true Shulammite shepherd's verse!" He covered her hand with his own. "Thank you. It's been years since anyone has spoken a shepherd's verse to me."

Abishag eased her hand away and sat down again beside his bed. Solomon's memories continued.

"Do you remember the way she answered me with a shepherd's verse each day? 'Come away from your troubles,' she would say. 'Be strong like a young stag on the spice-laden mountains.'"

"Solomon," Abishag said, "speak her name."

Tears spilled over his lashes. "I cannot."

"Say her name. You've held her captive in your heart long enough. Say her name." Moments passed in silence. "What are you afraid of, my king?"

"I'm afraid if I speak her name, the memories will escape, and I'll feel more alone than I've felt all these years." He looked at the only person who knew and loved his wife as much as he did. "Why did I give you to my brother Nathan? Why didn't I marry you myself?"

Her laughter washed over him and allowed Solomon to smile through his tears. "Because you don't love me," she said. "You loved Arielah. Your other women are simply entertainment."

Her words pierced him. No condemnation laced her tone, but in those few words, she'd summarized the essence of Solomon's life. His seven hundred royal brides and three hundred concubines had been pleasurable distractions from the deep ache left behind when Arielah died giving birth to their only child. *Arielah died giving birth* . . . If she hadn't been weakened by the beating, would she have lived? Why hadn't he loved her from the beginning? She was so easy to love. He'd wasted so much time—so much of his life. He squeezed his eyes shut, and tears streamed down his face.

"Solomon, what is it?"

"Have I ever thanked you for taking such good care of our daughter?"

Abishag's cheeks turned a lovely shade of pink, the color of one of the rare sapphires in his crown. "It was our honor and delight to care for Arielah's child, my king. Your wife and I were more like sisters than queen and servant in those last days of her pregnancy." Abishag stroked his brow, and her eyes became distant. "When Arielah realized she was dying, she asked me to care for her daughter—and for you. Just before you rushed into the room, she said, 'Love my daughter as you have loved me, and name her after Solomon. Name her *Peace*.'"

"Shalom-it . . . Shlomit." Solomon whispered his daughter's name reverently as Abishag played absently with a tassel on his pillow. "Abishag, where is my daughter now?"

The woman's hand stilled and then pulled away. When Solomon looked up, caution had replaced her tender expression. He reached for her hand. She tensed but did not resist. His heart convulsed at the suspicion in her eyes. "Abishag, I'm dying. I don't want to disrupt Shlomit's life. I simply want to know if she is well."

The woman stood and fidgeted nervously with the jeweled belt at her waist, her slender figure still beautifully formed after six children. "I must call for Nathan. He should answer your questions about our—I mean your daughter." Before he could form a reply, Abishag fairly ran out of his chamber.

"Wait! I—" He tried to shout, but he collapsed into a fit of coughing. His chest felt as though it was on fire. The palace physician offered him some sort of potion. "No! I will not sleep. I must speak to Nathan!"

More servants shuffled about until finally his brother entered with a worried Abishag trailing behind him. Nathan had become Solomon's best friend and most trusted advisor after Benaiah's death.

The physician drew Nathan aside. "The king is very weak. Try not to let him talk too much."

"I heard that!" Solomon tried to raise his voice, but coughing gripped him again.

"Brother, must you always have the last word?" Nathan crouched behind Solomon like a chair on the bed and lifted his brother's shoulders, enabling him to breathe easier. He'd done this dozens of times in the past weeks.

The coughing abated, and he tilted his head up. "Of course I must have the last word. I am the king." Solomon offered a weak but mischievous smile. He noted a timid grin on Abishag's face as she exchanged glances with her husband.

"All right, Solomon," Nathan said. Climbing from behind

his brother's shoulders, he motioned to the servants for help propping up the king with more pillows. "Shlomit is a beautiful woman with a family of her own." Casting a furtive glance at his wife, Nathan added, "She is wholly dedicated to Jehovah. Why this sudden interest in her?"

The mirth in the room evaporated, and Solomon realized Shlomit had been hidden to protect her from his pagan influence. "Nathan, after weeks in this bed, I've realized that my heart was wooed from the Lord by foreign wives and their gods." His eyes misted. "Surely the scrolls I dictated during the last new moon proved my conviction that only Jehovah provides meaning to anything under the sun." When Nathan seemed unconvinced, he continued. "I need to know Shlomit is well, and I want to talk about—her ima."

A guttural moan began in Abishag's throat and finally emerged in ranting. "No! We will not speak of Arielah until I hear her name from your lips!" This customarily meek Shulammite was trembling, her chest heaving. "Her name! Say it!" Sobs shook her as the words spilled out.

Nathan gathered his wife into his arms as Solomon watched, regret seizing him anew. He had caused them much pain. After Arielah's death, Solomon had devoted himself to wine, folly, and pleasure. He'd buried himself in projects: God's temple, palaces, fortress cities, gardens, and vineyards. He'd become greater than any man before him, using God's wisdom to build and guide, while trampling the hearts of those closest to him.

"Oh, Arielah." Shame drew her name from his heart. It was only a whisper, but Abishag heard him.

She quieted in Nathan's arms. "What did you say, Solomon?"

"Arielah. Arielah. Arielah." The name quenched the thirst of his soul and flowed from his lips. "Arielah!" he cried, and the coughing began. "Arielah . . ."

Nathan and Abishag rushed to embrace him but were

pushed aside by the physician. "Get me the loquat solution," he shouted at one of the servants.

Solomon tried to shove the doctor away but found his strength sapped by the coughing. Before he could protest further, a large spoonful of foul-tasting liquid was ladled down his throat. *Lord Jehovah! Let me die before my next dose of that!* Nathan held him upright while his coughing subsided. The room grew blurry, quiet, and then finally blackness covered him.

When Solomon awakened, Abishag was working her spindle again. Nathan was sprawled in the high-backed ivory chair—a gift from the Cushite ambassador—his ankles crossed. He was slouched and snoring.

"How long have I been asleep?" Solomon's voice sounded like wind through a shepherd's pipe with the holes uncovered.

Nathan let out an awful snort, returning to consciousness, and Abishag giggled like a young maiden.

"Well, long enough that my beard has grown three inches." His brother rubbed the neatly manicured gray growth on his chin.

Abishag issued a reproving glance to her husband. "Not long," she said to Solomon, her eyes kind, all fear gone. She leaned up, tenderly touching the king's arm. "We'll tell you about Shlomit if you like."

The familiar ache in his heart deepened, twisted, extending down his left arm. "Yes, but first . . ." He looked at Nathan. "I want to ask . . ." A racking pain replaced the ache in his chest, and he winced.

"Are you all right, brother?" Nathan's face registered alarm, and the hovering physician took a few steps toward the bed.

Solomon glared. "Tell that vulture to go feast on someone else's bones." His patience was wearing thin with that potion-wielding fellow.

Nathan chuckled and warned the doctor away. "He's just doing what you pay him to do." Solomon rolled his eyes, but

Nathan continued. "You've searched the world for the best physicians, the most knowledge, the grandest architecture. You've accomplished much, brother."

"But there's one more thing," Solomon said, his eyes filling with tears. "I need you to write something for me."

Nathan exchanged a puzzled glance with Abishag. "Solomon, you've written so many songs and proverbs already. What could I possibly write for you?"

"I wasn't talking to you. I want Abishag to write it." Solomon enjoyed the shock on both of their faces.

"What? I can't write," she said. "What would I write?" The pink sapphire shone again on her cheeks.

"I want you to help me write about her—about Arielah," he amended quickly, avoiding any more outbursts from this suddenly emboldened Shulammite.

Nathan watched with a satisfied grin, his gaze intent on his wife. *Look how he loves her after all these years.*

"At first, all you need to do is sit with me while I dictate memories to a scribe." Solomon squeezed his eyes shut. "But if Arielah told you things, feelings only a woman could convey, you must share them. And I want much of it to be written in shepherd's verse—as a song, a sacred song." Solomon chuckled, setting off a short coughing bout. "No matter how hard I try, I'm sure your shepherd's verse will outshine mine."

Abishag began shaking her head, her eyes full of tears, and Solomon's heart plummeted. "I understand, Abishag. I will not compel you. I don't deserve the honor of your help to write this sacred song." A lonesome tear made its way down Solomon's cheek. "But I would be grateful."

Abishag reached up to wipe the tear from Solomon's beard. "If Arielah's love taught us anything, it is that mercy is rarely deserved." Her hand lingered on his cheek while she spoke. "And what is Nathan supposed to do while you and I are hard at work?"

Another tear escaped when he realized she'd just agreed to

his request. "Thank you, Abishag." He reached up to cover her hand.

"All right. That's enough caressing of my wife." Nathan's eyes glistened.

Solomon's laughter had become more of a wheeze, but it still felt good to laugh. Mischief suddenly got the better of him. He ceased his laughter and donned his most serious expression. "Listen carefully, both of you," he said in a grave voice. Nathan and Abishag leaned close, their faces poised for Solomon's instruction. "If I should die before we finish Arielah's song . . ." Abishag gently drew his hand into hers. "You two must make it the best song *I've* ever written."

"Oh!" Abishag threw away his hand as though he had leprosy. "You'd better live long enough to write the whole song, or Nathan and I might take the credit!"

Nathan's laughter resounded in the king's chamber, and Solomon felt another moment's regret. He'd shared too few quiet moments in his lifetime with these precious people. The remaining days of his life would be different—in many ways.

With his heart at rest, memories of Arielah flooded his soul, and Solomon nestled into his pillows. He hadn't felt this shalom since . . . well, since his lion of God had left him. "We'll begin writing the song tomorrow, Abishag. But for now, tell me about my Shlomit."

AUTHOR'S NOTE

This story began in 1998, when I was intrigued by a one-page fictional summary of Song of Solomon written by Ann Spangler and Jean E. Syswerda (*Women of the Bible*, Zondervan). Like all good biblical fiction, the story sent me back to Scripture, and I found Song of Solomon extremely confusing! When I turned to commentaries, each scholar had not only a different approach to the interpretation of the original language, but a differing opinion on which character spoke what line of poetry. Being the determined (my husband would say *stubborn*) student that I am, I decided to read all eight chapters of Song of Solomon every day until I understood it. A year later, the story of Solomon and Arielah's sacred love had taken shape, and the foundation for a retreat topic and adult Bible study was born.

As the vehicle changed from speaking topic to Bible study to novel, over twelve years of research also evolved. Each new tidbit of knowledge changed the characters, the scenery, and the timelines. The geography of Lebanon, Shunem, and Jerusalem intrigued me, as did the seasons and festivals, the ancient wedding traditions, and Solomon's political reforms.

First Kings 6:38 says Solomon completed the temple in the eleventh year of his reign after seven years of construction. This single verse gave me a four-year window for his relationship with Arielah. Since most research on Solomon discusses his later reign (the building of his palace and God's temple), I aligned scriptural accounts with my best guess at a plausible timeline for this story.

I'm often asked, "How much of the book is fact?" My reply is always, "As much as possible!" You can find Solomon's birth in 2 Samuel 12:24–25 and the records of his reign in 1 Kings 1–11 and 2 Chronicles 1–9. Additional information on Solomon's early reign is included in the final days of David's life in 1 Chronicles 22:5–16; 28–29.

God is perfect and His Word inerrant. I and my writing are neither. I have made every effort to write an accurate historical novel. Accuracy is crucial, and though it is very important to me, it is not my only goal. Most important is the message of Arielah's love. It's my prayer that in the ferocious, unrelenting love of a simple shepherdess, you will catch a glimpse of God's lavish love and passionate pursuit of every heart. Jesus Christ adores you and won't settle for less than your whole heart. May we all learn to carry Him like a seal over our hearts.

Shalom, dear reader.

ACKNOWLEDGMENTS

Though it may sound cliché, I must first and foremost thank God for this story. When I began reading all eight chapters of Song of Solomon daily, I discovered the Lord's ability to shape and define characters and themes. No commentary or theologian devised the unfolding plot. It was His gentle whisper, revealing His ferocious love.

To my writing partner, Meg Wilson—you are tenacious, my friend! If it hadn't been for your repeated counsel—dare we say *nagging*—I would never have written my retreat topic in novel form. And then with every major plot overhaul, you plowed through these pages again, faithfully calling me to think more deeply, to express more emotion with fewer words.

To my second partner, Velynn Brown—thanks for giving up family time and your own writing time to help me stay "real" on the page.

To Michelle Nordquist, my email edit specialist—though we've met in person only once, the long hours of computer connection have made us kindred spirits! My undying gratitude for your steadfast efforts on that crucial last rewrite, my friend. You're awesome!

Huge thanks to Gayle Roper and her fiction mentoring clinic at the Mount Hermon Writers Conference in 2008, where this story found wings.

To Wendy Lawton—I would have stopped writing completely if it hadn't been for you, my friend. At my first writers' conference in 2001, you saw my discouragement, but you said, "I see the passion in your eyes when you talk about Solomon's story. Don't give up." Four years later, you picked up this rough and dusty novice and carried me in your pocket. You protected me from all those rejections, and you didn't let me fall. You were a godsend and are still a good friend.

To my editor, Vicki Crumpton—WOW! Where do I begin? You gambled big on this rookie author who didn't even know what "POV" meant! And then you lovingly, patiently taught me to write real characters rather than teach through allegorical cutouts. "Thanks" is simply not enough to convey my appreciation for the way you gently coach, tenderly challenge, and graciously stretch me.

To Michele Misiak, Jessica English, Donna Hausler, Karen Wiley, Cheryl Van Andel, and the host of other creative and committed folks at Revell—you've spoiled me with your kindness and efficiency!

Immense thanks to Karl Kutz, chairperson of biblical languages at Multnomah Bible College. I don't know any other busy professor who would sit down with a novelist and scour every word of Song of Solomon. You brought the Hebrew words to life and changed my perspective on several scenes.

And, once again, thanks to Suzanne Smith and Pam Middleton at the Multnomah University library. You're awesome! Your expert research help has given me access to online databases and ancient texts beyond my scope of understanding but well within my heart to learn.

To my faithful prayer team—only God knows how powerfully you've impacted this book. Your love and support means so much to me and to my family.

I couldn't have written about the healing love of Arielah's father and mother had I not experienced it so profoundly from my own dad and mom. Charley and Mary Cooley have shown me Christ's unconditional love throughout my life.

To Pat and Sharie Johnson, the parents of my heart—thank you for the tangible and intangible ways you love me.

To my father-in-law, Bill Kidwell—thanks for encouragement and impromptu suppers that help keep me at the keyboard.

To our kids, Trina and Jason, Emily and Brad—thank you for being easy to love, quick to forgive, and abundant with grace. Each of you shows me a different glimpse of Jesus's love in a unique way. It is a pleasure and privilege to watch you live lives of integrity.

Finally, to my sweet husband, Roy—I would never truly know the love of the Holy Bridegroom if you hadn't modeled it so beautifully. Thank you for pursuing me. Thank you for loving me. Thank you for being a godly example of sacred love.

Mesu Andrews is an active speaker who has devoted herself to passionate and intense study of Scripture. Harnessing her deep understanding of and love for God's Word, Andrews brings the biblical world alive for her readers. She and her husband enjoyed fourteen years of pastoral ministry before moving to the Pacific Northwest to pursue the next step in God's calling. They have two married children and live in Washington, where Mesu writes full time. Visit Mesu at www. mesuandrews.com.

COME MEET MESU AT
WWW.MESUANDREWS.COM

Read her blog, sign up for devotions, and
learn more interesting facts about her books.

STAY CONNECTED ON
🅵 Mesu Andrews
🅑 mesuloveshim

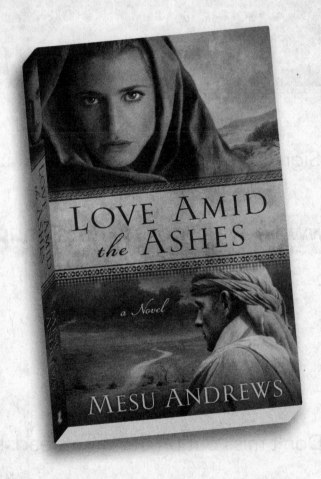